Another Kingdom

TURNER PUBLISHING COMPANY
Nashville, Tennessee
www.turnerpublishing.com

ANOTHER KINGDOM
Copyright © 2018 Andrew Klavan
All rights reserved.

Cover design: Mark Swan
Book design: Karen Sheets de Gracia

LIBRARY OF CONGRESS CATALOGING-IN-PUBLICATION DATA
Names: Klavan, Andrew, author.
Title: Another kingdom / by Andrew Klavan.
Description: Nashville, TN : Turner Publishing Company, 2019. | Series: Another kingdom ; 1 |
Identifiers: LCCN 2018022522 (print) | LCCN 2018024512 (ebook) | ISBN 9781684422654
(ebook) | ISBN 9781684422630 (hardback) | ISBN 9781684422647 (paperback)
Subjects: LCSH: Murder—Investigation—Fiction. | Psychological fiction. | GSAFD: Suspense
fiction. | Mystery fiction. | Adventure stories. | Horror fiction.
Classification: LCC PS3561.L334 (ebook) | LCC PS3561.L334 A66 2019 (print)
| DDC 813/.54—dc23
LC record available at https://lccn.loc.gov/2018022522

9781684422630 Hardcover
9781684422647 Paperback
9781684422654 eBook

PRINTED IN THE UNITED STATES OF AMERICA

18 19 20 21   10 9 8 7 6 5 4 3 2 1

ANOTHER KINGDOM

A NOVEL

ANDREW KLAVAN

TURNER
PUBLISHING COMPANY

THIS BOOK IS FOR *Jeremy and Ann Boreing:*

friends in both kingdoms.

"No one is told any story
but their own."

—C.S. Lewis

SUDDENLY, I WAS ON THE EDGE OF A
tremendous drop, at the ledge of a high window. Blue sky swirled
above me, filled with stone towers and conical roofs in tilted
confusion. Something sparkled and spun through the air beneath
me toward the sparkling water far below.

There was noise behind me. Thundering footsteps. Shouts.

My arm flew out for balance as I staggered back from the ledge.
I turned around. I looked around, stunned, confused.

I was in a stone room hung with tapestries. A woman lay on
the floor in a pool of blood. The woman was beautiful, and she was
dead.

She was twenty at most, with round cheeks and a noble brow and
golden hair spilling around her face like a halo. She was stretched
out on the cold gray stone and clothed in a long, elegant gown of
some fine white material. There was a bloody gash in the fabric right
below her breasts. Blood stained her bodice. There was blood in a
pool all around her.

And there was blood on the dagger—the dagger I was holding
in my hand. There was blood dripping off the point of it onto the
slab between my feet.

Someone started pounding on the door . . .

1

THE TRUTH IS? BY THE TIME EVERYTHING WENT CRAZY, I was pretty much crazy already. Edgy, anxious, hypochondriacal. Thirty years old and I hardly recognized myself. I mean, there was a time, I used to be somebody. Not somebody famous—just a dude— but somebody. I used to be able to look in the mirror and say, *That's me. That's Austin Lively.* Now? I was lost in a dark wood. Hollywood, ha ha. I'd been told that Hollywood was where you went if you wanted to sell your soul to make movies. I went, but I never sold my soul. No one would buy it. I just got tired of carrying it around.

I did sell a script once. Right out of film school. A daring, original, deeply personal take on the sci-fi epics that were all the rage. *Three Days in Forever*, it was called. I sold *Three Days in Forever* to one of the major studios, then spent the next two years in development meetings with producers and studio executives. You ever see jackals gutting the carcass of a once-beautiful gazelle? That's what the development meetings were like. My script was the gazelle. The producers and executives were the jackals. I was the asshole. The movie never got made.

After that? I wrote a script my agent couldn't sell. Then I wrote a script my agent wouldn't sell. Then . . . then came that day, when either I went berserk or the world did or we both went berserk together. I still don't know which.

I slumped into Hitchcock's Cafe that morning wearing my sorrows like a thundercloud hat. Hitchcock's was a NoHo tavern of stained wood and white fairy lights. Bar to your left as you came in. Liquor bottles glittering green and white and brown-red with the light from the flat screen where the TV news was flickering. Tables to your right. Hollywood hopefuls nursing coffee over their laptops. Posters from old suspense films hung on the walls here and there: glamorous stars of the forties and fifties making fearful faces with images of danger surrounding them, speeding trains and gunmen and heroes dangling from the Statue of Liberty's lamp. Somehow, the antique one-sheets gave the place an arty glamour.

There was my crew at the long table by the restroom door. Jane Janeway, Ted Wexler, Wren Yen, and Chad Valentine. Wannabes, sellouts, and hangers-on. Oh my. Not a one of us older than thirty-three and all of us gone so wrong so young. They were picking at their muffins and yogurts and coffee and reading the postings on their handheld devices. None of them said a word, not even hello, as I plunked down among them. Only Jane bothered to smile. But then, she was in love with me.

Schuyler Cohen pushed out through the kitchen door. She was the waitress but also one of us. A large, buxom woman ballooning the unofficial Hitchcock uniform of black T-shirt, black skirt, and black tights. Short, spiky red hair and a face at once cherubic and furious. She was trying to be a comic, working open mic nights at clubs. Slinging jokes about what pigs men are. Like all comics, she was angry and miserable. I never met one who wasn't.

She smacked my coffee mug down in front of me like a hanging judge's gavel. Schuyler hated me. Because she actually kind of liked me. But she loved Jane Janeway, who let her live in her house but wasn't interested in her because she was interested in me. It was complicated.

I lifted the mug to my lips and stared bleakly through the steam.

"What a bunch," I said bitterly. "Staring at our devices. We don't even look at each other anymore."

Ted Wexler raised his eyes from his handheld and studied me. Wex was assistant to a literary agent. He aspired to be a sleazy, unctuous dirtbag like his boss, and he was well on his way. "I'm looking at you," he said. "You look like shit."

Chad and Wren Yen gave me one curious glance apiece. Chad was a short, slim aspiring actor of the boyishly brooding type. I never knew what he did for money. I wasn't sure I wanted to know. Wren, across from him, was a Eurasian stunner, tall and lean. A receptionist in real life, a model in her dreams. I'm not sure I ever heard her speak, but the corners of her mouth lifted expressively sometimes. Now she nodded.

And Chad said, "Wow, you do look like shit. Almost exactly."

Schuyler paused in tidying up the crumbs around Jane's granola. Took a look for herself. "The resemblance is uncanny."

Jane—tenderhearted Jane—started to say, "Cut it out, you guys," but then she saw me too and said, "Oh. Wow."

Jane was mousey, slump-shouldered, and shy, but she could've been lovely. She had a slim, graceful figure, a sweet, gentle, oval face. She played her looks way down by wearing drab clothes and too little makeup and by letting her long, straight hair hang in limp brown strands. She was personal assistant to Alexis Merriwether, the once-gorgeous movie star. Part of her job was not to look too young and beautiful. That would've annoyed the boss.

"What the hell happened to you?" Schuyler asked me.

My sigh rippled the black surface of my coffee. "I heard from my agent," I said.

"He didn't like your new script," said Jane.

"Oh, is this going to be one of those Hollywood failures stories?" said Wex.

"I love those," said Chad. "They make me feel so much better about my life."

"He fired me," I said.

"Oh, Austin!" said Jane. She put a consoling hand on my arm. Which made me feel even worse.

"He can't fire you," said Wex. "He works for you."

"He told me I needed to find an agent who was a better fit."

"Wow," said Wex. "He fired you. The script must've really blown the big whistle. Must've sucked the hairy straw. Must've eaten the . . . "

"Ted," said Jane.

"What? I'm just saying."

But that was exactly the problem: the script had, in fact, eaten whatever it was Ted was about to say it had eaten. It was a terrible script, clichéd and lifeless. The work of a cynical no-talent trying to play to the market. I think I had talent once. I must have. All those awards I won in film school? But failure had beaten the vision out of me. I'd gotten so I'd do anything to avoid the goolie punch of rejection. I used to consult my muse before deciding what project to work on. Nowadays I consulted the box office charts. I would call my agent—my former agent—and ask him: "What are the buyers looking for? Zombies? Spaceships? Superheroes? Great. I have this idea about a superhero on a spaceship full of zombies. I'm really excited about it. I think you're gonna like it."

So the script was crap; I knew it. After I sent the final draft to my agent, I immediately caught a cold that lasted six weeks. When the cold cleared up and my agent still hadn't called, I sank into a depression so bad I finally had to take myself to a psychiatrist. She said I had a chemical imbalance and gave me a prescription for some pills. I filled the prescription and read the label. Possible side effects included impotence and constipation. I hadn't been with a woman for three months, but I did still enjoy a trip to the bathroom from time to time. So I flushed the pills down the toilet. Chemical imbalance, my ass.

For the next two weeks, I sat in my room with the lights out and waited for my agent to call and reject the script as it deserved. I wasn't expecting him to fire me though. Life retained its capacity to surprise.

"Hey, look," said Chad, lifting his chin toward the bar behind me. "Isn't that your famous and successful brother on TV?"

"Oh man," said Wexler. "That's gotta make you feel like shit. Doesn't it? You already *look* like shit, but that . . . "

"Ted," said Jane Janeway.

"What? I'm just saying."

I looked over my shoulder at the flatscreen behind the bar. And yes, there was my famous and successful brother, all right. With his great, handsome head and his Viking beard and his swept-back golden hair. And his broad-shouldered frame in his three-piece suit and his PhD in comparative sociology from Harvard. And the title of his latest best-selling book on the chyron: *Creating Equality*. And his name: Dr. Richard Lively, Orosgo Institute.

Which reminded me: he was in town today, flogging his new book. We were scheduled to have dinner tonight. My parents were coming down from San Francisco to join us. My brother had warned me in an email that we would "have to discuss" Riley, our little sister.

And yes, all of that did make me feel like shit. Almost exactly. The resemblance was uncanny.

WHEN I LEFT Hitchcock's, I drove to Global Pictures. I had a freelance job there as a story analyst. A "story analyst" is a fancy name for a reader. A reader reads things on assignment—books, screenplays, articles. For each thing he reads, he writes a synopsis and gives his opinion about why it would or would not make a good movie. This is called "coverage." His boss reads the coverage, and then he can pretend he read the book or the screenplay and has an opinion about it. I'm sure my agent had a reader read my script before he fired me. I'm sure he didn't read it himself. No one reads in Hollywood except readers. Like me.

My brother, Richard, had gotten me this freelance gig when the money from my script sale ran out. I had called him in a humiliating panic. *I'm broke. I don't know what to do.* My brother put me on hold for about three minutes. Then he came back on and told me I had a reader job at Mythos, a production company. My brother could do that because Mythos had a deal with Global Pictures, and Serge Orosgo, the billionaire who funded my brother's think tank, also owned Global, not to mention major newspapers, television stations, and publishing houses around the world. Richard and Serge were pals.

I drove to the studio in my eight-year-old Nissan, a sputtering, blunt, scratched-and-dented piece of scrap on wheels. A car in LA is like an accent in England: it instantly reveals everything about you. My Nissan sputtered along a freeway streaked with the afterimages of the sleek, low-slung racers that were flashing past me, each as quick as a dismissive glance.

The Global Pictures studio lot was a white-walled fortress that rose out of the long, dismal storefront flatlands of Melrose Avenue. The main entrance was the famous Da Vinci Gate, a victory arch of golden marble topped with elaborate iron filigree, a rococo relic of the industry's golden age. I thought of the two-toned Rolls Royce Phantoms that once carried actors though that gate into immortality. My Nissan farted pitiably as it idled in a line of Beamers and Teslas waiting to enter.

It was autumn. A cool and sunny day. I parked in one of the spaces near the gate and walked past sound stages, barracks-like buildings as large as dinosaurs. Some had their enormous doors open, and as I passed, I peeked in at the fake interiors of TV shows:

a police precinct, a suburban home, a set of law offices. I always liked being on the lot. It made me feel like I was still part of the city's glamorous enterprise. And how pathetic was that? Like the joke about the guy who shovels out the elephant pen at the circus.

Maybe you should get a better job.

What? And leave show business?

The production company was in the Edison Building, a long four-story barn of yellow brick, circa 1930. Inside, I walked through a maze of identical hallways past identical office doors and up sudden stairways that led to other hallways and other doors equally identical.

Mythos was on floor three, a flashy, modern suite of offices once you pushed through the Depression-era door. Posters decorated the walls behind the cubicles, one-sheets from the films they'd made, most of them in the *Captain Samurai* superhero franchise, a big-money series of comic-book tentpoles about a young man whose zen powers of something gave him the ability to something something something, who the hell cares. *Captain Samurai, Captain Samurai: Vengeance, Captain Samurai: Apocalypse, Captain Samurai: Origins* (the reboot), and so on.

My boss, the story editor, Candy Filikin, was on a call when I arrived. So said her assistant, a willowy boy named Ken with a face so bland it could've been featureless. He gave me a bottle of water, and I sat and waited in the chair beside his desk. Waited and waited. Twenty minutes. Twenty-five. Staring hypnotized at the posters. Thinking what utter shlock these *Samurai* pictures were, and how I would have sold my soul to have a screen credit on any one of them.

Finally, Ken said, "Candy is ready for you."

She was sleek and smart and pretty in an adamant sort of way. Sable hair just so, and bright brown eyes just so, and nose just so, and her smile and her gym-toned figure and her khaki slacks and her blue men's shirt all business-sharp. She shook my hand when I came into her office, and her hand was cool and dry. She sat in the big armchair in front of her desk, poised and confident, her legs crossed at the knee. I sat on the sofa in front of her, sinking deep into the cushions so that I felt small, a supplicant. Candy asked me if I had made any "discoveries" this week: if any of the scripts and novels I'd read might provide movie material for Mythos.

I snorted in answer. "Candy," I said, "sometimes, I swear, reading this crap day after day, I feel like a psychiatrist in hell, like I'm listening to the twisted fantasies of damned souls whose last desperate hope for redemption is to transform their perverse imaginings into something like a story."

"So that would be 'no,'" said Candy, with a mirthless laugh—a laugh that told me that I and my opinions meant nothing to her. She had seen a hundred smart-ass never-weres like me in this job.

I was out of her office in five minutes. Out again in the mazelike halls. My thundercloud-funk hat now settling down to embrace the whole of me, a thunder-funk shroud. Swathed in the brown fog of it, lost in gloomy thought, I lectured myself: I should give this up. This dream of Hollywood success. I should go to law school like my mother wanted. Get a PhD like my father said. Get out of the business, Austin Lively, before you wake up one day and you're fifty and you've never done anything but sit around coffee shops whining about how the movies are no good anymore, not like the old days.

It was at this point that I looked up and realized I was lost. Lost in the Edison Building. I wasn't sure which of the identical hallways I was in or which of the identical doors I was in front of or even what floor I was on. I read the plaques on the wall. *Netherway Pictures . . . Perdita Productions . . . Jess Newfeld & Co . . . .* I'd never heard of any of them. Had I gone down a flight of stairs? I couldn't remember. I didn't see a stairway anywhere. How was I supposed to get out of here?

There was a closed door at the end of the hall. I figured that was my best bet: a stairwell probably. I went to it quickly, feeling like an idiot. I tried the knob. It turned easily. I pushed it open and stepped through . . .

I let out a frightened shout, fighting for balance. Suddenly, I was on the edge of a tremendous drop, at the ledge of a high window. Blue sky swirled above me, filled with stone towers and conical roofs in tilted confusion. Something sparkled and spun through the air beneath me toward the sparkling water far below.

There was noise behind me. Thundering footsteps. Shouts.

My arm flew out for balance as I staggered back from the ledge. I turned around. I looked around, stunned, confused.

I was in a stone room hung with tapestries. There was a woman on the floor in a pool of blood. The woman was beautiful, and she was dead.

She was twenty at most, with round cheeks and a noble brow and golden hair spilling around her face like a halo. She was stretched out on the cold gray stone and clothed in a long, elegant gown of some fine white material. There was a bloody gash in the fabric right below her breasts. Blood stained her bodice. There was blood in a pool all around her.

And there was blood on the dagger—the dagger I was holding in my hand. There was blood dripping off the point of it onto the slab between my feet.

Someone started pounding on the door.

2

MAYBE I SHOULD HAVE TRIED TO ESCAPE OR THOUGHT
to drop the knife—or thought *something*. But I couldn't think at all.
I couldn't understand what I was seeing, how I was seeing it, what
was happening to me, where I was. Had I wandered onto a movie
set? And the knife in my hand . . . What the hell was going on?

I looked around in an idiot daze. Someone was still pounding
insistently at the door, and yet my eyes roamed stupidly over the
tapestries on the wall. Torches flamed in the spaces between them,
the wavering light giving life to elegant medieval scenes of reapers
in fields, huntsmen on horseback, gentlemen and ladies dancing
daintily hand in hand. The pounding, pounding, pounding at the
heavy wooden door seemed far away and unreal.

Then the wood tore with a terrible cracking noise, and the door
burst inward.

A small army of men flooded the room. Men in black leather
and chain mail. Men with drawn swords that flashed in the flame-
light from the torches.

"Ah, God! She's dead!" one of them shouted.

I stared at them, my mouth open. I thought this would have to
be over in a moment. It was some kind of hallucination, that's all. In
another moment everything would be normal again.

The men—there were six of them—parted into two groups of three as a seventh man came in behind them and pushed to the front. He was obviously the leader. Tall and fit and broad and ramrod straight. Black haired and black bearded. He wore a red vest with a gold dragon embroidered on it. He wore a sword in the scabbard on his hip. He wore an ironic expression of disdain for the world. He looked handsome and bold.

His eyes went down to the dead woman, then up to me. He sneered.

"You son of a bitch," he said.

Without thinking—because what could I think? What the hell was happening to me?—I gestured at him with the dagger in my hand.

He must've thought I was going to attack him. In a movement too swift to see, he drew his sword and swept it at me in a casually brutal arc. The flat of the heavy blade smacked into the side of my head. My mind seemed to go flying out of my body and then snap back into it and sink down and down into a murky distance inside me. The room, the men, the world all accordioned away, far away. My eyes rolled up in opposite directions. I felt my legs turn to jelly. The dagger dropped from my limp fingers and fell, twirling, to the floor. I wilted down after it.

The next thing I knew, I was dimly aware that two men were holding me, one gripping me under each arm. They were dragging me *thump-thump-thump* down a torchlit stairway, my legs trailing limp, my toes bumping along behind me. There was blood in my eyes and on my cheek. I shook my head, trying to clear it. I tried to speak, but my jaw hung slack. I heard myself groaning.

We reached the bottom of the stairs. I struggled to get my feet under me. I managed to stumble along as the two guards hurried me onward by force. My head started to pulse with pain—real pain, no hallucination—as if a big pain balloon were blowing up and deflating inside me, filling me with fresh pain each time. It was awful. My mouth still hanging open, I looked around. I caught glimpses of an underground labyrinth of dirt and stone. A third guard was striding ahead of us, leading the way. Corridors ran off left and right under sepulchral archways. Heavy iron doors were set, here and there, deep into the hewed rock. Torches flamed and flickered in sconces on the wall, set far enough apart so that the jittery shadows melded into brooding darkness between them. The air stank of shit and despair.

"What's happening?" I tried to say. "Where am I?" But the words came out blurry, like words in a dream.

"Jailer!" the lead guard shouted.

There was a loud clank of metal. Hinges creaked, the sound echoing off the vaulted ceiling. A door swung open somewhere. My head lolled on my shoulder as if it would come loose and fall off. My vision rolled sickeningly. I caught sight of fire. A torch, nearer, brighter than the others. I managed to turn toward it. I saw a horrid, insectile little man.

The jailer. He was no more than four feet tall. His bent and scrawny frame swam inside a worn gray robe. His head was cowled, but I could see the warty, bug-eyed, and absurdly beak-nosed face grinning weirdly out of the folds of the cloth. He held his wildly flaming torch aloft in his left hand. In his right, he held a ring of enormous keys. The keys clanked and jingled as he walked toward us.

"Who's this?" he said. He had a voice like a rusted machine, slow and creaky.

"His name is Austin Lively," said the lead guard. I blinked, shocked, because that was my name, my actual name. How could it be? How could he know me? "He's charged with the murder of Lady Kata Palav."

Even with my brain befogged and rattled, those horrible words shocked some speech out of me. I struggled weakly in the grip of the guards. "Murder?" I shouted. "Are you nuts? I didn't kill anyone! I don't even know what's happening! I don't know where I am!"

The words came out slurred, thick, indistinct. No one paid any attention. It was as if I'd made no sound at all.

The jailer started down a corridor, muttering to himself and giggling. Flipping through the keys on his ring. Quick and pigeon-toed, he skittered like a roach. The guards frog-marched me after him.

We passed under a brick arch. I turned from one guard to another, one stony, indifferent face to another, trying to tell them it was all a mistake, trying to push the thick words past my thick tongue. No one even glanced at me.

The jailer moved to one of the iron doors. The latch gave a hollow thunk as he unlocked it. The hinges groaned as he hauled the door open. A thick stench poured out of the deeper darkness in the cell beyond. Something within that hellhole gave a deep animal huff of rage and hunger.

My eyes went wide. This was real! This was really real! And now the guards were dragging me toward the cell's open doorway. The jailer stood back and watched, grinning with sadistic pleasure, holding his torch to light the way, his warty face hideous in the wavering flames.

Terror went off inside me now like a bomb. I tried to dig my heels into the dirt and stone of the floor, tried to stop the guards from dragging me into that cell, locking me in with whatever was in there.

"Stop! Listen to me! This is a mistake! I didn't do anything! I don't belong here!"

I had no chance. The guards were big men, much stronger than I was, and I was still weak and dazed from the blow to my head and from the shock of finding myself in this impossible place. They overpowered me easily. Forced me past the grinning jailer. Forced me over the threshold. Hustled me over the dirt floor as I struggled. Hurled me face-first into the cell wall.

I grunted as I hit the stone. Still, I spun around to try to fight. But one guard pressed his sword point hard into the hollow of my throat, making me gag, pinning me. The other guards grabbed my arms and snapped manacles around my wrist.

"What are you doing?" I shouted. "Stop! It's a mistake! I'm a story analyst!"

Too late. I was chained to the wall. It all happened in a second.

Then the three guards stood aside—and I saw the monster.

I had never heard myself scream before. Not really, not like this. It just broke out of me, beyond my control.

Across the cell, lit by the dancing orange flames of the jailer's torch, stood a massive and uncanny creature, savage, brutal, and utterly grotesque. It was at least twice as tall as the biggest guard and huge at the center, its torso a great ball of meaty flesh. It had arms the size of a bull's haunches and stout, short legs bulging with muscle. It wore nothing but a filthy rag around its loins, and its flesh was covered everywhere with thick, curling, filthy hair. Its face: horrible. Shaped like a squashed boulder with the wide, bloody, fanged mouth of a shark, a bulbous, streaming nose the size of a softball, and one eye—one immense and dreadful eye—smack in the center of its forehead. I would not have believed that a single eye could contain such depths of ferocity, such a rage for bloodshed and destruction. And it was staring straight at me.

The thing was in a frenzy, struggling against its chains, sending up a sort of squealing roar that spiraled up from one height of fury to the next. Its daggery teeth snapped and flashed as it tried to get at me.

The lead guard shared a laugh with the others. "You don't want to get too close to him," he advised me with a smile. "He'll take your head off with a single bite."

I gaped at the creature. I couldn't take my eyes off him. "Listen," I said hoarsely to the guard. "You can't leave me in here with that thing. This is all a mistake."

The guards all laughed some more, and the jailer laughed, trying to be one of them. Showing off, he stuck his torch in the monster's face. Taunting it, tormenting it, while it squealed and snapped at him, roared and strained.

"Oh no. You've had your share of heads this lifetime, ogre," he said to it—trying to impress the guards. "You're going to entertain the crowds by dying slow."

The monster squealed and bared its fangs and pulled so hard on its chains that I saw dust fly from the walls where the chains were anchored. My heart seized in fear that the anchoring rings would tear free.

"All right," said the lead guard. "That's enough. Leave him alone. Let's go."

The jailer gave a satisfied snigger. He lowered his torch from the ogre's face. The guards headed for the door.

They were leaving me—leaving me here with that thing.

I shouted at them, "Wait!" Staring at the beast who stared back at me with his single eye as he raged and wrenched his bonds. This had to be insanity. It had to be. It couldn't be happening. But it was. It was. "Wait!"

The guards marched out. The jailer grinned at me one last time, then followed them.

The cell's iron door slammed shut.

DARKNESS.

The ogre went on screaming his squealy scream, his chains rattling. I cowered, wild-eyed, against the rough wall, praying I would wake up. Because this had to be a dream. It had to be.

The moments went by with intolerable slowness. The stench was suffocating. So was the helplessness. So was the fear.

But after a while, I don't know how long, the darkness seemed to have an effect on the monster. His roars began to subside. The clanking of his chains grew intermittent. Finally, with a last low growl, he fell quiet. I heard him settling on the floor with a huff.

My eyes had begun to adjust now. The darkness, I saw, was not utterly dark. The torches from the dungeon corridors sent a faint, shivering glow through the square opening in the cell door. Soon I could make out the shape of the monster. I could see him sitting against the opposite wall. I saw his huge eye blink and then sink slowly shut. His great head tilted forward. His chin came to rest on his chest. He began to snore. It was a sound like the bowels of the earth shifting.

For the first time since I had come here, I had a moment of relative quiet, relative peace. I tried to breathe. I tried to calm myself. I had to think. I had to figure out where I was, what I could do.

I ran my hands over my clothing. Did I have my phone with me? My keys? Something I could use to call for help or to pry off these manacles. But no. These weren't my clothes at all, not the clothes I'd been wearing—when? . . . a few minutes ago—when I was in the hall at Global Pictures. I was wearing some sort of vest—suede, it felt like. And leggings of rough cloth. No pockets. No pouch. Nothing I could use to get out of here.

Frustrated, I looked around, squinting to try and see through the shadows. And now, with a small shock, I realized for the first time that there was someone *else* here—someone besides the monster.

There was another man, sitting in the corner to my right. He was chained to the wall too. I could see the links rising from his nearest wrist to the ring above and behind him. The longer I stared, the clearer I saw him: a starved, half-naked creature, with long, dirty black hair. His head hung down. His hair dangled, obscuring his face. I thought he must be asleep, like the monster. But then, as if he felt my eyes on him, he looked up. Looked at me. Even in that darkness, I could see the tears glistening in his eyes and on his cheeks. Then he lowered his face again. His body shuddered. I could hear him weeping.

"Hey," I whispered. I glanced at the ogre. I didn't want to wake the thing. But when the man just went on crying, I whispered louder, "Hey!"

The man lifted his head again—lifted it slowly as if it were a great weight.

"What is this place?" I asked him. "Where the hell am I?" He only stared at me as if he couldn't understand the question. "I don't know where I am," I said. "Tell me. Please."

He had to work to speak. His voice was hopeless, thick with tears. He answered as if I ought to already know. "It's Eastrim. The castle dungeon."

"Eastrim. In California? Are we in California?" And when he was silent again, "Where is Eastrim? I've never heard of it."

"It's the council seat of Galiana. On the border of the Eleven Lands."

This sounded so absurd—the Eleven Lands—like something out of a second-rate sword-and-sorcery novel—I thought at first maybe he was being sarcastic. But then this whole place—the dungeons, ogres, castle guards—it was *all* sword-and-sorcery stuff.

I opened my mouth to ask more. But I didn't ask more. I didn't say anything. I just stood there, my mouth still open.

Galiana . . . wasn't that what he'd said? Galiana? My mouth closed slowly. I licked my lips, thinking, thinking. Something had stirred in my memory. Galiana. I knew that name. I'd heard of that place before. Somewhere. Where? I couldn't remember.

"Galiana," I said aloud.

But now the man lowered his head back down. He made an awful noise and began sobbing again.

"Where is Galiana?" I asked him.

"Oh please, please, please," was all he said. Sobbing. "Please . . . "

I wasn't going to get any more out of him, not for a while. I scanned the cell to see if there was anyone else here. No one. Just the monster, still sleeping, still snoring, and the sobbing man.

Suddenly, I was aware of how weary I was, how heavy I felt, as if the weight of all this craziness was just now sinking down on top of me. I lowered myself to the floor. Propped myself against the wall. The thick shit-stench of the place was even thicker down here. It made my gorge rise and my stomach roll. I wanted to stand up out of it, but I was too tired. Exhausted.

My head continued to pulse with pain. I put my hand to the sore spot and flinched. I felt dried blood, skin scraped raw on a bump the size of a fist. I squeezed my eyes shut against the throbbing ache of the wound. I leaned my head back against the stone.

Galiana, I thought. Where had I heard that word before? Maybe if I could remember, I might begin to make some sense of this. Maybe . . .

What seemed like a moment later, I quickly lifted my head. It had fallen forward. I realized I'd been asleep. How long? I didn't know. But something had woken me. What was it?

With a jolt of fear, I thought: *the monster!* Maybe he'd woken up. Maybe he'd gotten free! But I located him in the dark, still on the floor, curled up on his side now, still snoring. The emaciated man in the corner to my right also seemed to have fallen asleep.

What had woken me up, then? I scanned the dark cell. Everything was still. Then—wait—yes—out of the corner of my eye . . . I had seen something for a moment, but it was gone now. I stared at the spot. Seconds went by. Then there it was again. A dim, colorful flash. A strange motley sparkling, very brief, there and gone. I leaned forward, peering at the place where the flash had been. It took a while, but finally, I made out a figure, a silhouette, a shadow there.

My stomach turned. It was some sort of animal. Something like a rat, but huge, the size of a small dog. It was sitting not two feet away from me. Just sitting. Just gazing at me. I could see the glint of its eyes.

My chains rattled as I drew back from the thing. But a few seconds later, it happened again: that dim, sparkling, multicolored flash of light. White, red, yellow, blue, green, and golden particles of illumination flew off the creature like confetti.

I gave a little gasp of amazement and disgust. In the momentary glow, I saw that the rodent had a human face, a woman's face, bizarre and haunting on that animal body.

A second later, the dancing sparks of light winked out and the rodent—or whatever it was—dropped back into the shadows again.

My mouth had gone stone dry. I had to lick my lips before I could speak. And should I speak to a thing like that? But I did. I said, "What are you? What do you want?"

But before she had time to answer—if she could answer—footsteps sounded on the dungeon stairs. I turned quickly toward the door.

I heard a shout: "Jailer! I'm here for the heretic!"

The emaciated man in the corner bolted upright, fully awake. "Oh, God!" he screamed. He scrambled to his feet, his chains clanking.

The monster stirred too, grumbling. I looked toward him, then looked toward the girl-rodent. But she was gone. She had vanished.

There were noises now all around me. The jailer's door creaking open. The emaciated man in the corner mewling to himself, "No, no!"

The ogre chained to the opposite wall snuffed and huffed and lumbered to its feet.

"Oh shit!" I said.

Footsteps were coming to the cell door. Torchlight coming through the opening. The key in the lock. The hollow thunk.

"God, forgive me! Help me!" wailed the emaciated man.

And the monster—the ogre—went wild again. Roaring its high-pitched roar. Rattling its chains, straining to break free.

Frightened, I leapt up. I tried to press my body through the stone of the wall behind me to get away from the monster. The monster went on shrieking. The emaciated man—the heretic in the corner—started whimpering. "Please, God!" He was in an agony of terror.

The door chunked open. The ogre roared louder. The heretic cowered and wept. The jailer stood just outside the cell doorway, holding his torch.

And into the cell came a figure of fear. I knew at once he was an executioner.

What else could he be? Dressed in a robe of midnight black, his head completely covered by a black mask with holes in it for his mouth and nose and eyes. They were eyes that expressed a brisk professionalism, jovial, contented, and merciless. I could see the same professionalism in his rolling gait and in his bare, blunt, powerful, cruel white hands. Here was a man who was happy in his work and good at it.

He strolled jauntily into the cell, and two husky guards strode in behind him. The jailer skittered in last, his beaked nose protruding from his cowl, his bug-eyes red with flame.

The heretic fell to his knees, his hands clasped in front of him. "Mercy! Mercy!" he cried.

My eyes flashed here and there in confusion and panic. The ogre went on squealing and struggling. For the second time, I saw dust fly up from the rings that anchored its chains to the wall. I thought I saw one of those rings wobble, loosening. But in the unsteady flame-light, with all the din and fear, I couldn't be sure.

"Mercy!" the heretic cried again.

The executioner laughed—not cruelly, I thought, but just because the prisoner's pleas struck him as amusingly predictable, like a child's whining at bedtime.

"You might want to save your screaming, heretic," he said. "You'll have plenty to scream about soon enough. Take him."

This last was to the guards. They moved forward at once and seized hold of the emaciated man. He howled and struggled wildly. Threw himself on the floor, clawing the dirt, trying to hold on. But the guards were skilled and swift. They pushed quickly past his flailing limbs. Detached his bonds from the wall. Then, holding a length of chain like a leash, one of them dragged the prisoner, kicking and screaming, across the floor and out of the cell. The whole operation took less than a minute, with the ogre roaring all the while.

The executioner glanced at me where I stood crouched and gaping against the wall. It was a professional glance, I thought, assessing me as his next project. It made my heart go hollow.

"Well," he said to me then with a friendly wave, "have a pleasant evening."

And he pivoted on his heel and strode out as jauntily as he'd come.

The jailer lingered only another moment to harass the monster with a few last passes of his torch. His sadistic giggles were drowned by the ogre's frenzied cries.

"Stop it, you idiot!" I shouted.

Because this time, as the ogre struggled, I was certain I saw the ring in the wall start to wiggle out of its moorings.

The jailer gave another nasty laugh and walked out, shutting the door behind him.

Again, there was darkness. And again, the ogre raved and strained, and his chains rattled. I cowered against the wall, waiting for him to break free, to leap across the shadows and rip my head off with a single bite of those massive jaws. Christ, would I even see him coming?

But again, slowly, he settled down. The roaring subsided. He sank to the floor once more and began to snore.

ABOUT TWENTY MINUTES later, the shrieking started.

I'd heard the expression before: *My blood ran cold.* But I'd never experienced it, not like this.

Those shrieks—that uncanny sound: it was not like any other sound I had ever heard, ever. It made my breath short. It made my balls tighten. And yes, it made my blood feel icy in my veins.

Somewhere deep in the belly of this nightmare place, the heretic was being tortured. That jolly, professional executioner was doing unimaginable things to him with expert skill. I knew this because the victim's cries of agony were coming through I don't know how many levels of thick stone and reaching me where I was as loud as if the man were right beside me.

"Jesus! Jesus!" I whispered. My flesh was all bumps and tremors. It wasn't as if I could feel the pain, but I remembered the executioner's glance, and I could feel my own vulnerability to pain, how easily what was being done to the heretic could be done to me.

Even the ogre stirred and muttered uneasily in his sleep.

The shrieking went on and on and on and unbelievably on, a kind of torture in itself, a mental battering. You would have thought the poor bastard would lose his voice. You would have thought he would lose consciousness. You would have thought he would die— just, for God's sake, die. But the executioner must have known every trick, every method to make the man suffer and yet keep him alive.

Assaulted by that noise, I sank onto the floor again. I curled my body up and pressed my hands to my ears to try to block it out. It didn't help at all. There was no blocking out those wails of agony. They were in my mind now, rising out of the blackest part of my imagination. On and on and on. They shrouded me, an acid shroud that ate away at whatever courage I had, whatever hope I had, whatever faith I had. What was happening to me? How had I gotten here? Was I going to die here? Like this? Like him? Tortured? Executed? Or ripped to pieces by a beast who couldn't even exist? What was this place? Was I crazy? Or was I crazy before, back in LA? Was my real life some sort of dream? Was this hell reality?

I curled on the floor, holding my ears, squeezing my eyes shut. The heretic's shrieks went on and on and on.

A tear ran down my cheek and fell into the dust on the dungeon floor.

WHAT HAPPENED NEXT happened with shocking quickness. I must have slept again. It was a small mercy anyway. Suddenly, the cell door came crashing in. Suddenly, the ogre was roaring again. Suddenly, there were men in the cell: two guards and that other man, the black-bearded man in the red vest with the gold dragon on it, the man who had struck me down. Suddenly, the jailer was back with his torch held high and his hideous warty face cracked open in a grin.

Groggy, confused, I was on my feet. The guards came at me and grabbed me. Freed me from the chains in the wall and wrenched my arms behind me. The man in the dragon vest stood directly in front of me, his eyes on mine, mine held by his. He gripped his sword in his hand, and I knew if I struggled he'd strike me down on the spot. So I just stood there while the guards manacled my wrists behind my back.

Over the roars of the ogre, over the rattling of his chains, the man in the dragon vest said in a voice of perfect calm, "It's time for your trial, Lively."

Then the guards grabbed my arms. The man in the dragon vest strolled out of the cell. The guards hustled me after him. I was forced across the threshold . . .

And the next thing I knew, I was standing in the stairwell at Global Pictures, the world swirling around me.

3

I REELED WHERE I STOOD. THE STAIRWELL SEEMED TO tilt and spin. I clutched my chest, swallowing hard, fighting down the urge to vomit.

I staggered toward the edge of the steps. I reached out blindly for the wooden banister. Felt it. Grabbed it. Held on with both hands to keep from falling over.

It took me a second or two to catch my breath, to get my bearings. Then my eyes ranged around the space.

Was it possible? It was! The nightmare, the hallucination, whatever it had been—it was over!

Gripping the banister, I bent double. I let out a gasp of relief. "What. Just. Happened?" I said—and for a moment, I was giddy with joy. I laughed out loud.

But then, the moment after that, I thought: *No, really. What just happened?* I lifted my head. My vision was blurred with emotion. *What the hell just happened?*

The only answer I could come up with was that there had to be something wrong with me, wrong with my brain, a tumor or something. Because that—what just happened—that was so insane, and so insanely real, too. The whole thing: the dead woman on the floor and the dungeon and the ogre and the shrieking heretic—it hadn't been like a dream at all. It was like I was there. Like it was really happening. That couldn't be normal. Could it? That was brain tumor stuff, for sure.

Still, it was over. For now, at least. That was something anyway. Because so help me, that ogre was about to pull those chains out of the wall, I was sure of it.

I laughed again, just once. "Ogre," I muttered. *Listen to me. Talking like there were ogres. Like there could really be ogres outside of a fairy tale or a movie or something.*

Still, I couldn't believe how real it had all seemed.

I started down the stairs. I kept a good, firm hold on the banister. My legs felt weak and unsteady. But with every step, the dizziness and nausea were receding. By the time I reached the bottom, I could feel the strength returning to my limbs.

I pushed through the door, out onto the ground floor of the Edison Building. There, at the end of the hall, were the glass doors to the lot outside. The blessed California sun was shining through them. The blessed blue California sky was visible above the rounded roofs of the sound stages.

I quickly made my way to the doors. I pushed out and took in a great big beautiful breath of the autumn air. How fresh it was! How free! Blowing away the stench of the dungeon, the shit and despair, erasing the memory of the manacles on my wrists, dispersing the suffocating fog of helplessness, confusion, and terror that had surrounded me.

I hurried across the lot to my car, trying to gather my thoughts, trying to make some sense of what had happened. I would have to go to the doctor, I figured, get some tests, maybe a brain scan. A thing like this—it couldn't be normal, could it? A hallucination that realistic—it was cause to worry, wasn't it?

It was. I knew it was. And yet, with every step, the entire bizarre experience seemed to be receding into a distant unreality. I glanced at my watch. It didn't seem as if any time had passed from the moment I stepped into that tower room where the dead woman lay to the moment I returned to the stairwell. The whole nightmare had come and gone in an instant. So, whatever had caused it, how bad could it really be?

By the time my battered Nissan came into view in its parking space, I was beginning to talk myself out of even my lingering anxieties. Maybe this little sword-and-sorcery fantasy of mine had just been some sort of harmless brain glitch, some little frizz of neural static. I was never a big drug guy, but I'd smoked some weed from time to time. The last time was more than a year ago but who knows? Maybe the dope had backed up on me somehow, caused a flash of dendritic weirdness, a sort of mental belch.

I continued across the studio lot. I saw people stare at me as I went by. I saw the way they frowned and narrowed their eyes. But I didn't really notice it. I didn't notice anything. I was too lost in my own thoughts.

I reached my car. I pulled the door open. I sank into the driver's seat. Started the engine. Glanced up into the rearview mirror to check for traffic behind me.

And I saw myself.

The shock of it was like a blow to the chest. It seemed to stop my heart and knock the breath right out of me. I stared at my reflection in the rearview mirror, my eyes wide and white and full of horror.

The side of my face was smeared with dried blood. On my forehead was the purple knot with split skin running across it—the wound I had felt with my fingers in the dungeon—the wound I had gotten when the man in the dragon vest had struck me with the flat of his sword and knocked me senseless.

It was there. The wound. It was real.

I looked at my hands. They were covered in dust. There were faint blue bruises around my wrists where the manacles had been.

I looked up into the mirror again, my mouth open. The blood. The wound. They were real. It was all real. The dead woman, the dungeon, the ogre roaring in his chains.

It had really happened.

As my mind raced, I heard a whispered word break from my lips: "Galiana."

I DROVE UNSTEADILY back toward NoHo. I was fighting panic now. My thoughts were going in circles, trying to make sense of something that just did not make sense. I kept looking at my reflection in the rearview mirror, hoping the wound and the blood would be gone, gone like the dungeon and all the rest, another hallucination.

But they were still there, always still there. And now that I knew they were there, my head began to throb and ache again. I began to feel weak and dizzy—maybe from the blow, maybe just from the shock and confusion.

I parked my jalopy in the garage under my apartment building, but I didn't go up to my apartment. I didn't want to be alone there, staring into the bathroom mirror, desperately trying to understand what could not be understood.

Instead, I hurried back to Hitchcock's. And now I did notice the faces of the people who looked at me, the way they started and stared when I staggered past them on the sidewalk. All I could think was that they didn't know the half of it. For all they knew, I could have gotten this wound falling against the curb or walking into a door. What if I told them how it had really happened?

It was quiet at Hitchcock's, the hour between breakfast and lunch. There was only a handful of stubble-chinned writer types sitting behind their laptops at the sidewalk tables. I scanned their faces. There was no one I knew. None of them even looked up from their work as I stumbled past them to the door.

I pushed inside the cafe. I saw at once my usual table was empty. All of my friends had gone off to work or whatever it was they did all day. There were just a couple of yoga class girls having coffee in one corner, their rolled-up mats leaning against the wall. An out-of-work actor reading a paperback behind the bar. A protest of some kind was on the news on TV, people shouting, raising their fists, the volume low. It was quiet here, very quiet.

My heart sank. No friends, no one to turn to, no one to help me.

Then Schuyler Cohen shot out of the kitchen like a cannonball.

She looked enormous as always, stuffed into her black T-shirt, and angry as always, with her red hair spiking off her head like a flame. She was carrying a plate with a sandwich on it.

She saw me and the plate dropped from her fingers and shattered on the floor.

SHE PRACTICALLY CARRIED me to her car, a colorless old Ford of some sort. Plunked me into the passenger seat. And drove me back to her house—which was really Jane Janeway's house—cursing at me the whole time. Because she didn't like men but she liked me but she didn't like me because she liked Jane who didn't like her, or not in that way, and she didn't think it was fair the way men got women to take care of them but something in me brought that out in her which a lot of times actually made me uncomfortable because it annoyed her so much but right at the moment I was very grateful for it. It was complicated.

"What did you do to yourself, you stupid asshole?" she said, glancing from the road to me. "Did you get into some macho ape fight? You did, didn't you? If you did, so help me, I will fuck you up, you understand me? You will rue the day, Austin, I'm serious."

This, from Schuyler, was tender loving care. I leaned against the passenger window, weak and sick, letting the warmth of her affection wash over me.

It was a lot of affection, twenty minutes of insults and obscenities. Jane's house was in Los Feliz, near Griffith Park: a beautiful Spanish Colonial manse with yellow walls and a red tiled roof and all sorts of towers and chimneys rising into the branches of the surrounding oaks. The house belonged to Alexis Merriwether really, her movie star. It was one of Alexis's smaller properties around town. She let Jane live there so to make sure she was available twenty-four hours a day, seven days a week.

Schuyler parked in the driveway. I got out of the car, but she rushed around to grab hold of me as if I were about to collapse.

"I can walk," I said.

"Shut up." She gripped me hard, holding me upright as we went together toward the house.

I was glad she did. Between the head wound and the insanity of it all, I really was pretty sick and dizzy by now. I drew strength and comfort from leaning against the generous feminine softness of her. She knew it too—she pressed me tightly against one enormous breast—though if I'd said it out loud she would've beaten me senseless.

"Jane!" she bellowed as she pushed through the door and hauled me in with her. Between this and being dragged around the dungeons of Galiana by prison guards, I felt I hadn't taken two steps on my own all day.

We came into a hallway decked with colorful Spanish mosaics and paved with elegant Spanish tiles.

"Jane!"

Whenever she wasn't picking up Alexis Merriwether's dry cleaning or shopping for her furniture or accompanying her from place to place or listening to her complain or helping her pick out her wardrobe, Jane was often home during the day, working on her computer, making Alexis's appointments, answering her email, and arranging her travel. I got the impression Alexis had two lives: the glamorous movie-star life she lived, and the life of everyday drudgery that Jane lived for her.

Jane came out of her home office into the front hall and saw me in Schuyler's arms, a wounded warrior carried off the field. She was wearing one of her shapeless sweatshirts and track pants—to hide her loveliness from her employer even now when she was nowhere near. And yet the look on her face was so full of compassion, so full of the feminine tenderness Schuyler felt but couldn't show, that it pierced through even my panic and confusion, and I saw that mousey Jane was really beautiful. For the first time I wondered, down deep, only just above the level of panicking consciousness: *What would it be like to actually earn the kind of devotion from her that her movie-star boss merely paid for?*

The two girls helped me into what I guess was a guest room: a small rectangular space with nothing but a bed and a writing desk and chair in it, plus a window onto a pleasantly weedy little garden out back. Jane took my shoes off while Schuyler laid me down on the mattress, my head on a fluffy pillow. Then Schuyler fetched a washcloth and brought it to Jane. Jane sat beside me and cleaned my wound, fussing over me with a womanly care that made me yearn up into her blue-green eyes. Schuyler, meanwhile, leaned darkly against the door, looking jealous of me for being with Jane and jealous of Jane for being the Jane-like way Schuyler could never bring herself to be.

"What did you do to yourself, sweetheart?" Jane asked me, swabbing the wound.

"He got in a fight," said Schuyler gruffly from the doorway.

"I didn't get in a fight," I said.

"What did you do?" asked Jane.

What could I say? That I'd been bodily swept off into some fantasy movie? Locked in a castle dungeon with an ogre in the imaginary land of Galiana?

"I tripped and fell off the curb at the studio. Smacked my head on the pavement," I said.

"Oh, Austin!"

I didn't like lying to her, but I liked the pity in her voice. I loved the pity. I drank the pity down like a healing elixir. How soft they were, those blue-green eyes.

She wrung the washcloth out in a small bowl. She examined her work: my head. "The cut's not so bad. I don't think you need stitches or anything. It's just a bad bump, really."

And so help me, as I live, she leaned down and kissed it lightly. To make it better, you know. And so help me—as I live—it *did* make it better. It made me feel better anyway. She was full of magic yin, our Jane, and all I could think was what a shame it was, what a waste to spend that supernatural girl power on a spoiled movie star who wouldn't even notice if her limo backed over her. A man of spirit, on the other hand, might live and die to make a girl like Jane proud and happy.

From the corner of my eye, I saw Schuyler avert her glance from the two of us, wincing with emotional pain.

Then I heard—we all heard—the phone ringing in the home office. Alexis calling Jane with one of her endless demands.

And yet she didn't leave me, not right away. "I want you to rest here a little, all right? Until you feel stronger." The phone rang again. She stood up off the bed. "Are you hungry? Do you need something to eat?"

I shook my head weakly, gazing up at her, mesmerized.

"All right. I'll make you some soup in a while. Just get some rest."

She lingered to smile down at me, but the phone kept insisting. At last, she hurried away.

I glanced over at Schuyler. Schuyler rolled her eyes and shook her head in disgust, then peeled off the doorway and disappeared down the hall.

Alone then, I lay where I was. Jane had worked her wonders on me. Everything that had been frantic inside me was quiet now; everything that had been sore was soothed and easy. I turned my head on the pillow to glance out the window at the pale-green tangle of garden framed in the pane. For the first time since my return to reality—or my return to Los Angeles, at least, which was as close to reality as I was going to get—I was able to think things over with a measure of calm.

What had happened to me? This journey to Galiana, what was it? If it was just a hallucination, how had it left its mark on me? I didn't just mean the bruise on my head either; it was more than that. The shock of my arrest, the fear of the ogre, the sympathetic agony that had curdled my skin as I listened to the shrieks of the tortured heretic. All that had scarred me too. If nothing else, I couldn't help but notice it had taken me out of myself a little, given me some emotional distance from my current Hollywood setbacks and irritations. In fact, I hardly felt them at all at the moment. Even if Galiana was an illusion, that mark remained, same as the knot on my forehead.

Galiana. Where had I heard that name before?

Gentled by Jane's gentleness, I let my eyes sink shut.

I WOKE FROM a fine, deep sleep, still peaceful, more peaceful than I had felt in what seemed like a long time. I had been so troubled for such a while, these many weeks at least. The long, quietly frantic wait to hear back from my agent about my new script. The hollow nausea of knowing the script was bad. The crushing grief—that's what it was, the grief—of having him reject me. The spiraling emptiness of feeling that the dream of my life was over, that I was not going to be what I wanted to be but was going to be nothing more than what I was right now. And then . . . walking through that stairwell door.

Galiana.

Where had I heard that name?

I went into the pocket of my jeans and fished out my phone. Still lying down, I held it up above me, working the keyboard with my thumbs. I brought up the Oh-Gee search engine and tapped in the word. *Galiana.*

There were over a million hits. It was both a first name and a last name and the name of several locations. Up at the top of the results, there was a Wikipedia entry. I clicked on that. It was a disambiguation page: a page giving all the various listings for the word:

Galiana may refer to:

- a town in Punjab, Pakistan
- a princess in moorish Spain
- a fictional country in the novel *Another Kingdom* by Ellen Evermore

The moment I reached the end of the entry, I felt a jolt of recognition.

"*Another Kingdom,*" I whispered to myself.

Yes. I knew that book, or at least I'd heard of it. But when? Where? I read so many books as a story analyst for Mythos I couldn't remember all of them, yet I felt sure I'd seen that title somewhere among them.

There was no link to any Wikipedia entry for the book, so I called up Amazon and searched for it there. Sure enough, they had it listed:

Another Kingdom

By Ellen Evermore

Murder and political intrigue stalk the dangerous halls of Castle Eastrim in the New Republic of Galiana.

There it was! Excited, I sat up quickly—too quickly. The room tilted and I felt dizzy and sick again.

"Woof," I said.

Slowly, I lay back down. I reread the page. Eastrim. In Galiana. Wasn't that exactly what the heretic had told me in the dungeon? Yes, it was.

I scrolled over the site some more but, surprisingly, there was nothing else to find. There should have been a longer description of the book, but there wasn't. There should have been a picture of the book's cover, but there was only an empty square containing the words, "No image." There were no reviews. No links to other sellers. Only a notice that said: "This book is not available at this time."

Not available? Anywhere? On the whole internet? Not available at all?

Moving cautiously, I turned onto my side and propped myself up on my elbow to get in a better position to work the phone. I searched other sites. Auction sites. Used book sites. I ran a general search for the novel's title. It led me back to Amazon. That was it.

I bit the corner of my lip. Strange, no? A book you couldn't find online? When the hell does that happen?

I took a breath, trying to come up with a fresh search tactic. And I thought: *My coverage.* Sure. If I'd read the book for Mythos, I would've written a report.

I tried my Cloud files but there was nothing there. Which didn't mean much. To preserve space, I usually moved coverage I no longer needed into a local file in my laptop.

I needed to get home and find that coverage. My hunting blood was up now. Something weird had happened to me—something very weird, mega-weird. The hallucination or dream or whatever it was, the head wound, and now a novel with the place-names Galiana and Eastrim in it, just like in the dream? It felt like I was close to finding an explanation for my experience—close and yet impossibly far because I couldn't imagine what explanation there could be. But whatever it was, I wanted to find out. Needed to.

I only had one clue.

Another Kingdom by Ellen Evermore.

I USED MY Orgo ride-share app to call for a car. Then, moving slowly, like an old man, I swung my feet down onto the floor. I found my shoes, slipped them on. I tried to stand, but the room began tossing and tilting again. I sat back on the bed hard, my stomach dropping. I stayed there a few moments, drawing deep breaths. I knew I must have a concussion. I knew I ought to go to a doctor or at least lie back down and rest. It was awfully tempting to think of staying here for a few more hours, even a day or two. Jane would sit with me sometimes. She would feed me soup. Schuyler couldn't hang around forever.

I pushed myself up and staggered from the room.

I heard voices as I came down the hallway toward the front door. I passed Jane's home office and peeked in. The room was empty. The lights were out. She was gone. I was disappointed.

The voices were coming from the living room up ahead. I continued down the hall and went in.

It was an elegant, colorful room. A wagon-wheel chandelier hung down from a dark wooden beam ceiling. The sofa and stuffed chairs below were bright sherbet colors, red and green. Everything was arranged around a tall white fireplace. High, arched windows made the space airy and light.

The television was on. That's where the voices were coming from. Some daytime talk show, loud women and lots of applause. At first, I thought there was no one watching, but then I saw Schuyler. I saw the red top of her head anyway. She was splayed inharmoniously in the armchair right in front of me. Her feet on the ottoman. One hand holding a beer balanced on her belly button, bare where her black T-shirt didn't quite meet her black leggings. She had her back to me as she watched the program. She didn't look around when I stepped into the open archway. I thought she didn't know I was there.

Then she said, "Jane had to go to the Big House." The Big House—that was where Alexis Merriwether usually lived when she was in town. Jane had shown me pictures of it. A massive estate you could have seen from the moon. "She told me to make you soup if you woke up," Schuyler said.

"That's all right," I said. "I'm not hungry. I called a car."

"Good. 'Cause I'm not making you any fucking soup."

I smiled. I nodded though she couldn't see me. I felt for her. I started to sidle away toward the door.

"Why don't you make your move, you dumb shit?" she asked me. "You can see she loves you."

Well, that made me pause. I searched for an answer—a true answer—but I didn't know what the answer was. I wasn't sure how I felt, I guess. And you don't make a move on a Jane Janeway unless you're ready, unless you're sure.

But before I could say even that, Schuyler said, "Christ's sweet sake, Austin, a girl like that, she'd serve you all her fucking days. Isn't that what men want?"

I felt the sting. Was I so selfish? Of course I was. But somehow I managed not to say, "*Hey, it's what you want too, isn't it? You're obviously crazy about her.*"

"You're not man enough, that's your problem," she said.

That hurt too, because I suspected it might be true. And on another day I might have barked back, "*Neither are you, if it comes down to it.*" But somehow, today, I managed not to say that either.

She swigged her beer. "You're just another wannabe artiste counting the days until you sell out and get a job."

Wow, that was merciless. Jesus. But even now, I felt for her. Even now, I managed not to say, "*Well, what the hell are you, then?*"

Schuyler belched. "You know what?" she said to the TV screen. "In the old fairy tales? You know how the beautiful princess gets the handsome prince? And people read that shit, and they think: *Well, why doesn't that happen to me?* You know why? You know why it doesn't happen? 'Cause they're not princesses, they're not princes, that's why. They're just messed-up freaks who want the world to make believe they're beautiful and give them a happy ending they haven't earned. And that's you, Austin. You're not what you wanna be. You're not who you oughtta be. And you're not what Jane deserves. So go fuck yourself, all right?"

I was reeling from the blows but I was swamped with pity for her as well. Because I knew it wasn't just me she was talking about. It was herself too. Maybe it was the whole stupid wannabe city. We're all so lost here, all of us.

Wobbly and sick, I moved slowly out of the archway to her chair and stood above her, looking down. She lifted her Angry Cherub face to me. Her cheeks were flushed, her eyes glassy.

"And don't pat yourself on the back for being kind to me," she said. "I can hear what you're thinking."

I reached down and lifted her free hand off the chair arm. I raised it to my lips and kissed it.

"Thank you for helping me back at Hitchcock's, Sky. You're a good friend."

"If you don't let go of my hand right now, I'm gonna use it to rip your heart out."

MY APARTMENT WAS an attic space in a charmless complex of concrete towers. Its sole redeeming feature was a window near my writing desk that looked out on the street. From there, I could see the spillover crowd in the parking lot in back of the corner bar, *The No-Hole*. Come Saturday night, if someone out there screamed or broke a bottle, I could look down and check on the noise and watch a couple of drunken louts shoving one another before they wandered off home.

Other than that, it was two small rooms with aggressively low ceilings. The bedroom was so small that when I unfolded the futon, there was no space to walk around it on either side. The living room-slash-kitchenette—where the precious window was—was filled by the writing desk and a couple of chairs.

I set my laptop up on the desk. I was raring to start my search, but before I could, I had to sit down and rest a moment, leaning my elbow on the tabletop, squeezing my eyes shut with my hand. When the concussion nausea passed, I went to work. I searched my computer for the title: *Another Kingdom*. Nothing. Then for the author: Ellen Evermore. Nothing again. I sat and stared at the screen, frustrated. I was beginning to doubt myself. Maybe I *hadn't* read the book for Mythos. Maybe I'd heard the word *Galiana* somewhere else.

In a desperation move, I tried the computer's trash files.

And there it was. A single page I'd discarded: *Another Kingdom*. I opened it. It was coverage all right—or that is, it was the beginning of a coverage report I hadn't finished. There was nothing there but the company form, the lines you fill out before you write your synopsis and your review.

Another Kingdom

FORM: Novel

GENRE: Fantasy

AUTHOR: Ellen Evermore

COVERAGE: Austin Lively

SUBMITTED TO: Candy Filikin

SUBMITTED BY: Sean Gunther

Plotline

Murder, intrigue, betrayal, and love all come into play as conspirators in the court of Castle Eastrim fight for power in the New Republic of Galiana.

List of Characters

QUEEN ELINDA: the exiled Queen of Galiana

EMPEROR ANASTASIUS: Lord of the Eleven Lands, betrothed to Queen Elinda

LORD IRON NETHERDALE: Head of the High Council of the New Republic

SIR ARAVIST TEM: Captain of the Eastrim Castle Guard

LADY BETHERAY NETHERDALE: Lord Iron's wife, one-time Lady-in-Waiting to Queen Elinda

LADY KATA PALAV: Lady Betheray's friend, one-time . . .

My breath caught. Lady Kata Palav.

Wasn't that the name the guard had spoken in the dungeon?

His name is Austin Lively, he'd said. *He is charged with the murder of Lady Kata Palav.*

But that was all there was. The list ended there. There was nothing else. No synopsis, no report. Just that abrupt ending. Why hadn't I finished the coverage?

I checked the document's date. It had been created three months ago. It was just starting summer then. I tried to think back. Something stirred in my memory. Candy had sent me an e-book as part of the usual package. I'd started reading it, but before I could finish, something happened. I couldn't remember what.

I searched for the title in my email files. Found it. An email from Candy:

Austin. Hope this catches you before you read Another Kingdom. The submission has been withdrawn, so we don't have to bother with it. Sorry! CF

I didn't remember what I'd done with the book after that, but I'd almost surely deleted it. I deleted all the books after I'd read them. Why wouldn't I?

I stood up from the desk. The room did a slow, sickening roll around me. I cursed. I had to reach out and grab the back of an armchair so I could lower myself into it. Close my eyes. Rest. Sitting there like that, I tried to remember more about the book but there was nothing—certainly nothing that would explain what had happened to me in the Edison Building.

Maybe Candy still had a copy, I thought. Doubtful after three months, but she might. Or she might remember something about it. Or something about the man who had submitted it, Sean Gunther. That name sounded familiar too. If I hadn't felt so lousy, I might've been able to remember.

I took a deep breath to steady myself and worked my way out of the chair again, back to the desk again. I got my phone. I dialed Candy. I gazed out the window as I listened to the ringing on the other end of the line.

That was the first time I saw the black Mustang.

4

THE MUSTANG WAS PARKED AT THE CURB IN THE RED no-parking zone next to The No-Hole lot. A racy old-school machine, jet black and shiny. I didn't take much notice of it. Not right away, not yet. It was just something to gaze at idly while I waited for Ken, Candy's assistant, to answer the phone. I did notice the driver though. Kind of a strange-looking guy—or a strange-looking girl, I wasn't actually sure which. He or she had boy-cut blond hair but a small round face with kittenish female features. He had a narrow, girly body from what I could see of it, but a bared bicep on his visible arm with muscles that had to be a man's. Call her a him then, for convenience's sake.

That was all I took in before Ken picked up the line. He said he'd "see if he could find" Candy, which meant he'd ask her if she thought I was worth speaking to. I guess I was. I was still looking down at the driver of the Mustang when she came on the line.

"Austin," she said curtly. I was just a reader, after all. I'd already had my weekly meeting. What did I want now? "Is there a problem with the assignments?"

"No. Look, I'm sorry to bother you, Candy," I said. I turned away from the window to focus. I already had my story prepared. "I was just checking my records and I found an unfinished report for a book called *Another Kingdom.* I was worried I hadn't completed the assignment. Do you remember that one?"

"Gee. No. I'm sure if it was important, I'd've asked for it."

"It was submitted by a guy named Sean Gunther," I said.

"Oh! Oh yeah. Sure. He's a pal of Henry's." Henry Quint was the head of Mythos, Candy's boss. "He was, like, some big writer back in the day, like, a million years ago or something." As she went on talking, I searched Gunther's name on my laptop. "Henry talks about him a lot. I guess he wrote this one famous novel at some point, and he was, like, the flavor of the month. Then he did that Hollywood thing they do, you know, where he came out here hoping to score the big bucks and he took a lot of meetings and people fawned over him and it was all sweet and dreamy except the years went by and nothing he wrote got made and then people stopped hiring him. So, by the time he decided to sit down and write something again, his glory days were over. Nobody cared anymore what he did." Gunther's Wikipedia entry came up on the screen. There was his picture: a noble countenance haloed by a leonine mane of silver-white hair. His first novel, *A Thousand Pages of Self-Referential Drivel,* had been short-listed for the Pulitzer Prize. Thirty years ago.

Candy went on: "He sent this *Another Kingdom* thing to Henry because he wanted to adapt it for the movies. It was supposed to be his big comeback or whatever. It was a mercy read, basically. Henry was just being nice to a friend."

"Right. Only you pulled it before I finished the coverage, right?"

"Right. Right. Now I remember: Gunther got cold feet about the whole thing and decided he didn't want to go through with it. I think the guy's basically an old drunk. You know. Henry humors him 'cause they were friends back when dinosaurs roamed the earth."

"You don't still have a copy of the book around, do you?"

"Nah. Why?"

Again, I had my story prepared. "When I stumbled on the coverage, I remembered how much I liked what I read. I was thinking if Gunther doesn't want to do anything with it, maybe I would. You don't happen to have his contacts, do you? I'd like to ask him if he'd let me read it again."

"I'll have Ken check with Gunther and get permission to send you his info," Candy said.

I thanked her and hung up. I turned back to the window. Glanced out, thinking.

And there was the black Mustang. The kittenish man behind the wheel looked away quickly, as if I'd almost caught him staring up at me.

I LAY DOWN on the sofa and slept again. When I woke up, my dizziness was gone. My head felt better. My mind was clearer. I touched the bump on my head, and it felt smaller, less sore. Maybe the worst effects of the concussion were passing.

I sat up and looked toward the bedroom window. The light was fading from the small patch of sky that was visible there.

"Oh, crap!" I said aloud.

I had suddenly remembered: my parents! My brother was passing through LA and they were coming down from Berkeley to have dinner with the two of us. At six o'clock.

I looked at my watch. Twenty minutes to six. No time to change clothes. I grabbed my denim jacket off the back of a chair and rushed out of the apartment.

THERE ARE TIMES in LA when the traffic is so bad, you just sit in your car, motionless, and wait for the earth to turn and bring your destination to you. Fortunately, this wasn't one of them. The traffic was only hellish, and I made it the ten miles to Beverly Hills in a mere forty minutes, twenty minutes late.

Had to be Beverly Hills, of course, the most expensive restaurant in the most expensive neighborhood. Because my brother was just so important and successful, nothing less would do. I left my car with the valet and rushed inside. The maître d' was a tall brunette so beautiful she seemed unreal. Her glance up and down me made me aware of what a mess I was: still in old jeans and an untucked shirt with the denim jacket over it, my face pale, the bruise on my head still darkly visible. Nonetheless she consented to let me join my party, and I followed the heartbreaking sway of her unobtainable backside across the white floor between the white tables past the diners all done up in sleek suits and spangly dresses specifically designed, it seemed, to make me feel ashamed.

There were my parents and my brother already seated at their corner table in the coveted brick patio out back. I was preparing to tell the made-up story of how I got the bruise on my head, but you know what? No one asked me. No one said, "How'd you hurt yourself, darling?" Not even my own mother. When I leaned down to kiss her offered cheek, she just said, "Well. You did come after all."

My father gave me a thin, absent-minded smile. My successful and famous brother stood up to give me a successful and famous handshake and slapped my shoulder as if with brotherly affection. And by the time I took my seat, the three of them were doing what they usually did: talking among themselves, as if my arrival had been nothing more than a rather irritating interruption.

Instantly, I was twelve years old again, feeling ignored, excluded, insufficient, angry, and depressed. My bizarre mental journey to Galiana was forgotten. The impossible mystery of my real-life bruises was forgotten. My quest to explain it all: forgotten. What was remembered, what came back to me—like an anvil dropping on a cartoon villain's head—was my failure: my script rejected, my agent dumping me. Not only was I so much less successful than my brother was, I was even less successful than I'd been just a day before.

Wine came. Food came. I still felt unsteady from my concussion, and I barely ate. I just gazed morosely at my parents and my older brother as their conversation went on without me. They had always had a way of doing that, of discussing their big ideas in a sort of shorthand, so that I could never quite catch up with their meaning and so could not contribute ideas of my own. I always felt I wasn't meant to.

"Well, of course, the populace will bristle, that's to be expected," my mother was saying at some point. "The nation-state, after all, is their warm and fuzzy blanket, isn't it?"

"World War I," my father murmured wisely. "World War I."

"This is the whole theme of my new book," said Richard, circling a glass of white wine beneath his golden Viking beard. "Revolutions travel downward, not upward."

"Ah," said my mother, fingers to her chest, as if her darling little boy had just brought her a picture he'd made all by himself. "Wonderful. Of course."

She was thin as a needle, my mother, flat as a blacked-out window in her dress of sequined lace. Her body all lines, her face all angles, her lips sharp, her cheeks high, her eyes narrow. Her hair sprung out about her crown in brittle curls like steel wool. She was my mother! Shouldn't she have some soft place to burrow into? Just looking at my mother made me feel motherless.

And my father—where was the manly meat and muscle on him? His body was like a willow wand. A breeze might have rippled it. His salt-and-pepper hair, cut close to his head, seemed solid as a helmet. Owlish, musing, preoccupied features. Sharp, narrow glasses. Mom and Dad both wore sharp, narrow glasses. They both had those vague, distant, distracted stares.

"Reviews," my father was saying now. "Essential. Connections. Reviews."

I think this was by way of paternal advice to my brother.

"Has Serge read it yet?" my mother asked him.

Serge, of course.

"Serge says it's my best," said Richard proudly.

"Well, Serge . . . " murmured my father with a chuckle, as if this were all that needed saying: Serge.

Well, maybe it was all that needed saying: Serge Orosgo—another factor that linked the three of them and excluded me. My father held the prestigious Orosgo chair in Psychology at Berkeley, which the billionaire endowed. My mother, also a professor at Berkeley, did sociology research, which was often funded by the Orosgo Foundation. Mom and Dad had introduced Richard to the great man, and now Richard was a senior muck-a-muck at the Orosgo Institute think tank and the billionaire was his mentor and friend.

Of course, I suppose I was linked to Orosgo now too, since it was his charity, his favor to my brother, that had gotten me the reader's job at the production company at Global Pictures, which Orosgo owned. But somehow, it wasn't quite the same thing, was it?

The waiter brought us after-dinner coffees. I don't think I'd said five words since I'd sat down. Somewhere along the line, I stopped listening. My mind drifted, drifted back into time. A wistful memory returned to me. I was a little boy, maybe five or six or so. I was sitting on the floor in the back room of our house in Berkeley. My parents and my brother were in the next room over, the living room. My brother was seven years older than I was, so maybe twelve or thirteen then. The three of them were discussing big ideas, just as they were now.

My little sister, Riley, only two or three, had vanished into a long storage space hidden behind a sliding wall panel. She liked to crawl around in there and then return to tell long-winded stories about the secret hiding holes she'd found.

But I—I was aware of none of them. I was completely immersed in an imaginative universe of my own. I was arranging plastic figures against a backdrop I'd made out of colored paper taped to a cardboard box. Space knights and alien monsters and villainous galactic tyrants were doing battle in front of my crayon drawing of starry darkness. I whispered their dialogue to myself as I moved them into their various positions. Creating tableaux. Acting out scenes. Making movies of the mind.

And there was within me a stillness of complete delight—I remembered it—as if, in the act of creation, my brain waves had arranged themselves into their native patterns and my flesh was speaking the silent language of my original spirit. Delight, delight. Creation and delight.

Where had the purity of that impulse gone? I asked myself. Where had that original spirit gone? What had Hollywood done to me? What had I done to myself?

"Well, she can't. She simply can't," my mother said.

I snapped back into the moment, suddenly aware that the subject of the conversation had changed.

"A time. A place. Then . . . no," my father muttered. "Just . . . no."

"I mean, really. It's for her own good. Aliens!" my mother said.

Ah. Finally. The ostensible purpose of this gathering. Just as my brother had warned me: we were discussing Riley now, our little sister.

"Listen, we're lucky there are aliens," said my brother with a laugh.

"Well, this new one though. Juan or Pedro or . . . "

"Marco," my brother said. "And not an alien, in that sense."

"It's not funny. It really isn't, Richard."

"Venezuela," said my father darkly.

For the first time that evening, my mother turned to address me directly. "Really, Austin, you have to talk to her. You're the only one she listens to."

In every family drama, each person has a role to play. In my family, my older brother, Richard, was obviously the big success, my parents' pride and joy. Me?—well, I guess I was the misguided wastrel, frittering away my life in Hollywood until I came to my senses and got a real job or went back to school.

Riley, though—she was the black sheep, the lost cause. She lived up north near my parents. She lived off my parents too, dependent on their money although she did have a job, or a sort-of job, a part-time job on weekends as an "actress" at the Happy Town Amusement Park near Walnut Creek. She would play a farm girl at the petting zoo there or a ghoul at the funhouse, jumping out at passersby.

But her "real work," if you could call it that, was as a "video artist." She spent most of her time making this insane video series called *Ouroboros: Dark Dreams of Reality*. In the videos, she lay on her bed, kicking her legs in the air like an adolescent girl. She looked into the camera and spun conspiracy theories out of stories she'd read online. These theories involved aliens from outer space trying to take over the world with the help of an international cabal of human plotters. I could never tell whether these videos were serious or ironic. But the funny thing was: people liked them. They had tens of thousands of viewers, sometimes over a hundred thousand.

My parents had worked their way out of a Midwestern nowhere to become what they were. They were proud of their status and their elegant, intellectual friends. Riley's videos—her videos and her endless series of disastrous romances—embarrassed my folks no end.

But me, I loved Riley, loved her like crazy. I'd practically raised her, playing dolls with her, telling her stories when my parents were too busy professoring to do the job.

And so I didn't want to be in this conversation—yet another in the endless series of what-are-we-going-to-do-about-Riley family discussions.

"Excuse me," I said abruptly.

And abruptly, I got up. I weaved my way through the white tables quickly, as if making my escape. With a sense of freedom and release, I entered the main room of the restaurant and found the door to the restrooms. I opened it and went through into a narrow corridor paneled in old wood. I just wanted to stay there, hide there.

But I went down the corridor toward the men's room.

AS I STOOD at the urinal, I checked my phone. There was an email from Ken, the assistant at Mythos. He had sent me a phone number and street address for Sean Gunther, the author who had submitted *Another Kingdom* to the company.

I flushed and stepped away from the porcelain. I was alone in the room. I glanced at my watch. It was still early, not yet eight. Without really thinking about it, I punched in the number.

Mostly, it was just a way of stalling, staving off the moment when I would have to return to my family at their table. I had absolutely no idea what I was going to say to Gunther if he actually picked up the phone.

Hi, my name is Austin Lively. Earlier today, I was transported into an alternate reality, and I was wondering . . .

He picked up on the third ring. A gruff voice: "Yeah."

"Mr. Gunther?" I said, startled.

"Yeah."

"Hi, my name is Austin Lively. I . . . "

"Oh yeah, come on over."

He hung up.

I took the phone from my ear and stared at it. I thought: *Okay, that was weird.*

But weird or no, it had changed the entire tone of my evening. Suddenly I was charged up, on the hunt again. I was going to get out of this place, get out of this dinner, get out of this conversation, and find out what the hell had happened to me.

I slipped the phone into my pocket. I hurried to the men's room door and pushed through.

And I let out a wild shout of horror: "Oh no!"

Suddenly, two guards had me gripped by the arms, and I was being hustled up the dungeon steps to face my trial for murder.

5

IT WAS A BRUTAL SHOCK. A HAMMER BLOW TO THE GUT,
knocking the air and life right out of me. Why hadn't it occurred
to me I might walk through another door and find myself swept
back into Galiana? Because shit like that doesn't happen, that's why.
I still didn't really believe it had happened to me the first time, and
to find myself back here, in manacles again, facing murder charges
again—the jolt of despair was so sudden it was nearly crippling. Was
I going nuts? Or was this real? Why hadn't I gotten that brain scan
while I had the chance?

One of the guards gave me a rough shove.

"Come on, let's go! Hurry up! Stop stalling!"

The man in the red vest walked ahead of us, leading the way.
Sir Aravist Tem, the captain of the guard. Even in the whirl of
hopelessness and confusion, I knew his name now. I remembered it
from the character list in my computer.

We reached the top of the stairs. Went down a short stone
hallway. Pushed through a heavy set of doors. I prayed that crossing
the threshold would transport me back to Los Angeles and save me.
No such luck. We came into a small chamber. A cohort of guards
was waiting for us there, all with their swords drawn. Why?

Then a sound reached me, and I understood. It was the sound of a mob, just outside. An angry mob. People shouting, chanting.

"Bring him out!"

"Bring us the murderer!"

"Murder! Conspiracy!"

"We'll strangle him with his own innards!"

I looked around wide-eyed at the guards surrounding me. I swallowed hard. "Wait, are they screaming for me?"

No one answered. No one even looked my way. The guards focused only on Sir Aravist Tem.

Sir Aravist said, "Keep him surrounded. Don't let them get at him. Let's go."

"No, wait! Wait!" I said.

The Captain pushed through the doors and the guards marched me out after him.

"There he is!"

"Let us at him!"

"Murderer!"

"Get out of our way!"

Everything was chaos, noise, and motion. I was in a courtyard, a square of sky above me, stone walls rising on every side. I was jostled hard. Rough faces, contorted and purple with murderous rage, lunged at me over the guards' shoulders. Hands reached for me, grabbed at me, clawed the space in front of my eyes. The mob's cries filled the air like the roar of a surging sea. They pushed and shoved at the guards who veered and stumbled left and then right, dragging me with them. With my hands manacled behind me, I had to fight to keep my balance. I could barely see beyond backs and shoulders, angry faces, and wheeling glimpses of the sky.

It occurred to me, in jumbled flashes of panicky thought, that I could die here, really die, right here in this ridiculous fairyland. I'd been smacked with the flat of a sword here, and the bruise was still on my head when I returned to LA. So wouldn't I be dead in LA if I was torn to pieces by this mob or tried and condemned and executed? And what if—almost worse—what if I was sentenced to life in the dungeon? What if I never got a chance to pass through another doorway and could never return to my life at home? Would I rot away in my cell, chained to the wall, dying in this dream while I dreamed of my lost life in Hollywood?

"Burn him!"

"Draw and quarter him!"

"Let us have him! Murderer!"

"We'll cut him to pieces!"

The crowd kept roaring. The faces and hands kept trying to get at me. The guards kept shoving their way through, carrying me along with them.

It wasn't far, thank God. The trip across the courtyard couldn't have been more than twenty yards. After a few terrifying moments, two massive dark-wood doors loomed high above me just ahead. The doors swung open as the guards fought their way to them.

The mob charged us one last time. The guards stumbled into me. Hands reached. Contorted faces screamed. There were curses. There were clawing fingers. There were flashing silver blades.

"Get back, you animals!"

Then I was hurried through the doors, and the doors swung shut behind me with a boom.

The guards sheathed their swords and stepped away from me. My hands still manacled, I bent forward, panting for breath. Then, slowly, I straightened. I looked up.

I was in a small but majestic courtroom, lit by fire, by torches flaming from sconces and candles burning in the rims of chandeliers. In oaken boxes of tiered spectator benches to my left and right, lords and ladies and priestly types and who knows who else sat looking down at me. Their pitiless expressions flared and darkened in the shifting light and shadow. Behind them, wooden strips made chevrons on the yellow walls. Above them, shields and battle axes formed cornices beneath the dark wood ceilings. Like the eyes of the spectators, the murderous blades caught the orange fire glow and reflected it back to me.

Straight ahead at the end of a long, broad aisle was a high judge's bench. It was an awful sight, towering almost to the rafters. A rampant red dragon was carved into the front of it, six feet tall at least. And seated at the top were two terrifying figures: the judges. They wore black robes, and their eyes burned red from the depths of the cowls that covered their heads and shadowed their faces. I took one look at them and I knew I was doomed.

Now two guards gripped my arms and marched me down the aisle between the spectators. They brought me to a railing under the high bench and left me there. I stood, manacled, blinking up at the judges.

Sir Aravist Tem swaggered up beside me, stroking his neat black beard with one hand, the thumb of his other hand hooked insouciantly in his sword belt.

"Lord Judges of the High Council," he said in a soldierly voice that echoed in the reaches of the ceiling. "I deliver the prisoner Austin Lively to be tried for the murder of Lady Kata Palav."

The room was deathly silent then. Not even a curious murmur stirred the stillness. The two judges way up there above me solemnly nodded their hooded heads. The one to the left spoke in the gravelly voice of an old man, though his face was hidden in shadow and I couldn't tell his age.

"Summon Lord Netherdale," he said.

Lord Iron Netherdale. Head of the High Council of the New Republic. I remembered his name from the character list too. And even in my daze of fear and confusion, it occurred to me now how bizarre that was. You know? That I should have read a name in a fantasy book. And that I should be there—in Galiana—wherever the hell that was—and that name should be called as if it were attached to a living man.

A bell tolled, a massive bell tolling massively, sonorously, somewhere in some tower nearby, out in the courtyard. There was a shuffling sound, and I turned to see that everyone in the courtroom was standing, the judges and the pitiless lords and ladies and priests in the spectator benches. Everyone.

And in came Lord Iron.

He entered from a doorway high up in the wall and moved briskly across a raised platform toward the bench. As he went, he smiled at someone in the audience and pointed at someone else and smiled at yet another. A public man. A politician, just like the ones we have back home in reality. If I held any hope of getting justice here, it died right then and there when I saw him.

He was in his fifties, tall and substantial, straight-backed and broad-shouldered, fit and trim. He had a thick head of brown-blond hair speckled with gray and a handsome, confident countenance that went before him like the prow of a ship. I could see at a glance he was smart and schemey, the master of the place. Whatever happened here, it would be his doing or by his will.

He was followed close behind by another man, a much smaller man, very short and very wizened, very thin. He wore a robe of deep indigo that flowed about his desiccated frame like liquid night. He had a face like a raisin with small, glittering eyes buried deep in the wrinkled flesh. A gray tuft of hair rose like a little wave up top; a gray tuft of beard hung limply from his chin.

Lord Iron settled into his seat between the two other judges, and when he sat, all the others in the hall—the judges and the spectators—sat down as well. The little man in the indigo cape took up a place directly behind him, standing.

"This tribunal is in session," Lord Iron said in a voice that was both relaxed and strong, casual and yet authoritative. He looked down at me from his great height. I felt his power over me, the power of life and death. It made my guts curdle. "Austin Lively," he said—and I hated to hear him speak my name. It was disorienting, unreal, as if my name should have been on the character list on my computer along with his. "You are charged with stabbing Lady Kata Palav to death. How do you plead?"

I didn't want to answer. I didn't want to admit that this was happening, that I was actually here. But what could I do?

"I'm not guilty," I said as forcefully as I could.

The little graybeard behind Lord Iron leaned forward and whispered into the Lord's ear. The Lord smiled knowingly and gave a little snort. My heart sank. Doomed.

"Summon Lady Betheray to the stand," he said.

Lady Betheray. Yes, I remembered that name from the character list too, like Sir Aravist's name and Lord Iron's. And now—she was coming here? How crazy was this? Really, what the hell? Had I become a character in a novel?

Everyone turned, and so I turned. I saw a small door set in the wall at the rear of the room behind the spectator's box. The door swung open, and out from the darkness within walked a woman into the firelight, a woman like no woman I had ever seen before.

She took my breath away. It wasn't just that she was beautiful— though she was beautiful, she really was. She was young—in her early twenties at most. She had lush, raven hair held in bangs on her brow by a silver tiara studded with gems. The rest of it spilled with heart-stopping abandon down the sides of her rose-and-ivory valentine of a face. Her lips were soft and rich, and her eyes were brilliant green. A golden chain with a round, golden locket set off the grace and elegance of her throat. Her long gown of white and gold draped a shapely figure at once sensual and majestic. She was beautiful, no question. But I lived in LA. I saw beautiful women all the time.

No, it was more than that. It was the grace with which she came down the aisle as if floating on air. It was the way she never turned, never glanced either left or right at the staring, murmuring spectators. It was the way she kept her hands clasped beneath her breasts in a position of such modesty and self-containment. Everything about her—it was all just so incredibly . . . what was the word?

Womanly. So incredibly womanly.

I watched her walk past me. I couldn't stop staring. Sir Aravist Tem opened a gate in the railing for her. She inclined her chin half an inch in thanks and passed through. I watched her as she climbed up the narrow stairway to the witness box beside the high bench, climbed so smoothly she almost seemed to levitate.

She took her place in the box, stood there behind its low rail, erect, dignified, her hands still clasped before her.

"The witness will state her name," Lord Iron said.

"My name is Lady Betheray Netherdale," she answered. Her voice was like silver bells.

"And your station."

"I am honored to be your wife, my lord."

Lord Iron smiled blandly. "And it is my great pleasure that you are," he said.

As the watching crowd tittered its approval, I thought: *That's right.* I remembered that from the character list: she was Lord Iron's wife. A recent prize for him, I would have bet, considering what had to be the more-than-twenty-year difference in their ages.

"Before the fall of the queen and the rise of the New Republic, did you have another station as well?" Lord Iron asked her.

"I did, my lord. I was lady-in-waiting to Queen Elinda."

"And in that capacity, you served with Lady Kata Palav, the victim in this case, did you not?"

"Yes, my lord."

Yes, I remembered this too. Lady Kata had been Lady Betheray's friend. Which meant Lady Kata's death—her murder—must have really grieved this woman. I couldn't see any signs of grief on her face—of course not; she was too poised, too seemingly serene. But I had to wonder: Was she sorrowful enough to be angry, angry enough to want vengeance, vengeful enough to assume I was guilty, to actively try to condemn me here in her testimony?

There was a brief pause as, once again, the wizened graybeard in the wizardly robe leaned forward and whispered in Lord Iron's ear. The politician's large head inclined in agreement.

Then he said, "Lady Betheray, during the time you were a lady-in-waiting, did you ever have occasion to witness Lady Kata in a secret meeting with a man?"

"I did, my lord."

"Would you describe that occasion?"

Lady Betheray went on in her silvery voice, gazing straight ahead, never turning, her hands still clasped in front of her. I couldn't take my eyes off her. She was radiant in her womanly dignity and modesty.

"It happened one evening at the end of summer, just at twilight, shortly before the fall of the queen. I was doing my handiwork, sitting on the window seat of the ladies' chamber in the queen's quarters in order to catch the last rays of the sun to see by. As the daylight failed, I put my work away in its basket. I was just preparing to leave when I happened to glance down into the hedge maze in the garden directly below me. I saw Lady Kata there. She was walking in the maze, moving toward its center."

"You could identify her even in the fading light?" Lord Iron asked.

"I could, my lord. There was still light enough, and I knew the lady well."

"Very well. Go on."

"I was curious as to what Lady Kata was doing in the maze at that hour, so I stood and watched for a few moments. She made her way to the center and sat on the stone bench in the statue garden there."

"And then?"

"And then she waited. And it got darker. And after a few minutes, when it was full night so that I could no longer make out anything of her but her silhouette, a man approached her."

"You saw him enter the maze?"

"I did not, my lord," said Lady Betheray. She spoke into the air before her, looking neither to her husband nor anyone else. "It is my belief he had been standing in one of the maze's alcoves, hidden behind a statue. I remember it seemed to me as if a statue had come to life and approached her."

Again, the little wizard guy hovering behind the bench whispered to Lord Iron, and again Lord Iron nodded.

"Please go on, Lady Betheray."

"The man made his way to the center of the maze and joined Lady Kata in the statue garden," she said.

"And in what manner did she greet him?"

"She—Lady Kata—leapt from the bench on which she was sitting and rushed into the man's arms." Even from where I was standing far below her, I saw a faint flush of pink tinge the ivory of Lady Betheray's cheeks. It occurred to me somewhere in the back of my mind that I had never seen a woman blush like that before— blush because she was speaking about romantic stuff, I mean. I had only read about women doing that in books. But here it was in real life—if real life is what this was.

"She embraced him, you mean?" Lord Iron asked.

"Embraced him passionately and then kissed him, my lord."

"Kissed him like a relative?"

"No, my lord. They kissed as lovers kiss, and for a long time." The crowd murmured, and Lady Betheray's blush deepened, and something about it, I don't know what—the old-fashioned, ladylike modesty of it, I guess—but whatever it was, I felt it pierce me through like a sword point, even here, even now.

Lord Iron had one of those gavels without a handle that just fit in the palm. He banged it on the bench.

"Order!" When the spectators had fallen silent, he turned back to his wife. "Lady Betheray, would you describe to this court your reaction to what you witnessed."

"I was quite startled, my lord. I was shocked. I had always known Lady Kata to be a woman of virtue and true religion. She was married to Lord Gaunt, who was still alive at that time. And though he was much older than she was and had been sick of late, I had always known Kata—Lady Kata—to be faithful to her vows. I had not expected this."

"And did you confront her about her infidelity?"

"I did, my lord. I considered it my duty as a friend. I spoke to her in private the very next day."

"And can you describe that conversation?"

"Lady Kata was in great distress, crying grievously. She begged me to say nothing to the queen or to her husband. And yet she feared she would be undone in any case."

"Undone. Because?"

"Lady Kata confessed to me . . ." And now, for the first time, the lady faltered, lowering her eyes almost imperceptibly.

"Go on, my lady."

She drew a breath and lifted her head, willing herself back to composure. "Lady Kata confessed to me that she feared she was carrying her lover's child."

You could hear that pass through the crowd like a bolt of electricity, the murmur moving from one end of the hall to the other.

"And she knew that it was her lover's child and not her husband's?" asked Lord Iron calmly.

"She did, my lord. Lord Gaunt had been grievously ill for many months, as everyone at court was aware. Lady Kata feared that when her condition became known, she would face trial for adultery."

"As she would have," said Lord Iron. The wizard type behind him leaned in again to whisper, but he held up his hand to silence him and continued. "Lady Betheray, did Lady Kata confess to you the name of her lover?"

"She did, my lord," the lady replied.

It sounds crazy, I know, but to that point, I had been so hypnotized by her loveliness, so wrapped up in the narrative of her testimony, so completely convinced down to the bottom of my soul that that narrative had nothing to do with me, it was only in the moment before she answered that I realized with horror what she was going to say.

Until then, she had spoken almost without moving, her hands clasped before her, her eyes straight ahead. But now, she turned her face, just a little, just enough, so that her piercing green eyes were directly on me.

"She said that her lover was Austin Lively."

"What? No!" I shouted. I'd always wondered why people in courtroom dramas on TV shout out like that. It makes them look so bad. I always thought they would be smart enough to control themselves. It turns out, you can't help it. "It isn't true!" I shouted, straining against my manacles as a nearby guard grabbed hold of me. "I never touched her! I never met her! She isn't . . . "

I was about to say, "*She isn't even real in my world!*"—but Lord Iron hammered his palm gavel against the bench and I caught myself.

"Order!" he commanded. "Thank you for your testimony, Lady Betheray," he said then. "You may step down."

One more thing happened then—one more thing, I mean, to set my whirling mind whirling even faster.

Lady Betheray descended from the witness box, floating down the stairs as she had floated up them. She glided beneath the judge's bench to the railing. Sir Aravist opened the gate, and she glided through.

And just then, just as she was gliding past me, close to me, near enough to touch me, near enough so that I thought I caught a wild, yearning scent from her like the scent of night-blooming jasmine, she turned and faced me—fully faced me. There was no mistaking it. This was not some subtle gesture like her nod of thanks to Sir Aravist, or her modest glance downward on the stand. She turned her head. She looked right into my eyes, *gazed* right into my eyes. And as I gawked back, my mind still reeling with horror and bewilderment, I saw . . . I couldn't have said just then what I saw. Just then, I was too crazed to figure it out. But her gaze struck me like a broadside blow and an image came to life in my mind, a memory—more than a memory, a visceral flashback—her lips on mine, her soft shape against me. And in her eyes, I saw . . .

I thought about it later. And when I thought about it, what I thought was: I saw in her eyes that she loved me.

It was impossible. It was insane. I didn't even know her—plus, she'd just condemned me. But then, all this was impossible. It was all insane. And the more I thought about it, the more certain I was of what I saw. Her eyes condemned me, her eyes were furious with me, but it was the condemnation of betrayal, the fury of her pain, of her love.

And there was that kiss, that remembered kiss . . .

AFTER THAT, AFTER all that, I was in such a stupor of confusion that the rest of the trial passed by like a procession seen through deep fog.

There was other testimony. I remember a physician of some sort took the stand. He testified that what Lady Betheray said was true: Lady Kata had, in fact, been pregnant when she was stabbed to death.

And I remember Sir Aravist. He told how I had appeared in the city suddenly, how I insinuated my way into court. *Insinuated* was the word he used. He said he had suspected me from the first of conspiring to overturn the New Republic and restore the monarchy. He said he had had his agents follow me, and they had eventually followed me to my meeting with Lady Kata in the tower room. He told how they had come to fetch him then and how he and his men had broken through the locked door and found Lady Kata dead of a dagger wound and the bloody dagger still in my hands.

That was the worst part of it for me—the locked room, the bloody dagger—because I'd been there. I knew it was true.

But all this, as I said, went by in a fog. And if it was horrifying to hear the witnesses building a case around me like a coffin, well, it was all *so* horrifying that I could barely feel it except as a general deadening atmosphere of horror.

Oh, but that was before the end of it. I felt the end of it, all right. The final horror broke through the horror fog like a horror freight train and ran right over me.

At the end of it, when the testimony was done, the creepy wizard guy bent down again and whispered in Lord Iron's ear. Lord Iron listened and nodded and smacked his gavel on the judge's bench. He looked down at me from his great height so that I quailed with fresh fear even before he spoke. And then he spoke.

He said, "Austin Lively, the court has determined that the testimony of the witnesses has created substantial doubt about your claim of innocence. Therefore, we decree and command that you should be returned to the dungeon and placed into the custody of the executioner to be tortured until you admit the full truth."

"Wait, what?" I whispered.

"Take him away," said Lord Iron.

I shouted, "Wait! No. You can't do that. It's unconstitutional! You can't!"

But they could. Two guards grabbed my elbows. I struggled as they forced me up the aisle toward the great doors, toward the angry crowd—toward the dungeon.

"I'm innocent!"

In my mind, I could hear the endless shrieks of the tortured heretic as the guards dragged me away to suffer his same fate.

6

THE DREARY NIGHTMARE SCENES REPLAYED IN REVERSE. The angry crowd trying to lynch me as I was hustled from the tribunal hall back to the castle. The stone stairway down into the hell of the dungeon. The beak-nosed jailer with his giggle and his torch leading the way into the cell. The one-eyed, fang-mouthed ogre going batshit, roaring and squealing and straining against his chains so that dust flew from the walls and I expected the anchoring rings to fly free at any moment.

Then the jailer and the guards were gone again. The ogre settled down and slept again. I sat in the dust again, manacled to the wall. It was all just the same as before. Except for the heretic. He was back now, chained in his corner, naked—but he was not the same. While the jailer remained with his torch, I could see everything that had been done to him.

I won't describe what he looked like. It was unspeakable.

And I was next. The executioner was coming to do the same to me. Any minute now, any second. Hours and endless hours of torment would begin. And when they were done, my life would be over, worse than over. I would be that—that thing—in the corner there. I could hear him in the shadows. Trying to express his pain and anguish with what was left of his mouth. Even if I made it back to LA, I would be that. That thing.

I realized I had never been afraid before. Not really. Not like this. I remembered, back in elementary school, being scared the teacher would call on me when I didn't know the answer. I remembered being scared I would be grounded after I set the backyard shed on fire while sneaking some cigarettes. I remembered finding a lump under my arm and how I thought it might be cancer. I remembered a minor car accident I'd been in. That was my history of fear. All of it. What a life I'd lived till now. What an easy life.

Because this—this was unbearable. Sitting in the dark. Waiting for the executioner. Waiting for the hours of agony. Staring through the shadows at what I would be when it was over: the remnant of a human being, the weirdly surviving pieces.

I turned away from him. I gazed down at the dust. My whole body trembled. I tried to swallow. I couldn't. I tried to hold back my tears. I couldn't. A high, puling whine of supplication and misery came out of me. I was helpless with horror.

Then—a shock. Something caught my eye. Some dim momentary something to my left.

I turned—and gasped, startled.

That thing was back. That rodent with a woman's face. It was sitting right next to me. A deformed beast. Creepy. Staring at me, its black eyes glittering in the shadows. The sight of it made me start back and gag.

"Holy shit!" I cried out in a thin, hoarse voice.

It just sat there. Part rat, part woman. A hideous mutant. It just went on staring with its bizarrely human eyes. After a second, it glowed again the way it had last time, briefly throwing off a confetti of colored lights, then going dark.

Horror added to horror forced the words out of me. "For God's sake, what are you?"

She—it—snorted. Snorted with derision. She was mocking me. Such a human sound—but coming from this monstrosity made it seem all the more monstrous.

"What?" I said. "What are you?"

It spoke. Even that was awful, even the fact that it spoke, that such a creature could speak. "What are *you*?" it said—she said—because it had a woman's voice, though so high-pitched and nasal it sounded as much like a mouse's squeal.

"What?" I said again, barely able to get the word out, strangled by my fear of what was coming for me any minute, any second.

"What are you?" she said again. "I'm Maud. That's who I am. What are you?"

"What am . . . ? I'm a man," I said through my tears.

She snorted again—snorted derisive laughter. Rolled her eyes. "A man!" she said. "Look at you!"

"What the . . . ?" I could barely think, I was so terrified. Every word we spoke meant a second passed, every second that passed brought me closer to the torture chamber. "You're a rat! And you're talking to me! You're some kind of . . . what are you? Why are you here?"

"It's a long story," said Maud the mutant rodent-woman. "A sin, a curse, a quest. You want to hear about it, or you want to get out of here?"

"What?"

"You want—?"

"Get out! You can get me out? I want to get out!" I eagerly turned toward her—toward her and away from what was left of the heretic. I tried to focus. "What can you do?"

"Not much," said the rodent-girl. "I have no magic of my own, but if I can channel the forest king's, I might be able to get those manacles off you."

I thrust my hands toward her eagerly. No clue what she was talking about, but if there was any chance . . .

She looked me dead in the eye and spoke with maddening slowness. "But I can't do it with you mewling like a hungry kitten. A man!" she muttered derisively again.

"Just do it! Just get these things off me!" I held my hands out again so that my chains rattled. "Can you get the door open too?"

"Maybe. Like I said, I have to channel Tauratanio. So you have to shut up and let me focus."

"I'm quiet, I'm quiet—do it!" I said.

I glanced over my shoulder toward the door. It was silent out there in the dungeon maze. In here, in the cell, the ogre snored. The heretic in the shadows made his terrible low laments. That was all.

I faced the awful rodent-girl again. Maud. She was gazing at the manacles on my wrists. Taking deep breaths that made her furry front rise and fall.

"Come on, come on!" I whispered.

"Shut up! I'm focusing."

I managed to bite back my curse.

Once again, the rainbow sparkle of light flew off her. As it did, I saw her quickly raise her forepaws with their clawed, twiglike fingers, like the fingers of a squirrel. It seemed like the colored light was sucked back into her—*swoosh*—all at once. And then colored lightning sparked out of her claws. There was an electric fritz and I felt the heat on my wrists and saw the manacles leap and tremble under the flashing current.

Then the sparks died. I pulled at the manacle on my right wrist with the fingers of my left hand. It held fast.

"It isn't . . . " I started to say.

But Maud hissed at me, "Shut up! You think this is easy?"

"Well, do it. Do it!"

Again, she sat there breathing, focusing, waiting. Again, the colored lights came off her. She raised her claws. She gave a little high-pitched grunt of effort. The light was sucked back into her, and the sparks flew and hit the manacles. I felt the metal jump and tremble against my flesh. I willed the manacles to snap apart.

But then—then horribly—footsteps—footsteps on the dungeon stairs!

"Jailer!"

It was the executioner. The heretic in the corner heard him and gave a squeaking moan of fear through the hole in what was left of his face.

"Jailer! I'm here for the prisoner Lively!"

The sparks from the rodent's claws winked out. I tried to break the manacle again. Again, it wouldn't budge.

"Jailer!"

I heard the jailer's door come creaking open. I saw the glow of torchlight spilling through the window-hole in the cell door.

"I'm coming! I'm coming!" I heard the jailer say.

The mutant rodent was just sitting there again. I whimpered at her, "Please!"

"Stop it!" she spat in a harsh whisper. "You say you're a man. Be a man!"

I heard the jailer's keys rattle as his footsteps approached the door. Other footsteps joined with his, the heavy footsteps of big men. The heretic's tongueless moans of fear grew louder and more awful.

I tried to compose myself. I thought: *Be a man!* I drew a deep breath. I said a prayer. My parents had taught me there was no God, but I prayed anyway. It just came out of me. I held my hands out and was silent, letting the rodent-girl focus.

The jailer was at the door. I heard his key slip into the keyhole.

The confetti of colored lights flew off the rodent-girl again and was sucked back into her again and shot out of her forepaws again and the manacles heated and shook and rattled on my wrists.

I looked on in hope—but desperate hope. What good would this do me now? Even if my hands were free, how could I fight the executioner and his armed guards? They would cut me down with their swords or batter me senseless, and in the end, they would carry me off to the torture hole no matter how I tried to stop them.

The jailer's key turned in the lock. The heavy latch clunked back. The heretic let out a pitifully inarticulate moan of terror, and at the same moment the giant ogre leapt to its feet, roaring its squealy roar and rattling its chains as its one eye rolled wildly in its forehead and its mouth opened wide to show its sharklike fangs.

The manacles burst apart on my wrists.

"Yes! *Damme!*" cried Maud in triumph.

The cell door swung open. There was the jailer with his flaming torch and his warty face and his sadistic grin. There was the blithe executioner in his mask, striding in to fetch me with his two husky armed guards right behind him. The ogre squealed and roared and tried to get at them, straining at his chains. The jailer gleefully tormented him with his torch flames.

I leapt to my feet.

The executioner saw at once that the manacles were off me.

"Ah, hell, he's got free—grab him!" he said. He spoke quickly but casually. He wasn't worried at all. It was obvious why not. The two guards were tall and thick and muscular, with swords dangling from their belts. I had no chance against them.

The cell was full of noise: the ogre roaring and squealing, the heretic moaning and groaning.

The guards rushed past the executioner on either side, charging at me.

I threw a punch at one of them. A weak, sloppy, pathetic punch. My muscles, such as they were, had gone wobbly with fear. The guard blocked the blow easily and grabbed my arm. The other guard grabbed my other arm. Just like that, they had me locked up between them. Even struggling with all the strength of my terror, I was helpless.

"All right, fellows, bring him along," said the executioner in his blithely competent way.

But before they could start to drag me to the door, the colored lights came up out of my rodent friend again. Quickly, Maud threw her forepaws out and the lights were sucked back into her and the sparks flew from her forepaws.

This time, she pointed her claws across the cell. The sparks leapt the long distance and struck the ring in the wall that anchored the ogre's chains. The ring was already so loose, it shuddered and fell from the stone immediately.

All at once, the ogre was free.

In an unthinkably swift instant, the one-eyed monster's great horse-haunch of an arm lashed out and knocked the torch from the jailer's hand. The flaming stick went flying past my head. And in the same second, as we were all turning to look, the ogre grabbed the jailer in his two huge fists and lifted him off his feet as if he had no weight at all. The jailer shrieked like a little girl on a roller coaster—or shrieked one-half a shriek that was cut off as the ogre brought him to his gaping mouth as you would a chicken leg and bit through his throat with those gigantic fangs.

All this took a moment—less. Then the jailer's cowled head tumbled to the floor, landing with a wet thud while a geyser of blood gouted from his severed neck. Roaring, the ogre hurled the spasming corpse at the executioner. The corpse hit the masked man and sent him stumbling back as yet more blood spouted and sprayed from its neck. The ogre squealed and reached for the next nearest man: the guard who held my left arm. The monster tore him off me. The guard threw wild punches at the creature, screaming as he was hoisted off his feet. The guard on my right arm let me go and drew his sword with a swish of metal.

The executioner cursed. The heretic tried to yell.

And the rodent-woman Maud screamed, "Run, Lively! Run!"

I ran.

I sprinted for the open cell door. There was no one to stop me. The executioner was down near the heretic, tangled under the jailer's spouting, juddering corpse. One guard was rushing at the ogre as the ogre began to devour the other. I shot through the door into the dancing shadows of the dungeon labyrinth. I started to turn toward the stairway.

But then the mutant rodent-woman came flying out of the cell, all four legs splayed. As she leapt off in the other direction, her high cry reached me over the screams and shouts from within the cell: "This way!"

I dashed after her.

She ran down a corridor of cells under an arch, and I was right behind her. Springing ahead of me on her four legs, she arced up over a wall as she skittered around a corner, down another hall. I made the turn a second later and plunged blindly into a long, torchless corridor that led away into blackness. The shouts and cries from the cell faded behind me, and the glow of the flamelight faded too. I raced down the corridor, deeper and deeper into the dark. I saw something straight in front of me and only just managed to duck before I smashed my head against a low ledge.

I had entered another corridor, its ceiling lower, its walls tighter. I had to slow down, had to raise my hands to either side of me to feel my way between the walls as the dark grew thicker and thicker. Only the feel of the rough stone under my fingers guided me, only the occasional confetti of pastel lights from the rodent-girl kept me from stumbling on the uneven floor.

The rodent turned another corner, and I lumbered after her. I lost sight of her in the darkness and was about to call out when I heard her voice again.

"Here."

She sparkled with colored light and I was stunned to find her suddenly right at my feet.

"I'm not strong enough," she said. "Help me! Quick!"

She had her forepaws raised again. The magic glimmer came off her, swept back into her, shot from her claws in sparks to hit an arched grate set into the stone wall. The grate was about four feet tall and three feet wide, made of heavy iron. It jumped and trembled as the sparks battered it, but it didn't come free.

"Come on!" she said.

I knelt down and braced my feet against the ground. I grabbed the bars in my two hands. I pulled. It rattled but held fast.

"Wait for me, damn it!" squealed Maud.

Panting, I waited, kneeling there, gripping the grate by the bars, white-knuckled.

And now I heard the shouts of men approaching: the executioner and a guard, the surviving guard.

"Come on! He's on the run!" the executioner was shouting.

"Which way?"

"There! There's his footsteps! This way!"

I don't know how they'd gotten away from the ogre, but they had, and they were coming for me.

I glanced at the rodent-girl. She sat there in the dark, still, gathering her energy, steadying her focus. I wanted to urge her on, but I pressed my lips tight and kept silent.

I heard the executioner. "He can't be far! Come on!"

His voice was heart-stoppingly close, one corridor away. I could see the glow of torchlight now, growing brighter as my pursuers came on.

I breathed deep, trying to stay silent, stay calm.

And there it was! The rainbow sparkle off the rodent Maud. The flash of sparks from her forepaws. The double stream of colored electricity hit the barred gate and made it leap in my fingers. At that same moment, I yanked hard on the bars.

There was a loud scraping noise. Then I toppled backward onto my ass as the grate broke out of the stone and came away in my hands.

Instantly, the rodent sprang through the opening. "Come on!"

"There he is!" came the shout from the end of the corridor.

I turned and with a jolt of sickening fear, I saw the executioner come chasing around the corner, his masked countenance lit by the fire of the torch he held high. The remaining guard was running right behind him, his sword flashing in his hand.

I threw the grate aside and scrambled on my belly over the dirt floor to the opening. I slithered through as fast as I could, and instantly found myself standing in the narrow hallway of the restaurant in Beverly Hills with the men's room door swinging shut behind me.

I stood there, looking around me, openmouthed, wild-eyed. My heart was hammering. My knees were quivering. My mind teetered on the edge of madness.

7

I DON'T KNOW HOW MANY SECONDS PASSED WHILE I stood there gaping at nothing. I couldn't have been more dumbstruck if I had found myself lost among the stars in deepest space. I turned this way and that, my hands lifted, my mouth still open. I saw the wood-paneled walls on one side of me and on the other. I sucked in breath, trying to still my heart, the way you do when you come out of a nightmare.

I had no idea why I was standing there. I could not remember how I'd gotten there or where I had been going. I couldn't think at all, in fact. It came to me that there was something I was supposed to do, somewhere I was supposed to be.

My parents. My brother. They were out there in the restaurant, on the brick patio, waiting for me. I ought to go back to them before they wondered where I'd gone.

I walked unsteadily down the narrow corridor. I reached the door to the main room of the restaurant. Stretched out my hand to open it—then froze in place.

What if I went through and found myself back in Galiana? Racing through those dungeons with the executioner right behind me . . .

It took me several seconds to work up the courage, but what choice did I have? If anyone came in and saw me like this, they'd call an ambulance. I'd be put away. Tentatively, I touched the door. I pushed it open. I peeked through. There was the restaurant, all right, just as I had left it, white tables full of fancy diners in their fancy clothes.

But what would happen to me if I crossed the threshold and went in?

I stepped over it slowly, gingerly, as if that would prevent my being teleported—or whatever the hell it was—back into the dungeon. I made it through into the large dining room. I let the door shut behind me and let out a held breath. Then I wobbled my way toward the brick patio. I returned to the table where my parents and my brother were still chatting, unconcerned. They hardly noticed when I dropped down, deadweight, into my chair.

They went on talking. I didn't listen. I felt lost in a state of disjointed consciousness that was as close to insanity as I had ever come. I had to calm myself down before I became hysterical. If my parents or my brother looked at me, would they see the crazy on my face? Would they notice? Would they care?

What was happening to me? What was happening?

It had to be psychosis or a brain tumor or some drugs I'd taken by mistake or . . . something. But how would anything explain the bruise on my head from Sir Aravist's sword? Or the purple marks on my wrists from the manacles? I glanced down at my own trembling hands. I tugged up the cuffs of my denim jacket. The bruises were still there on my wrists—plus I saw red splotches where the sparks from the mutant rodent-woman's claws had singed me.

I shook my head. *The mutant rodent-woman!* How could those words even make any sense, let alone describe something real that I had seen with my own two eyes?

Slowly—slowly—I got hold of myself, at least to the point where

I could start to string some thoughts together. What had I been doing here—here in this life before I'd been carried back to Galiana?

This life! I thought. *My* life! *Real* life!

It came back to me. The book. *Another Kingdom* by Ellen Evermore. That's right. I had talked on the phone with Sean Gunther, the writer who had submitted the book to Mythos Productions, submitted it and then withdrawn it before I could read it through. The book was linked to Galiana. It took place in Eastrim, where the castle was and the dungeon. The characters in the book were the people I had seen there: Sir Aravist, Lord Iron, Lady Betheray, and the rest. The book was the connection, the only connection I had between Galiana and LA. It was the only clue I had to what was going on. I had to try and find it.

Without thinking, I stood up. My parents turned to look at me in surprise. My brother stopped mid-portentous-sentence and narrowed his eyes at me.

Dizziness and nausea came over me in a wave. I almost had to sit down again. Maybe instead of finding the book, I should get to a doctor, I thought. But no. I needed to know what was happening to me.

"I have to go," I murmured vaguely. "I have an appointment. I have to go."

"Well, that . . . you know . . . it's the sort of thing . . . " murmured my father. We sounded just like one another.

"You will speak with her though, won't you?" said my mother.

I gaped down at her. What the hell was she talking about?

"Riley," she said. "Really, Austin. She has to stop."

Oh. Right. Riley. My kid sister was doing something she wasn't supposed to do. As always. I nodded dumbly.

"Well . . . " I said.

"Good to see you, buddy," said my brother.

I nodded again, dumbly again. Then I turned and walked away.

Back into the restaurant, back through the tables, to the front door this time. I put my hand on the cold metal of the door handle. But I couldn't pull it. I was paralyzed—paralyzed with the fear that I would step across the threshold and find myself back there, back in the dungeon, on the run.

I stood there long seconds, unable to move.

"Be a man," I whispered.

Then I pulled the handle, opened the door, and walked out into the night.

THE VALET BROUGHT me my battered Nissan and returned it to me, sneering. I drove away along the evening streets. I was still in a daze, my mind flashing from one impossible image to another. I let out a shuddering sigh as I remembered the moment when the ogre had ripped off the jailer's head. I remembered the spout of blood and the wet sound the head made when it hit the cell floor.

"Jesus, Jesus," I whispered as I drove.

There were other memories. The jostling crowd raging at me. The judges on their high bench, looking down at me with cold doom in their eyes. Lady Betheray . . .

The thought of her seemed to draw me even deeper into a dream state. The thought of how she looked. In her tiara with her raven hair spilling down. In her flowing gown of white and gold. How she moved in it. How she spoke like silver bells ringing. And as I thought of her, it happened again just as it had happened in the courtroom when she faced me: I felt her kiss warm on my lips, felt her arms around me, her body pressed against mine—a visceral memory that could not be a memory at all because it had never happened. All the same, the absurd realism of it made my body stir.

I drew a long, deep breath, forcing myself out of my trance. I looked around to get my bearings. Where was I?

I was stopped—the Nissan was stopped—at a red light at an intersection on Santa Monica Boulevard. The rush hour was over now, the traffic thinner but still LA thick. A theater in an old Spanish-style building with a tiled roof was to the right of me; a little park, shadowy beyond the street lamps, was to my left. Lady Betheray melted from my vision as I focused on the bright red taillights in the two lanes ahead of me, the bright white headlights in two oncoming lanes to my left. Then I glanced up into the rearview mirror.

That's when I saw the black Mustang.

"SHIT," I SAID aloud.

In all the craziness of life and madness and transition from one world to another, I had forgotten all about it: that car that had been parked outside my building in the red no-parking zone. Under the bright lamps of the boulevard, I could make out the maybe-transgender-maybe-guy-maybe-girl sitting behind the wheel staring right at me. I could see through his windshield the bland, eerie smile on the kittenish face beneath his short blond hair. I could see another man sitting in the passenger seat beside him, a great hulk of a man: shaved head, enormous chest, enormous arms, expressionless face, a thug if ever there was one.

They were following me! Was I paranoid to think that? No, they had to be. I remembered now how they had sat outside while I slept, how I had caught the driver looking up at my window. And now here they were? Come on. I wasn't being paranoid at all. They were watching me, keeping tabs on where I was going.

The light turned green. I drove on, checking the rearview every few seconds. The Mustang sank back a small distance behind me so that another car, a red Passat, pulled into my wake and got between us. A space opened to my right so I changed lanes—quickly, without a turn signal—just to see what would happen. The Mustang changed lanes also, now two cars behind.

What the hell? Why would anyone follow me? It made no sense. Did it have something to do with this nightmarish fantasy I was bouncing in and out of? It had to. Right? Who was I? A story analyst. A reader. Another nobody show-biz wannabe, one of a zillion in LA. It had to be about this, about Galiana. Why else would anyone even bother with me?

And what was I supposed to do about it? That was the real question, the urgent question. Should I just ignore these guys? Just let them trail me all the way to Sean Gunther's house? That didn't feel right somehow. What business was it of theirs where I was going? And why should Sean Gunther be caught up in my troubles? But what other real options did I have?

I kept moving along with the traffic. There were no left turns allowed here, and nowhere to go on my right. The traffic kept on moving smoothly. Looking up in the rearview again, I spotted the Mustang still lurking two cars back, keeping its distance but sticking to my tail. I tried to convince myself I was imagining things, but I knew I wasn't.

I faced forward. In my job, I must have read at least two dozen books or scripts in which the hero got followed by the bad guy or vice versa. I tried to think about how they had handled it. I remembered one scene in one novel that had stuck with me because it had an air of realism. I couldn't remember the book's title. *Officer in Trouble*. *Officer Down*. Something like that. It was this gritty crime thing. The narrator had talked about how hard it was to follow somebody, especially if you didn't want to be obvious about it. It really required teams of people, he said. One car alone was too obvious, and made it too easy for the target to slip away.

That encouraged me. If it was easy to give a single tail the slip, then maybe even I could do it. It was worth a try.

I remembered the rest of the scene. It was a street scene, just like this one. City driving, four lanes, thick traffic. I remembered how the hero had lost the tail . . .

I made my decision. My heart sped up, but I wasn't afraid. Well, I was afraid, but I was excited too. Hollywood schmuck becomes Hollywood hero. I liked the idea. Be a man.

It was all in the timing. I signaled and pulled into the left lane again. I checked the mirror. Sure enough, the Mustang edged over with me. But they lost some distance in the exchange. Now they were three cars back. Ha. That was the exact same mistake the bad guys had made in the novel I read!

I looked ahead. A road opened to my left. The sign indicated no left turn. The oncoming traffic was streaming steadily. I slowed, just a little. Dropping back from the taillights in front of me. Waiting for any opening I could get.

There it was. Just a small gap. I hit the gas. Shot forward. Hit the wheel. A horn bellowed as my Nissan swung in front of the oncoming traffic. Brakes screeched as I blasted for the intersection. I could only hope there were no cops around.

Then I was through, off the boulevard. The oncoming traffic closed ranks behind me. I looked into my rearview mirror and saw the Mustang passing the intersection, unable to make the turn. I saw the driver glaring at me. The shaved-headed hulk beside him was leaning forward, giving me the Sneering Stare of Cold Death.

Well, bite me, Sluggo. Bullied by honking horns, the black car drove helplessly on until it was gone from view.

I drove away into the curling, elegant web of side streets they call the Flats. I made turn after turn, traveling block after block past big lawns and big houses, making my roundabout way north toward Sunset Boulevard and the hills. I kept checking the rearview, but there was no sign of the Mustang. I had lost it.

For the first time in what seemed like forever, I laughed with pure glee.

SOON I WAS winding high into the Hollywood Hills. The twinkling starlike lights of the city danced below me, going in and out of view on the snaking roads. I made my way to Sean Gunther's address and pulled the Nissan to the curb across from his steep driveway. I shut off the engine and stepped out.

The driveway was blocked by a heavy metal gate. A small wooden door, painted black, stood beside the gate. A bell and intercom stood on a concrete column beside the door. Curb, driveway, gate, door, and bell all stood under the pines and oaks that lined the quiet road. There were no streetlamps. It was dark everywhere except where a single hooded bulb burned dimly on the concrete column.

I still felt pretty good—pretty hero-like—about losing that car. But who was it? What the hell was it all about? Would Kitten Face and Billiard Ball be parked in the red zone outside my apartment when I went home?

Lost in these thoughts, I walked up the drive and stood under the single bulb and pressed the bell button. If it made a sound, I couldn't hear it. I stood and waited, listening to an owl going *whoo-whoo* in the trees. Nothing else happened. I pressed the button again.

Beyond the gate, a door opened and closed. I felt that surge of sort-of-fear-sort-of-excitement again. I heard footsteps. A woman's. High heels on stone or slate. I smelled her before I saw her, a rich, dark, sensual perfume that would have been overpowering indoors.

The latch on the door clacked. The door swung open, and there she was. No doubt in my mind what she did for a living. A prostitute. A cheap streetwalker, judging by her ridiculously short shorts and the latticed tank top that let her breasts show through and her ridiculously tall, ridiculously red high heels. She had a cheap face too, hard and cynical. But her hairstyle—that was kind of odd. I don't know much about these things. I don't know what kind of hairstyle you call it. But it was not a hooker's hairstyle, not long and loose like I saw hookers wearing on the street sometimes. It was elegant, a complicated 'do, the hair piled up, the blond strands interwoven. Something like what I've seen brides wear. Anyway, that's what it looked like to me.

I started to introduce myself. "Hi, my name is . . . "

"Save it, baby. I'm just leaving." She strutted by me, *clack, clack, clack.* The door began to swing shut behind her, so I had to reach out fast and grab it. "Thanks for the distraction," the hooker said. "If you hadn't rung the bell, I'd've never gotten out of there."

I watched her move off into the darkness, wobbly on those heels. She worked her phone as she maneuvered down the slope of the driveway to the curb. Calling for a pickup, I guess. I had a brief, instinctive gentlemanly urge to offer to keep her company in the dark till her car arrived, but it seemed a kind of dopey notion, given what she was. I went inside and let the door shut behind me.

The house was a big boxy white stucco, with long windows reflecting the distant lights of the city. I walked over the slate path along the side of it, looking for a door. I found one, but before I could knock, I heard a low muttering from around the corner. I continued along the path to the back of the house. I found Sean Gunther there.

The author was on the mountaintop patio, pacing a staggered trail back and forth on the slate paving stones. The water of a kidney-shaped pool flashed under night-lights behind him. There were deck chairs here and there and small round tables. Beyond, far away and far below, was Hollywood, twinkling colors on a sable bed of night.

Gunther was a tall man, well over six feet, and lanky. He still had the swept-back lion's mane of silver-white hair I'd seen in his picture online. But from what I could see of his profile when he paced past, his high, flat, white, noble, majestic face was pitted and scarred by an oozing red rash that curled up the side of his cheek to his brow. He wore deck shoes with no socks and white slacks and a long-sleeved white pullover. His slender body waved like a reed in soft breezes. He gestured with the plastic yellow tumbler in his hand. I noticed a whiskey bottle and an ice bucket and another tumbler, this one purple, on one of the little tables near him.

"Actually, I don't think women really have personalities," he was declaring. "Not like I think of personalities, individual characters. Each man is the man he is, but every woman is all women, really. A principle more than a person, if you see what I mean."

He was talking to the hooker. He hadn't even realized she had slipped away. It made him seem like kind of a dick: the fact he hadn't even noticed. That and the adolescent crap he was spouting— spouting in that voice men use when they're secretly angry but want to play it cool and philosophical. I disliked the guy on sight.

I came closer to him and stopped. I caught a whiff of the hooker's perfume on the chill night air. I could understand why the poor girl had seized on my arrival as a chance to get out of there.

"That's why this is honest, you see, an honest transaction," the author went on, swirling his plastic yellow tumbler in the air. "Everything I want from any woman I can get from you and my imagination. And money is cheaper than lies or affection. I don't have to—"

"Mister Gunther," I said.

It really startled him. He was maybe two yards away from me and so immersed in his own bullshit, he hadn't seen me there at all. He jumped and spun, his silver mane jouncing. It was kind of comical, really.

"How the fuck did you get in here?" he said, glaring at me.

"My name . . . "

"I didn't ask your name. Who gives a shit? Where's my whore?"

"She left. That's how I got in. When she opened the door to go."

He blinked at this, puzzled. Then he gazed into space through a haze of alcohol. His head tilted. He looked like a dog who's heard a strange noise. I could see the story assembling itself in his mind. The hooker slipping out, me slipping in. A humiliating story when you come to think about it. He couldn't even pay a girl to listen to his crap. I felt for him, kind of.

"My name . . . "

"What?" he said, coming out of his fugue.

"My name is Austin Lively. I called you."

It took a moment, but this got through. He remembered. He nodded with great seriousness, as if it were some deep truth he had just comprehended.

"Oh. Oh yeah. Yeah," he said. "Austin Lively."

He took a staggering sideways step. It brought him to one of the deck chairs. He flumped down into it, draining his tumbler even as he went so that the ice rattled against the plastic.

"*Three Days in Forever*," he growled.

I don't know what he could have said that would have surprised me more. That was the name of my script, the script I'd written while I was still in film school, the one that got optioned and then destroyed in what screenwriters call Development Hell.

"You read it?" I said. I couldn't keep the astonishment out of my voice.

"I read everything," he said, draining his tumbler again, just for show this time, just for the gesture.

He leaned forward in his chair and snagged the whiskey bottle off its table. Dumped some whiskey in his tumbler. Then put the bottle back and plucked some ice from the bucket and plopped that in the tumbler too.

"Help yourself," he said.

The only other tumbler was the purple one by the bucket. It had lipstick on the rim: the hooker's glass.

"No, thanks," I said. "Why did you read my script?"

"I told you. I read everything. Trying to remember how it's done," he added with morose self-pity. He drank. "It was good. Your script. You're good."

"Thanks." It seemed stupid to feel pleased by the praise of a guy like this, but I was. It had been a long time since my last compliment.

"*Another Kingdom*," he went on, leaning forward with his elbows on his thighs and his tumbler in his two hands, speaking down between his parted knees to the patio slates. "That's why you're here, right? *Another Kingdom.*"

I was surprised again—and excited now too. Because it felt like I was getting somewhere, that I was on the right track. He knew who I was, why I was here—he must know something more about what was happening to me, right?

"That's right," I said.

"Ellen Evermore," he said. He spoke the author's name in a wistful, faraway tone, smiling sadly to himself.

"Yes," I said. "*Another Kingdom* by Ellen Evermore."

He was already stretching back in the chair, reaching into the pocket of his white slacks, dragging out his phone. Woozily, swaying where he sat with the effects of the drink, he worked the keys with one hand. Then he held the phone out to me, dropping back hard in his chair when I took it, as if the effort had exhausted him.

I looked at the phone, at the photograph on the screen. Ellen Evermore. And now, suddenly, I understood this whole scene I'd wandered into.

The picture was a candid, taken in what looked like a museum. She was turning to face the camera, turning away from the wall where there hung a painting of a primitive muscleman clothed in fur with a woman on either side of him. Gunther must've called to her and taken the picture when she turned. She was smiling slightly, the way a woman does when she catches you admiring her, you know, and she's pleased but she wants to scold you a little, too, to show her modesty, how silly you're being. She had a nice face, a hell of a nice face actually. Not beautiful, not like a model or a movie star is beautiful, but there was something about it. It came right out of the picture at you. You could tell: this was somebody. A personage. A whole woman. Young, thirty at the most, but with a sort of serenity and firmness and humor about her—in her eyes, at the corners of her mouth—that made her seem older than her years. You could see she was kind and feminine and gentle, same as you could with Jane Janeway when you looked at her. But she had this authority too. That also made her seem older. Like she had seen things and was honest about what she'd seen and it had made her quiet and wise.

Anyway, I noticed all this, and I noticed she had a fine figure, not skinny and muscular like a lot of girls these days, but full and soft in a modest, old-fashioned dress of royal blue. Most of all I noticed—I couldn't miss—her hair. Her hairstyle. Because it was the same 'do the hooker had had, her golden hair piled high and interwoven. Of course, the elegant style of it was more suited to Ellen Evermore because you could tell she was elegant all through to her soul, but in its particulars, it was the same as the hooker's. So that explained what Sean Gunther had hired the streetwalker for, and it explained the crap he was spewing when I walked in, that one girl was the same as another, that one could stand in for all. Trying to convince himself, I guess. The poor bastard.

I handed the phone back to him. "Nice," I said.

He took the phone and studied the picture himself. And you know how sometimes you can see a man's whole history on his face? It was like that then with Gunther. The big first novel, the early fame, the wrong choices that grew out of his own personality and the disappointments that grew out of his choices—and the drugs and booze—and finally this, this loss, Ellen, symbolic of all the other losses and capping all the rest and leaving him to live out the down-swirling pattern of his now-indelible character: you could see it all right there.

"Eh," he said finally, as if none of it mattered, as if who cared about Ellen Evermore or any damn thing. He stuffed the phone back in his pocket and went after his tumbler hungrily. Then he dropped back in his chair again. "She read my book," he said. He said it as if he was recalling a distant dream of youth.

"*A Thousand Pages of Self-Referential Drivel.*"

He nodded—to himself more than me. "That's why she came. She read my book. Just showed up at my door one day. Looking like that, like what she looked like. With one of those big purses, satchel purses, on her arm. She had her own book in there. *Another Kingdom.* She had it printed up with this whole elaborate binding . . . "

He went into another fugue state, remembering, maybe daydreaming. His eyes fluttered as if he might fall asleep right then and there. The booze, you know. It was getting to him.

I tried to keep him going. "She wanted you to read it," I said. "Right? Young author. Admired your work, and she wanted you to read hers."

"Happens," he barely managed to say. "Now and then. Still, sometimes." He took a deep breath through his nose. It seemed to revive him. He straightened a little in his chair. "You read a page or two, you screw 'em, then you talk some shit about the writing life. They feel encouraged and go away. You know."

I nodded. I didn't know actually, but it was easy enough to imagine.

The author's expression turned inward again. He stared into low space. "She wouldn't though."

"Wouldn't . . . go away?"

"Screw." He snorted. "I thought they all screwed nowadays, the young girls. I thought that was the whole point of them."

I laughed. The guy was so much himself, you sort of had to. "Did you read the book?" I asked him.

He shrugged. Took another slug of booze. "Couple of pages. Enough to get her to do me. Then when she wouldn't . . . " He shrugged again.

"So she left?"

Gunther frowned. Shook his head. "No. I mean, yes. But she came back every day. To read."

"Sorry?"

"My . . . " He pointed vaguely to the house with his tumbler-free hand. "My stuff. My . . . whatever . . . collection. She came every day. Every morning. She . . . " He gestured weakly with the tumbler, looking for the right phrase. Or not the right phrase, I think. Something more vague than that, something that wouldn't tell as much truth as the right phrase would have. In the end I think he just gave up and came out with it, truth and all. "She took care of me." I could imagine that too. Her cleaning the vomit and piss off him after he drank himself stupid. Feeding him. Bringing him back to some semblance of his squandered humanity. No wonder he fell in love with her. "Then . . . she read. My . . . stuff, my . . . collection. That's how she found you."

That stopped me. I felt the excitement again, that sense again that I was getting somewhere. I needed a second or two to think it all through, but I could see I didn't have much time. Gunther's eyes were sinking shut again. He was going to pass out, and soon.

"She found me," I repeated, trying to keep him on task while I figured it out.

"*Three Days in Forever.*"

I was thinking as fast as I could, trying to put it all together before I lost him. Ellen Evermore had read Gunther's book and had thought he would understand *Another Kingdom.* But when she got to him, she found this ruin, this self-pitying drunk of a lost soul, wasting himself in cynical dissipation, unable to understand anything beyond pleasure and pain. So she started to read . . . what? His collection, whatever that was. Maybe a collection of writers he admired. The writers he studied to—what was the phrase he'd used when I first came in?—to try to remember how it was done. Looking for someone else who might understand. She'd found my script and . . .

"She wanted to send her book to me," I said. "She liked my script, and she wanted me to read her novel."

He barely had the strength to speak anymore, but he nodded.

I raised my voice, trying to rouse him. "What happened then? You looked me up. You found I was at Mythos." Again he nodded, his head listing to one side, his mouth slack, drool collecting at the corner of his lips. "So you submitted the book to me through your friend at Mythos, Henry Quint. For her. Not yourself. You did it for her." Now even nodding seemed to be too much for him. "What happened then?" I asked him, nearly shouting to try to wake him up. "Why did you withdraw it? Or was it her? If she wanted me to read it, why did she withdraw it? Mr. Gunther . . . "

I actually stepped forward then, actually gripped his shoulder and shook him. It made his eyes fly wide. He struggled to sit up straight. He looked up at me where I stood over him as if he was startled to find me there.

"Mr. Gunther, why did she withdraw it?" I asked again. "Do you have a copy? Do you know where Ellen Evermore is now?"

His answer came out slurred to the edge of incomprehensibility. " . . . lobal."

"What?"

He tried again. "Left me . . . disappeared . . . Global . . . "

With that, the plastic yellow tumbler fell from his slack fingers. It clattered onto the patio, spitting a stain of whiskey onto the slates, spilling a few melting chunks of ice. Gunther's head fell forward, and he started snoring heavily, unconscious.

I SHOOK HIM again, but it was no use. He was all gone. I stood there, looking around me, at the glittering pool water and the glittering city lights below and the glittering stars beyond. I sighed, frustrated.

Then I decided to search the house.

It was a crazy idea. The minute it popped into my head, I could see how crazy it was. Gunther might wake up and find me inside. He could call the police on me, have me arrested. He could even shoot me dead, if he had a gun handy.

Sure—but on the other hand, it'd be kind of an adventure, wouldn't it? Daring, even fun. After all, I was still the dashing hero who had pulled that maneuver that dumped the black Mustang. Wasn't breaking into a house the sort of thing a swashbuckler type like myself would do next?

Anyway, the more I thought about it, the more it seemed to me there wasn't much choice. I needed to find that book. It was my only clue to what was happening to me. I knew Ellen Evermore had brought a copy here. Maybe she'd left it behind. Or maybe she'd left a forwarding address or an email address or something like that.

By the time I finished explaining all this to myself, I had already left the snoring drunk slumped in his chair poolside. I was down the slate path. I was at the front door.

Gingerly, I tried the knob. The door was unlocked. I pushed it open just a little and listened for an alarm. No alarm, none that I could hear at least. I slipped inside.

Well, right off the bat, there was another part of the story clarified: what Gunther meant by "my stuff, my collection." It was all over the place. Manuscripts, hardcovers, paperbacks, loose pages, even a few e-readers and a couple of computers—they littered the room. Nice room too: a small foyer and then two steps down into a broad sunken living room, an expanse of elegant tile with a black-metal fire pit in the center. There was a wall of windows beyond that, a view of night and stars and the lights of Hollywood. There was a black leather sofa in front of the pit. It was practically upholstered with pages and books. There was a long, low coffee table with a mosaic surface covered in volumes and a computer and more pages. There were two armchairs, one to either side of the fireplace, both buried in pages, e-readers, books.

Everything else was books too. Walls, nooks, crannies. Fine wooden shelves packed tight with volumes, all well thumbed, well read, well worn. Lampstands with shelves underneath. A writing table near the window with shelves for a backboard. A couple of side tables with shelves. All the shelves crammed tight with books and pages. *Trying to remember how it's done.*

I came down the foyer steps slowly, nervously, as if I was expecting the books to jump up suddenly and rush at me from every side. I stepped cautiously amidst the mess, moving little by little across the room. My eyes passed over the bindings and pages, pausing here and there on a title or a name I recognized. Famous titles and famous names, names and titles from today's best-seller lists, and some titles I only recognized because I'd read them for my job.

I could imagine—I could almost see—Ellen Evermore, seated here then there, different places around the room, going through them all. Each book, each script, each page. Paying for the privilege with her patient care of the stinking drunk who used to be an author. I wondered if she'd realized how the helpless wreckage of a man was helplessly falling for her. Or was she too busy searching through the volumes? Searching for me, as it turned out. Why me? Why did she want me to read her book? Or had she made a mistake in having Gunther send it to me? Is that why she had withdrawn it? And where had she put it? And where had she gone after that?

I tiptoed past the fire pit. And then I saw it. The sight made me stand still. I drew a long, slow breath, trying to keep myself calm.

In the middle of the bookshelf against the wall to my left, the last in a row of bookshelves, right up beside the writing desk at the window, there was a low, inset cabinet: more shelves behind two glass doors. I could see even from where I was standing that this was where Gunther kept his most cherished volumes, old leather-bound antiques. Smack in the center of them was one thick red volume with golden letters on its ribbed spine. I couldn't read the title from there, but I knew right away what it was. I just knew. I took a slow step toward it, then a second, then a third. Then, yes, I could make out the words: *Another Kingdom.*

I went the rest of the way to the cabinet. Tugged on the knobs of the glass doors. Locked. I tugged again. Still locked, locked for sure. There was a keyhole on one door, near the middle where the doors met. The keyhole seemed to stare at me. It reminded me of the ogre in the dungeon, the ogre's single eye.

I hesitated, at a loss. I thought of grabbing the paperweight off the desk and breaking the glass, but I couldn't quite bring myself to do it. Seemed wrong, vandalizing the man's home while he slept. Instead, I took out my phone and hunted up a video online: *"How to Pick a Lock with a Paper Clip."* There were several videos of that title to choose from. I selected one in which the lock looked like the lock in front of me. I pressed play.

"Okay then!" said the willowy, long-haired man in the video. "Today I'm going to show you how to pick a lock with a paperclip . . ."

A few minutes later, I was on my knees working with a pair of paperclips from the writing desk's front drawer. I had the video playing through for a second time, and I followed the instructions as the willowy man gave them. I'm not sure I actually believed it was going to work, but lo and behold, the latch snapped back just like the willowy man said it would. The cabinet door swung ajar. Yay, internet.

I tossed the paper clips to the floor. Swung the door open the rest of the way. Reached for the red volume. Touched its red leather spine.

Then someone screamed. Sean Gunther. Sean Gunther screamed out on the patio. I leapt to my feet. Looked toward the window— but I couldn't see the patio from there. Sean Gunther screamed again and there was a splash.

Something was wrong. I had to go help him. I turned to the door.

The kitten-faced man or woman from the black Mustang was standing there, standing in the open doorway.

He—or she—was holding a gun pointed at my chest.

8

"IF YOU MOVE, LITTLE PEACHES, I WILL KILL YOU," HE
said. He spoke in a feminine voice but a man's voice—that is, a
deep man's voice with a sickly sweet, feminine tone. He was wearing
tight, skinny black jeans that showed off the womanly shape of his
legs. He now had a black windbreaker on over his copper T-shirt,
so I couldn't see the big man muscles of his arms anymore. Still, his
upper torso was man-sized, no question. His small, kitten-like face
had a coy, flirty smile on it. His eyes appraised me sexually, going up
and down my length, even as he held the gun steady.

Out on the patio, out of sight, Sean Gunther gave a strangled
groan of anguish. Kitten Face pouted at me, as if it was all such a
pity, wasn't it?

"Who are you? What do you want?" I asked him.

"Quiet, baby, or Mama spank," he said, lifting the gun a little.

Sean Gunther screamed again, tears in his voice now. It reminded
me of the screaming heretic in Galiana. Not as bad, not that high-
pitched agonized wail from the bowels of the castle dungeon. But I
could hear that Gunther was in pain, real pain. I thought of the thug
who was probably out there with him.

I considered Kitten Face. It's a funny thing about having a gun pointed at you. How many movies had I seen, how many books had I read, where the hero had that happen? Sometimes I'd watch a scene or read a scene and think: Why doesn't he just go for it? You know? Why should he do whatever the gunman tells him to do—put his hands up or get in the car or get on his knees or lie down on his face—if the killer's going to kill him anyway once he's helpless? Why not just go for the main chance, whatever's left?

Turns out, in real life, there's not a whole hell of a lot you can do. Kitten Face was clear across the room. I couldn't reach him. And even if I could, I doubt I would have had the courage. That black bore staring at me—and me one finger twitch from kingdom come. My brain went on the fritz as it searched itself for options and came up with nothing. So I just stood there, like the heroes in the movies. I even put my hands up instinctively, or maybe because it was what heroes in the movies did. Plus, I was afraid. Not to state the obvious, but I was afraid of getting shot, afraid of dying. I tried not to think about how afraid I was, but I didn't have to think about it. I just was.

Now there were footsteps outside. Heavy, thumping footsteps. To the left of the gunman, through the window, out there in the night, I saw Billiard Ball moving over the path by the house, from the patio, approaching the front door.

Kitten Face glanced his way, then sashayed a step or two into the foyer to make room for him. He swung his hips elaborately as he moved and eyed me as if he thought I might be watching his hips and how they swung. He made a big show of it. I felt he was mocking me. It pissed me off. That and the gun. He kept the gun trained on me the whole time.

Billiard Ball walked in. He was dragging Sean Gunther by the ankle, dragging him behind him as if he were nothing, no weight at all, the way a little kid tows a security blanket. Gunther was drenched from his sopping silver hair to the darkened knees of his white slacks. Billiard Ball must have held him by the ankles and dunked him head first into the pool.

The author lay on his back, dazed, with his hands lifted and his eyes open and his mouth open as he was dragged helplessly over the floor. His nose was smashed and there was fresh blood on his upper lip.

Billiard Ball slung the writer's body into the living room like you might sling a stick for a dog to fetch. Gunther cried out as he flew down the two stairs from the foyer. His cry was cut short as he landed hard on the tiled floor, sending scattered papers flying. He groaned then. He rolled over onto his front, propping himself up, dripping water and blood onto the pages still underneath him.

He started to rise. Kitten Face watched him. There was something really awful about the expression on the androgynous gunman's face. He was smiling, like it was cute, you know, cute to watch the broken Gunther try to stand. As if Gunther were a toddler just learning to stand and he, Kitten Face, was the toddler's admiring mother. Billiard Ball meanwhile stood with his massive arms crossed on his massive chest. He sneered cold death at me, just as he had from the window of the black Mustang.

Gunther pushed up onto his knees. Every move he made brought another grunt of effort out of him. He wiped the blood off his mouth with his hand, grimacing at the pain in his nose. Then, grunting some more, he rose to his feet. I could tell he was still drunk from the way he staggered a step, his body swaying like a reed in the wind.

"Who the fuck are you people?" he said, gingerly touching his nose again. He was talking to Kitten Face even though it was Billiard Ball who'd given him the beating. "Huh? What the hell did he rough me up for? I told him I didn't know anything."

Kitten Face pouted and smirked and glanced over at Billiard Ball.

"He doesn't know anything," Billiard Ball said. He had a surprisingly high voice, almost mousey. Strange to hear it come out of a guy that size.

"See?" said Gunther. "What did I tell you? It's nothing to me if—"

Kitten Face shot him dead.

THE MURDER OF Sean Gunther was so nonchalant I couldn't take it in at first. Still pouting and posing and sticking his hip out provocatively, Kitten Face simply flicked his wrist to move the gun from me to Gunther then pulled the trigger and flicked his wrist to point the gun at me again. The shot was loud and flat, like a ruler whapping a desktop. I hardly would've known what it was if I hadn't seen the burst of smoke and flame from the barrel. Even so, I couldn't believe it. I stared at Gunther as if I expected him to finish his sentence.

He didn't finish his sentence. He staggered again. He turned—turned toward me with his head down, looking in stunned surprise at the ragged black hole that was now in the middle of his white shirt just beneath his sternum. Then he lifted his eyes to me. The expression on his face was terrible. He was just beginning to realize that the story of his life was over. Any plans he had—for change or renewed success or personal redemption—they were all off. Time was up.

He crumpled to the floor and let out a throaty breath. Finally, he lay utterly still, staring sightless at the ceiling. That terrible expression was now frozen on his face forever.

"Aw," said Kitten Face. "Poor thing."

I think if I could have, I would have killed him then, killed him with my bare hands. I was that angry. It was such a dismal thing to do, just shoot the man like that for no reason. And the girly gay humor made it worse somehow. Like it was nothing. Like Gunther's life was nothing. Like it was all about Kitten Face. His cute little joke. His cute little show.

But it wasn't nothing to me. The reality of the author's death was beginning to register in my brain now, as final and inarguable as a brick wall. I had never experienced death before, never seen a man die, never even known anyone who died, not anyone I cared about. There was the jailer in the dungeon when the ogre bit his head off, I guess. But that wasn't like this, not real like this. Cowled jailers with torches, ogres, dungeons. All that was just too insane to be real. Not like this.

Kitten Face was coming toward me now. Swinging his hips elaborately. Daintily stepping over Gunther's corpse as if it were a puddle.

"What's the matter, peaches?" he said to me as he came. "You look pale. Something troubling you?"

My eyes flashed to the body on the floor. Kitten Face glanced back at it. "Oh. Yes. Poor darling. But then, he didn't know anything." He came up close, then closer, keeping the gun on me. "What about you, sweet cheeks?" he said. He reached out with his free hand and squeezed my cheeks between his thumb and fingers as if I were a child. Holding his gun on me so I couldn't push him off—or anyway didn't dare. "What do you know? Hm? Do you know anything? Hm?"

I didn't. I didn't know anything, and I figured when I said so, he'd kill me too. And I was even more scared than I was before, and I had been plenty scared before. But I was also furious—helplessly furious—at being mocked and manhandled like this.

"Tell Mama," Kitten Face said. And he let go of me and slapped me, not hard but hard enough to hurt.

I wanted to jump at him. I wanted to kill him. He was muscular but small, smaller than me, and I might've been able to do it, angry as I was. But the gun held me in place. I didn't have the courage to try.

"Tell Mama what you know," he said.

"I don't even know what you want," I said. My voice came out thin and tight. I was strangling on my helplessness and rage.

"Ooh, baby's angry, isn't he?" Kitten Face said. He patted my cheek, more softly this time. "Don't be an angry baby, peaches. You know what I want. I want what you want. The book. The woman. Ellen. What do you know about those?"

What could I say? What could I tell him that would keep me alive? I just stood there, staring at the gun barrel, staring past the gun barrel at his pouting, preening feline face. Waiting for him to pull the trigger. Wishing I had the guts to attack him—and why not, since I was going to die here anyway? But I didn't attack him. I just stood there.

"You're being very naughty," he said, waggling the gun back and forth, the way he had when he'd turned it on Gunther and fired. "Don't make Mama punish you."

An idea came to me. Something to say, anyway. My mouth was so dry I couldn't get the words out at first. I had to lick my lips and swallow hard before I tried. I tilted my head toward the cabinet.

"It's in there. The book. If that's the book you mean."

Kitten Face followed my gesture. He touched his lips with a finger and made a theatrical moue of surprise when he saw the big volume with the red binding: *Another Kingdom*. He kept the gun trained on me as he slinked over to the cabinet. He kept the gun trained on me as he lowered himself gracefully and plucked the volume from the shelf. Then he wagged the book in my face.

It wasn't a book. It was a fake. Just a binding. The pages had been torn out, leaving nothing but a few ragged shreds.

Kitten Face tossed it at me. I knocked it out of the air. It flapped to the floor.

"So that's no help, is it?" he said. "Is that the only copy?"

"It's the only one I know of," I said. I felt like I was signing my own death warrant.

And sure enough, Kitten Face stepped toward me and pressed the barrel of his gun hard into my forehead. My brain told me I had nothing to lose. I could make my move. Grab the gun. Turn it on him. Kill him like he deserved. Maybe even shoot down Billiard Ball too. *Be a man,* I thought.

But I couldn't do it.

"So you're not much use to me either, are you?" he said. I didn't answer. He pressed the gun against me harder, making me hurt. "Are you, you naughty baby?"

I still didn't answer. Because screw him. I was a dead man anyway, so screw him. I waited for him to pull the trigger, afraid of death and furious at my killer and sad that I was going to die. But I didn't have the courage to go for the gun.

Then, from across the room, Billiard Ball made a noise. A little cough. Barely audible.

Kitten Face drew the gun away.

"All right," he drawled. "Let's go."

HE MARCHED ME at gunpoint out of the house. Along the path. Through the driveway door. Down the drive. Back to my car where it was parked across the street in the shadows. Billiard Ball walked just behind us. I caught a glimpse of him in the car window, hands in his pants pockets as he strolled along barely paying attention, eyeing the night as if this were just a stroll in the garden.

Now that it seemed Kitten Face wasn't going to kill me right then and there, my frozen mind started to work again. And I realized: this—this, now—what was happening to me right here and now—made no more sense than my insane, supernatural trips to Galiana. Who were these people? What did they want from me? Why me? I thought of Gunther lying back there in the house, all his plans over, all his hopes gone. For what? What was it about? What *could* it be about? Had Gunther known the answer? Had he understood why his future was erased like that, his life, such as it was, erased just like that?

We reached my Nissan. Kitten Face spoke to Billiard Ball. "You take the 'Stang. Peaches and I will drive back in his car." He added to me: "Won't that be cozy, peaches?"

Billiard Ball didn't answer, just obeyed. He strolled off to the black Mustang, which was now parked at the curb just a few yards up the road.

Kitten Face prodded me in the back with his gun.

"Get behind the wheel, darling," he told me. "And don't try anything, or I'll blow your balls off. You won't like it. No one ever does."

I unlocked the door and pulled it open. I took a quick glance back at Kitten Face. I don't think he was expecting me to do that because I caught him with an expression on his mug that wasn't part of the whole showy camp repertoire. It was a hollow expression, slack and dead-eyed: the expression of a man sitting alone in his room as the sun went down, contemplating a life of emptiness and despair.

I lowered myself into the car—and like the snap of a finger, I was blind. I couldn't see anything. Had he shot me? Was I dead? Everything was blackness.

Then the next moment I felt my body sliding downward, bumping downward over a rough surface, then flying off the surface and into the empty air.

I heard a shout from above and behind me: "Go after him!"

I heard another voice, urgent in the pitch blackness: "This way!"

There was a moment of stunned confusion before I recognized the nasal, squeaking female voice of the mutant rodent Maud from Galiana. Christ, I was back in the dungeon again! I was running for my life again with the executioner and the guard right behind me. I remembered: I had pulled the grate out of the wall and scrambled headfirst through the opening. I must have slid through some sort of chute into this blackness.

I smelled shit. All around me. As if I were in a sewer.

I saw a light up ahead of me—a flash of sparkling colored lights. Maud.

I started running toward her.

9

I GUESS IN SOME BIZARRE WAY, I WAS GETTING USED TO
this: stepping through doorways from one world into another.
Whether it was a brain tumor or the onset of psychosis or actual
magical teleportation from reality into fantasy land, I was starting to
get a handle on it. It only took me a second this time to realize I was
no longer facing death at the hands of a gun-wielding androgyne
madman but was, in the blink of an eye, facing death instead from
a medieval sword-wielding dungeon guard while I escaped in the
wake of a mutant rodent.

As a side note, psychosis seemed the most reasonable explanation.

Anyway, I ran after Maud's sparkling lights, but I didn't get far.
The lights went out. The dark was absolute. The ground underneath
my feet was uneven. I took a couple of steps and tripped on some
sort of rise and went sprawling to the ground. I skinned the side of
my knee and lost my bearings utterly.

I started to get up. I heard my pursuers shouting behind me. By
luck, something had delayed them. There was some confusion about
whether the guard should bring his torch into the chute with him.

"You know what's down there?" shouted the guard—and I could
hear raw fear in his echoing voice.

"Damn it!" answered the executioner. "He's getting away! Let's go!"

What's down here? I wondered.

And then something sank its claws into me. I let out a high-pitched shriek.

"Oh for pity's sake!" said Maud, disgusted—she was right beside me now. She pulled her claws out of my shoulder.

"Well, you startled me!" I muttered. I climbed to my feet.

"Just come on! Follow me."

"I can't see anything."

She sparkled, and I did see her then in the spray of light around her. She was clinging to the rough wall beside me like a squirrel. "This way," she said. And she scrambled off along the stone, winking out into darkness as she went.

I stumbled to where I'd seen the wall and felt my way along it, moving more slowly, more carefully now.

Behind me, I heard a body hit the ground. A loud, gruff curse. The guard must've come through the chute. I glanced back, but the darkness was complete again. The guard had obviously decided to leave his torch behind him.

What's down here? I thought again.

"God, the smell," I heard him say.

It was bad, all right. Raw sewage. A lot of it. The stench burned in my nostrils. And it was getting worse with every step I took.

"Stop," said Maude. Then more urgently: "I said stop!"

I stopped. There was a pause. Then she glittered—and by the vibrating confetti of colored lights, I saw that I was standing inches from the edge of a pit: a sharp drop into nothingness. The shit smell rose up out of the depths in a wet gust so strong it made me want to vomit.

The lights around the mutant rodent went out. I heard her voice. "Find the rungs. Go down."

I lowered myself to my knees. It was so black, I could barely find the ground. I felt around for the rim of the pit. Felt past the rim until I touched a horizontal bar of rusted metal in the pit wall: the first rung.

Maud's weirdly human, weirdly nasal, weirdly animal voice now came up from the depths below me. "Climb down."

Nothing could have made me descend into the thick, nauseating stench of that pit—nothing except the sound of the executioner tumbling out of the chute behind me. His voice and the guard's voice . . .

"Come on, move it!"

"I can't bloody see!"

"To hell with that! Don't let him get away!"

. . . closing in behind me.

I began the climb down the side of the pit, rung by rung, hand over hand. With every foot of the descent, the stench grew thicker, worse. It was like a living putrid shroud of wet excrement folding itself around me, covering my mouth, my nose, my eyes, tightening on my lungs, smothering me.

"God!" I choked out, strangling on the miasma.

But I could hear the guard and the executioner cursing and shouting at each other as they stumbled after me through the darkness. So I kept climbing, down and down, deeper and deeper into the thicker and thicker stench.

I touched bottom—not a solid bottom. No such luck. A wet, thick, moving, stinking bottom of God knows what loathsome stuff that rose around my ankles and squeezed up over my feet and soaked my leggings while the stink of it lived and breathed around me. I gagged. I shuddered.

"Make your mind go blank," Maud said. She glittered—and there she was, clinging to the wall beside me. Her bizarre deformity of a woman's face eyed me eagerly, like a Halloween mask hung on the head of a rat.

"What?" I said, barely able to speak, barely able to breathe.

"There is no magic here but Tauratanio's," she said. I still had no clue what this meant. But she went on, "You have to let it in. You have to open a path for it in your mind. Like I did when I broke your chains."

"Well, why can't you do it now?"

"This is bigger. It takes a human mind. Come on!"

Above me, there was a rough shout. Then a cry: "Watch it!"

"Bloody hell!"

The guard and the executioner had come to the edge of the pit. Another second and they'd be climbing down after me.

"What do I do?" I whispered, swallowing what felt like a solid chunk of stench.

"I told you," said the rodent. "Clear your mind."

I looked behind me as I heard a man's heavy tread on the iron rung of the pit wall.

"Clear your mind!" Maud commanded.

"Damn it, how'm I supposed to do that now?"

"Just do it!"

I heard my pursuers steadily descending after me. I faced forward. I breathed out. Then I breathed in—and it was like swallowing the contents of a toilet. I bent forward, clutching my throat, gagging.

"There's no time for that!" said Maud. "Clear your mind!"

Panting, I forced myself to straighten. I forced myself to breathe more evenly. I forced myself not to think about the *clank, clank, clank* of the two men climbing down the iron rungs above me. I forced myself to stare into the dark and let the dark become my thoughts and think of nothing. And for a second, I did it. Just for a second, but it was enough for me to feel what Maud was talking about: the magic. It was a steady pulse of energy flowing from somewhere into my mind. I gasped at the strength of it—and lost hold of it. It snaked away like a live wire. But I tried again and found it quickly.

And this time, once I found it, it was easier to keep the channel to the energy open. And as I did . . .

As I did, a swarm of colored lights came into view before me. The swarm was about twenty yards away, approaching swiftly through the air: a flying throng of sparkling reds and greens and yellows, blues and whites, dancing, rising and falling in the darkness as gnats rise and fall on currents of air.

"What is it?" I whispered—but the moment I spoke, the lights began to dim and wink out.

"Clear your—" Maud began to say.

"I know, I know."

I steadied myself. I focused. The colored lights grew bright again: a Christmas cloud of them still rolling and tumbling toward me. I was aware of the clank of the rungs behind me. The guard and the executioner were about halfway down, only seconds away. But here was a revelation: as frightened as I was, I could make myself be *not* frightened, I could release the frightened part and keep my mind focused wholly on the colored lights.

I had never done that before—but I did it now. And the cloud of colored lights grew brighter, came closer. Now, by their glow, I could see the corridor ahead. A few feet away, it opened up into a much larger space that ran off a long way beneath an arched stone ceiling. A narrow, flat walkway stretched out through the oncoming glow-swarm until it faded into shadow and then into the invisible darkness beyond. On either side of the flat stretch, the stone slanted down into a broad gutter, each gutter a good eight feet wide at least. Both gutters were full of sewage, a thick, brown, fuming concoction of polluted liquid and solid waste. The liquid shifted and flowed, lapping at the slanted stone, bubbling and churning at the center as if it really were alive.

I stared. I realized I was going to have to walk along that path between the filth-choked gutters.

And just then, in a thrumming, whispering rush, the dancing lights surrounded me.

I let out a noise I'd never heard myself make before: a little breathless cry of wonder. They were people! The lights—they were small, flying people! Men and women, each about five inches long but perfectly formed. Each gave off a multicolored radiance of his own, and the glow of each blended with the others, and the glow of all together created the twinkling, rainbow cloud. The little people surrounded me, rose and spun and fell around me. They were naked. They were beautiful. And they had wings! Transparent, gossamer wings like the wings of a dragonfly. That's what made that sound, that stuttering thrum as they swarmed.

"Fairies!" I breathed. "They're fairies!"

"Don't let their lights go out," said Maud.

I could see her now too, lit by the fairy lights. Still clinging squirrel-like to the wall, her eerie woman's face bright-eyed and anxious. I stood there with the cloud of fairies swirling around me. The mutant rodent gazing at me. The swordsman and the masked executioner chasing after me. This had to be some kind of brain damage, right?

"Let's go," said Maud.

My breath caught as she leapt off the wall—just like a squirrel—leapt through the air and landed on the corridor to scramble out onto the walkway up ahead of me. I could feel the cloud of fairies moving after her. I moved with them to stay within their light.

We entered the high-ceilinged hall and stepped onto the walkway between the steaming, shit-filled gutters. At first, I was so awestruck by the sight of the fairies it was easy to keep my focus on them. I could feel the magic energy flowing in and out of me from somewhere far away, powering the fairies as it passed through them as if they were bulbs on a circuit. The cloud of light and I moved as one, traveling briskly together along the narrow path.

Then there was a splash and a grunt behind me. I looked back over my shoulder and saw through the misty rainbow that the guard had reached the bottom of the ladder. He was standing in the thick puddle of crap that covered the passage there. He saw me, and he drew his sword with a metallic swish. His eyes glittered, and his lips went tight with determination. A moment later, the fearful masked figure of the executioner dropped down behind him, cursing at the mess around his feet.

"Never mind them!" Maud told me. "Keep the lights on!" Her voice was now coming from somewhere down the tunnel up ahead.

I faced forward and saw what she meant. While I was distracted, the fairies had grown dimmer. Their naked bodies were turning gray. Their thin wings were fighting frantically with the air.

All the same, I stole another quick glance back at the guard. He was still standing where he had been, watching me, sword in hand, fading into darkness as the fairy lights faded. He seemed reluctant to follow me onto the walkway.

Why? What's down here?

The executioner shoved the guard in the back. "Come on, move!" he said.

Maud's voice, hollow with distance, called to me again: "Ignore them! The fairies will protect you! Keep your mind clear!"

Breathing hard, I forced myself to look ahead. Scared as I was—of the guard, of the sword, of the executioner, of the endless night of torture that awaited me if they caught me, and the endless life of deformity after that—I had to use all my mental strength to concentrate. A frantic second passed and then another. I couldn't focus. Then—yes!—I did it. My mind caught hold of the snaking wire of magic and held on. The fairies' colored lights grew bright. Their thrumming buzz grew louder as their wings beat faster and they rose in the air and surrounded me.

In a cloud of rainbow light, I walked on.

Behind me, I could hear the executioner angrily urging the guard to chase me. I could hear the guard muttering, "All right. All right." Their voices grew closer, but only slowly. Why were they so wary? What were they afraid of?

I couldn't think about it. I had to focus on the magic. I had to keep the twinkling fairies bright, hovering in the air around me, lighting the great hall of the sewer.

Then, a splash. Out of the corner of my eye, I caught a glimpse of motion: something humped and enormous rising up out of the burbling shit in the gutter to my left. I gasped and swiveled to look. I heard the guard behind me let out a curse.

But whatever it was, it was gone. Only the ripples it had made remained, making the sewage lap against the slanting stone.

The fairy lights began to dim again. How was I supposed to focus now? I remembered what Maud had said: *The fairies will protect you.* But would they? From that? That thing that had just splashed in the sewage? It was big. I could tell even from that sidelong glimpse of it. It was *really* big.

I took a deep, shuddering breath, and as I let it out, I let my fear steam away into the surrounding shadows. Once more, the fairy lights grew brighter. I focused. I focused hard. *The fairies will protect you.* But in the back of my mind, I couldn't help wondering: What would happen to me if I let the lights go out?

The grisly answer came almost at once.

Whatever had risen from the shit, the guard had gotten a better look at it than I had. It had made him lose his nerve.

"Did you see that?" I heard him growl.

"Never mind! Go on! He's escaping!" barked the executioner.

"Are you crazy? That thing will . . . "

But then his gruff voice pinwheeled up into a falsetto shriek of absolute terror. I couldn't help myself. My focus broke. I spun.

I saw the beast arising. Living excrement. A soulless, breathing hulk of hungering shit. Its immense, vaguely human shape burst out of the sewage with a gurgling roar. It rose up like a wave, and like a wave it fell upon the guard even as he reeled back in horror. He tried to wield his sword against it, but the fear took the strength out of him. The blade glanced weakly off the fetid body of the beast and fell from the guard's slack fingers. Then the creature poured itself over him.

As I gaped in horror, the fairy lights went dim. And thank God for that—thank God—because even what I saw was almost more than my imagination could bear. In the moment before the hall went black, I saw the Shit Thing swallow the guard. The next instant, it forced its way into him through every pore, both engulfing him and entering him so that his figure appeared dimly through the edge of its substance. His mouth was still open on a scream, but the scream was silenced by the influx of sewage. Sewage filled him. It bloated him. It burst from his eyes and tore through his belly and then—thank God, thank God—the light went out, and there was a terrible liquid explosion as everything was enveloped in blackness.

My mind was white with incandescent fear, but even in that fear, I realized the beast would have me next if I didn't clear my mind, and fast. Somewhere I could hear Maud screaming the same thing to me, the same thought. And somehow—I truly don't know how—but somehow, I managed to remake my mind into the blackness all around me and catch the invisible magic by the tail and hold on to it for dear life.

The fairy lights flickered on again. The little creatures thrummed their dragonfly wings and flew around me. In the rainbow glow, I saw the beast receding down the sloped stone into the gutter. All that was left behind on the walkway was a patch of pooled sewage and a few unspeakable remains of the guard and his fallen sword.

As for the executioner, he was not so scary now. He was running for his life full speed. I watched him by fairy light as he raced blindly for the narrow corridor beyond the sewer—the corridor that led back to the pit and the rung ladder. Then he was out of sight in the darkness.

I stood and gaped at the dreadful aftermath another moment, the cloud of sparkling lights surrounding me, the fritter of gossamer wings filling the air.

So that's what happens if the lights go out, I thought.

Then I turned and started to move away.

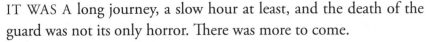

IT WAS A long journey, a slow hour at least, and the death of the guard was not its only horror. There was more to come.

That thing—that Shit Thing—followed me the whole way. Or maybe there was more than one, maybe the sewers were full of them, I don't know. But now and then, I saw it from the corner of my eyes. It bubbled up from the bubbling offal and splashed and grumbled and sank away again. Every time, I shuddered. Every time, the fairy lights dimmed. Every time, I forced myself to clear my mind again and seize hold of the magic current and keep the circuit open and the fairy lights on.

It was exhausting work. At first—after the guard was destroyed like that—the fear was so intense it kept me focused. What choice did I have? It was focus and walk and keep the fairy lights burning or literally be covered with shit and filled with shit and destroyed by shit from within. Still, you know, after a while, everything becomes normal, doesn't it? Suffering, danger, slow death—it's all just life in the end. So, after a while, as I walked on—on and on through the long tunnel with no end in sight—my mind began to wander, my attention began to flag. It happened so incrementally, so subtly, that I didn't even notice that the sparks of light coming off the flittering fairies had begun to grow just a bit duller, then just a bit more. The little pink naked bodies surrounding me grew just a bit more and then a bit more gray.

Maud was running up ahead of me, sometimes within the reach of the glow and sometimes just beyond it off in the darkness. She hadn't said a word to me in a long time. She didn't want to break my concentration, I guess. And maybe she'd gotten into the routine of the journey too, maybe she was getting lost in her own thoughts too, because she didn't notice the fairy lights dimming either.

But now, I looked ahead through the thrumming rainbow cloud, and I saw the mutant rodent had stopped. She was sitting like a rat sits, her front paws raised before her. She was looking back toward me with her creepily human face. I peered through the glow and saw that she had reached the end of the walkway. She was waiting for me there, waiting for me to catch up. A few yards beyond her, the gutters ended and there was a sort of stone alcove. And though the alcove was dark, I saw—or thought I saw—a faint misty glow of white light as if a sunbeam were falling into the darkness from a great height.

After the long trek through this stench and filth, I felt a thrill of hope—and only at the last second did I realize that my concentration, already slipping, was now utterly broken, not by my fear this time but by my excitement, my anticipation of escape. The fairy lights flickered—which finally drew my attention to them.

"Oh no!" I said.

And the beast attacked.

It came up so suddenly and was so huge that it overwhelmed me. Its gurgling roar, its ghastly stink, its hungry eyes, its awful presence—a mountainous, looming, living creature of liquid waste—blasted every thought right out of me. Any chance I might have had to regain my focus and relight the protective cloud of light was washed away in my fear of the rising shit wave.

I saw it was about to drop on me. The image of the guard's horrific death filled my mind. I panicked. I ran.

The fairy lights went out, and the long hall was plunged into utter blackness.

Or no—not utter blackness. I could still see that dim beam of light shining down into the alcove at the end of the walkway. Ignoring the sting of my skinned knee, I ran for it with all the speed of fear.

The Shit Thing crashed down onto the walkway right behind me—right on the spot where I'd been standing half a second before. I heard its roar become a thick, gooey splash. I felt its thick blanket of stench envelop me. It had missed me on its first attack, but I heard, then felt, its living substance burbling and thrashing over the walkway, coming after me.

I screamed. I ran faster. It grabbed my ankle.

I was shocked by the strength of it, by the solidity of it when it had seemed to be made of nothing but offal and goo. It grabbed me like a giant's hand. It roared like a giant as it seized hold in order to drag me backward into it. I reached out wildly in the darkness, reached out in wild despair for that faint misty beam of light.

My fingers touched the entry to the alcove. I grabbed hold of the edge of the wall with both hands.

Just as the Shit Thing strengthened its grip on my heel, I yanked myself forward with all my might. I broke the creature's hold and went spilling forward into the alcove, falling onto my backside in the midst of the dim gray light from above.

I heard—I could not see—the beast receding. The smell faded, and I heard the liquid creature sinking back into the gutter with a disappointed groan.

I swallowed the copper vomit of fear and disgust. I raised my knees and rested on them, sitting on the hard stone, breathing fast. After a second or two—or an hour or two, I don't really know—I noticed the silence around me. I fought to bring my breathing under control. I fought to focus again. I cleared my mind and—there!—the flow of magic came back into me. There was a slow flicker of color, a stuttering hum of wings. And then the cloud of fairy lights came back on again, the beautiful naked creatures orbiting my head.

In the multicolored glow, I saw Maud. She clung to the alcove wall, looking down on me. She had an expression on her face—how can I describe it? Disdain? Disappointment? Condemnation? All of these. She looked as if she could not believe what a cowardly wimp I was.

"What're you looking at me like that for?" I said.

She shook her head, disgusted.

"Because I screamed?" I said.

She averted her eyes.

"What? Did you see that thing?"

She sighed. "You better start climbing," she squeaked. "It's a long way."

Disgruntled, I pushed my way to my feet, muttering under my breath. "It was a gigantic shit monster! It was gonna eat me! For Christ's sake!" Maud didn't speak again and didn't look at me either. *Stupid bizarro hamster. What does she know?* I thought. I'd have said it aloud too, but she was the only ally I had. Still, she was making me feel like crap.

The sparkling fairies and I moved deeper into the alcove. The pale beam of light was brighter there. I tilted my head back, and my heart lifted a little. Way, way up above me, there was daylight, a little pinprick of white brightness. Rodent Girl was right about that anyway: it was a long climb.

I found the rungs on the wall and started up.

10

AFTER THE DUNGEON, AFTER THE DARKNESS, AFTER THE
stench and the terror, it felt almost miraculous to climb out into the
daylight and the open air. The moment my head and shoulders emerged from a narrow street sewer, the fairies dispersed like birds frightened
by a gunshot. Off they flew in all directions, their little bodies vanishing
in the distance. I didn't even have a chance to tell them thanks.

I climbed out the rest of the way. I was in an empty alley formed
by the stained walls of two shabby houses. Either way I looked, left
or right, the alley opened onto streets lined with buildings. A green
stenchy fog hung over me, giving the sky a sickly hue.

Maud came up after me. She scrambled up the wall to the level
of my head.

"Where are we?" I asked her.

"The town of Eastrim," she said.

"It smells weird," I said. "It smells bad."

"Come on. We have to hurry. Once the executioner sounds the
alarm, they could close the city gates."

With that, off she went, up the wall and onto the eaves of the
roof above me. She leapt along the gutter there, and I followed after
her, out of the alley, into the town.

Eastrim was a dismal place. A small city of narrow streets and lousy air. That weird and awful smoke hung over everything, and it stank. The streets were paved with cobblestones. Low wooden buildings leaned toward each other from the curbs as if they would topple together into the roadway at any moment. The people moved in dense packs, shoving and cursing one another. They all seemed to have the same flat, round, pale, and dirty faces, the same dulled and gaping expressions, as if they were dumb beasts rather than women and men. They wore torn, dirty, colorless robes belted at the waist by ropes. They trudged beneath the overhanging eaves, carrying buckets, loads of wood, sacks of potatoes, or caged, squawking birds and animals. I saw men beating mules with sticks, trying to get the stubborn creatures to pull wagons full of hay or lumber. I saw women sweeping thresholds, emptying chamberpots out of windows, or cleaning house and tending children, visible through their open doors.

I gaped at all of it. I had seen paintings like this. Renaissance paintings, medieval scenes. I felt like a traveler in imagined time, a three-dimensional modern on the flat backdrop of the fantastical past. Was I a real man in a make-believe world or a make-believe man in the real world? Whatever—it mesmerized me. I had to force myself to stop staring like an idiot, just to glance up now and then and check on Maud's progress as she leaped from roof to roof and wall to wall.

I followed after her through the bizarre maze of streets.

Now and then, through a gap between the buildings, I caught a glimpse of the castle from which I'd just escaped. It was an impressive sight: six mighty towers and a central keep, the walls fierce and formidable. It stood on raised earth above the city, in cleaner air above the smoke. A moat of dull water surrounded it. I wondered which tower I'd been in when I was arrested beside the body of Lady Kata. I couldn't tell for sure.

The rodent and I continued along the stinking, smoky streets. After a while, we came out into a broader plaza surrounded by shops and bordered by an official-looking structure decked with flags. The smoke was thicker here, the smell was worse. Soon I saw why. There was a bonfire in the middle of the square. The noxious green-black miasma was pouring up out of it.

On another side of the open space, a crowd was gathered, raising a great noise. The sound drew my attention. I looked over as I passed through the plaza—and I found myself staring at a dreadful spectacle.

Prisoners were being put to death, right then, right there, out in public. There were five of them, all men, each held in a small cage, each cage suspended by a chain on a pole, holding it only a few feet off the ground. Guards, much like the guards who had arrested me, were sticking the points of their long spears through the bars, piercing the flesh of the men within. The men shrieked in agony, helpless to avoid being punctured and shredded. The guards chose their spots with care, keeping the victims alive as long as they could. They were laughing as they worked. And the spectators were cheering them on with wild fervor, their peasant faces contorted with glee and rage. They were shouting "Traitor! Traitor!" They were shouting "Give it to them!" and "Make it last!" It was like a sporting event in a madhouse.

I slowed down to watch. A woman passed by me. She was large, grimy faced. Carrying a basket of laundry in her hands. She seemed to have paused on her way somewhere. She was watching the torture too—watching and snickering through a toothless grin.

"What did they do?" I asked her.

"These?" she said in a hoarse crow's caw of a voice. "They're the latest to betray the revolution, that's what. They plotted to bring back the queen."

The queen. *Elinda.* I remembered her name from my computer's character list and from the testimony against me at the trial. Lady Kata, the woman I was accused of murdering, had been her lady-in-waiting. So had Lady Betheray, the raven-haired beauty who had testified against me.

"These are the latest, you said?" I asked the laundrywoman.

She nodded. "These are the latest—and those are the last." She gestured with her basket toward the bonfire.

I looked. I had only noticed the burning pile of wood before, but now I saw that, mingled with the logs and boards, there were bones, human bones—limbs and hips and grinning skulls—some with a last coating of boiling flesh just now bubbling away. That explained the awful smoke, the awful smell.

I grimaced and swallowed my gorge and turned my eyes away. As I did, I caught a glimpse of Maud on a ledge above me. She beckoned me urgently. I had to go.

I hurried out of the square, down another narrow street, and to a small mews not far away. The stables were lined up here, one after another. Blacksmiths working at their anvils and forges, grooms brushing down horses, stablers pitchforking hay. The smell of animal dung mingled with the more deathly, more dreadful smell from the bonfire back in the plaza.

I hesitated. Several streets led out of the mews, and I didn't know which one to take. I looked up at the rooftop, searching for my rodent friend. I didn't see her. But even as I looked, I heard her whisper to me over the clanging anvils and neighing horses.

"Psst. Over here."

She was clinging to the corner of a small building just beside me, just head high. I moved to her.

"See that man over there?" she asked softly. She gestured across the mews with her weirdly human face. I followed the gesture.

Across the way, there stood a big man—a blacksmith, well over six feet tall, broad in the chest, domed at the belly, and muscular in his shoulders and arms. He had a great black beard and bright eyes and a few loose strands of black hair across his bulbous head. He wore a leather apron over his robe and held an iron pair of tongs in one hand and a hammer in the other. He was holding a piece of iron in the tongs, turning it in the bright orange fire of a forge, watching it as it started to glow red.

"I see him," I said softly.

"He's our contact. Go over to him," Maud whispered. "Say to him, 'I go my way.'"

"I go my way," I repeated. "Is it code?"

"It means we are with the queen."

"Right, we're with . . . Wait, what?"

Annoyed, Maud began to repeat it slowly, like I was an idiot. "We are with—"

"Yeah, no, I heard you. But isn't that why they were killing those people back there? For supporting the queen?"

"Yes, that's right."

"And we're with them?"

"Of course we're with them," said the squirrel-girl. "Look around you. This was a great city before the revolution."

"I'm sure it was but—"

"But what?" she snapped.

"I'm already wanted for murder."

"Then you have nothing to lose."

"Ha ha," I said. But I guess she had a point at that. I sighed. "All right."

"And keep it quiet. Don't let anyone hear you. The council has spies everywhere."

"Great."

Looking at the scene all around me—as if I could somehow spot the spies among the mews workers—I crossed over to the blacksmith. He had begun hammering the hot iron now, shaping a shoe. The ringing blows were loud, too loud to speak over. I stood close, waiting for him to take a break.

He was in the midst of lifting his hammer into the air when he noticed me.

"What the hell are you looking at?" he said. His voice was guttural and ferocious.

I began to whisper, "I go my . . . "

"What?"

"I go . . . "

"Speak up. I can't hear you! What the hell's wrong with you?"

I looked around the mews. Either everyone was listening to me while pretending to go about their business or I was imagining it. Probably I was imagining it. I tried again, leaning as close to the blacksmith as I thought I could without him bringing that hammer down on my head.

"I go my way," I said.

The blacksmith just stared at me ferociously.

I dropped my voice even lower. "It means I'm . . . "

"What?"

I leaned even closer, spoke even lower. "I'm with the queen. I go my way."

Still, the blacksmith didn't react. He just stood there, just glared at me, his hammer lifted. I thought for sure he was about to raise an alarm. I could already see myself locked up in one of those cages in the plaza. I could already feel the spears going into me, gouging and shredding my flesh.

But no. Now, without a word, the blacksmith simply lay his iron and tongs and hammer down on the anvil. Without a word, he turned and walked into the stable just behind him.

Standing alone now, I looked around me at the mews, at the other smiths and the stablers and the grooms working away on the horses. No one seemed to be looking back at me, but I felt they were. I felt they were all stealing secret glances my way, getting ready to call for my arrest.

A few endless moments went by. Then the blacksmith came back out of the stable. He was leading a sleek, black stallion, already saddled and reined.

It was a magnificent beast. I'd ridden horses before, but they were tamed ranch horses rented for an afternoon on some family summer vacation or other. They were nothing like this. The glistening stallion snorted and tugged at its reins. Its hooves danced restlessly on the cobbles, kicking up dust. The blacksmith handed the reins to me. I stared at them. I looked up at the horse. The horse whinnied. It threw its head this way and that, its white eyes rolling.

The blacksmith leaned close to my ear, so close I felt his hot breath on me. "Let wisdom reign," he murmured low. His eyes were filled with hot passion. When I drew back and looked at him, he nodded gravely as if to confirm that we were brothers in a great cause.

Well, what could I do? I nodded back in the same manner, trying to look like I knew what the hell was going on. Then—there seemed no choice—I mounted the stallion. I tried to do it all in one swift motion—you know, to catch the royalist fervor of the moment by heroically swinging into the saddle and dashing away. *Let wisdom reign. Giddyap!* In fact, the best I could do was claw and scramble and climb inelegantly into the seat, my face pressed stupidly into the stallion's mane. Finally, I worked myself upright, holding the reins in my hand and trying to look as much as possible like an equestrian statue.

Then I nearly fell on my head as the horse took off.

It moved as if it knew the way. Stepping high and lively, it cantered to the edge of the mews, then pulled up short, tossing its head. There was a shocking streak of gray-brown something, so near my face it almost toppled me backward. Maud. The rodent-woman had leapt from the wall and now landed expertly on the pommel. As if this was what it had been waiting for, the stallion trotted away.

We rode through the streets. The peasants grudgingly stepped aside to let us pass. I tried to sit straight and look authoritative, as if I were guiding the beast, but it really did seem to know where it was going. Whenever it hesitated, Maud whispered in its ear, and on we went again.

We trotted down one street, then another, then another. Then I looked up and there, ahead of us, were the gates of the city.

My insides twisted, instantly tense. I could see this wasn't going to be easy. There were high stone walls, two high, arched iron gates, and guards with swords and spears posted all along the ground and up on the battlements. The gates were open, and a steady flow of people, vehicles, and beasts were passing in and out of town under the guards' watchful eyes. Merchants with carts piled high with jugs and boxes, pilgrims with sacks on their backs and staffs in hand, peasants on foot and knights on horseback, and farmhands, men and women both, dusty from the road with their sheep and cows trudging along beside them.

With Maud whispering in its ear, the stallion took its place in the flow of people heading toward the exit. With every step that brought us closer to those guards, my guts twisted tighter. Did they know I'd escaped? Were they watching for us? Waiting for us, ready to spring a trap?

When we were only a few yards away from the gate, Maud pulled back from the stallion's ear and turned to me. Close-up like this, it was creepy and even a bit disgusting to see her woman's face protruding from her ratlike head.

"Try not to act like such a fugitive," she said.

Then, without waiting for my answer, she leapt off the saddle.

"Wait, where . . . ?" I started to say—but she had already disappeared into the dust around the feet of the pedestrians. And of course I understood: if the guards were looking for me, a man traveling with a mutant rat would be hard to miss.

All the same, with Maud gone, I felt very alone and uncertain. My horse and I moved closer and closer to the gate and to the guards. I tried to calculate how long it would've taken the executioner to get out of the sewer and raise the alarm, how long for the guards to bring word down to the gate, how long it had taken me to travel out of the sewer and through the town. But it was no good. I'd lost all sense of time amidst the danger and confusion. I had no way of knowing whether the guards at the gate were ready for me or not.

The crowd of jostling people and carts and animals moved along, and I moved with it, closer and closer to the exit, closer and closer to the sharp, scanning gazes of the guards. No one said anything. The dust of travel swirled around me. I tried to focus my mind as I had below ground. Now the gate was right in front of me. Now the arch was over my head. Now I was passing out of the city.

And before I fully realized what had happened, I felt the gun pressed into the base of my neck. I looked up, startled, into the rearview mirror and saw the feline face of the androgyne assassin.

"Drive," he said.

11

I HAD ALMOST FORGOTTEN ALL THIS. THE KITTEN-faced killer in the back seat of my Nissan. The author, Sean Gunther, in his house, on the floor of his living room, dead, shot dead. All this inexplicable madness had been swept from my consciousness by the inexplicable madness back in Galiana: the guard and the executioner after me, the Shit Monster hunting me from the gutters, the work of keeping the lights of the protective fairies bright . . .

I felt a wave of hysteria pass over me. It wasn't the gun—the gun that had killed Gunther—ready to fire into the base of my brain. It wasn't just the gun, anyway. It was everything. The whole lunatic situation. The lunatic thoughts in my own head. Shit Monster! Fairy lights! Galiana! Christ, it had all seemed so real just two seconds ago. It had felt real, even smelled real. The death of the guard, watching the guard destroyed as his screams were smothered in his throat by sewage. It had seemed totally real at the time.

But now—now all at once—it seemed like it must've been a dream, some sort of elaborate subconscious psychological metaphor for who the hell knows what. This—the killer, the corpse in the house, the gun at my neck—*this* was real. And yet this also seemed impossible, a nightmare.

"Don't make me say things twice, baby boy," Kitten Face said, tapping the back of my head with the gun barrel. "Get going. Follow the 'Stang."

The Mustang. Right. Billiard Ball, the shaven-headed thug, was in the black Mustang just in front of me. The car was just now pulling away from the curb, speeding off with a screech of tires. I got the Nissan going and shot after him, following his red taillights through the darkness.

I drove in silence at first. I was trying to reorient myself, to reassemble what was happening here in LA. I tried to remember: my talk with Sean Gunther. *Another Kingdom.* Ellen Evermore. Her picture in his phone. It came back to me. She had read my script. She had wanted me to read her book, and then she had withdrawn it. Why? *Global.* That's all Gunther had been able to tell me before he passed out. That was his last word to me on the subject before his brutally casual murder.

All these thoughts were vague and tangled, mixed up with other thoughts, flashbacks of my escape from the dungeon and my journey through Eastrim to the gate. I felt a sense of regret. I wished I could have used my time in that other world to give some thought to this one. Maybe I could have come up with a plan of escape or figured out a way to smuggle a weapon from that dimension into the here and now.

But how could I have? I'd been so desperate just to stay alive. Just to get out from below ground without being devoured by the Sewage Creature from Hell. There had simply been no time to think about anything else. So here I was, a prisoner again, helpless again, under threat of death again.

I glanced up in the rearview mirror. Kitten Face saw me and pursed his lips to send me a taunting little kiss. *Mwah.* Oh yeah, I remembered that too. His campy bullying and how it got under my skin.

We traveled through the Hollywood Hills in purple darkness, on winding roads between trees made silhouettes by deep night. Now and then, I stole a glimpse at the killer in the rearview. He was barely paying attention. He looked bored. He looked as relaxed and indifferent as he had when he flicked his wrist to snuff out Sean Gunther.

"Where are we going?" I asked him.

With an off-handed gesture, he thwacked me on the back of the head, hard enough to make me grunt. "Ow!"

"You didn't ask Mama's permission to speak," he said. And he gave me a pout, as if this was all just some sort of flirty game between us. What a psycho.

We came down onto level ground and cruised over to Sunset Boulevard. The late traffic on the strip was thinning. The Mustang up ahead of me passed smoothly under billboards and neon marquees. The colored lights played over my windshield as I followed. We headed toward Beverly Hills.

I tried to think. What should I do? My eyes scanned the scene outside. What if I saw a cop? Could I honk the horn and try to get his attention? Could I leap out at the next red light and run for it?

But that gun. The killer's gun. I remembered how it had held me frozen back at Gunther's house, how I'd stood there paralyzed by it while Kitten Face tormented me. I hadn't had the courage to make a play then, and I doubted I had it now.

I wished I had my fairy bodyguards swirling around me. I wished all I had to do was focus my mind and have their lights glow and protect me. But that world was worlds away in who knew what fantastic territory of my obviously broken brain. The best I could do here was try to concentrate as I had back there, try to focus through my fear and clear my mind.

I did. I let the anxiety come off me like steam. I steadied my thoughts. Once I took the heightened emotion out of it, I could see things more clearly. I couldn't risk an escape attempt, even if I had the nerve. Kitten Face was too crazy. He might blow me away in a fit of pique and then take his chances in a shootout with the police.

No. The best I could do for now was try to get some information out of him, try to get a better picture of the situation I was in. It might cost me a few more raps to the skull, but it would give me a sense of what was possible. He obviously had orders to bring me in, so he wasn't going to shoot me if he could help it. At least I didn't think he would.

"So how come you killed him?" I asked into the mirror. Kitten Face seemed surprised that I'd dared to speak to him again. I waited for him to give me another swat with the gun barrel. He didn't. Not right away, anyhow. I pushed on: "I'm just curious. You're looking for the book, right? *Another Kingdom.* Isn't that what you're after?"

In the rearview, I saw the killer consider me. He narrowed his eyes. He pursed his lips to make his high cheeks hollow. Did he want to shut me up, or did he want to talk a little to pass the time? I met his gaze in the reflection and he met mine. I was surprised by my own cool. So was he, I think. I think that's what decided him.

"Well . . . " he answered. "Daddy wants it."

"Daddy. Your father?"

He gave an elaborate feminine roll of his eyes. Not his father. Of course not. His boss. His man. Daddy. I nodded. I shifted my eyes back to the windshield. I followed the Mustang's taillights away from the bright lights of the strip and on into the grassier stretch of the boulevard.

"I get it," I said. "So that's what I mean. If Daddy wants the book, why kill Gunther? He's the last one who saw it, isn't he?"

He gave me a girlish little shrug with his narrow shoulders. "Maybe I just wanted to."

I looked at him in the rearview.

"I like killing men," he said. "Men especially. They think they're so *there*, you know. Then *pow*. They're gone. They're nothing." He wrinkled his nose at me as if he'd said something cute.

"Uh huh," I said. I tried to keep what I felt out of my voice. It wasn't easy. The guy was a horror show. "But you couldn't kill him if Daddy didn't want you to, right?"

"Don't talk about Daddy," said Kitten Face—and his kitten face darkened as he said it. So I didn't talk about Daddy. He turned away and looked out the window at the passing mansions on their acres of grass. "We knew what he knew," he murmured as if explaining it to himself. "There was no point in leaving a loose end. We only kept him alive till now in the hope he would draw out someone like you."

Up ahead, through the windshield, I saw the Mustang turn right off Sunset. I followed him onto dark residential streets. The road began rising steeply.

Someone like me, I thought. *Someone . . .* "How did you know?" I said. "It was me you were following, not Gunther. How did you know I was looking for the book?"

He gave me a sidelong look, raising an eyebrow. He lifted his gun and pressed the muzzle to his lips: *Ssh.* It was a secret.

We traveled uphill, past fine homes and lofty estates. We rose higher and higher above the city.

I thought it over as I drove. I thought: it must've been my search. I had searched for *Another Kingdom* on my phone when I was at Jane Janeway's house recovering from that sword blow to my head. Then when I got home, the Mustang showed up outside my building. They must have seen the search somehow. How else would they have known I was looking for the book? And then . . . my phone . . . After I had lost them in the Flats, they must have hacked into my phone somehow and found my call to Sean Gunther. Or maybe they had put a tracker on my car . . .

These thoughts made me sick inside, sick and cold. Who were these people anyway? The government? The police? Foreign spies? Crazed super-hackers? Who else could monitor a search engine waiting for someone to look up a book? Who else could break into your phone and find out where you were going, just like that? And who else could kill a man—just like that—without worrying about the consequences?

That thought made me sick too. If they had killed Sean Gunther because they knew everything he knew . . . and if they were taking me somewhere to question me . . . what would they do to me when the questioning was over, when they knew everything I knew too? You didn't need heavy math to figure that one out.

The wave of hysteria began to rise in me again. I caught it, forced it down. I focused, just like I'd learned to do in the sewers of Galiana. I made my mind dark. I let the fear go. Incredibly, it worked. There were no fairy lights, no magical protection. But it calmed me down anyway.

I glanced out the window. I had no idea where we were anymore. High in the Beverly Hills somewhere and even beyond. We turned and turned again. The roads got smaller, steeper, higher.

Now, a few yards away, the Mustang turned into a driveway and came to a stop before a large filigreed iron gate. The gate swung in. The Mustang went through. I followed in my shabby Nissan, the gates looming over me. Then both cars, the Mustang and mine, began the climb up a long, winding lane. The moon became visible over the far horizon. The moonlight and the city light bleached away the stars.

Up into the night we went, a long way with nothing but grass and trees on either side of us, no signs of habitation. This was bad. Bad twice. At least twice. One, it was deserted up here, so that was bad because with no one in sight, and no houses, there'd be no one to witness what happened to me, no one to call for help. And two, this was expensive property, which was bad because it meant whoever owned it was rich—really rich, and probably powerful. Rich and powerful enough to have Sean Gunther killed without a qualm, and so therefore plenty rich and powerful enough to erase a minor character like me.

"So who . . . ?" I began to ask.

But Kitten Face said, "Ssh. Quiet now, peachy-poo. I want to deliver you undamaged if I can."

Man, oh man, I had to give it to him: the guy had a way of getting under my skin. Every time he pulled that sweety peaches shit on me, I wanted to rip his head off with my bare hands.

I drove up and up after the Mustang. And with a start, I suddenly realized we were not alone. There were people here—dark figures lurking by the side of the road. They were guards. They were patrolling the hilltop. They were holding rifles on their hips. They were dressed in black. They were almost invisible in the night.

Then a house hove into view above them.

It was a fine, modern ranch, built to seem a part of the hill-side. Constructed on a long rolling line, it fit the contours of the setting exactly. It was fashioned of brown stone and tan stucco, surrounded by brush, lit by soft spotlights. The indoor and the out-door spaces blended one into the other. I could see a dining room without walls leading into an enclosed den with a fire blazing in an enormous hearth. The den had glass doors, and the glass doors led out again onto a broad, flat patio of clay-colored brick.

The Mustang stopped on the wide pavement before a four-car garage. I stopped behind it. A black-clad rifleman stepped up to the Nissan's door.

"Out you get, baby boy," Kitten Face said.

I opened the door and climbed out into the cool of the autumn night. Billiard Ball was already out of the Mustang. He had crossed his arms over his chest and was watching the scene with lidded eyes.

Kitten Face emerged from the car behind me. He tossed his fluffy blond hair and slipped his pistol into his windbreaker. He winked at the rifleman and gave him one of those pursed-lip kisses. The rifleman was a bearded, hard-eyed military type. I saw him curl his lip with annoyance, but he didn't say anything. I wondered if he was afraid of the psycho too.

What happened next took me by surprise, but maybe it shouldn't have. It had been a long night. A long night and a long day. In this world and the other. I'd been roughed up and chased down, slapped around and forced to witness a murder by a crazy-as-shit assassin who treated me like his catamite. Now I was heading who knew where to face who knew what, and I was trying to stay focused, trying to keep my attention trained outward on the situation around me and not inward on my own mental state. I guess I didn't realize just how jacked up and pissed off I was.

The rifleman said to me, "This way."

He gestured with his head toward the open-air dining space. There was no one there now, but the long table was set with two places. It was lit by candle globes and an elegant chandelier. Beyond it was the cliff and the city lights and the moon hanging in the dark blue sky making the setting spectacular. It was a good guess that Daddy was on his way and would be joining me for dinner.

I began walking toward the house over a slate path. Focusing my mind, controlling my breath, taking in my surroundings. The rifleman walked a half step behind me. Billiard Ball was trailing somewhere off to my left. I'd lost sight of Kitten Face. The rifleman kept his weapon on his hip, pointed upward. He wasn't worried about me making a run for it. Where would I go? We were on the highest peak of Mount Nowhere, and there were men with guns in every direction.

So that was the scenario. I was about halfway along the path to the dining space. Then, for no reason other than that's the kind of punk he was, Kitten Face stepped up behind me and gave me a slap on the ass.

"Hurry up now, little one," he chided me.

I turned around and punched him.

I didn't mean to do it. That is, I did mean to do it—of course I did, you can't slug a guy that way by accident. What I mean is, I didn't *intend* to do it, I didn't think about doing it before I did. If I had, believe me, I would've stopped myself. He was a stone-hearted killer, after all, with a gun under his jacket. But he did what he did and I did what I did and there it was.

I came around fast and my fist came with me. I'd never hit anyone before. I'd never been in a fight in my life. I had no training. But it didn't matter. Where he was walking and the way I had to turn to get at him—our positions created a perfect punch. Hips, arm, fist. *Boom.* My knuckles connected with his cheek, dead-on. His face was soft. It didn't hurt my hand at all. And he—well, he was in good shape and fierce and all that, but when it came down to it, he was a girly little guy, and there wasn't much to him. The blow sent him spinning sideways, and he dropped to the ground. He propped himself up on one elbow right away, but then he just stayed there, staring, conscious but dazed.

I gaped down at him, shocked at myself. I glanced at the rifleman. He had his tongue stuck in his cheek as if to keep from laughing. I glanced over at Billiard Ball. He was standing still, blinking. I think he was as shocked as I was.

"Hmph," I heard him say.

That was putting it mildly.

My predicament had already been bad, but it was bad squared now, maybe bad cubed. There was no point in trying to run away. One of the riflemen would shoot me down or tackle me. There was nothing to do but stand there until Kitten Face recovered. Then what? He was sure to kill me. Or beat me senseless. Or beat me senseless and then kill me. Whatever—it wasn't going to be pleasant.

So we stood there, the rifleman, Billiard Ball, and me. We stared down at Kitten Face, all of us. After a while, Kitten Face shook his head. The fog cleared from his eyes. He looked around. He looked at me. He smiled. It was not a pleasant smile. It was a smile that sent a chill from my balls to my brainpan.

"Oh," he said in a throaty whisper. "Oh. Oh. Oh."

With that, like some sort of supernatural feline beast, he leapt to his feet in a single swift motion. I caught my breath, waiting helplessly for whatever would come.

Kitten Face took a slow step toward me. His smile became a full-fledged killer grin, mirthless and furious. "Oh," he said again, drawing it out this time.

He took another step and came up close.

Just then, a blinding light struck all of us. A vibrant guttural stuttering filled the air. The stuttering grew swiftly louder until, in another moment, it became a thunderous roar.

Kitten Face froze, his smile faltering. A murderous fury flamed in his eyes. His fists clenched at his sides. His hair—my hair too—began blowing wildly in a newly risen wind. He stayed where he was, but he didn't attack me. Something had made him hesitate.

The hilltop grew brighter, louder. The wind rose higher. I lifted my eyes.

A helicopter was descending out of the night sky. It seemed to have come from nowhere. It seemed to be heading directly toward us. The wind off the rotor blades was blowing over us. The noise enveloped us. The chopper's spotlight grew brighter and brighter.

I lowered my eyes to the assassin again. His face was red where I had punched him and red where I had not punched him too, just red with passionate rage. His grin was forced and savage now. His eyes were white hot.

He spoke to me. His mouth moved anyway, but the words were washed away in the chopper noise. It didn't matter. I knew what he was saying, more or less. He was telling me what he was going to do to me—what unimaginable thing—the very first chance he got.

But not right now. The helicopter continued its descent, and as my perspective on it changed, I could see it was coming down not on top of me, but on the patio over there just beyond the den. As I was watching it, the black-clad rifleman caught my attention with a gesture. He tilted his head: *Follow me.* There was still a little humorous quirk at the corner of his mouth. He'd enjoyed watching Kitten Face get punched. I think he wanted to get me away from him as quickly as possible. I followed him to the patio.

The chopper wind grew stronger, the noise grew louder, and the light grew brighter and then dimmer as it narrowed on the point just beneath the craft. With a wobbling tremor, the copter touched down. The engine kept running, and the rotors kept spinning. The door slid open and out stepped a little man, ducking his head beneath the turning blades.

Daddy.

He was old and bent and exceptionally short—four foot something probably, maybe five foot nothing, but not more than that. He was wearing a dark suit, the jacket flapping in the rotor wind. Since his head was bent, all I could see of him was a fine crop of unruly silver hair and his hands, so wrinkled they seemed made of crumpled paper.

Then he came out from under the rotors and looked up. Big surprise. I had never seen him before in the flesh, but I recognized him all right. From pictures in the news and from the framed photographs on the mantelpiece in my parents' living room back home and other photographs on the wall of my brother's fabulous New York apartment. Because my father held the Orosgo chair in Psychology at Berkeley and my mother funded her research with grants from the Orosgo Foundation and my brother worked for the Orosgo Institute and, hell, even I worked for Global Pictures, which Orosgo owned.

And lo and behold, here he was right in front of me: my father's benefactor, my brother's mentor, my own employer, Serge Orosgo.

12

IT'S STRANGE TO SAY, BUT I'D NEVER GIVEN MUCH thought to Orosgo. You'd think I would have, wouldn't you? His presence wound like a golden chain through my family—Mom, Dad, Richard, me. When you think about it, even my sister, Riley, took his money if you count the handouts she got from my parents, which ultimately, one way and another, came from him. Yet, somehow, though I had been vaguely aware of his existence since I was little, I had never really considered him as a person, real, with skin on. He was just too far above me somehow, too rich, too powerful: more an influence than an individual, more an atmosphere than a man.

Now, though, here he was walking toward me, and it was disorienting to see him in his humanity, to say the least. He was ancient yet vital—for all his years, a casual, confident, even youthful figure. He wore no tie, just a white shirt open at his wattled throat. His face beneath the silver hair was square and very pale, the skin almost transparent where it wasn't pocked with liver spots. His cheeks weren't wrinkled much. I guess he'd had some cosmetic surgery since they were weirdly smooth, as if he were wearing a plastic mask. His pale blue eyes were wide the way very old men's eyes get wide. Smooth cheeks and wide eyes: the overall effect made him look kind of like an infant, a perpetual baby perpetually startled by the brand-new world.

As the chopper gave a wobble and lifted up into the sky behind him, the old man offered me his hand. Dazed by his presence, I took it, looking down at him from my greater height. His hand was cold and dry like a lizard's skin.

The chopper tilted and shot away. The wind around us subsided. The noise grew dimmer.

"Austin. Good to finally meet you," Orosgo said. He had a faint, romantic-sounding accent. I couldn't quite place it. "Come. Sit with me. We'll eat."

He walked toward the dining area. The rifleman met him along the way. Orosgo touched his shoulder in a paternal manner as the big soldierly man leaned down and spoke low in his ear. Orosgo nodded. Glanced at me. "Go on ahead. I'll be right with you," he said.

He walked off to where Kitten Face was standing apart from us. The killer had not moved to greet the chopper but was still where we had left him on the path. He was sulking like a child, kicking the slate of the path with the ball of one foot. Orosgo gently took his chin in his fingers and tilted his face so he could examine the place where I'd punched him. He murmured some consoling words. He patted his cheek, then sent him off toward the house with another pat on his backside.

I, meanwhile, moved to the open dining area, stealing glances over my shoulder at the conference between the billionaire and the murderer as I went. To say I was confused, to say I was stunned, to say my head was spinning is not to say enough. Thoughts were whirling through my mind like tornados. In the last . . . had it even been twenty-four hours?—I had seen sights beyond believing. I had traveled from world to world in ways I couldn't—in ways no one could—understand. I had seen a man's head ripped off by a one-eyed ogre. I had seen a man shot dead by an androgyne psychopath. I had seen a man torn to pieces by a monster made of shit. Made of shit! Yet somehow my brain had managed to incorporate all that into its conception of the possible. But this . . .

My father's benefactor. My brother's mentor. My own employer. The founder of my family's feast. The friend of presidents. The owner of media outlets. The funder of political campaigns and charities and popular movements. And he was the one who had brought me here at gunpoint. He was the one who had dispatched that murderer to snuff out Sean Gunther like a candle. I couldn't take it in right away, not fully, but I understood that somehow the entire story of my life had just been rewritten.

As if in a dream, I stepped up onto the platform where the table was set. I waited there for Orosgo to walk back through the night to me. It occurred to me in the midst of my confusion that when I had searched for *Another Kingdom* on my phone, I had used the Oh-Gee search engine. Oh-Gee—that name—it was a cute little way of branding the engine as part of the Orosgo empire. That confirmed my suspicions about how they knew to come after me. They had been monitoring the engine—Orosgo's engine—waiting for someone to make the search.

The little old man stepped up onto the dining platform with me. He lay a paternal hand on my shoulder as he had with the guard. He smiled a charming smile. It was almost possible to forget that he had had a man killed in cold blood. Almost possible.

"Sit. Sit," he said.

We sat. Me at the foot of the table and him at the head, the candles and the chandelier burning brightly in between. A refreshing breeze came in from every side and was toasted to a mellow perfection by the outdoor heaters. It was a charming place to dine.

And, in fact, I was hungry. I'd eaten almost nothing at my dinner with my parents, and now, in spite of everything, I was ready to dig in. There were several courses, all of them very delicate and delicious. An elaborate mix of lettuces with pralines and chèvre and pears. Thin pastries filled with meat-like somethings and shredded vegetables with an exquisite sauce. Strawberries dipped in chocolate for dessert. Each course brought to the table by a brace of waiters who seemed to shimmer in and out of the shadows as if they were shadows themselves. Through it all, there was wine too, a rich red wine so good and so refreshing I had to exert all my will to keep from drinking myself silly. I had to keep reminding myself that I was dining with a billionaire who had men snuffed out with casual indifference. It seemed wise to keep my wits about me.

So we ate and drank, and all the while, Orosgo talked. Talked and talked and talked ceaselessly. I remembered my brother, Rich, had said something to me about this once.

"Billionaires talk. They don't listen," he had told me—ruefully, but not without humor and affection. "It's true of every billionaire I've ever met. It's what their money buys them: the right to hold forth. Why shouldn't they? They know they're smarter than you. If they're not smarter, how come they have so much more money?"

Myself, I'd never met any billionaires before, so I had no way of knowing if Rich's observation applied to the breed in general or just to this guy. But it sure applied to this guy. All through dinner, his monologue rambled on—on and on almost without pause. Rich had made this billionaire logorrhea sound like an endearing eccentricity. It wasn't. It was unpleasant. First, because of the monotony, the one voice droning. Even a billionaire ought to shut the hell up and let someone else say something now and then. Second, because of the suspense. He'd already had one man killed tonight for not having the answers he wanted. What was he going to do to me, and how long would I have to wait to find out? And third, after he'd gone on for a while, it became clear to me that Serge Orosgo—the founder of my father's chair, the leader of my brother's institute, the owner of the studio where I worked—was not just evil but batshit crazy too.

"Memory. Fascinating," the old man was saying. He rolled the red wine in his bowl-like glass so that its mulberry depths reflected the yellow candlelight. "As one gets older, one begins to suspect that many of the things one remembers may not be, strictly speaking, true. Essential, even formative chapters of one's biography may be whole-cloth inventions. And yet if these false memories shaped you, aren't they real enough? Real enough to have an effect on the world, at any rate?"

I nodded attentively, because it felt like nodding attentively was my role here. But I was not attentive, not really. I was too busy wondering whether I was going to die tonight, and wondering also what it meant to my own memories to realize that my entire family had been in orbit around this murderer since I was a child. I couldn't process that and listen to him and fear for my life all at the same time.

Orosgo took another sip of wine. I had to wait in silence for him to continue. I picked at my meat-filled—what was it called?—phyllo pastry, that's it—just to have something to do. Finally the billionaire emerged from his glass with a satisfied gasp. He continued.

"A perfect example. I remember—at least, I seem to remember—a conversation I had many years ago, a conversation with a strange, pale, starved, rather monkish person wearing a sort of robe with a . . . a whatchem—" He drew a circle around his head with his free hand, trying to describe what he meant. "A cowl. Just like a monk would wear. Who could he have been? What was the occasion? I no longer know. I remember we were in my dacha outside of Moscow, so it must have been before I emigrated but after the fall—the fall of the Soviet Union—because I must've already made my fortune in the privatization, you see. And we were speaking about that, about one's aspirations, one's ambitions:

what's left to strive for after one has made so much money that any more would make no difference."

He bowed low over his plate. His wizened hands worked his knife and fork. He lifted a bite straight to his mouth in the European fashion. He went on talking even as he chewed.

"I can remember we talked all night, sitting side by side before the fire. But the words themselves . . . they're faded, vague. Was I describing my desires, or was he offering me advice? I'm not sure, but at some point one of us articulated a . . . a vision, call it: the idea that one might write one's name upon the human singularity, one might be enshrined in every grateful heart forever as the architect of the era of perfected man. The Orosgo Age." He said these words with irony, but there was no irony in his wide, bright, infant eyes, neither the first time he said them nor when he repeated them again, "The Orosgo Age," savoring them on his tongue as he had savored the wine. "What would it cost? That was the gist of the conversation. To be that man? What would I be willing to give in the reckoning?"

Somewhere during this soliloquy, we finished the main course. Two waiters appeared from the edge of night, removed our plates, and evanesced. I couldn't help but be aware that every bite, every course brought us closer to the end of dinner. It was like watching the sand run out of an hourglass. And what would happen then? The next time I lifted my wine, I couldn't hide the fact my hand was trembling.

Orosgo, meanwhile, dabbed his lips with his napkin. Sat back in his chair. Somehow he managed to seem relaxed and intense at the same time. "My point is—that conversation—I can't remember who it was with or when exactly it happened or even if it truly did happen. And yet it set the entire direction of my life from that point forward, which makes it real enough. And now, of course . . . " He made a nonchalant gesture, tilting his head, lifting his hand, as if he were confessing some charming vulnerability. "Now that I am approaching the end of my life, it comes back to me. *He* comes back to me. In dreams. Or are they dreams? A figure in the dark corridor. A face in the mirror that is not my face. Someone standing behind me. Even his voice. Indistinguishable whispers at first. Old age, I told myself. But they're louder each time. More real. More insistent. *The reckoning. The debt must be paid."*

Again, two waiters oscillated in from nowhere and set the chocolate-covered strawberries before us. And when they had vibrated back into nothingness, Orosgo lifted his wine glass again and said, "I need that book, Austin."

I don't know whether I'd been mesmerized by the monotony of his jabbering or whether I'd lost the train of his thought or what. But those words took me off guard completely. They rang in that charming hilltop dining space like a bell, like a great tower bell knelling the hour of decision. Whatever clouds of inattention had gathered in my consciousness, they were shaken away and gone, all gone, just like that. I sat there. I stared at him. I thought: *What has he been saying all this time?* I didn't know. It had seemed random, meditative, half-meaningless, and now . . . it turned out to be— what?—his explanation of why I was here? Of why he had had Sean Gunther killed? Of why he would kill me after we'd enjoyed the chocolate-covered strawberries?

"The book," was all I could choke out, echoing him. And though I had tried to go easy on the wine, I had to drink some now to keep the inside of my mouth from going dry as dust.

He nodded, still leaning back, still relaxed—and also not relaxed, intense, his eyes so wide, so bright, that I wondered if he was afraid too, maybe even more afraid than I was. *"Another Kingdom.* You were searching for it, Austin. Why?"

It was at this point I felt a presence behind me. I looked over my shoulder and saw Billiard Ball standing just beyond the dining space in the half-lit dark. He had his arms crossed on his chest and his eyes trained on my head. Dull, merciless, strangely witty eyes, judging just where he would strike when it came time to deal me pain.

I faced Orosgo again, licking what felt like ashes off my lips. "It was submitted to me to read at Mythos—where I work."

"I know where you work."

"But it was withdrawn before I had a chance to read it."

"I know that too." How did he know that? Could he look into my e-reader? I figured he could. "Who submitted it?" he asked. "Do you know?"

"Sean Gunther." It hurt to speak the author's name to the man who had had him executed. "But he did it at the request of the author. Ellen Evermore. That's what he told me."

"She submitted it. And she decided to withdraw it?" Orosgo asked.

"That's what he said."

I knew he was about to ask me *why*—why she had withdrawn it— and in the second before he did ask, I suddenly realized why. *Global.* That's what Gunther had said when I asked him. Ellen Evermore must have realized that by submitting the book to Mythos, she had sent the book into the realm of Global Pictures and therefore within the grasp of Orosgo. That had to be it. She knew he was after it, and she didn't want him to have it.

"Why?" said Orosgo. "Why did she withdraw it?"

I hesitated. Should I tell him what I thought? I remembered the photograph of Ellen Evermore in Gunther's phone. I remembered the serenity and humor and wisdom in her face. I looked at the desiccated surprised-baby face of the billionaire across from me. Not hard to tell who the good guys and bad guys were in this story. Not hard to know which side to be on.

"I don't know," I lied. Because screw him. He was probably going to kill me no matter what I said.

"And why did you search for it?"

Well, that was the question, wasn't it? How far would I get into my absurd tale of being transported to Galiana before Billiard Ball knocked me senseless? Luckily, I remembered the story I'd made up to use on Candy Filikin at the office. I used it again.

"The book stuck with me. What little I'd read. I thought it might make a good movie. I'd been looking for a new direction."

"Because your agent rejected your last script."

God, he knew everything. One misguided lie, and he'd catch me cold. "That's right," I said.

"And is that the only reason?"

"Yeah, sure. What else could there be?"

I thought I saw an expression of frustration, maybe anger, cross his plastic mask of a face, but it was gone in a moment. "And so you went to Sean Gunther," he said.

"That's right."

"But he couldn't tell you where the book was or where the author was."

"He didn't know."

"No. He didn't. And so you don't know."

Well, now we were right down to it, weren't we? This was the point in the conversation where Gunther had been shot—shot dead for not knowing the answer to Orosgo's question. I wanted to ask if I was going to be shot dead too, but it seemed such a weak, pathetic thing to say. So instead I said, "Your man. Or whatever he is. The girly guy with the cat face."

"Sera."

"Sara?"

"Sera. Short for Serafim. An old Russian name. I gave it to him when he was a child."

For some reason, these words sickened me, but fortunately I didn't have time to figure out why.

"He killed him," I said. "Gunther. Sera shot him."

Orosgo never took his over-wide baby-blue eyes off me. He picked up his wine without looking away, drank without looking away. "Mm," he said. "He does that. When I ask him to. Sometimes when I don't." He put the wine down again, still without looking at anything but me. Man, those eyes were wide! "I think he likes it, really. I think he pretends the victim is me. Daddy issues. Why? Does it trouble you, his killing Mr. Gunther?"

"Well, it is murder," I managed to say.

He shrugged. "Murder. Don't be a small man, Austin. We're talking about big things. Humanity perfected. The world that is to be."

The Orosgo Age, I thought, trying to put the pieces of this insane conversation together.

"Sera says you struck him," Orosgo said.

"I did."

"That was unwise."

"I didn't plan it. I wasn't thinking. He made me angry."

"Ha! Yes. He can do that. But unfortunately, he wishes to kill you now. Actually, killing you is only the last thing he wishes to do to you."

Since he raised the issue, this seemed like a good time to ask the question that was really foremost in my mind. "Are you going to let him? Kill me? Is that what this is all about?" I indicated the table between us. "My last supper?"

Orosgo seemed to give the issue a moment of serious consideration. "The truth is, I can't always control what he does. Our relationship is complex. The moral authority shifts back and forth, depending on who committed the latest sin against whom." He leaned forward, pinning me in my seat with a no-nonsense glare. He rapped the tabletop with his index finger. "But I do want that book, Austin, and he knows that."

Well, that was clear enough: if I gave him what he wanted, he might be able to talk Kitten Face out of revenge. Maybe? For a while?

"I don't know what I can do," I said. "I've told you everything I know."

There was a soft shifting sound behind me. Orosgo's eyes lifted to the place where I knew Billiard Ball waited. Almost imperceptibly, the billionaire shook his head no. Whatever the bald thug was about to do to me, he didn't do.

Orosgo plucked a chocolate-covered strawberry from the dessert cup before him. He lifted it to his eyes and examined it, a jeweler with a gem, or maybe a cat with a mouse. "Your family have been friends of mine for a long time, Austin," he said.

These words sickened me too, sickened me more, and chilled me. "Is that just a coincidence?" The question occurred to me so suddenly I asked it without thinking. "That they know you, work for you, and I got the book? Did that just happen?"

"I doubt it," he said, and he ate the strawberry. "But that's not my point," he said around the mouthful. He swallowed. "My point is only that I want to be your friend too. I want you to be my friend, like your father and mother and your brother are. I don't want anything unpleasant to happen to you, son."

"Unpleasant like with Gunther," I said.

"Nothing unpleasant happened to Mr. Gunther until there was no longer any chance that he could help me. Is there still any chance that you could help me, Austin?"

By this time, I felt I was beginning to make some sort of sense of things, to fashion some sort of narrative out of it. It was such a bizarre narrative—so bizarre and so surreal—that it was hard for me to take it seriously. This long-ago man with the cowl he'd talked about, for instance—was he real? And if he was, what exactly was the conversation they had had all night by the dacha fireplace? What was this mysterious reckoning that was coming? Would finding the book somehow keep it at bay? And did I have some cosmic part to play in the whole thing? Or was I just a fool who had been sucked into the whirlpool of his delusions?

"This must be a very valuable book," I said.

His surprised-baby eyes looked even more surprised and more babyish. "A thing is worth what someone is willing to pay for it," he said. "So for me, yes, in this case, it's priceless. Which brings me back to my original question. Do you think there's any chance you might be able to recover *Another Kingdom* for me?"

He was watching me closely as I thought over my answer. Not that there was any question what my answer would be. We both knew I was going to say yes—yes, I would try to find the book for him. What else could I say? He had made it clear he would have me killed if I refused. The only real mystery was whether I would be lying or not when I said it. That's what he was watching me so closely for. That's what he wanted to see.

"Yes," I said. "I'll do my best, anyway." And yes, I was lying. That is, I was going to go on looking for the book. I had to. It was my only hope of explaining my interworldly condition, my only hope of curing it before I got myself killed by some fantastic Galianan beast or other. But if I did find the book, there was no chance I would give it to him. Not willingly anyway. Whatever trouble Orosgo had gotten himself into with the cowl guy, I'd be damned if I was going to ransom him out of it.

He continued to study me for a long moment after I spoke. Did he believe me? Could he tell what I was thinking? He had hacked into my search engine, after all, and my phone records and my e-reader. Could he hack into my mind as well? Could he tell I was not like my parents and my brother? That I was not his friend but his enemy?

"Good," he said finally. "And this unfortunate Gunther business—let's put that out of our minds for now, all right?"

What could I say? I nodded.

"And for my part," Orosgo continued, "I will do my best to keep Sera from acting out his anger on you."

"I'd appreciate that."

"He is volatile. I can't guarantee anything."

"Neither can I."

His smile was mirthless and razor thin. "Well . . . " he said softly. It was all he needed to say. It was a threat of death. Fail to find the book and you die. Go to the police about Gunther and you die. That simple.

And with that, my dinner with Orosgo was over. The next moment, he gestured to the bald thug behind me. And the moment after that, the bald thug stepped forward and slapped my car keys down on the table where my plate had been: *jingle-whap.*

Now, a potent mixture of too much wine and sudden relief and sneaking, gut-curdling suspense swam up into my head. I felt as if I was in a hazy, slo-mo dream as I walked along the slate path back to my Nissan. It wasn't a good dream either, because I was thinking about how, in the gangster movies, they always pretended to let you go just before they garroted you and sent you to sleep with the fishes. I glanced over at Orosgo's ranch, and just inside, a shadow within the shadows, there stood the figure of the assassin, his kitten face barely visible within the darkness. And on that face and in his eyes, I saw what anyone could see: his daydreams of my blood-soaked agony and my agonizing death.

I reached the car. I checked the back seat quickly to make sure no one was hiding there with a garrote. I pulled open the door and slipped inside.

"Oh, shit!" I shouted furiously.

I was seated on the black stallion again. I was back in Galiana.

13

THE STALLION AND I HAD JUST PASSED THROUGH THE Eastrim city gates. The horse was still traveling slowly amidst the crowd of pilgrims and the cloud of their dust. I was still a little hazy on Orosgo's wine. I looked around me unsteadily. Peasants and merchants and a knight on horseback were all staring at me because—I suddenly realized—I'd shouted out in exasperation to find myself back here again: "Oh, shit!"

As I struggled to come to terms with this latest transition, it occurred to me that I didn't need all these curious eyes staring at me, especially not when I was being hunted by the authorities and still within arrow-shot of the guards on the city wall.

I snapped the horse's reins and guided him off the road. I urged him into the surrounding grassland with a brisk clucking noise, trying to put some distance between me and the rest of the travelers. My mad dinner with Orosgo and the strange story he'd told me and, yes, the fear and the wine were all still sloshing around in my brain, and really I just wanted to lie down somewhere and make this whole ordeal stop for a while. I would have said that this going back and forth between two worlds was driving me crazy except . . . well, except I must have already gone crazy or none of it would have been happening in the first place.

The stallion and I had moved a couple of dozen yards away from the dense crowd of people exiting the city when I felt a pinch on my foot. I looked down and saw Maud. The mutant rodent had leapt up out of the high weeds and grabbed me. And now she scrambled lightly, quickly, up my leggings and over the side of my saddle to take her place on the pommel again.

I groaned loudly. The rodent turned to me. "What? What's the matter?"

What's the matter? I wanted to say. What's the matter? You're a fucking rat with a woman's face, that's what's the matter! You can talk, that's what's the matter. Best case scenario: You're the emanation of a brain tumor. And even if I could cure the tumor and make you and this entire la-la land disappear, I'd only find myself back in la-la land proper with an insane billionaire and his gender-bending psycho killer after me. That's what's the matter, I wanted to say.

"Nothing," I muttered sullenly.

The mutant creature gave a curt nod then leaned over to whisper in the horse's ear. Because, of course, the horse could understand what the rat-woman was saying. Because that's what it's like when there's a black growth the size of a cantaloupe devouring your cerebral cortex.

"To Shadow Wood," the rodent said to the horse.

Huzzah. To fucking Shadow Wood.

And off we rode.

I WILL SAY this much for Galiana. It was a haunting gothic ruin of a country, sere and desolate and starkly beautiful. Once we broke full away from the others, we rode for hours in majestic loneliness across a blasted landscape under a looming, gathering dusk. Solitary, leafless trees bent wearily in the wind here and there, their branches rattling. Empty huts and broken towers rose on the horizon, grew large as they approached, and grimly hunkered over us then fell away behind. Now and then, at some abandoned window, in some fallen wreckage of a fortress or a home, or on some dusty path that once had been a highway, a wide-eyed starveling would turn to watch us pass, the remnant of what had sometime been a man or a woman. I saw the wistful hunger wreathing the faces of these people. They looked as if they half-remembered a longed-for time of human warmth and connection, but that time was gone. I wanted to ask them: What happened here? What happened to this country? But the effect of the wine was wearing off. I was exhausted and didn't have the energy to listen to an answer. I just rode on in silence over the windswept land.

AS THE SUN was descending toward the horizon, we crossed a long, flat autumn vale. In the fading distance, I could make out the front line of a forest, red oaks and orange elms and yellow hickories and smoky-green conifers and cool, shadowy depths within.

"Is that it?" I asked the rodent. "Is that Shadow Wood?"

"Yes," she told me. "Tauratanio's kingdom."

WE REACHED THE forest at sunset. Maud jumped down and told me to dismount, and I poured off the saddle like spilled gelatin. Leading the horse by the reins, I followed the mutant rodent into the trees.

Almost at once, the mist gathered around us, and the leaves folded over us, and the last light of day went dim. We were suddenly moving through a deep gloom, already shading into darkness.

Maud scrambled ahead like a squirrel and quickly blended, like a squirrel would, with the tangled latticework of vines and branches. That latticework seemed to close in on me so that each direction looked the same as every other. The mist drifted eerily like fingers between the trees, further obscuring the way. Occasionally, the last red glint of the falling sun shot through a gap in the branches and reached me. Otherwise the deep twilight simply grew deeper as night came on.

Soon, I could barely see a foot in front of me. Soon after that, the forest came alive with noises. Peeper frogs came out and held their high-pitched conversations. Crickets jabbered. And things I couldn't name moved along the ground, rattling the duff. A breeze coiled through the branches, and their brittle leaves shivered. In the thickening darkness, the forest seemed to fill with whispers.

I slowed down, looking around me. I was a city boy. I didn't like it here. Even back home—in real life—if I found myself alone in the middle of nowhere after sunset, I got nervous. Scenes from horror movies would come into my mind. Vampires, werewolves, ghosts. Stupid, I know. Stupid there, anyway, back home in real life. Here—in Galiana—who could tell? There might actually *be* vampires and werewolves and ghosts lurking in the darkness. And by the way, where had Squirrel Girl gone? I could no longer find her in the darkness.

"Maud?" I called. It came out a dusty whisper. My mouth had gone dry.

I stood very still. I listened, hoping to hear her answer. For a moment, there was only the living noise of the forest. But then— then, faintly amidst the creature chatter and the sough of the breeze and the creak of branches and the rattle of leaves—there came another sound, a sound like music.

It was eerie, uncanny: a lingering melody, just off-key. It chilled me, like a specter's touch. I don't think I had ever heard a song so strange, so otherly. I felt I had lost the power to move. I couldn't do anything but stand there, listening, waiting to see what would happen next.

What happened next—so help me—was this.

The eerie melody grew louder. I caught glimpses, among the distant trees, of twinkling lights and swirling rainbow-colored clouds. The forest seemed to grow a little brighter, the tortuous shapes of vines and the skeletal fingers of branches that had moments before become invisible as the daylight died began to reemerge as the black of night turned indigo.

The eerie music filled the woods, surrounding me. I could hear it more clearly now. Pipes and tambourines and a ghostly choir of inhuman voices, high and wild. The sparks of light and the clouds of light grew brighter. Soon these surrounded me as well.

The air was fluttering, full of fairies. The shadowed woods were dancing with imps and antlered fauns and satyrs with their pipes of Pan and peak-capped trolls and sentient creatures I couldn't name crawling along the duff and on the branches.

In the swirling mists of light, I saw a broad stream winding toward me between the tree trunks. And out of the water, nymphs were rising like mist, glowing nude women of an ivory perfection that made me swell with a kind of bold, natural, robust erotic desire that was nothing like the clammy lust I felt leering at the wannabes on LA's streets or at the naked girls on my computer. It seemed I hadn't felt like this in ages.

The weird, weird music played and played. The colored lights glittered and swirled. The fairy-tale creatures flew and gamboled and danced around me in an impossible vision of secret forest life. And the nymphs approached and circled me in the rainbow glow, their faces lovely, their bodies exquisitely rounded and soft. I watched breathlessly as they closed in. I gasped as they touched me. Some caressed me, some undressed me, some took me gently by the arms and led me to the stream. I could not have resisted them if I had wanted to. I didn't want to.

They drew me naked along the banks of the water. We came to a clearing where the stream gathered in a pool. The fairies and the fauns and the imps and the satyrs were dancing here as well with their lights and music. The nymphs took me into the pool.

The water was warmer than I expected. It was velvety smooth and soft and only waist high. The nymphs bathed me and kissed my neck and cheeks and stroked my body until I raised my face to the stars and cried out in mindless ecstasy, purged of every dark and dirty thing. My weariness was gone. My fear of the forest dark was gone. Even my skinned knee and the pulsing bruise on my head from where Sir Aravist had struck me with his sword was healed and gone. The music played, and I lowered my eyes and gazed in wonder at the tender faces of the nymphs eddying around me in the eddying water. I didn't care that there were creatures on every side who might be watching. I didn't care about anything just then. All I knew was that I never wanted this to end.

But now the nymphs gently led me up out of the pool into the clearing. I felt calm and satisfied and clean. They dried me off with some soft white wool and dressed me in my clothes again, and my clothes felt crisp and clean as well.

I noticed now that the piping, jingling music of the wood had changed. It had grown steady and rhythmic and ceremonial, almost martial. I noticed that the creatures were slowing in their dance, and now they stopped. They stood where they were and turned to gaze into the distance. I followed their gazes and looked to where the colored outglow ended and the forest sank back into the blue-black dark beyond.

Now, out of that darkness, there came a stately procession. What I thought at first was a brigade of cavalry was coming through the trees in double file at a slow march. As they grew nearer, I saw they weren't cavalry—not mounted men—but centaurs, men with the lower halves of horses, and their top halves muscular male figures carrying sabers at their shoulders. Female centaurs—lighter in color but with the same muscular grace—rode on the outskirts of the ranks, in attendance on their soldier men.

They marched closer. And in the midst of them, two figures seemingly all of light manifested themselves. First the darkness glowed a little in the two places, then each glow expanded, then each congealed into a radiant figure, and then the figures grew solid while still remaining luminous. The figure to the left was a rotund, heavily bearded man, his eyes bright and merry, his cheeks red, and his high forehead crowned with leaves. He rode in a chariot made of light, and the chariot was drawn by four horses of light who pawed the empty air above the ground as they flew along, pulling him after. The figure in the chariot to the right of him was a woman the color of the moon, long and lithe and unbelievably beautiful, with moon-colored hair and drifting robes that seemed to flow off her like water.

"That's Tauratanio and Magdala. They rule the forest," whispered Maud. She had suddenly reappeared, clinging by her claws to the trunk of the tree beside me. Her weird woman's face was giving me an ironic, knowing look. My cheeks went hot as it occurred to me she might have been watching when I was getting it on with the nymphs in the water. But there wasn't much I could do about it now.

I turned again to watch the oncoming parade.

ESCORTED BY THEIR centaur cavalry, the king and queen entered the clearing in their chariots of light. I have to admit, if this was a hallucination caused by a brain disorder—and, let's face it, what the hell else could it have been?—it was a damned majestic one. The two forest royals dismounted and moved hand in hand to two thrones of light that had manifested themselves miraculously out of the dark at the center of the grove. They sat, and the court formed around them—nymphs, satyrs, fauns, peak-capped trolls, and all the rest—in semicircular rows at their feet, while the fairies sparkled in the surrounding trees like Christmas lights.

The king's voice boomed, jovial and mellow, "Show me the man!"

That, apparently, meant me. The nude nymphs took me gently by my arms and led me before the thrones. I stood before the king and queen, squinting into their light. Tauratanio looked me up and down. I could see the smile buried in the thick beard beneath his twinkling eyes. Magdala, his queen, examined me too with a sweet, serene regard. I was still swathed in the post-coital calm of my encounter with the nymphs, so I was not as nervous under their gazes as I might have been. Still, instinctively, I bowed my head to the two light figures. Somehow I found I wanted to please them. I wanted them to like me.

The king now cast a look beyond me at Maud. He nodded to her as if, I thought, to thank her for carrying out my rescue. I turned in time to see the girl-rat shrug her rodent shoulders as if to say: *He's not much, I know, but he's all I could find.*

Tauratanio laughed a Santa Claus laugh. "So," he said—and I faced him. "So you're Austin Lively."

How crazy was it to hear this king of silver light speak my everyday name? Crazy. But at this point, crazy was my default setting. I nodded. "Yes."

"And Queen Elinda sent you?"

I raised my hands helplessly. "I don't know the queen."

"She knows you, apparently."

The forest lady spoke from beside him. Her voice flowed like her robes and her hair. "And the important thing is: you've come."

It was the oddest thing. They were speaking as if everything that was happening made sense to them, as if all this were real and even normal instead of impossible and insane. And you know what else was bizarre? Besides everything, I mean? What was also bizarre was that this conversation I was having now was no more incomprehensible to me than the conversation I'd just had in LA with Orosgo. In some ways this—this here—was not even as disturbing as that, because it didn't mean I had to reconsider my entire life and who my parents were and what my brother did and how I fit into it all. I just had to—I don't know—accept that what couldn't possibly be happening was happening.

"But how?" I asked them, turning from one to the other. "How did I get here?"

"That's the wrong question, my dear," Magdala said sweetly.

"The right question," said Tauratanio with a deep chuckle, "is why?"

I raised my hands again, just as helplessly as before. "All right, then. Why?"

"To find the queen's talisman and deliver it to Emperor Anastasius," said the king, as if this ought to have been obvious to anyone. "So he knows to return from the Eleven Lands and restore her to her throne."

Right. The talisman. The Eleven Lands. The Emperor Anastasius. Of course. What the hell was he talking about?

"But . . . why me?" I said. It was the first of the million questions in my mind to come tumbling out of my mouth.

"Because there are no more men here," said Magdala.

"No fighting men," Tauratanio said.

"No fighting men of brave heart and right belief," added Magdala.

At this, I couldn't help but look over my shoulder again at Maud. The rodent rolled her eyes. Now I understood her impatience with me, her disapproving looks, that snappy order: "Be a man." Queen Elinda had sent me to Galiana because there were no more men here? No more fighting men of brave heart and right belief? She had sent me? Me? Were they kidding? What the hell was she thinking? I was no brave fighting man. I was from Hollywood. No one was brave there. Not brave-brave where maybe you died at the end with nobody watching. No one in show business had to be brave like that. You just had to pretend to be brave while they took pictures of you pretending. That was the whole job.

And right belief? As I turned back to the forest king and queen, all of a sudden and for the first time in my life, it occurred to me to wonder: What were my beliefs? And the answer came to me with a plummeting nausea that broke clean through my nymphean satisfaction: I had no freaking idea. None. I believed . . . what everyone believed, I guess. Be good? Be nice? Be fair? Sell a script and direct a movie and become a star so I could give interviews on TV about how good and nice and fair I was? How brave?

"No men . . . " I said in an ashen whisper.

"The knights have all been corrupted by Lord Iron," Tauratanio explained with a tone of sorrow that sounded strangely not-so-different from his tone of joy. "Just as Lord Iron has been corrupted by the wizard Curtin."

The wizard Curtin? I thought in a daze. Who was he, now? I didn't remember that name from the character list in my computer. But I did remember that spooky, raisin-faced guy in the night-blue robe who had stood behind Lord Iron during my tribunal, whispering in his ear. I guessed that must've been the wizard Curtin.

"And as for the men of the land, well, you saw them," Tauratanio continued. "Iron seduced them into rebellion with promises of a perfect country, good and nice and fair, where each is equal in all things to another."

He echoed the very words swimming in my swimming brain.

And Magdala, with her own majestic sorrow, added, "They tried to kill the wisest queen in all the world in the name of that illusion.

They would have succeeded too, if my husband had not used his magic to transport her to another kingdom."

More echoing words. Another kingdom. Like the book? And this illusion of a perfect country—was it anything like the Age of Orosgo? Was it possible the story of my life in LA and the story of my life here were the same story?

Tauratanio went on. "I would have done more. But Curtin draws his magic from the minds of men and grows stronger in cities where men congregate. My magic is of the woods, and I did not have the power to defeat him on his own ground."

I remembered my escape through the dungeon sewers, how I had to focus my mind to receive the power of Tauratanio's magic in order to keep the fairy lights glowing. I remembered how Maud had sparkled from time to time in the dungeon and grew powerful as the magic came through her. Now I understood. The king had used us somehow to cast his power from a distance, but its source was here.

Abruptly, the expression on Tauratanio's face—and Magdala's expression too—were transformed from sorrowful gravity to gladness and even celebration. It was as if, in spite of the poverty and meanness and cruelty I had seen on the toxic streets of Eastrim, the horrors of its torture chambers, and the injustice of its counsel, all was suddenly right with the world. And why?

"But our hero has come!" Tauratanio declared—gesturing with his light-made hand toward me.

I swear: *toward me.*

"AND NOW, AUSTIN Lively," the king continued, his tone still joyful. "To give heart and hope to my people, prove to them you are the one Queen Elinda sent to us by claiming the gift she left for him, as only he can do."

Uh oh, I thought.

But the truth is, I didn't know whether to be terrified or relieved. I mean, obviously, if they were looking for a fighting man of brave heart and right belief, they had missed their target by about a mile. So whatever test I was supposed to pass now was going to result in some sort of low comic moment of total failure. And on the one hand, that would get me off the hook for whatever the hell quest I and my brave heart and right belief were supposed to get ourselves killed over. On the other hand, some of those saber-carrying centaurs looked like pretty rough characters, and I hated to think what their reaction was going to be when they found out they had the wrong guy.

As Tauratanio spoke, he shifted the hand with which he was majestically gesturing at me in order to majestically gesture at something behind me. I turned around to see what it was.

It was an oak tree. A big one. The kind you find growing for, like, a thousand years in some forest in England or someplace. I hadn't noticed it before, which was kind of odd, given the size of it. But there it was now anyway, near the edge of the grove. Its trunk was as thick around as . . . well, as the trunk of a gigantic oak tree. I can't actually think of anything thicker around than that. Its branches sprang from it in all directions and rose into the forest night and fell to the forest floor like the legs of an alien spider in a science fiction film. Lit by the rainbow light of the fairies and the silver glow that emanated from the king and queen, its leaves showed themselves a rich copper gold that touched me somehow with their perfection and loveliness.

This was the gift Elinda had left for her chosen hero? A big tree? What was I supposed to do with it? Hug it? Put it in my pocket with thanks all around?

I glanced Maud-ward for help. But all the rodent-woman did was tilt her head toward the big tree, indicating I should approach it. I approached it. Got a closer look. It was a big old tree, all right.

I glanced around me. From every nook in the glowing forest, eyes looked back at me. The eyes of the forest king and queen, yes, and the eyes of the martial centaurs and their ladies, the eyes of the imps and elves and the trolls with their peaked caps held humbly in their gnarly hands, the eyes of buzzing fairies hovering all aglow in the sable air, the eyes of fauns and satyrs with their pipes of Pan, and most moving of all, the tender eyes of nymphs with their forms and faces of heart-melting beauty—what would I not have done to please them? All those eyes were staring at me in hope and anticipation, waiting for me to do . . . what? To do the thing that would assure them I was who they so desperately needed me to be.

And what the glorious hell was that?

I glanced at Maud again. Her womanly eyes urged me on: *Do it.* Do what? I turned back to the tree. It was still a tree. I stared at it. The moments passed. Nothing happened. I felt all the eyes of the forest on me, all their hopes in me, and I did not know what I was supposed to do. Well, of course I didn't. I was not the guy! It broke my heart to admit it to myself, but I just wasn't the one they were waiting for. You only had to look at me to know it.

More moments passed. More nothing happened. It was excruciating. I was about to turn to them all and confess the truth. But unable to bear the thought of destroying their hopes—unable to face, most especially, the thought of seeing the disappointment in the eyes of the nymphs—I hesitated another second and another. Finally, in pure panicky desperation, I tried the only strategy I could think of, the only trick I'd learned since I had come here.

I let go of myself. That is, I opened up my mind like opening a hand and let every thought of who I was fly free. And do you know what came to me then? What came into that empty space where my thoughts of myself had been? That child came, that child that I once was. Remember? That boy of five or six or so? Sitting on the floor in the back room of my parents' house, sitting there while my parents and my brother talked and my sister explored her secret spaces, sitting there and arranging plastic figures in stories and tableaux. That little boy, lost in his own imaginative universe, in an act of creation, in a stillness of complete delight. For a moment, just a moment then, I not only remembered that little child, I became him.

And in that moment, I saw a light—a bright pinpoint of white light shining out at me from deep within the giant trunk of the giant oak. Just a pinpoint at first, but then it grew into a dragon-toothed star, a pulsing gleam in the core of the wood, and then that gleam grew—grew and spread and became a cloudy glow that flooded up through the trunk and out to the very tips of the great oak's branches. And as the oak filled with that ghostly light, its bark and wood seemed to lose their substance. They became transparent so that standing there, amazed, I could see right into the oak's heart.

I saw a sword.

It was held there, hanging there, right in the center of the oak's trunk. Oh, it was a wonderful weapon! Compact, yet lithe and graceful, silver-white and gleaming like the light that revealed it. My eyes filled looking at it, not just because of how beautiful it was but because I could see it. I—I could see it!

The wisest queen in all the world had left it there for me.

Before I really knew what I was doing, I took a slow, mesmerized step toward the oak, and then another, as if the glowing sword in the glowing tree were a magic magnet pulling me to itself. I lifted my hand. Reached out to the oak.

And then, impossibly, my fingertips, my fingers, my hand, my arm passed directly through the bark and into the wood. I grasped the sword's hilt.

I gasped as a shock of energy went through me. I heard a gasp . . . a dozen . . . a hundred gasps in unison all around me: a collective sound of relief and gratification, one single sigh of joy. Openmouthed with shock, frozen with surprise, trembling with wonder, I watched as the light of the sword began to spread up over my arm like quicksilver. It reached my shoulder in a second, and in another second bathed my whole torso, sped down my legs and up over my head at once, until I was all clothed in it as in a suit of luminous liquid armor.

Then—with a great electric *swish* and another shock of energy—all that silver light was sucked as if through my pores up into my body. There was an enormous flash—and the light went out.

I was hurled back from the tree. I staggered on my heels, my arms pinwheeling for balance. I almost fell before I managed to steady myself.

I stood there, dazed a moment, marveling. Then, my mouth still hanging open, I turned to look around me at the king and the queen and the waiting creatures of the wood.

They were gone. My sword and armor were gone. I was dressed as I had been. And the forest was empty. Dark. The spectral music had ceased and the sounds of peepers and crickets filled the night. I was alone.

Or not quite alone.

"You better get some rest," Maud said, her nasal squeak coming from somewhere nearby. "We'll have to get an early start in the morning."

Rest? I thought. Rest? Are you kidding me?

But before I could even finish the thought, exhaustion washed over me like a great wave. I wilted under the weight of it, sinking down to the earth beneath the branches of the giant oak. I lay down there. I curled up on my side.

In another second, I was fast asleep.

I WOKE TO FIND THE FIRST LOW BEAM OF THE RISING
sun piercing the autumn foliage to touch my face. And the horse—
the black stallion—he was touching my face too, nuzzling me to get
me up.

I sat up quickly, stiff and shivering from sleeping on the cold
earth. I blinked and looked around me at the morning forest, bright
with light, loud with birdsong. My mind was blank for a second and
then—then, the memories of the night before crowded in on me.
You want to talk about some crazy, crazy shit? Try my memories.
Serge Orosgo landing in his helicopter . . . the king and queen of the
forest escorted to the dance of fantastic creatures by ranks of armed
centaurs . . . a gender-bending assassin shooting a drunken author
dead . . . me pulling the sword out of the oak . . .

And if all that weren't nuts enough, a giant rat with a woman's face
was looking down at me from the pommel of the stallion's saddle.

"We better get going," she said.

I leapt to my feet, my heart pounding. I remembered the rest of
it, in LA. I had to find the book or the assassin would kill me, and
here in Galiana I had to find the queen's talisman, whatever the hell
that was.

"Going where?" I asked the squirrel-girl groggily. "Where are we going?"

"You're the hero," she said drily. "It's your quest. You tell me."

I stared up at her on the pommel. She stared back—a droll, sarcastic stare. Never mind that I had pulled the silver sword out of the oak tree. Maud no more believed I was the hero sent by the queen than . . . well, than I believed I was the hero sent by the queen. Because the truth was: I had absolutely no clue what I was supposed to do next.

And then—then strangely enough—I kind of did.

Out of the jumbled craziness of my impossible memories, one memory suddenly stood out. It was that moment when Lady Betheray had left the witness stand at my tribunal. She had just finished testifying that her friend Lady Kata, the woman I was accused of murdering, had told her I had gotten her pregnant. She had descended from the stand and walked past me. And she'd looked at me. It was a look full of betrayal and wounded love. And it came to me in that instant—it came to me like a memory from someone else's life—that I had kissed her sometime in the past, I had held her in my arms and kissed her, and we had loved one another.

"We have to find Lady Betheray," I said. "She thinks I betrayed her with Lady Kata. She thinks I killed Kata."

"Well, didn't you?" said the rodent-woman.

I felt a flash of anger and was about to bark at her. But had I? I didn't think I had. But if I couldn't remember my love affair with a lady as spectacular as Betheray, what else had I forgotten? It seemed in coming to Galiana I had walked into a story about myself that was already half over. What else had happened to me—what else had I done—before I arrived? Murder? I didn't know.

Well, I wasn't going to discuss it with a big girl-rat. A man has some dignity, after all.

"Do you know where we can find her?" I asked her.

Maud sighed and looked away and shrugged her rodent shoulders. "I know her home is Netherdale. We can look for her there."

"All right," I said. "Let's go to Netherdale, then."

And after a few pathetic attempts to swing myself heroically into the saddle, I finally crawled up over the horse's side and dropped into place, and off we rode.

LONG BEFORE WE reached Netherdale, whatever courage I had—and it wasn't much—began to fail me. We had been riding for hours, out of the woods and through the open country. I've never had a good sense of direction, but as near as I could tell, we were traveling at a narrow angle to the line between the city of Eastrim and the point where we'd entered the forest. That meant we were getting closer to the dangerous city precincts where the guards would be hunting for me, looking to bring me back to the torture chamber. The ruined Galianan landscape with its broken towers and abandoned villages, its withered plains and lonesome, leafless trees, its staring phantoms of once-human beings—a landscape that had held some small measure of ghostly charm when we were escaping—just seemed threatening now as I felt the Eastrim castle and its dungeons growing near.

Then we came up over a low rise and I saw Netherdale.

It stood alone amid blasted trees and weedy gardens: a big, looming, gloomy place. A great gothic manse of gray-brown stone with frowning gables and louring turrets and ivy clinging dark around black windows that suggested a soulless emptiness within. A road of dirt and broken cobbles with brown grass growing in between ran from the overgrown cul-de-sac before the house's front door and wound off to the vanishing points on the left and right.

On the right, under a blue-and-white sky of swiftly moving clouds, a greenish pall hung over the low hills. I figured that must be the hellish smoke of Eastrim, the smoke of burning heretics and traitors.

Instinctively, I drew back on the reins. The stallion came to a slow stop, whiffling. I looked down over the scene of tortuous, naked black branches and tangled weeds. I admit it: I wanted to turn around and ride out of there as fast as I could. I was afraid.

I glanced at Maud to see if she had noticed. She had. Of course she had. She was looking off into the distance, shaking her head with disgust, as if she couldn't believe she'd gotten stuck babysitting such a wimpish weakling.

You and me both, sister, I thought.

"Let's . . . " I started to say. But I didn't know what to say. "Let's . . . wait here awhile," I finished lamely.

The mutant rodent snorted. I felt ashamed. But I wasn't just going to charge down there like some gung-ho idiot to prove my manhood to a giant deformed squirrel. If Lady Betheray was there, her husband, Lord Iron, might be with her. And even if he wasn't with her, she wouldn't be unguarded. She thought I had slept with Lady Kata and then murdered her to cover up our affair. So the minute she saw me coming, she'd have me under arrest and on my way to the Eastrim dungeon, to torture and death.

I dismounted and led the stallion back down the rise a little way so it wouldn't be visible from the house. Then I returned to the crest and lay down to watch the place, waiting for . . . what? Well, I guess to see if I could get a sense of just how much trouble I was walking into. That's what I told myself anyway.

For a long while, nothing happened. The autumn sun angled down the far arc of the sky, and the shadow of the gothic manse grew long and dreadful on the stark face of the landscape. Now and then, I thought I saw a movement at one of the windows, but the place was so dark inside, I couldn't be sure.

Maud, meanwhile, sighed and snorted and rolled her eyes and ran back and forth down the hill for exercise and basically did everything she could to make me feel like crap, thank you very much.

As the sun sank lower and lower, I grew more and more convinced that this whole adventure was a bad idea—very. I was just wondering how humiliated I would feel if I got the hell out of here when the front door of the dismal place swung open—and out stepped Sir Aravist.

"Shit!" I hissed, pressing myself as close to the earth as I could.

Maud scampered up beside me, sitting on her hindquarters to see what was going on.

"Get down! Get down!" I whispered.

She gave me a glance full of scorn and stayed right where she was.

I watched through the weeds. Sir Aravist's red dragon vest blazed bright against the drab stone of the house. His black hair stirred in the autumn breeze. With his bright eyes and his handsome young face and his trim, sharp beard, he was the very image of a warrior. Even though the lump he'd given me had been healed by the nymphs, I thought I could feel it throbbing on my forehead.

My heart thundered against the ground. "What's he doing here?" I said.

"He's the captain of the castle guard," said Maud. She didn't even bother to whisper. "He's smart and loyal to Iron, who's given him everything he has. And he's deadly with a sword. My guess is he's waiting for you."

"What?"

"Ssh. Do you want them to hear you? Look."

Now, two other guards stepped out of the house and flanked their captain. Aravist gave them instructions, the wordless sound of his voice carrying to us on the breeze. The guards moved off to walk around the house, checking the windows and doors and looking into the distance to see if anyone was nearby.

If I had pressed any closer to the earth I would've sunk into it. I clutched the dead grass with sweaty hands. What the hell was I doing here? Forget the sword in the oak. I was not the right guy for this kind of work. I was a jackass to have even thought I could handle it.

"Hmm," said the mutant rodent beside me.

I glanced up at her from the dirt. Her eyes had shifted back to the house. I followed her gaze.

Lady Betheray. She had appeared on the small balcony outside a third-floor gable window.

Seeing her there, I held my breath. I was struck to the heart again by her serene and regal femininity. She was standing as she had stood on the witness stand, very straight, very still, her hands clasped before her. She was wearing some sort of white, full-length, flowing gown, belted at the waist so that her full, soft shape pressed through the fabric. God, she was beautiful.

She gave a brief glance down at Aravist—a glance of pure disdain. Then she looked away, off into the distance to her right, as if searching the horizon for someone's approach.

I looked too—and I saw a cloud of dust on the horizon.

"Maud!" I whispered.

The mutant rodent looked at me, then off down the road, the weird squirrelly eyes in her weird woman's face narrowing. As if I needed something to increase my already over-brimming anxiety, I saw the line of her mouth tighten as if with fear.

"What?" I said. "What is it? What's wrong?"

She didn't answer.

Tense as a bowstring, I lay where I was and watched the cloud of dust move over the rim of the furthest hill. It descended swiftly along the broken road, growing closer, larger. Soon, the ghostly shape of an ornate carriage appeared within the cloud.

It was a fine vehicle, drawn by four white horses. Golden trim twined around the windows and along the edge of the roof, and there were golden shields at intervals on the sides and a golden crown on top. It had burnished brown doors with elegant paintings on them—cherubs, I think, though I couldn't see clearly from so far away.

"That's got to be Lord Iron, right?" I said.

Maud nodded grimly. "And Curtin."

"The wizard? I thought he could only work in the city."

"He's strongest in the city, but we're not very far away."

"You sure it's him?"

Another grim nod. "The driver."

I turned from her fearful face to watch the carriage pull up before the mansion door, its horses straining and whinnying in their traces. Sure enough, there was Curtin. He was sitting up in the driver's seat, the reins in his hands. He was unmistakeable in his flowing robe of liquid darkness, with his wizened little raisin face sporting its tufts of white hair on the crown and at the chin. From where I was, I couldn't make out the glittering eyes in the folds of his wrinkles, but I remembered their wicked gleam.

"Iron must have a reason for bringing him here," Maud said. "And not a good one."

The next moment, Lord Iron stepped out of the carriage. I could see his light hair capping his broad, virile figure. Curtin descended from the high seat, his dark robe swirling. Both men stepped up to greet Sir Aravist.

I glanced from them up to the third-floor balcony. Even as far away as we were, and even with the afternoon shadows bathing her, I saw Lady Betheray's pale cheeks grow paler. It was the sight of Curtin. She was afraid of him.

She stared down at the men below her for a long moment. Then she swiveled around quickly and vanished into the house.

"What are they going to do to her?" I asked Maud.

But the mutant rat-girl only shook her head.

The two guards who had searched the perimeter of the house now returned to the front door. All five of the men went into Netherdale. I could hear the door of the house shut behind them. For the first time since we'd arrived, I felt a fear even greater than my fear for my own safety.

"I have to go down there," I said.

Maud snorted at me with disdain. "What do you think you can do?"

"I don't know."

"Then what's the point?"

"Well . . . Jesus, you're the one who's always rolling your eyes at me."

"Because look at you."

"Okay," I said. "So now I'm, you know, going to do something."

"Yes. You're going to get yourself killed."

"Well . . . "

"Well, don't expect me to wait around for you," she said angrily.

"I don't," I said. "Go."

"Don't think I won't."

"Go ahead."

"I will."

I got to my feet.

"This is ridiculous," Maud said. "I don't care who Tauratanio thinks you are . . . "

But I was already moving toward the mansion.

I BENT LOW and traveled quickly. I used the trick I had learned down in the sewers where the Shit Monster lived. I focused beyond my fear. I kept hidden among the high weeds as much as I could.

I reached the garden surrounding the house. It was a haunted place, or felt like one. The stems of dead flowers and branches of leafless shrubs wafted and waved around me like phantoms in the lengthening shadows. The plants did not seem to have died a natural death but to have been sucked lifeless by some toxic something or other in the local earth and air. As their cold, dead tendrils and spines snatched at my arms and legs in passing, I lost my concentration. I suddenly had this sure, clear sense that something terrible was about to happen.

But I reached the house without being seen—at least, I thought I had. I went to the far right corner and pressed as close to the wall as I could, hoping with all my heart that I was out of sight of the windows.

I'm not sure what I was planning exactly. I had some vague and stupid idea of grabbing Betheray and making a run for it. My stallion ought to be able to outrace their carriage, right?

But how the hell was I going to get to her?

I craned my neck to look up at the looming, frowning, soulless house. Ivy grew thick and heavy down the walls, twining over the brick facing that capped the corner. It was old growth, the vines stout and deeply entrenched in the stone. I thought maybe it would hold my weight if I tried to climb it—hold me long enough, anyway, for me to grab onto the ledges and gargoyles that jutted out from the second floor upward.

I was never much of an athlete. Climbing? I was always the guy who couldn't shimmy up to the top of the ropes in the high school gym. Girls with arms like twigs used to scramble by on the other ropes around me. They would slap the ceiling and slide down while I was still twisting and dangling at the halfway mark.

But there was no other way to get to Betheray without being seen, so I went for it.

The next few seconds—well, they were harrowing. My muscles ached and strained as I pulled myself up the vine hand over hand. The ivy creaked and rattled like an antique car on a gravel road. I felt sure one of the guards inside would hear it. The cold stone scraped against my bare forearms and my face. The whole house seemed to hang over me like a movie monster, claws upraised. Only that sense that something terrible was about to happen kept me from giving up and letting go.

I reached the second floor. One more pull—and then one more—and then I reached up, stretched my fingers, and—yes!—I seized hold of the jutting ledge above me. From there, I managed to get my knees onto it and grab the next ledge and get my knees on that. Then, balanced precariously, I reached up and grabbed the dragon gargoyle above my head. Holding on to the stone beast's neck, I stretched my free arm out until I could grab the rail of the balcony where Betheray had stood moments before. I grabbed with one hand then with the other.

And my knees slipped off the ledge.

A split second of terror—the earth spinning under me—my hands on the rail, my feet dangling. Then, with the strength of fear, I scrambled up and spilled down onto the balcony.

Through the glass of the doors, I caught one glimpse of the room inside: a spacious bedroom with a large four-poster in it. I saw Lady Betheray, lit by the light of two candles, kneeling at the sculpted wooden prayer desk on which the candles burned. Her hands were clasped beneath her chin, her valentine face was turned toward heaven, her raven hair spilled down behind her. She looked like a saint about to be martyred.

Then the lady turned to the door. Leapt to her feet. I pulled back quickly against the wall to hide myself from view.

It was Lord Iron. He had come marching into the bedroom with the evil little wizard guy scuttling after him.

I pressed close to the balcony wall and listened. I could hear their voices clearly through the glass doors.

"I've disturbed you at your prayers, my dear. I'm so sorry." That was Iron. He didn't sound sorry at all.

"What's the meaning of this, Winton?" That was the lady. "Am I your prisoner here? Is that it?"

"My prisoner? Of course not. Don't be ridiculous. You're my beloved wife."

"Then why do you . . . ? Keep him away from me."

"He only wants to help you."

"I know what he wants. He uses his power to cloud my mind and shape my will."

"Shouldn't a wife's will be shaped to her husband's?"

"Not by demon magic. Is that what he did to Kata? Put a spell on her? To make her accuse Austin Lively?"

"You're confused. You don't know what you're talking about."

"No. No, now my mind is finally clear. It wasn't Austin I saw with Kata in the maze that night at all, was it? I remember now. It was you."

There was a long, ominous silence. A chill autumn wind blew off the blasted heath below me. It washed over me where I hid in the afternoon shadows. It made me shudder where I stood pressed against the cold stone.

Lord Iron spoke again, his voice thick with bitterness and sarcasm. "My poor, fine, noble, loyal, and ever-so-moral wife. Who was the first of us to commit adultery?"

"I never did."

I stiffened as I heard the sound of a sharp slap. Until then, I had felt nothing but fear. Fear for myself, fear for her. But now a raw fury washed the fear away. I had never felt anything like it before, not since I was a child anyway. Like a child, I wanted to jump through the window and strangle the man. Like a child, I was helpless. I stayed where I was.

"Liar," Iron said. "You think I don't know? You played the whore with Lively."

Lady Betheray's voice was thick with shock and with tears. "I wanted to. I should have. He's ten times the man you are. But I said my marriage vows before God."

"Oh! God!" Lord Iron laughed, as if it was the stupidest word he'd ever heard in his life.

Then—a shuffling movement.

"No!" Lady Betheray cried out, half in fear, I thought, but half in anger too.

Then another man spoke. I knew right away that it was Curtin, the wizard. More than the wind that blew across me, the sound of that voice chilled me to my bones. I had never heard a tone of such dead malevolence. It wasn't violent or threatening or cruel in any way. Just malevolent. Just dead.

"Look at me, my lady. Don't be afraid. Don't be foolish. You know you can't fight me."

"I can. I will," she said. "I was confused before by Kata's lies. I thought Austin had betrayed me and that made me weak. But now—I know you can't control me if I won't let you."

There was another long silence. I could feel the struggle of wills going on beyond the doors, Lady Betheray trying to shield her mind from the hypnotic power of the wizard, the wizard trying to wear away her defenses. I could imagine the two fields of energy pushing against one another, vying for supremacy.

Then: "Damn you!" This was Lord Iron again, angry now. "Never mind, Curtin. It doesn't matter. I don't care whether you believe me anymore, my lady. I only need you to be here. To draw him. You're nothing but bait to me now."

"He won't come. He saw me betray him at the trial."

"That's exactly why he will come. To set you right. He loves you. He needs you to know he didn't betray you. He'll come. And when he comes, we'll have him—and this will be over. And I'll have no more need of you."

There was a pause. A sound of motion. Iron was leaving—Iron and Curtin both, I thought. I heard Lady Betheray call after them.

"He won't come. He won't."

But there was no answer. And the moment after that, I heard her give a wild cry of despair. She began sobbing miserably as if something had broken inside her.

I understood. She must have realized that what Lord Iron said was true. She must have realized that I would come, that I would walk right into her husband's trap to try to save her.

She was right. I would.

15

LADY BETHERAY WENT ON SOBBING. I WANTED TO GO
to her then and there, but I remained where I was until I heard the
door of the house open below me. Quickly, I crouched down to hide
myself beneath the balcony wall. I heard footsteps on the dusty drive.

"He'll be here, I'm sure of it," Lord Iron said. "I'll leave the rest
to you—best if I'm nowhere near. Just make sure it's Lively who
takes the blame."

Sir Aravist answered him with an easy drawl, "My lord."

I waited, crouched there. Waited. I heard the carriage take off,
the horses' hooves pounding against the earth. Still I waited. Silence
below. Sir Aravist must've been standing in the drive, watching the
carriage go. A few more seconds of waiting and I heard his footsteps
as he returned to the house. I heard the front door open and close.

This was it. This was my moment. My only moment, probably.
The time was short—very short. I had to move.

I sprang up. I stepped to the balcony doors. They weren't locked.
I pushed them open and stepped out of the chilly day into the
shadows of the candlelit bedroom.

There was Lady Betheray. She lay sprawled on the bed, her face
buried in her arms, her sobs loud and violent.

How long before Sir Aravist and his men came up to check on her? Minutes? Seconds?

"Betheray," I said.

Her sob caught on a startled gasp. She lifted her head and saw me. She leapt to her feet.

"Austin! My darling!"

She threw herself into my arms.

It was an impossible moment. Intoxicating. Surreal. I knew we had to go—we had to go now, right now. But I couldn't move from her embrace. It was too good, too full. I couldn't leave it.

I held her, surrounded by her scent, swimming in her softness, my cheek pressed against the velvet smoothness of her hair. My whole body was enveloped in such a cloud of longing, it went beyond the erotic into an almost holy devotion.

And more than that. More than that. Bizarrely, in that moment, there were other moments too, memories I had not lived through, cherished experiences I did not know I'd had. I caught glimpses of shared glances. I heard whispers of whispered secrets. I could half-remember her half-pulling away from me, resisting my desire in the name of her vows.

It was crazy, like one of those crazy quantum things you read about on science blogs where phenomena only exist when you're there to observe them. Lady Betheray and I had had a whole relationship that hadn't actually taken place until now, when I remembered it. A great passion I'd never felt. A grand endeavor I hadn't been there for. A whole dangerous conspiracy of good against evil, a mission for the sake of the country and the queen that had brought us together in a past where I'd never been.

I did not remember falling in love with her, but I knew I had. I had not lived it, but suddenly I remembered it. Maybe some Great Observer in the Sky had seen it all from the beginning, but I was only coming to it in this moment, in this embrace.

I knew we had to go, but still I didn't go. I went on holding her, feeling our whole fantastic history coming to life inside me for the first time.

At last, she drew back slightly. She tilted her tearstained face up to me. The sight of it filled me with something I had never felt before: a fever to fight, to fight for her, even to die for her. She had told Lord Iron I was ten times the man he was. Just then, and for the first time in my life, I felt I was ten times any man.

"Can you ever forgive me?" she whispered.

"Ssh. We have to go."

"Tell me, Austin. Tell me you don't hate me for what I said in court. I was under a spell . . . "

I let out a laugh. Hate her? I kissed her. I thought kisses like that were just in the movies. I whispered again, "We have to go."

"Aravist has his men guarding the stairs."

I looked around me. "We'll go out through the balcony, then. Come on. We'll find a way down."

Finally—finally—I worked up the will to push her gently away from me.

That's when I saw Sir Aravist standing in the doorway.

Crap, I thought.

AMAZING HOW QUICKLY all that romantic courage turned to steam and flew away. I remembered what Maud had said: Aravist was deadly with a sword. I remembered how fast he'd drawn his blade and struck me down in the tower room—so fast I'd hardly seen it.

I was unarmed. And even if I had been armed—unless I was armed with, like, a .38—I would've been no match for him, no match for anyone.

It occurred to me again—occurred to me with a wave of nausea—that I was a fool to have come here, an unrealistic idiot. I was not the guy for this fight, or for any fight. What was I going to do now?

Sir Aravist stepped forward. His thumbs were hooked arrogantly in his sword belt. He was smiling. Utterly relaxed. Well, why wouldn't he be?

Instinctively, I pushed Lady Betheray behind me. Aravist snorted to see it. Sure he did. What the hell good was that going to do her? How was I going to stop him?

"Not even armed, Lively?" he said. "You might have brought a sword just to make it entertaining."

"Look, let me get her out of here," I said. The words came out almost before I thought them. "That's all I want. Let her go and then you've got me."

He lifted a finger to stroke one side of his mustache. He pretended to consider it. Then he said, "That's one idea. Or I could hobble you and then kill her while you watch and then have you taken away to be tortured until you tell us where the talisman is. Yes, I think all in all, that's the option I prefer."

This time, I saw him make his move. I guess I was expecting it the whole time he was talking. I saw his hand go to the hilt of his sword just as it had in the tower where Lady Kata died. Just as before, he drew his sword in a flash of steel and swung it in a cruel arc at my head. I threw up my arm in a useless gesture of defense.

And with a loud clang, his blade struck the blade of the sword that was suddenly—magically—gripped in my hand!

I gaped at my blade crossed with his. It was the queen's sword, the silver sword I had drawn from the heart of the oak! Just as it had vanished into me, so it had sprung out of me in the moment of need. Likewise, the mercurial armor that had been sucked into my body now emerged from my skin and clothed me head to toe in liquid metal!

Whoa! I thought. And Sir Aravist looked like he was thinking something similar—because he was standing there just like I was standing there, staring, gaping at the sword just like I was.

But I understood it first. I recovered my wits first.

I lifted my foot high and kicked him in the stomach.

I don't know where I came up with that move. Something I once saw in a movie fight scene maybe, I don't know. I just thought of it, and I did it. I planted my foot hard in Sir Aravist's leather-clad belly. I don't think it hurt him much, but it was a square-on blow, and it sent him reeling backward.

I didn't charge after him. It would have been suicide. I mean, yes, I had a sword now, but I hadn't the faintest idea how to use it. If I got into a duel with him, he would cut me to pieces, armor or no.

He was already recovering his balance, already straightening on his feet, ready to fight.

I grabbed Lady Betheray's hand and rushed with her across the room.

It was a desperation move. How was I going to outrun Aravist? How was I going to get past the other two guards? I had no idea. But this was the only thing I could think of.

Sword in one hand, lady in the other, I reached the bedroom door. I swung Betheray through it.

"Run!" I cried.

And I leapt after her into the house's hallway.

Except not the hallway. Not the house. I suddenly wasn't anywhere I recognized.

Then I did recognize it. My Nissan! I was in my Nissan! Sitting behind the wheel of my car in the driveway outside Serge Orosgo's hilltop ranch!

I didn't know whether to scream at the insanity of it or to say a prayer of thanks for my salvation. Second after second, I just sat there in the car, panting with terror and excitement, my heart fluttering in my chest as if I'd just awoken from a nightmare. Which I suppose in some way is exactly what I had done. Except I'd awoken from a nightmare into another nightmare, because now I was back in LA, and I had to find the book *Another Kingdom,* or Sera, the girl-boy assassin, would be set free to torture me to death—unless I was teleported back to Galiana first. Then Sir Aravist would torture me to death. Either way, there seemed a high probability that I was going to be tortured to death.

It took me three tries before I could steady my violently trembling hand enough to slip the key into the ignition and get the Nissan going.

SHATTERED, TREMBLING, CONFUSED beyond reason, I drove home through the snaking darkness of Coldwater Canyon. I kept telling myself I needed to think—*Think! Think!*—but I couldn't think. Bouncing back and forth between the fatal dangers of Los Angeles and the fatal dangers of Galiana had left me in something like a state of waking coma. I stared through the windshield without seeing the road. I steered the car without knowing where I was headed. My mouth hung open like an idiot's mouth or a drunk's. I did everything but drool, and I probably would have drooled too if I'd thought of it. But I couldn't think of anything, nothing at all.

Somehow—by habit, I guess—I made my way back to North Hollywood. I found my apartment building. I drove into my garage and parked. I reached for the handle of the car door.

And I froze with my fingers on the metal.

The old Galianan doorway problem. What if I stepped through the door and was back in Netherdale? Sir Aravist had been two steps behind me at most, his sword drawn. A second after I returned he would be on me. He would strike me down a second later. Lady Betheray would only live a few moments after that.

I sat there in my dark car, surrounded by dark cars in the half-lit garage. I didn't know what to do.

Finally, I went into my pocket and brought out my phone. The glow of the screen filled the Nissan's shadows. I searched for a video: "How to Fight with a Sword." Guess what? There was a whole series of three-minute instructional sword-fighting videos. No kidding. Yay, internet.

I sat in the car and watched the videos. Each video covered one type of blow or defensive move. I watched each one three or four times, trying to memorize the instructions. When I had gone through six of them—as many as I thought I could remember—I set the phone on my lap and closed my eyes. I imagined how I would use the moves in the video to fight with Sir Aravist. There was one I liked especially: a forehand slash down to the hand that knocked the sword aside, then a back slash to the face. I knew I would only have one chance to catch my opponent off guard before he killed me, but I pictured in my mind what it would look like if I pulled it off. It calmed me down a little. A little, anyway.

I stuffed the phone back in my pocket. I sat and stared at the car door some more. I realized that the moment I passed through it might be the moment of my death. I took a deep breath. I opened the door and stepped out.

No transformation. No Galiana. I was still in Los Angeles. Still in the garage.

I stayed there a few more minutes. I rehearsed the sword fight moves I had learned in the videos, moving about the concrete floor, imagining the sword in my hand, slashing my arm down to my opponent's wrist, up to his face. After a while, another car came into the garage, and I was caught in its headlights, playing at the duel. It made me feel like an idiot. I headed into the building.

I went up to my apartment. Each time I passed through a door—the building door, the elevator door, the apartment door—I braced myself. Each time, I thought I might be hurled back into the hallway of Netherdale with Sir Aravist right behind me. I couldn't even enter my own bathroom without being afraid it would send me back to die at the point of Aravist's sword.

By the time I went to bed, I was a nervous wreck. I lay there wide awake, watching the sword-fighting videos on my phone again and again. And when that exhausted me, I put the phone down and just lay there, staring into the darkness.

My weary mind returned to Lady Betheray. The feel of her in my arms. The sight of her tearstained face turned up to me. What a woman she was! So feminine, so passionate, so steadfast, honorable, and loyal. I had never met anyone else like her. How was it possible I had won her love? A Hollywood nobody like me. In those snatches of half memory that had come to me out of nowhere when I was holding her, I seemed a different person. Better. Braver. More heroic. How would I ever be able to live up to that quantum man whom I had never been but only remembered? In a way, I thought bitterly, I'd be lucky if Sir Aravist killed me the minute I returned. At least I'd never have to see the disappointment in Betheray's eyes when she realized I was not the man she thought I was.

It was almost dawn before I drifted off to sleep.

THE BOOK!

That was my first thought when my eyes opened in the late morning. Somehow I had to find that book, *Another Kingdom*. If I didn't find it—and if I didn't find it fast—Serge Orosgo would let Sera kill me. Who knows? Sera was so crazy and so angry, he might come after me and kill me even if Orosgo didn't let him.

That is, if I didn't flash back to Galiana and get killed by Sir Aravist first.

But where was I supposed to find the book? I had no idea where it was. I didn't even know where to begin looking.

I went to the bathroom—after hesitating on the threshold for several minutes, afraid I might be flung back into the sword fight. I brushed my teeth and shaved, looking in the mirror. The bruise on my head was totally gone, washed away by the nymphs in the magic river of Shadow Wood. The marks on my wrist, same thing—gone as well. Even so, I looked like crap. Exhausted. Eyes full of worry. My hand so unsteady I nicked myself with the razor twice. Some hero.

As I was wiping the last of the shaving cream off me, I heard my phone buzz in the living room. Reflexively, I went to answer it, crossing the bathroom threshold again, only this time without thinking. The moment I realized what I'd done, I pulled up short, terrified Aravist was about to run me through. He wasn't. I was still here, still in LA.

I hurried to the phone, which was recharging on my desk by the window. It was a video call. My kid sister, Riley.

I plopped down into the desk chair and answered it on the laptop so I could see her on the bigger screen.

There she was, as she almost always was when she called me, as she always was in her crazy conspiracy videos, lying tummy down on her unmade bed, her legs bent at the knees so that her tiny feet in their ankle socks waggled up in the air behind her. She was only three years younger than I was, but she seemed a childlike creature, small with straw-yellow hair she wore in braided pigtails and a round, cute face that got all pinched and wrinkled when she was upset, like a baby's face when she's about to cry. Her body was more a girl's body than a woman's, with no shape to speak of, and she always wore tattered jeans and baggy T-shirts that gave her a gamine charm. I couldn't look at her without wanting to feed her and tuck her into bed as I had often done when she was little.

"Hey," I said.

"Hey. What's up?" she said.

For a moment, I wondered if I should tell her what had happened to me after my dinner with Mom and Dad last night—tell her about my second dinner on the patio with Serge Orosgo. Should I let her know that our family's benefactor was a homicidal nutball with a gunsel who wanted to kill me?

Probably not. Riley was so crazy already with all her alien invasion conspiracy theories, I didn't want to make her any worse. So I just said, "Nothing's up. What's the matter with you?"

"Who said anything's the matter?"

"You only call me when something's wrong, Riley."

"That's so untrue!"

"Okay, how's everything?"

"Everything sucks," she said. And she kicked one little foot pettishly into the mattress. "I hate our parents."

"Which means they've cut off your money."

"That's such a shitty thing to say, Austin. Not everything's about money." It was my turn to roll my eyes. "All right, yes, they cut me off," she said. "But it's still shitty to say it."

"Well, whatever you're doing to annoy them, they want me to talk you out of it."

"I'm not doing anything."

"Which means you're going out with some awful guy again."

I remembered my mother had said something about this: *This new one . . . Juan or Pedro . . .* Unfortunately, the same girlish vulnerability I found endearing in Riley was a magnet to the sort of men who wanted to use her and mistreat her. Which, sadly enough, seemed to be just the sort of men she was attracted to.

"Not everything is about a guy, Austin!" Riley said. Then she said, "His name is Marco," and she coyly twined her stockinged feet together and smiled at someone standing behind her camera.

On cue, Marco entered the picture. He plopped down on the mattress beside her and gave her a smack on the backside: a gesture of ownership she clearly enjoyed. It made me wince. Plus the guy looked like a drug dealer—assuming he wasn't something worse, like a pimp or a hitman or a serial killer. He was long and sinewy with blue ink tats on his neck, chest, and arms, all of which were visible because he wasn't wearing a shirt. He looked aggressively good shirtless too, with his washboard abs folded neatly into the enormous silver belt buckle at the front of his jeans. He had long, shaggy hair and long vulpine features and olive skin like some brand of Latino. He smiled at me, hand still resting on Riley's bottom. It was a domineering and insinuating smile, a strong-man-to-a-weak-man smile, an I-have-my-hand-on-your-sister's-bottom smile. The bastard.

"Austin, this is Marco. Marco, Austin," Riley said. "Isn't he cool?" she added fondly, rubbing her head against him as if she were a kitten.

"Jesus, Riley," I said. "Of course Mom and Dad won't give you money. What did you expect?"

"It's not because of Marco."

"Of course it's because of Marco. Look at him."

Marco smiled wider, showing me his white predatory teeth.

"Well, okay, they do hate him," Riley said affectionately. "But it's my vids they're angry about. They say they're not going to help me anymore until I stop posting them. They say I'm humiliating them."

"Well, you know, Ri, the whole alien-Illuminati-world-takeover thing: it does kind of embarrass Mom and Dad in front of their intellectual friends."

"It is because she is getting too close to the truth," Marco chimed in at this point. He had a deep, mellifluous voice with a fake-sounding Latin Lover accent. He was the whole bad-news package, all right. No wonder Riley adored him.

"Yeah, too close to the truth," I said drily. "That must be it."

"Marco was a documentary filmmaker in Venezuela during the collapse," Riley said proudly. "He saw my videos online and came to help me."

"I'll bet he did."

"We are very close to exposing the whole conspiracy, my friend," he said. And he lifted his hand off my kid sister's butt long enough to indicate the mess on the shelf on the wall behind them. Books about UFOs and Illuminati stacked up or leaning lopsided. Purple crystals and plastic pyramids and a big pile of ragged pages tied together with twine.

"We just need a little more time," Riley wheedled. "If they would just give us enough to live on for a few more months, we'll be famous."

"Riley . . ."

"Could you ask Richard for us? Please?"

"Richard won't give you money if Mom and Dad won't."

"But he'll argue with Mom and Dad if you ask him to. They love him and he loves you and you love me—that's how our family operates."

I was about to ask *"Who do you love, Riley?"* but then Marco replaced his hand on her backside and gave me his toothy grin again, so that answered that.

Riley rolled over and pressed the back of her head into Marco's bare belly. "Please, Austin?" she repeated. She stretched the words out as far as they would go.

I looked at her, sprawled on her side with her T-shirt bunched up to expose her navel, and her jeans torn to show the white flesh high on one thigh. I thought about my parents and my brother being funded by Serge Orosgo and Serge Orosgo threatening to kill me for a book about a world I kept teleporting into. I thought maybe Riley was the only sane one among us. It sure as hell wasn't me.

"I'll think about it," I said finally. I gestured toward Marco. "Meanwhile, dump this clown. He's trash."

Marco grinned even wider. The bastard. I broke the connection.

I sat back in my chair. I ran my hand through my hair and sighed. My family. Serge Orosgo. *Another Kingdom.* The sword fight at Netherdale. Too much stuff. So much stuff! I gazed dolefully out the window.

And I saw the black Mustang parked across the street. Sera was at the wheel. The killer was staring up at me, his eyes bright in his kittenish face, his teeth bared in an insane grin.

I felt my whole body clutch like a dry engine. Look at him! Gun in his jacket, murder in his heart. I had to get out of there, and fast. I didn't know whether Sera had come to kill me or just to watch me for Orosgo. I didn't know if Sera knew either. But I knew if I stayed in my apartment alone and did nothing, I'd be completely unprotected. I couldn't call the police—it would be sure to get back to Orosgo. No, I needed to get myself to a public space, somewhere there were people, witnesses, who might make Sera think twice.

Hitchcock's. It was past breakfast time: My people might have come and gone. But there'd be others there. And Schuyler would be there, working the day shift. Schuyler might be pissed off at me because Jane Janeway loved me instead of her, but I still thought she'd probably object if Sera shot me dead in front of her—if only because she wanted to do the job herself.

It was an unpleasant journey. I was afraid of every doorway—afraid it would take me back to Netherdale—afraid Sera would be waiting for me on the other side.

Down in the garage, I searched under my car for a tracker. I didn't find one, but it didn't matter much. Sera didn't need a tracker. He and his Mustang were still right there at the curb when I came driving out of the garage. The minute he saw me, the slender blond pulled away from the curb and followed after. He wasn't subtle about it either. He kept his front fender pressed close to my rear. I could see his bright eyes and eerie grin in my mirror. Stopped at a traffic light, I saw him pout at me flirtatiously and wink.

He followed me right into the restaurant's parking lot, but he didn't get out of his car. He just sat there behind the wheel, just watched me as I walked to the restaurant door.

I went into the restaurant without thinking about the door. There are so many doors to walk through in life, you can't be afraid of all of them, even if you know one of them might be your last.

It was a relief to be in my old hangout. The familiar brown wood walls and white fairy lights, the TV news dancing on the liquor bottles behind the bar—it was all so familiar, it created an illusion of normalcy and even safety. Sera wouldn't just walk in here and open fire. I didn't think he would, anyway.

There were plenty of starving artists still sitting at the tables, drinking their coffee concoctions under the old suspense movie one-sheets. Even a couple of my disreputable crew were still at our usual place by the kitchen door. Ted Wexler, the aspiring asshole agent, was scrolling through the emails on his phone with one hand and picking at the crust of some dry toast with the other. The inscrutable beauty Wren Yen was inscrutably blowing the steam off a cup of tea while inscrutably staring into space, a living Eurasian stereotype.

Schuyler pushed out of the kitchen just as I was sitting down with them.

"What the hell happened to you?" she said, scowling.

Both Wexler and Wren Yen glanced at me with minimal interest, then looked away.

Holding a tray in one hand, Schuyler stood next to me, her enormous figure hanging over me like a tight deadline. With her free hand, she gripped my cheeks painfully and turned my face to her.

"Uhwuh?" I said, the word squeezed into incomprehensibility by her painful grip.

"Your forehead. The bruise is gone. It's not even discolored."

Oh, right. In spite of everything that had happened, only a few hours had passed since I'd last seen her.

"Some nude nymphs bathed me in the healing water of a magic grove, then stroked me to the greatest orgasm of my life, renewing me body and soul," I didn't tell her. I said instead, "I ess it wuh . . ."

"What?" Schuyler barked.

I pulled her fingers out of my cheeks. "I guess it wasn't as bad as it looked," I said.

Schuyler continued to stare down at me with harsh, unforgiving skepticism, but it made no difference. Even if I told her the truth, she wouldn't believe it. A second later, she lifted her eyes. I saw her angry cherub face go soft beneath her spiky red hair, and I knew Jane Janeway had come in.

It was an intricate moment. I turned and saw Jane by the door in all her slumped, mousey, secret loveliness. There was no mistaking the pleasure in her eyes at the sight of me, even though she shyly turned away so I wouldn't see it. There was no mistaking Schuyler's gloomy brooding as she hurried off to deliver someone's breakfast. Wexler smirked. Wren Yen watched through her tea steam. The whole thing was fraught with social complexity.

Myself? It was strange. As soon as I saw Jane, I knew something had changed in me since yesterday. I had changed, and my feelings toward Jane had changed as well. I couldn't figure it out just then. Not with all the threats hanging over me from every side. Not with my mind churning and burbling with anxiety. But before, the sight of Jane had always filled me with guilt and uncertainty. I knew she liked me. And I—well, everyone—liked her. She was so incredibly sweet, so nurturing, so kind—the sort of girl you wanted to build a life with.

But was I willing to build a life with her? With anyone? Was I willing to risk hurting her if I wasn't ready? And not to sound like some shallow Hollywood cliché but . . . well, but what about my career? Schuyler was right about Jane. She was the sort of woman who would give all of herself to her family, her husband and children. Was I ready to support a woman like that? A family like that? I had always fancied myself a high-minded artist in the making. Would I give up that dream to make the money we'd need?

Those were the questions that had paralyzed me before—just yesterday. But now . . . ? I was different. The misty nymphs of Shadow Wood had brought out some natural manly something in me I'd never quite felt before. And my bizarre, preternatural memories of Lady Betheray—and my memories of the man who was me when I was with Lady Betheray in the past, if you get my drift—had planted a new idea of myself in my brain, or maybe an old idea, or maybe just a different idea than the one I'd been operating on until now.

Anyway, the upshot was, when I saw Jane this time, I felt something—a quick, deep, bright premonition that she was going to be mine, and not mine in a polite, modern, equitable, easygoing partnership sort of way either, but totally mine, in my possession and in my care, body and soul, forever.

Well, the feeling came and went, just a flash of insight here and gone, a split-second shock of raw, organic understanding. It was crowded out immediately by a fresh rush of worry about what I was going to do next. Still, a sort of undercurrent clarity lingered as I watched sweet Jane, in her oversized sweater and ugly tennis shoes, shuffle across Hitchcock's to our table.

She stopped when she reached me. Her gentle blue-green eyes went wide. Her cheeks pinkened.

"Austin, your head," she said.

"I know. It healed fast, didn't it?"

"Well . . . yeah! I mean, it's crazy how fast."

I pulled out the chair beside me. "Sit down with me, Jane. I need to talk to you."

Holding her teacup to her lips, Wren Yen's eyes shifted toward us inscrutably, brightened inscrutably, and shifted inscrutably away.

Jane sat down next to me, all earnest and caring and Jane-like. "What's the matter, sweetheart?" she said. "You look worried."

It wasn't a romantic "sweetheart." It was just Jane being darling Jane. She probably didn't realize yet that one day soon I was going to lay claim to her flesh and spirit and fill her belly with children and redefine her life by the force of my passion. Actually, I wasn't sure I knew that either, but I sort of did know it too. Like I said, the scenery in my brain was moving too fast for me to get a good view of it.

"Aw, what's da mattuh, sweetie-tum-tums?" Wexler mimicked her, making a kissing noise in his best asshole-in-training manner.

"Shut up, Wex," said Schuyler. She had returned to the table in order to assure Jane that her morning yogurt would fly to her with wings as swift as meditation and the thoughts of love. She loomed immensely, glaring mournful death, first at Wexler, then at me. Then she returned to the kitchen.

Jane went on gazing into my face expectantly in that sisterly-motherly-loverly Jane way of hers, waiting for me to tell her my troubles so she could kiss them and make them better. Not for the first time, I reflected what a waste of womanhood it was for her to spend such sweetness taking care of a movie star who didn't give a crap about her.

"I've got a problem," I said.

"Tell me."

"It's this script I'm working on. I've written myself into a total corner, and I need to talk it out with someone." I dreamed up this story on the spot. I knew it would sound natural. Jane was sometimes dragooned into reading script submissions for her movie star boss. I had used her as a sounding board for ideas myself once or twice. She was at least as good a story analyst as I was. "It's been keeping me up at night."

"I can see. You look so tired."

"Snookums," muttered Wexler.

Schuyler came out of the kitchen again and set Jane's yogurt in front of her. Jane barely interrupted our intense eye contact to smile her thanks. Which made Schuyler glower at me before she charged back through the kitchen door.

"Okay," I said, "it's about this ordinary guy who finds himself in a totally locked room with a murdered woman, and he's got amnesia so he doesn't know how he got there."

"Oh, that's original," drawled Wexler, rolling his eyes.

"It is the way I do it," I snapped at him.

"Stop now, Wex," Jane told him quietly.

Wexler rolled his eyes again, but he shut up and returned his attention to his phone. Because Jane was Jane.

"So now he's on the run, and the police are after him for the murder," I went on. "And all he knows is he's got to find this book that will explain how he got into this situation. But the woman who has the book has totally vanished, and he doesn't even know where to begin to look for her."

"Is the woman with the book hiding from him?"

"No. No, she actually wants him to have the book, but she's afraid if she gives it to him her enemies will get hold of it."

Jane gave a slow nod, raising her eyes thoughtfully to the ceiling. I used the moment to steal a glance out through the glass of the restaurant storefront to make sure Sera hadn't left his car to come and get me. There was no sign of the kitten-faced assassin out there—but as I was turning back to Jane, my eyes passed over the television set behind the bar.

My lips parted. My breath caught. I felt the blood drain from my face.

The local news was on—and they were covering the murder of Sean Gunther. There was a picture of the house in the Hollywood

Hills where I'd been last night. There was video of Gunther's body being carried out on a stretcher. A caption under the picture read: "Death of an Author."

It wasn't that I'd forgotten Gunther's murder. Not exactly. It's just that so many other dangers had been weighing on me it had kind of fallen to the bottom of the pile. I hadn't reported the murder, of course, because Orosgo had hinted he'd have me killed if I did. But now, for the first time, it occurred to me to think about how that would look. I'd witnessed a man being killed and I hadn't said anything. If the police found out I'd been there . . .

"Okay. How about this?" said Jane.

"What?" I said, startled. I turned from the TV to stare at her, my head swimming.

"If the woman actually wants your hero to find this thing, but she's in hiding because she's afraid of her enemies, would it be plausible for her to find a way to slip the hero a clue?"

"A clue . . . " I murmured gormlessly.

"Yeah, you know, something subtle enough to lead him to her but without the bad guys catching on."

"I . . . like . . . what?"

Jane smiled. She couldn't hide how beautiful she was when she smiled. "Well, come on, sweetheart! You're the writer. That's your superpower! Come up with something."

I went on staring at her. The thought of Gunther's murder was still pinballing around in my head, and for a second, I couldn't even take in what she was saying. But then I did take it in and . . .

Well, it was nuts, I know, but yes, it was plausible when you thought about it. What Jane was suggesting—it made total sense. If Ellen Evermore had sent me *Another Kingdom* but had withdrawn it when she realized I worked for Orosgo, mightn't she have left a trail to help me find it again?

A new thought came to me at once: the picture! The photograph of Ellen in Gunther's phone. Had she meant for me to see it? Did it contain a clue?

"You know what?" I said softly. "You're right. That's good, Jane. That's actually possible. That might work."

Jane's face went bright. She was so pleased to have helped me. Even her shlumpy getup and her limp hair couldn't hide how lovely she was just then.

Was it possible? I wondered. Could Ellen Evermore really have left that picture with Gunther in order to lead me to her—to her and *Another Kingdom*? I remembered the shot. She was in a museum. She was standing in front of a painting on the wall behind her.

I took out my phone. I called up my search engine. I tapped in a description of the painting as I remembered it: a man in a skin of some kind standing between two women.

Yay, internet. It came up almost at once. *The Choice of Hercules.* There were several paintings of the subject, but the one I wanted was right here, in LA, at the Getty Museum. I looked at the picture. I didn't see anything particularly unusual about it. But maybe there was some message in the museum itself . . .

"Hey, look. It's you," Wexler said.

"What?" said Jane and I in unison.

Wex held his phone out toward us. I felt something stick in my throat as I looked at the picture on the screen. It was a grainy photo—like a photo taken from a security camera. It showed two figures standing at the gate of Sean Gunther's house. It was me and the call girl, the girl who had seized on my arrival to make her escape.

Wexler drew the phone back and read the photo's caption aloud: "'Police are looking to question two people who were outside the author's residence on the night of the murder.' So like—you killed a guy now?"

"I didn't kill a guy," I said, trying to make it sound as if the idea were ridiculous.

"That did sort of look like you," said Jane.

"It is you," said Wexler.

"It's not me," I lied.

Wex showed the picture to Wren Yen. She shrugged her graceful shoulders inscrutably.

So many thoughts were racing through my mind at once, I could barely make sense of any of them. Would the police be able to identify that picture? Had I left fingerprints? Were my fingerprints on record? I had called Candy Filikin at Mythos to get Gunther's address. Would she hear about the murder, see the picture, and call the police? Maybe I needed to go to the police myself no matter what Orosgo was threatening. But how could I?

No. I knew what I had to do. I had to get to the Getty Museum. I had to see if Ellen Evermore had left a trail for me there to lead me to the book. I didn't know—I couldn't imagine—what good *Another Kingdom* would do me. I only knew it was the one thing that linked all my troubles together: Galiana, Gunther, Orosgo. Everything. If there was a cure for the madness that was happening to me, it was in that book.

"I have to go," I said.

"Sure," said Wexler. "Run away, but you won't get far."

"Just shut up, Wexler."

"You can't outrun John Law," he said.

"I'm not trying to outrun anyone. I just . . . "

Schuyler came out of the kitchen with another tray.

"Hey, Schuyler," Wex said. "Look at this. Austin is wanted for murder."

"I'm not wanted for murder!"

"What?" said Schuyler—and I couldn't help but notice the note of hopefulness in her voice. She took Wexler's phone with her free hand and examined the photo there.

"It isn't me!" I said. I turned to Jane again. "It's just . . . you've given me a great idea. I have to go work on the script, that's all.

That's all it is." I reached out and touched her hand in gratitude. "You really helped me."

She squeezed my hand back and I saw the pleasure of the touch in her wonderful eyes. "I'm glad."

"She'll wait for you—won't you, Jane?" Wexler said. "Hell, he'll probably only do twenty-five years to life."

"Wex," said Jane, blushing with irritation.

"That is you," said Schuyler. "Look, he's wanted for murder," she told Jane.

"It's not me," I said. "I'm not wanted."

"Then why are you running away?" said Wexler.

"I'm not running away!" I got up from my chair to get the hell out of there.

"Would you guys stop it already," Jane scolded the others.

"He's trouble, kid. He'll only break your heart," Wexler told her.

"No, I'm serious, this is really him," said Schuyler. "Look. Isn't this him?"

"It's not me. I gotta go. I'll see you soon," I said to Jane.

I rushed across the restaurant, leaving my friends squabbling behind me. I reached the glass door. I was so confused and in such a rush to get out of there, I didn't even think that I could be charging right out of Los Angeles and back to Netherdale, back to the sword fight with Aravist, back to the final seconds of my life.

16

BUT NO. I WENT OUT THROUGH THE DOOR AND WAS still here, in real life, or in Los Angeles anyway, racing through the fine, warmish autumn day toward the restaurant parking lot. What's more, I came around the corner and saw that the black Mustang was gone. Sera was gone. I had no clue what that meant, but I was glad to be rid of him if only for the moment. I hurried to my Nissan and pulled the door open. This time, I did brace myself for the transition, trying to remember some of the sword-fighting moves I'd gleaned from the videos.

Again though, there was no transition. I was in the car.

I peeled out and headed for the Getty.

I raced along the cliffs of Mulholland with the valley spread out far below me, hazy and serene in the morning sun. I wanted to use the drive time to calm my mind and think. I couldn't. I wanted to try to figure out some strategy to evade Sera . . . and the police . . . and Sir Aravist . . . but nothing came to me.

By the time my car was sputtering up the rising road to the museum complex, I had lost hope, even in what I was doing right now. What real chance was there that Ellen Evermore had left a trail for me? I had seized on Jane's idea out of desperation back in

Hitchcock's, but now that I was here, it seemed too outlandish to believe.

I parked in the museum garage and jogged out to catch the monorail up to the top of the hill. The little white tram car was uncrowded in the midweek morning. I sat and stared through the window across from me. A recorded announcer droned something over the address system. As the freeway sank beneath me and green, hilly wilderness rose on the horizon, I drifted into a hazy fugue state, barely thinking anymore at all.

The tram wound its way up to the museum. The trees of the surrounding park crowded in close. I was still gazing distantly into the leaves when for a second—really just a split second—I thought I saw Sera again. I thought I saw the kitten-faced killer standing amidst the purple blossoms of a willowy jacaranda tree. I blinked out of my fugue state, my blood racing. But he was gone. The blossoms drifted over empty space in an autumn breeze.

Had he followed me here? Tracked me? Had he withdrawn from Hitchcock's parking lot so I would reveal where I was headed?

But there was no sign of him. I must have imagined it.

Still, when the tram reached the top and I stepped out onto the platform, I was wide awake and all vigilance. I headed into the museum complex wide-eyed. Were there dreamy gardens and plashing fountains all around me? Majestic white towers of cleft-cut travertine linked together by bridges of sunlit glass? Were there stately views of the far-off city that made it seem the capital of an antique paradise rather than the rootless mall-and-freeway maze it seemed up close? It didn't matter. I saw none of it. My eyes were studying faces, face after face, searching for my assassin.

He was nowhere, nowhere I could see. I kept telling myself I was spooked, fantasizing. He wouldn't kill me here—not with the tourists all around. He wanted a private place where he could do his dirty work slowly, a place where no one would hear me scream.

I explained all this to my paranoia, but it didn't help. By the time I made it to the European galleries, I could barely focus on the pictures there. I was so busy seeking out that weirdly sexless, weirdly sensual kitten face of his.

All the same, I found my painting. It was there in a fine hall of sky-blue walls and misted glass. There were only two other visitors wandering here, a middle-aged Japanese couple. The moment I came around the corner, I spotted two framed pictures hung one on top of the other. They were on the far wall, flanked by two statues, one of a nymph and one of a hero—I didn't know their names. The bottom painting—that was the one I wanted, the one in Gunther's snapshot. It gave me a mystic thrill to stand before it, to stand where Ellen Evermore had stood.

For a few seconds, I lost myself in the painting. I forgot my fear of Sera. I stepped out of the traffic jam of troubles and dangers crowding my mind. I found enough focus to really study the picture and to read the description on the plaque to one side.

This was Hercules choosing between Virtue and Pleasure. Virtue was a stern helmeted woman, pointing upward toward a climbing, narrow path. Pleasure was arrayed at Hercules' feet, beckoning. She was a beauty, her clothing in disarray, revealing tempting swaths of rounded flesh. Hercules leaned on a post and listened to Virtue's lecture with a quizzical expression, as if he were trying to figure out what possible argument there could be for leaving behind the luscious babe below him in order to climb the rocky, strait-and-narrow way.

I gazed at the painting for long seconds, searching desperately to see some relevant meaning in it, some clue to the whereabouts of *Another Kingdom*. But there was nothing. Nothing I could figure out at least. And I had lost faith in the whole idea anyway. How could Ellen Evermore know I would find Gunther, that he would show me her picture, that I would understand the clue? It was all ridiculous, I thought. A dream of desperation.

And then I thought: *Wait.*

The woman pointing upward. Maybe . . .

I lifted my eyes to the painting above the painting. I knew at once that I had found the clue that Ellen Evermore had left for me.

I didn't understand it. Not then, not yet. It was a painting of a queenly woman in a chair: Wisdom—that's who the plaque said she was. Like Virtue, she had a soldierly helmet on. She held a shield with the emblem of a dove like the Holy Ghost. There were angels around her—cherubs—"putti," the plaque said, though I'd never heard the word before. One of the cherubs held a mirror to the woman, symbolizing self-knowledge, I guess. One overhead held a snake coiled into a perfect circle, its tail in its mouth—a symbol, the plaque said, of eternity.

But what drew me, held me, excited me, was the third cherub sitting at the woman's feet. He held an open book, a radiant book. He was pointing to the words on the page. The words were in script, hard to make out, but the word just beneath his finger was "kingdom."

"The kingdom of God cometh not with observation: Neither shall they say, Lo here! or, lo there! for, behold, the kingdom of God is within you."

I held my breath. I leaned in close, trying to read more of the words. This had to be it, didn't it? This had to be what I was looking for. The photograph of Ellen here. The seated queen—like Queen Elinda maybe? An open book with the word "kingdom" in it. It couldn't all be coincidence. This had to be the clue that Jane had said there'd be.

But what did it mean? What?

I went on gazing, so intent I felt I might almost fall right into the picture. But all at once, I snapped back into myself. My sense of dread returned to me—stronger for my having forgotten it. I turned quickly to survey the gallery, to make sure no one was creeping up on me.

No one was. In fact, I was all alone here now. The Japanese couple had left. There was no one else in sight. There wasn't even a museum guard. It felt eerily deserted.

I heard footsteps approaching from the far hall. I felt a chill go through me. Sera?

It couldn't be. But it didn't matter. I was too nervous now. I couldn't stay there. I hurried out the nearer door. Came into a broad sunlit stairwell. Went down a winding flight and found the bridgeway. There were a few people here, walking to the next building. I joined them, looking back over my shoulder as I went.

Down another flight of winding stairs to the ground floor, into a broad atrium encased in glass and striped with beams of light. There were exit doors on either side, to the panorama of the city to the east and out to the fountains in the museum courtyard to the west. I don't know whether it was superstition or phobia or a sixth sense, but I felt danger closing in on me. I chose a way. I hurried through the sunbeams toward the eastern exit.

And there he was: Sera. Coming toward me. Coming for me. Cat's eyes bright. Cat's mouth open on a toothy grin. Walking with purpose straight my way. He was three steps from the door, no more than that.

I froze. Should I run? Where would I go? Could I escape him? He took another step. Another. He was at the door.

Then his smile went out like a light, and the light in his eyes went out as well. He was looking over my shoulder, looking past me.

I turned. Followed that look.

Two people, a man and a woman, were approaching the atrium from the west, coming toward the door with three jets of a fountain springing high into the air behind them. They were walking with just as much purpose as Sera. And like Sera, they were walking straight toward me.

The man was shortish, white. He seemed to have been assembled out of blocks. His head, torso, arms, and legs were all cuboid. Even his thin mustache was rectangular. The woman was black, a head taller than the man and big, around 250, maybe 300 pounds. She had a smooth, almost featureless face, oval. A wry expression stuck on the corner of her lips, suspicion implanted permanently in her eyes.

I knew who they were—what they were—in a flash. Police detectives. Looking for me. Looking for a suspect in the murder of Sean Gunther.

I turned back to the eastern door. Sera was gone. He'd seen the cops and run for it. That way was open.

I rushed to it, threading between two tourists who were in my way. It occurred to me that I was making myself a fugitive, but what could I do? If I talked to the cops, Orosgo would have me killed.

I pushed out into the daylight, looking back over my shoulder.

I saw Sir Aravist charging at me, his sword upraised.

17

LADY BETHERAY SCREAMED MY NAME: "AUSTIN!"

I turned toward her and saw Aravist's two other guards just cresting the stairs down the hallway, their swords drawn. They were driving toward us, one just behind the other.

I still had my silver sword in my hand, Elinda's magic sword. I still had my mercurial armor on me. But any small knowledge I had gleaned from those internet videos—well, that had been blown completely out of my head by the whirlwind of troubles I was in and the sudden shock of this latest transition.

I turned back to Aravist. Already too late. He was right on top of me. Bringing his sword down from on high in a killing stroke. His handsome, bearded face was contorted into ugliness by his murderous rage.

In fact, it was his murderous rage that saved me. He was so furious—and he had me there so helpless, at his mercy—that he didn't even bother to use his famous sword-fight mastery. He simply brought the edge of the blade whipping at my neck as if to swipe my head off.

On pure instinct, I dropped down low, went almost to my knee before I stumbled and fell on one hand. Not only did the sword stroke sweep right over me, but Sir Aravist kept coming with the force of his charge and tripped over my legs and fell headlong on the faded carpet.

I used the moment to leap to my feet. I swung around to face him.

I saw Lady Betheray pinned in terror against the wall beside a slender vase set on a tall pedestal there. She watched helplessly as first one burly guard and then the other came rushing past her to get at me.

They were already close—but they weren't prepared for Aravist's fall. Guard One nearly stepped on the captain's hand where it lay stretched out on the runner. Trying to dance around it, he lost his balance and came stumbling toward me.

I killed him.

It was the most shocking moment of my life, more shocking than when I first stepped into Galiana, more shocking than all the mad creatures of this brain-tumor fantasy world, more shocking than all the dangers I'd faced both here and in LA.

The way it happened: it was almost an accident. The thickset guard was falling my way, still coming on fast. I half lifted my sword in a half-hopeless half attempt to defend myself against him. He stumbled into the point belly first, and I guess I pushed and the blade went into him, into him deep.

Shocking. Shocking in the ease of it, shocking in its simplicity. Shocking in its completeness and existential finality. The look in his eyes, just a few inches from mine. The sudden understanding there that every dream and hope of life was over utterly. And then life left him—all in a second—I saw it go, a whole unique experience of the world suddenly made nothing.

My mind frizzed like a broken machine, all sparks and fragments, flashing thoughts. I tried to deny the enormity of it. I tried to tell myself he wasn't real. He was just a character in a book, a hallucination in this whole hallucinated kingdom I was in.

But I didn't believe it, couldn't. I'd seen him. I'd seen him die, seen his humanity snuffed out. I'd killed him, and all I really knew just then—knew all through me, knew without words—was that I never wanted to kill anyone ever again.

Then the other guard reached me, and I killed him too.

It was all happening in a chaos out of time, slow motion and high speed at once. The dead weight of the falling guard pulled my sword down across my body. The corpse slipped off the blade and thudded to the floor. I looked up, and my vision was filled by the roaring face, the deadly blade, of Guard Two, attacking. He'd brought his sword back over his shoulder for a backhand blow. I was out of position. No way to defend myself. I was a second from dying.

Then the vase hit him in the head. Lady Betheray had snatched it off its pedestal and hurled it at him in a panic of fear for me. She hadn't had time to put any force behind it. The vase didn't even break when it struck him. It just thumped him behind the ear and dropped to the rug. But the guard thought he was under attack from behind, and it confused him. He threw his sword up to defend himself, leaving his front unguarded.

I brought my sword up quickly and slashed it blindly across him. To say I cut his throat is not to tell it. I nearly took his head clean off. It tilted back unnaturally as he spun away from me. He spattered the wall with a geyser of blood and dropped to his knees. There was a brief horror show of convulsions. Then he lay still.

By now Sir Aravist was on his feet.

The traffic of the battle had kept him off-balance. Two men dead in—what?—five seconds? The hall was a jumble of flying bodies and slashing swords. Aravist had had to roll away before he could stand. Then the second guard, charging, had shouldered him, and he'd staggered against the wall. Even now, as he steadied, it took him a second to get his bearings so he could read the situation.

He was standing maybe six feet away, with the first guard's corpse between us and the second guard's corpse against the wall. Lady Betheray—red faced, her raven hair wild—had been brought forward by the motion of throwing the vase. She was standing a little off to my left, equidistant from the both of us.

Both of us—both Sir Aravist and I—realized in the same frantic instant that she was the key to the battle. If Aravist grabbed her, he could use her as a shield and I'd be helpless. We both reached for her at once.

But she lunged for me, and I got her.

I grabbed her reaching hand. I pulled her quickly behind me. I let her go and squared off against the captain. We stood face to face in the broad hallway, a corpse on either side of us.

Aravist was angry at the death of his men, I could see that. Still, he smiled. He raised his sword for battle. He crooked his free hand at me.

"Come on, then," he said.

FROM THE VERY start, there was no question who was going to win this fight. I was going to die here. I knew it. He knew it too. The man was obviously a master with a blade. You could see it in the way he stood, the spring and flexibility in his legs and torso, the way he held the sword as if it had no weight, the alertness and certainty in his eyes.

And me? Well, I had my magic sword, I guess, and the liquid armor that seemed to move with me like a second skin. And now that we were man-to-man, the few techniques I'd learned from the sword-fight videos came back to me—forehand down to the hand, back slash up to the face—came back to my memory, at least, for what they were worth. Somehow, too, I was steady inside myself, more steady than I would have expected. After all, just a few hours ago I'd stood paralyzed in front of my own bathroom, unable to step over the threshold for fear of coming back here, coming back to this.

But now that the worst had happened, now that I was here . . . I don't know. Maybe it was some magic in the sword that strengthened me, or maybe all the terrors I had faced had made me brave. Or maybe it was just that Lady Betheray was behind me, and I knew I had to do my best to protect her, even if it meant dying. Whatever. The point is, I was not afraid. Not as afraid as I would have thought I'd be, anyway.

All that said, I knew I didn't stand a chance.

He came at me, and if it hadn't been for some magic in my armor, I'd have been dead in the first second, in a single exchange. His sword was everywhere, so fast I couldn't follow it. His blows were a criss-cross of blue-white arcs in the air. From the very start, he had me staggering backward, awkwardly turning my blade to defend against his last attack even as his next attack was coming from a new direction. In the first few moments, he scored three strikes, any one of which could easily have killed me.

My armor seemed to have some magic quality in it that made it flow and thicken at the spot where it was needed. Whenever Aravist's sword came at me, the metal rose like living water to turn aside the blade. So his first strike hit me hard on the side and should have cut into me, but the armor somehow made it glance off harmlessly. His second strike went directly into my left shoulder, but the armor dulled it so a slash that should've taken my arm off only scratched me. His third strike should have been a killing thrust, but I managed to twist a bit, and the armor carried his blade away to the side.

I never got to use any of the techniques I'd learned in the videos, not one. He never gave me the chance. The only time I managed to hit him at all was with a clumsy backhand flick after he'd nearly skewered me and was off-balance. It took him by surprise. The edge of my blade struck his chest, but there was no power behind it. He leapt back just in time, and I only managed to take out a piece of his doublet near his breast. I didn't even nick him.

We drew apart and faced each other again. I was already completely out of breath, gasping for air behind my mercurial helmet. Sir Aravist—he was fine, calm, breathing easy, smiling. He had forced me back down the hall, almost to the door of the bedroom again. Lady Betheray must have still been behind me, though I couldn't see her.

I had a moment of clarity then at the end. My whole position came to me. Austin Lively, story analyst, Hollywood hanger-on. Standing here in armor, holding a sword. Fighting for my life and the life of a lady in this gothic pile in a fairy-tale kingdom.

What a crazy way to die, I thought.

Then the end came. It was quick and awful. Aravist moved in on me, light on his feet, his sword swirling. He feinted high with the blade, and I lifted my sword to block it. His sword was already gone from the spot. He had drawn it back, and in a flash he thrust it into me.

I could feel my armor rush to gather at the spot and deflect the blade. But too late—and there was too much power behind the blow. The point of the sword pierced right through the liquid metal. The blade sank into me, deep into my flesh. I could tell right away he'd killed me.

Somewhere in the distance, I heard Lady Betheray scream my name again: "Austin!"

But I was lost in the shock of an obscene agony, the blade filling my guts, slicing through my guts. I saw Sir Aravist's eyes, bright with victory.

I heard Betheray scream my name again: "Austin!" I felt black grief at having failed her, at leaving her here unprotected.

But now I was falling helplessly into darkness, and the world was flying away from me. The whole business of life was fading into a distant irrelevance. I fell and fell toward the black pool of emptiness that was opening up beneath me.

The last thought that went through my mind was of Jane Janeway: her face, her tender blue-green eyes, the children we had never had a chance to have.

Sir Aravist lifted his foot and kicked me off his sword. All the air and all the life went out of me. Every thought was gone from my mind and every feeling gone from my heart. I was simply toppling sideways into—who knows?—oblivion or eternity.

18

"AUSTIN!"

And still, the voice kept calling out my name. It seemed to have been calling for a long time. I tried to answer: *Betheray*. But I didn't have the strength.

"Austin! Listen to me!"

I listened. Slowly, it came to me: This wasn't Lady Betheray at all. It was a man's voice, very far away.

"Austin! Damn it . . ."

I struggled to open my eyes. It was hard. Hard. I used all my strength but my eyelids only fluttered like wounded butterflies before they settled closed again.

"Austin, you have to wake up! Okay? You have to listen! We haven't got much time!"

I drew breath, gathered myself, tried again. My eyelids rose a little, just enough to let in a blur of light. An unfocused figure was at the center of the brightness. I fought to make the shape come clear.

It was a face. For a moment, I saw it, the familiar features. Swept-back golden hair. Blue eyes. A grand Viking beard moving with the motion of his lips.

"Austin!"

My eyes shut again. But now I whispered, "Rich?"

It was my brother.

"Can you hear me?" I felt his hot breath on my face. He was leaning down over me, very close. Speaking very softly but very urgently too. "Do you understand?"

I tried to nod. I wasn't sure whether or not I succeeded. The effort exhausted me. I rested a moment, then tried to open my eyes again. When I did, there was no one there. Rich was gone. Had I dreamed him?

And where was I? I was too weak to lift my head and look around. But I turned an inch or so to one side, then the other.

I saw I was in a hospital room. I saw a TV hanging over me, the monitor dark. I saw a window with venetian blinds, morning daylight pouring through the slats.

My eyes sank shut.

"Austin!"

I opened my eyes and my brother was back again. Some time must have passed. Yes: the light in the room was different, softer, afternoon light coming through the windows indirectly.

How had I gotten here? I couldn't remember. I tried to think. I saw Sir Aravist's face, close, twisted in triumph. I felt the obscene intrusion of his sword . . .

I shook my head. That didn't make sense. It must have been a dream. Everything I remembered must have been a dream. Galiana, Orosgo, *Another Kingdom* . . . Soon I would remember what had really happened. A car accident or something. I'd been in a coma, hallucinating . . . I tried to speak. I tried to say, "What happened to me?"

"What?" said Rich. I felt the mattress sink as he sat down on the edge of the bed beside me. I tried to speak again. "Never mind now," he said. "Just listen to me, okay? I don't want them to get to you first."

I nodded weakly. I drew a deep breath. I felt a little stronger than before, a little clearer. I felt the way you feel when you first break out of a fever, like I had come through a crisis, like the worst had passed.

I lay still, gazing up at the white ceiling, trying to assess my condition. I could tell I was on drugs, pain meds probably. Everything seemed a little muffled, a little blurred. Even so, the pain was terrible. A sense of hollow weakness at the core of me. Nerve ends on fire as if my entire torso were one big rotten tooth.

Sir Aravist's face. His sword . . .

I groaned and closed my eyes. When I opened them, Rich had vanished again. I turned my head to look around me. The hospital room was small. Just the one bed, one bedside table, one armchair. There was a clear plastic bag hanging on a pole. The bag was full of fluid. A tube ran from the bottom of it into my arm. There was an electronic device on the bedside table next to me. It had red numbers on a readout: my vital signs. The device beeped steadily.

It was night now. I could see the glare of streetlights through the slats of the Venetian blinds. It was weird, the way time kept passing.

I looked in the other direction. There was a door leading out into the hallway. A man was sitting in a chair just outside. A man in uniform. A cop. Was he there to protect me? Or to make sure I didn't escape?

I was aware of falling asleep this time. I was aware I'd slept when I awoke. I felt Rich's weight on the mattress, and when I opened my eyes, sure enough, there he was again. Morning light was coming in through the blinds in sharp rays. I licked my crusted lips.

"Water," I croaked.

Rich glanced furtively toward the door, toward the cop in the hall. He took a plastic tumbler from the bedside table. It had a cap on with a built-in straw. He held the straw to my lips. I sipped the lukewarm water gratefully.

"How long . . . ?" I managed to say then.

He made a gesture with his hand, pressing down on the air: Keep your voice down. "You've been here three days," he whispered. He leaned closer, whispered more softly. "Do you remember what I told you?"

I shook my head no. I didn't.

He sighed. "Damn it. All right. Listen. You have to remember this time. They'll be coming back soon. They're going to question you."

"Who?"

"The police! But don't worry. We have lots of friends, plenty of friends, high up. In the police department, the city, the state, everywhere. But they can't protect you if you don't say the right things."

I looked up at him dully. It was all true, then. No dream. Orosgo. My family. The book. *Another Kingdom.* There was so much I wanted to ask him. Did he know? Who Orosgo was? Did he know the man was a mad monster? Did our parents know? Had they always known? Were they complicit in his madness? What had our family been up to all these years?

"We're going to give them Sera," Rich went on in low, secret tones. "Serge has agreed to it. It wasn't easy, let me tell you, but I convinced him. Sera's crazy. Serge can't control the guy anymore. He has to get rid of him before he does something that drags us all down. All you have to say is that you went to visit Gunther about a book you were interested in. While you were there, Sera came in. You'd never seen him before. Sera and Gunther had a quarrel. Like a lover's quarrel. Sera was in love with him, but Gunther was only into women. Sera shot him. Then Sera put the gun to your head and told you he'd kill you if you went to the police. You were afraid, so you kept your mouth shut. But Sera must've gotten worried you'd talk. He followed you to the Getty and stabbed you. Just tell it like that and you'll be all right. The important thing is: you never mention Serge. Never. He has nothing to do with this. Understand?"

It took some effort, but I shook my head. I didn't care what Orosgo did to me. I was done covering up for him.

"What are you doing?" I whispered. The words ground against my throat like gravel. "You. Dad. Mom. With Orosgo . . . the guy's a fucking lunatic."

"Shut up!" he hissed, leaning close, his lips red and glistening amidst the heavy beard. "Don't say his name. Don't ever say his name." He glanced over his shoulder toward the open door, toward the cop in the hall, then he leaned down close to me again to whisper. "You don't understand anything. He's a great man. He's given so much of himself. He's going to transform the world in ways you can't even imagine."

I only had enough strength to bring up one word: "Murder . . . "

"Dah!" It was a noise of frustration. "Don't be a small man, Austin." I remembered. Those were Orosgo's very words: Don't be a small man. "This is the future of the world we're talking about," Rich went on. "A new age. Riley was bad enough, but at least she's crazy. You . . . You think he's going to let the likes of you get in the way of global transformation? Huh?"

I blinked. "Riley?" What did my little sister have to do with anything?

"If you don't care about yourself, think of her. Serge's my friend but his patience won't last forever."

I was gathering strength to ask him what the hell he was talking about, when Rich suddenly stood up off the bed.

The two detectives had come into the room.

THE DETECTIVES WERE named Graciano and Lord. Graciano was the short white guy all made up of rectangles. Lord was the big black woman with the bland face and the permanently suspicious expression. They stood at the foot of my bed. Graciano kept his hands in the pockets of his wrinkled khaki slacks. Lord scribbled in a notebook with a pen. Rich stood in the far corner of the room, impeccable in his three-piece suit. His blue eyes never left my face.

"Okay, just once more to make sure we've got it right," Graciano said. "You went to see Gunther about a book."

I nodded weakly.

"And this man came in. You never saw him before."

"Gunther called him Sera," I said.

"They argued." This was Lord, gesturing with her pen. "And just like that, the guy shoots Gunther dead right in front of you."

"Yes."

"And then threatens you," said Lord.

"He said he'd kill me if I called the police. I was afraid."

"But then the next day he shows up at the museum and stabs you anyway," said Graciano.

I nodded again.

"You're lucky we were right there," the detective went on. "The doctor said you'd have died if we hadn't been on the scene to stop the bleeding. Even so, she said it was a miracle."

"She said it looked like you'd been run through with a sword," added Lord. "The chances a blade that size could go through you and miss anything vital. She said it was like it was guided through this narrow slot between your stomach and your liver."

"And then somehow missed your spine," said Graciano.

"A miracle," Lord agreed.

But no, I thought. It was the armor. Queen Elinda's magic armor. When it couldn't stop the blade, it guided it through.

I licked my lips. "I don't remember," I said.

THE QUESTIONING WAS over very quickly, or at least it seemed quick to me, oddly quick. I'd expected to be grilled like a suspect on a TV cop show. You know: *"Come on, Lively. Don't insult our intelligence. We know you killed Gunther."* I thought they'd go over my story again and again, searching for inconsistencies, challenging me, trying to catch me out. But there was none of that. Graciano and Lord had me tell the story once, then once again. Sometimes I wasn't sure whether I was telling it to them, or they were telling it to me and I was repeating it back to them. When we were done, they asked a few final questions. Then they turned and nodded to one another.

"I guess we have what we need," Graciano said.

"Looks that way," said Lord, though the wry, suspicious look remained on her face the whole time.

It was only now that it occurred to me—drugged up and bleary minded as I was: Maybe these two detectives were some of the "friends" Rich had spoken about. Friends high up, in the police department, the city, the state, everywhere. Maybe this whole interrogation was a setup, all arranged in advance.

Graciano and Lord thanked me for my help. They gave me a business card and told me to call if I thought of anything else I wanted to tell them. Then they nodded a goodbye to Rich and left. The moment they were gone, Rich moved quickly to the door and shut it. He came back to my bed and stood over me.

"Good job," he said.

I looked away, sneering. I was angry. I didn't like lying. I didn't like covering up for Orosgo. I didn't want to be part of any grand and murderous plans to change the world. I only said what Rich told me to say because I was afraid for my sister. And because I didn't know who to trust.

"Well . . . get some rest," said Rich—and for the first time, I thought I heard something in his tone that might have been remorse or at least embarrassment.

I turned back to him. "What happens now?" I said hoarsely.

He averted his eyes. "You don't have to worry about that. I'll take care of it."

"Won't Sera talk? If he knows he's taking the fall?"

He shook his head. He still wouldn't look at me.

"What's in the book, Rich?" I asked him. "*Another Kingdom.* Why does Orosgo want it so badly?"

He made a vague gesture. That was his only answer.

My wound was beginning to throb again. I needed some more meds, but I didn't want to get muzzy or lose consciousness, not yet. I pressed on. "What's Riley got to do with any of this? Is she in danger? Look at me, you bastard. Is our kid sister in danger?"

Rich gave me a quick and angry look. "She's my kid sister too," he snapped. "You think I haven't had to work to keep her alive this long?"

"Keep her a—? For Christ's sake, Rich. What have you done? What have you all done?"

Rich hesitated. He looked like he was about to answer, like he wanted to answer. Finally though, he just repeated, "Get some rest, bro."

And he walked out of the room.

THE NEXT DAY my mother and father came down from Berkeley to visit. My mother sat in the chair by my bed. She wouldn't stop talking and couldn't stop fiddling with her phone. An endless stream of meaningless musing and gossip came out of her, and the whole time she was thumb-scrolling through her emails and her social media.

My father, meanwhile, wandered around almost silently, examining the room as if there was something to find under the bed or behind the bureau. He'd answer my mother now and then with a grunt or a bit of muttered sarcasm. Studying the wardrobe. Looking out the window at the courtyard. Rambling out into the hall and rambling back in again. And my mother talking all through.

I lay on the bed and stared at them, like a dead man staring. All of this was typical of them, their typical behavior, and yet today, they seemed particularly awful to me. Sexless, lifeless, nearly inhuman. Had I always found them awful? Or was I just noticing it now for the first time?

As I looked at them, that same old moment came back to me. That same memory: myself as a little boy sitting in the back room of our house, creating tableaux with figures, space knights battling monsters amidst the stars. My mother and father in the living room, talking to my brother. I could hear their voices, their lockjaw tones of intellectual superiority.

What were they talking about? I wondered now. Had I ever known? Had I known back then and since forgotten? Is that why I had escaped into the still delight of my figure stories, to forget?

And what about Riley? My little sister, a mere toddler. Crawling around in the storage spaces behind the wall panels. Could she hear their voices in there? Did she understand what they were saying?

If we want a perfect country—good and nice and fair—we have to kill the queen . . . I closed my eyes. That wasn't right. That wasn't my memory. That was Tauratanio and Magdala in Shadow Wood describing the revolt in Galiana. Or was it all the same thing somehow? The pain meds made me feel confused.

"It's not that I don't feel for them, of course," my mother was saying, "but it is an institution of learning, after all." I had no idea what she was talking about. Her words pounded at me like a headache. Plus I had a headache. "Does it really take four janitors to sweep a hallway?" she went on. "If you can save one entire administrative position by having a single person push a broom instead of . . . Well, really, I mean it's about the students, isn't it?"

"Too bad there's no tenure for janitors," my father muttered, gazing out the window at who knew what.

"Well, that isn't the point at all," my mother said. "That isn't what I'm talking about at all." And she went on to talk about whatever it was she was talking about—on and on and on.

I opened my eyes and gave them my dead man's stare again.

My mother kept rambling. "At some point, these jobs are all going to be automated anyhow and then we're going to have to . . ."

"What is it you two do?" I asked.

My voice was hoarse and weak. Maybe they didn't hear me at first. Or maybe they just pretended they didn't hear me. My mother went on talking.

Louder, I asked, "What is it you do for Serge Orosgo?"

My mother stopped. She looked at me as if I'd said something grotesquely rude. My father glanced over his shoulder at me with an expression of bemused irony.

"What is it *Orosgo* does exactly?" I said. "And what part do you play in it?"

"Well, there's no need to take that tone, sweetheart," my mother said—and that "sweetheart" of hers clinked like ice in a glass. "You work for him too, after all."

"Yes. What is it *you* do?" my father said with a chuckle, as if he had hit on just the right response, as if he had scored a point against me.

"The Orosgo Age. What the hell does that mean?" I asked them. My voice sounded like a corpse's voice, even to me. "This perfect world you're going to make. Who has the power in it? Who makes all the decisions? How many people have to die to make it happen?"

"Who said anything about dying?" my mother said, looking around as if she might find the culprit crouching in some corner of the room.

"Don't criticize what you can't understand," murmured my father, singsong. He had wandered from the window to my IV bag now. He was studying it as if it were a work of modern art in a museum.

"Yes, please don't go all Riley on us, Austin," my mother said. Then, looking at her phone, she pointedly changed the subject, saying, "Oh, here's another hysterical email from Bert. It takes almost nothing to set him off these days. He sees Nazis under the bed!"

"Who can blame him nowadays?" my father murmured back.

I stared from one to the other of them. My dead man's stare.

"You haven't even asked who stabbed me," I said.

That seemed to stop them both for a moment. My mother stopped talking. My father stopped wandering around. But only for a moment.

"I'm sure the police will sort it all out," my mother said then, thumbing her phone.

"Yes, the last thing the world needs," my father murmured, "is more paranoia."

MORE PARANOIA.

That night, after the aide cleared my dinner away, I called Riley. I got no answer, not even a voicemail recording. I sent her a text, then an email. No answer. Half an hour later, I called her again. I got no answer again.

I turned off the light and lay in the dark, my gut throbbing. They'd given me a morphine machine for the pain. I could press the button for more meds whenever I needed to. I didn't press it. The meds made me groggy. I wanted my head clear. I wanted to think.

I thought about Riley. My little black-sheep sister. With her straw-colored pigtail braids framing her round baby face.

Don't go all Riley on us, my mother said.

Riley, my brother said, *was bad enough. You think I haven't had to work to keep her alive this long?*

I thought about lying next to her in her bed when she was little. Her big blue eyes inches from my cheek, gazing at me like I was an island of love in her sea of loneliness.

Put Riley to bed, would you, darling? my mother would say.

And I would put Riley to bed and Riley would say, *Tell me one of your stories, Aus.*

So I would lie down next to her and spin one out while she gazed at me like that, like I was an island of love.

I phoned her again and texted her again. No answer. Well, it was only fifteen minutes since I'd tried her before. The last thing the world needed was more paranoia.

I thought of the last time I'd seen her, on the video call. Lying on her bed on her tummy. With her little girl's body. With her white stockinged feet kicking up behind her. And Marco. Pimpy Marco, with his vulpine smile, sitting next to her. His hand on her ass. The bastard.

My eyes filled. The meds—they were making me emotional. But also it was unbearable to think of her as she was when we were kids—*Tell me one of your stories, Aus*—gazing at me from her lonely ocean inches away. To think of her then and to think of her as she was now, with some man always around to use her and abuse her, and her messed-up, lost, empty "video artist" life.

Had she known? About Mom and Dad and Rich and Orosgo? Had she listened to them from her hiding places behind the paneling? Is that what drove her crazy? Because she was crazy, there was no question about that. With her nutty conspiracy theories. Aliens seeking to take over the world with the help of their international human cabal.

I looked at the phone, still in my hands. It couldn't be about that though, could it? Her conspiracy theories. Her crazy videos. *Ouroboros: Dark Dreams of Reality.* That couldn't be why Rich had had to talk Orosgo out of killing her. Could it?

She is getting too close to the truth, Marco had said. *We are very close to exposing the whole conspiracy.*

I remembered how he had said that, and I remembered how he had lifted his hand off my sister's butt just long enough to point to the books on her shelves, the books and the purple crystals and the pyramids and . . .

I straightened up in bed, so quickly my guts seemed to shift within the hollow, wounded place in my belly. The scar there sent up a bright, metallic flash of pain. I grimaced, my hand on the place where the sword had gone in.

I thought: wasn't there something else on those shelves? Yes. A manuscript, tied together with twine. A stack of papers with ragged edges. I thought: ragged edges. As if the pages had been torn out of something.

I remembered the book I had found in the cabinet in Sean Gunther's house. A bright-red binding and gold inlaid letters spelling out the title: *Another Kingdom.* But inside, there was nothing—nothing but shreds of paper, as if the pages had been torn out.

Could those have been the pages on Riley's shelf?

No. No, of course not. That made no sense. It was ridiculous.

But even as I thought that, I was bringing up the video app on my phone. I searched through the app for Riley's video series.

I stared down at the phone, openmouthed.

There was nothing there. No videos. Not even a sign there had once been videos that had since been removed. The kooky chat rooms where people went to discuss the videos—those were gone too. Even the Wikipedia page about the videos was gone.

It was all gone, all of Riley's work, as if it had never existed. The only thing that came up was the Wikipedia page for *Ouroboros*, the word *Ouroboros*. I clicked on it.

"An ancient symbol depicting a serpent or dragon eating its own tail," it said.

I already knew that. Or I had known it at some point. But now that I saw it on the page, I remembered it. I remembered it, and it reminded me of something else too. But what? I searched my foggy brain.

Then it came to me: the painting! Of course. The painting of Wisdom in the Getty Museum, the one just above the painting in Gunther's snapshot of Ellen Evermore, the one I'd been looking at just before my last transition.

There had been cherubs in the painting—little angels—putti. They fluttered around the seated Wisdom figure. One held a mirror representing self-knowledge. One pointed at a book, his finger hovering over the word *kingdom*.

And one—one held a snake coiled in a perfect circle. A symbol of eternity. Ouroboros.

Riley? Is that what the clue meant? Was Ellen Evermore trying to tell me that she had passed the book on to Riley? Had she torn the pages out of the binding at Gunther's house and given the manuscript to my sister to keep it safe from Orosgo until I could track it down?

With trembling fingers, I called Riley again.

No answer.

There was no answer the next day either. And no one came to visit me in the hospital, not Rich, not my parents, not anyone— though Jane Janeway sent me an animated Get Well e-card with valentine hearts that rose on the page like bubbles. She had heard about the stabbing on the news, she said. She said she had tried to come see me, but the police wouldn't let her in.

So for the time being, only the cop at the door kept me company. I knew now he was there to guard me, not arrest me. I knew that because Detective Lord and Detective Graciano had told the news media I wasn't a suspect. They hadn't named me, and they hadn't revealed I was the same man who had been stabbed at the Getty in an apparently random and unconnected incident. They just said they had interviewed the man and woman in the security photo taken at Gunther's gate and they were no longer considered suspects. The reporters didn't ask much more about it.

That was it. I'd been cleared. Cleared and forgotten. Just like that. Just as quickly as Riley's videos had vanished.

How powerful was Orosgo anyway? How high, how far, how wide did his influence reach?

THE NEXT DAY, some of the gang from Hitchcock's dropped by: Schuyler and Chad Valentine and Wren Yen. Wexler didn't come because—said Schuyler—it would've harmed his burgeoning reputation as a Hollywood dickhead. But Schuyler knew that wasn't why I looked disappointed when they came in, why I stole a glance around her massive presence to see if anyone else was coming through the door behind her.

"She had to go to New Zealand," she told me gruffly. "It was all of a sudden. Alexis is meeting a director there. You know what she's like."

I nodded. I pretended it didn't matter, that it was fine.

"She said to say hello," Schuyler added grudgingly. "She says she'll try to call. She says she's afraid of disturbing your rest with the time difference and everything." I nodded again. Then she confessed the whole truth: "She says to send her love."

Later, when it was time for them to leave, Schuyler let Chad and Wren go out before her. Then she leaned in very close to me. Her cherubic and furious face was terrifying at that distance.

"What the fuck is going on with you?" she said in a hissing whisper. "First your head is practically caved in, then it's suddenly fine. Then you're wanted for murder. Then you . . . "

"I wasn't wanted for . . . "

"Then you get stabbed," she said. "Stabbed! At the Getty? No one gets stabbed at the Getty, Austin. It's a fucking museum!"

I started back against the headboard as she lifted one hand to me, clawlike, as if she was going to rip my face off. I really think she would have done it, too, if I hadn't looked so weak and pitiful. But her hand sunk down then, though her eyes went on burning with rage.

"She's been crying," she whispered. "You understand me. She thinks I don't hear her but she's crying because she's so worried about you. And if you feel good about that, so help me God, I will kill you right here and now."

Well, I did feel good about it a little, but I felt bad about it too. I didn't want to make Jane cry. I just wanted to possess her body and soul and fill her womb with a new generation. Even just to see her and chat would've been nice.

"Asshole," said Schuyler.

And she turned her elephantine bulk away and thundered to the door.

"Tell her I'm fine, Schuyler."

"Fuck you," she said, giving me the finger as she stormed out of the room.

When she was gone, I called Riley. There was no answer. I called Rich. I got his voicemail. I left a message.

"Get the hell over here," I said.

BUT RICH DIDN'T get the hell over, even though I called him several times again. Another day went by and then another. There was no sign of him.

I was starting to feel better now, starting to get stronger. The stitching on my ribs was still ugly, the shaved spot white and pale, like my flesh was rotten. But the wound no longer gave me that bizarre feeling it had given me at first, as if I were empty in there, as if my innards were rattling around in a space too large for them. Schuyler went to my apartment for me and brought me some clothes to wear: track pants, sweatshirts. I started taking twice-daily exercise walks along the hallways. I was even off the intravenous antibiotics, so I could walk without carting my IV pole around.

The cop who was guarding me—whichever uniformed patrolman happened to be on duty that particular day—would walk along behind me. Whenever I'd glance back, he'd be there, following me, his eyes scanning the nurses and doctors and patients and visitors who passed along the halls.

"Who are we looking for?" I asked him.

Stone-faced, he shook his head, said nothing.

That's how I knew they hadn't found Sera yet, that Sera was still out there somewhere, still after me.

SOON, I WAS cantering up and down the stairs in the stairwell. The cop still followed me. I could hear him panting above me on my way down, below me on my way back up. I would do the routine once in the morning and once in the evening. My wound burned a little as I worked up speed, but the painful throbbing was gone.

On my tenth day, my last day at the hospital, when I returned from my evening jaunt, I stepped into my room and found Rich there waiting for me. He was standing at the window across the room, his back to the door, his hands in the pockets of his sky-blue slacks. His bearded face was reflected on the pane, where night had fallen.

He must've seen me reflected there too. He turned around before I even spoke. His suit was impeccably pressed. His golden tie seemed to flow naturally from his golden beard. Only his eyes betrayed anxiety, laced with red, ringed with gray.

We looked at one another silently for a moment, then I went into the bathroom to get a towel. I wiped the sweat off my face as I stepped back out into the room. I noticed I didn't hesitate anymore when I went over a threshold. I wasn't afraid of being whisked back to Galiana, or at least I wasn't thinking about it. After ten days here in the hospital, the whole Galianan experience seemed completely unreal to me. I had even begun to wonder if maybe the lie I'd told the police was true: maybe it was Sera who stabbed me. Maybe that first thought I'd had on waking here in the hospital—that Galiana had been some sort of coma dream—maybe that was true as well.

I lowered the towel. I looked at Rich.

"Where is she?" I said. He pretended not to understand me, and I said, "C'mon, man. Riley. Where is she?"

He averted his eyes. He shrugged. "I don't know."

"Is she all right?"

"I don't know."

"Well, is she alive, damn it?"

"Damn it, I don't know!"

He turned his back on me again, looking out the window. I moved over to the bed. I threw my towel down on it angrily.

Rich muttered, "What did you expect, Austin?"

"I didn't expect anything," I said. "Because until now, I didn't realize my parents and my brother were agents of an international conspiracy to—"

"Keep your voice down."

"Well, to what? To do what? Install space aliens in government? Are the aliens real?"

I meant this as a bitter joke. At least I thought I did. At this point, I wasn't entirely sure. I found myself waiting tensely for his answer.

After a moment or two, he snorted. "Thank God for the aliens," he said. "It's the aliens that saved her."

I let out a sigh of relief. No aliens, then. Well, that was something, anyway. My sister's videos were such a crazy version of Orosgo's crazy plans that even Orosgo wasn't crazy enough to take them seriously. That's how Rich had managed to keep her alive. Until now, at least.

My brother still didn't turn around. He kept on staring out the window through his own reflection at the night beyond.

"He wasn't always like this," he said after another little pause. Our eyes met on the pane. "Serge. It's only recently he's gotten like this. You know, with old age coming on. The prospect of the end."

"Don't kid yourself," I told him. "He didn't create Sera overnight. That took time. God alone knows what he did to that child."

He didn't answer right away. I took that for an admission.

"Even great men have flaws," he said finally.

I laughed. Mirthlessly. "Jesus Christ, Rich."

He swung around to face me. His voice was firm and angry, but his eyes . . . I could see all his doubt and decency in his eyes. Whatever Orosgo had drawn him into, Rich knew he was in it too deep.

"Is it so wrong to believe that things can be better than they are?" he asked me. "A world without war, where no one's bigger or better than anyone else?"

I didn't know what to say. He was my successful, brilliant big brother. The guy wrote books, for crying out loud. He was interviewed on TV. He gave speeches about his big ideas on how to change the world. People paid to hear him. Me, I was a Hollywood nothing. I hardly even followed the news day to day. How could I tell him about what I'd seen on the streets of Eastrim, the heretics and traitors in their cages, the guards torturing them to death while the degenerate, bloodthirsty crowds cheered them on?

Iron seduced them into rebellion with promises of a perfect country . . . where each is equal in all things to another," Tauratanio had told me.

They tried to kill the wisest queen in all the world in the name of that illusion, Magdala had said.

But what did it all mean, here, in Los Angeles, in real life? I didn't know.

Still, Rich reacted as if I'd spoken out loud, as if I'd accused him of something. "Well, what do you do for anybody?" he said irritably. "Huh? Mr. Show Biz. I mean, you think what I believe is so terrible. What do you believe?"

The question drew my gaze to him. I was still thinking about Shadow Wood and the forest king and queen. I remembered how they said to me that Queen Elinda had sent me to them because they needed fighting men of brave heart and right belief. Me, ha ha. Austin Lively. A fighting man of brave heart and right belief.

So . . . what did I believe? It was a good question.

I met my brother's eyes and he met mine. "What's in the book, Rich?" I asked him. "*Another Kingdom.* Why does he want it so badly?"

He made a little noise of frustration, shaking his head. "He's obsessed with it. I don't know. It's like . . . he thinks it has some sort of power or something."

"Power? What sort of—"

"I don't know. I don't know. He's old, Austin. He's old, and he's afraid of death."

"Oh, he's afraid of more than that, brother. I mean, has he told you his whole story about the all-night conversation in the dacha with the cowl guy?"

I couldn't interpret the gesture he made in response. It either meant he'd never heard the story or he'd heard so many stories he couldn't recall one over another. I'm not sure.

"Do you know where it is?" he asked me. "The book. Do you know where the book is?"

The image of Riley flashed in my mind again. Riley lying on the bed, Marco sitting beside her, gesturing toward the bookshelf. Was the manuscript there really *Another Kingdom*?

Well, if it was, I wasn't going to tell Rich, that was for sure. Whatever else happened, whatever happened to me, I had to find my kid sister before Orosgo's people did—any of Orosgo's people, including my mother and father and Rich himself. I had to get to her first to make sure she was safe.

I made a helpless gesture. Shook my head.

"Are you sure?" Rich said. "I mean, don't fuck around about this, Austin. Serge can be a good friend but . . . "

I sneered. "But what? But cross him and he kills you? Don't do what he says and he kills you? I thought you'd convinced him to spare me and throw Sera under the bus."

He started to answer but thought better of it. He turned away again, back to the window, back to the night.

"It's a big bus," he said quietly. "If Sera should happen to turn up and murder you, and then . . . " His voice trailed off.

"And then if Sera gets arrested or killed by the police." I finished the thought when his voice trailed off. "It takes care of a lot of problems. Is that why you came here tonight? Is that what you came to tell me?"

Rich didn't answer. He just stood looking out at the darkness.

I gave another derisive laugh. "The Orosgo Age," I said.

THAT WAS MY last night in the hospital. The doctors had wanted to keep me another day, but I had to go. I couldn't reach Riley on the phone or by email, and I couldn't just sit there and wait for her to turn up dead. I was still a bit weak, but I felt strong enough to do what I had to do. I talked the docs into springing me.

I fell asleep that night around ten o'clock. I had a dream—a terrible dream. I dreamt I was in the hallway of a gothic mansion. I dreamt I was in a sword fight like in some old knights-in-armor movie on TV. I dreamt I killed a man, ran him through with my sword, and watched at close quarters as the life and the hope of life drained from his face. But then, dreamlike, the next moment, the dying man was me. It was me with the blade buried deep in my body. It was me feeling all the soul-light flickering into blackness. I knew the last thing I would ever see was the triumphant face of the man who'd killed me, filling my vision. The last thing I would ever hear was his roaring, victorious laughter . . .

I woke up with my heart hammering, my pillow soaked with sweat. I lay staring up at the ceiling. The lights in the room were off, but the light from the hall came in through the open door and everything was visible in the gray shadows.

My dream came back to me—in fragments, but vivid enough for me to piece them together. Was that what had really happened to me? A sword fight in a gothic manse? Or was it an assassin outside the museum? Either scenario was too crazy to be real. And yet, if either scenario was unreal, then what did that mean about me? About my brain? About my sanity?

My eyes filled in the semidarkness. I wasn't sure of anything, not anything. What the hell was happening to me? What the hell was happening to my life?

Miserable, I rolled my head on the pillow so I could look out the door at the lighted hallway. I saw right away that something was wrong, but it took me a moment to figure out what it was.

It was the chair, the chair out in the hall by the door. It was empty. The cop was gone.

I SWUNG OUT of bed, my gut aching. I pulled my track pants off the chair and put them on. I stepped through the room's shadows out into the hall.

The whole hall was empty! The entire hospital hall from one end to the other: empty. The questions went through my mind again: How powerful was Orosgo? How far did his influence reach? Could he have me killed right here, right now, with no one around to stop him?

Somewhere, out of sight around the corner to my right, I heard a swinging door pushed open. I heard it swing shut. I heard footsteps coming my way. I stood there, indecisive, helpless, almost surrendered to my fate, as the footsteps came closer and closer.

Then a nurse came around the corner, reading charts on her tablet. She glanced up and smiled at me briefly as she went past.

The hallway was empty again. Quiet. I went back into my room.

IN THE MORNING, an aide came to fetch me with a wheelchair. It was hospital policy, he said. I wasn't allowed to walk to the front door on my own. I sat in the chair with an overnight bag in my lap. As the aide pushed me along, I watched the faces rolling past.

And the faces watched me. Or at least, I thought they were watching. I thought there was more than one nurse and doctor and aide and security guard who followed my passing with expressions that blended fear and guilt and pity. It could have been my imagination. It must have been.

We rounded the semicircular reception desk and reached the big glass doors of the hospital exit. The aide brought the chair to a stop. I stood up. I said goodbye to him. He was a young, cheerful, caramel-colored guy, six feet tall and broad shouldered. He gave me a grave nod of farewell.

"Be careful out there, my man," he said. Then he winked and turned around and wheeled the chair around the reception desk and out of sight.

Be careful. I wondered why he had said that. But really, anyone could have said it, just to be nice.

I turned back toward the exit. I approached the doors. I put my hand on the metal bar that opened them. I hesitated and looked through the glass, surveying the scene.

The hospital was part of a medical complex, a small maze of streets and structures set apart from the traffic-packed boulevards and leafy residential lanes of Beverly Hills. It was like a small town set in the midst of a big city. Beyond the doors, across the street, medicos in scrubs and patients in day clothes walked on the sidewalk, passing by the open maw of a blocky parking structure set between a tower of glass and a tower of white stone. There were cars parked by the curb and cars and delivery trucks cruising along the street. Everything looked normal out there, even serene.

I pushed outside.

It was a fine autumn day, warm and mellow, bright and clear. My plan was to get some air and exercise after my long confinement by strolling out to the main road and then summoning a car on my phone.

But before I took a single step, there was a piercing tone—a series of piercing tones. I jumped and stiffened. But it was only the warning signal from a van that was backing up from my left, edging slowly toward me.

Smiling ruefully at my own nerves, I stood and watched as the van drew up in front of me. It was a white van with pictures on the side of loaves of bread. I guessed it was delivering fresh baked goods to the hospital cafes.

Still emitting those sharp, high tones, the van backed slowly past me until its large windshield came into view. The windshield was dark and reflected the street in front of it.

I saw Sera's image on the glass.

19

THE ASSASSIN WAS STANDING ON THE CORNER TO MY left, standing at the corner of the white building there, watching me.

I held my breath. I spun to face him. I caught one glimpse of the feline face beneath the boy-short blond hair, one glimpse of the girl-slender legs in hug-tight jeans and the man torso in a leather jacket with a red T-shirt underneath. He was smiling a louche, sensuous smile. I knew he was there to kill me.

One glimpse. One second. Then he was gone. Slipping behind the building and out of sight.

Had I really seen him? Or was I worked up to such a state of suspense my mind had conjured him out of nothing? I wasn't sure. For the last few days, I'd thought I was being transported back and forth between LA and a land of nymphs and ogres. How the hell could I be sure of anything?

My heart was hammering just as rapidly as it had hammered after my nightmare last night. Maybe this was a nightmare too.

I swallowed hard. I turned away from the spot where Sera had been standing. I started walking quickly in the opposite direction, toward the boulevard. I tried to be cool about it, but I was not cool.

I kept looking back over my shoulder to make sure the kitten-faced killer wasn't following me or hadn't snuck up right behind me.

There was no sign of him. I kept walking.

Then I reached the corner and saw him again.

He must have moved quick as thought. Somehow, he had circled the block and come out from behind a medical building across the next street. I was sure I saw him this time. He was standing by the point of a wall, grinning at me. At this distance, I could even see the threat of death in his lunatic eyes.

A truck rumbled between us and, like in a conjuring trick, Sera vanished once again. The truck went past and he was gone, just like that.

I cursed. Enough. This was no dream. I shifted my overnight bag to my left hand, took my phone out of my pants pocket with my right. Slipping the bag handle over my wrist, I clumsily worked the business card the detectives had given me out of my shirt pocket. I tapped in the number.

"Detective Lord," came the big woman's matter-of-fact voice.

"This is Austin Lively," I said.

I could almost feel the detective sit up and take notice. I could hear the sudden focus in her tone. "Yes?"

"He's here. The man who stabbed me. The man who killed Gunther. He's following me."

There was a long pause. It was unnerving. What the hell was there to pause about? This was an emergency, wasn't it? Shouldn't she be sending help?

"Where are you?" asked Detective Lord carefully.

I heard my own voice spiral higher with growing panic. "I'm just outside the hospital. Just at the corner of San Vicente." I looked longingly across the boulevard. I wanted to keep moving, to get out of there. But the traffic light was red. There was nowhere to go.

"Do you see him now?" Detective Lord asked me.

"Not right now. But he was there just a second ago. Twice. I think he's toying with me. He shows himself, then disappears. You said to call . . . "

Again, that pause. It made my stomach drop. What the hell was going on with her? Even in the fine, clear weather, I felt a clammy sweat break out on the back of my neck.

"Hello?" I said.

"So you don't see him right now," said Detective Lord. She was still speaking very carefully, very slowly.

"Not right this minute but . . . "

There was a beat of silence. Then Detective Lord said, "Uh huh."

The light changed. I started moving across the wide avenue. Somehow, I already knew what Lord was going to say next. All the same, when she actually said it, I felt my whole body fill with a bleak gray atmosphere that I recognized as despair.

"Well . . . " she began—and now she put on a bland, official, mock businesslike tone. "We can't really do anything if you don't see him at the moment. What I would suggest: why don't you give me a call if you see him again, and we'll try to check it out."

An answer started to rise up into my throat, but it stuck there like a solid thing, like plastic letters all jammed up and jumbled together in my gullet. I wanted to cry out to her: *If I see him again? He's a murderer! If I see him again, I'll be dead!* But I didn't say that. I didn't say anything. I knew there was no point. Detective Lord had her instructions from on high. I hadn't found *Another Kingdom.* To Serge Orosgo, I was now just a loose end, another witness who could link him to Sean Gunther's murder, a stumbling block on the way to Utopia. In other words: a dead man.

I cut the connection. To hell with her. To hell with the cops. I pocketed the phone. I upped my walking speed.

Up ahead of me, there was a construction site, a massive indoor shopping mall either undergoing renovations or being torn down,

I wasn't sure which. One half of it was a sleek white stone-and-glass commercial palace several stories high, the other half was a skeletal ruin of dirt, girders, cement, and rebar rising above wooden street-level fencing. Here and there in the fence were open corridors and dark doors, mysterious entrances and exits in and out of nowhere. It was an immense, haunting monument to failure or promise, one or the other. I eyed it as I approached, wondering if I might duck into the mess of it and make my escape.

I reached the curb. There was a trash can on the corner. I dumped in my overnight bag. It was weighing me down, slowing me up. I glanced back over my shoulder and took a long scan of the landscape behind me. The traffic rushing along the big avenue. The medical complex across the way. No Sera. The assassin was gone.

I faced forward—and there he was.

How the hell did he keep doing that? Suddenly, he was right in front of me, sashaying along the length of the mall fencing in that aggressively feminine way of his. The motion made his short blond hair bounce gaily around his feline features. He smiled at me, sweetly, his bright eyes mad.

There was no one else on the sidewalk. This was LA. No one walked here. People were in their cars, grinding, honking, rushing past. Here, it was just him and me converging quickly.

He slipped his right hand into his jacket pocket. The pocket bulged and stiffened, protruding in my direction. Was it my imagination, or could I see the outline of a gun muzzle shaping the fabric? I did not think it was my imagination.

I figured I only had a single second before he pulled the trigger. No one would hear the muffled shot with all this traffic roaring past. I would simply wilt to the sidewalk like a dying flower. Who knew how long it would be before someone even noticed I was dead?

Instinctively, I turned to avoid the shot—a useless gesture. But in turning, I saw an entryway. A sign: *Escalators to Shops*. Without breaking stride, I ducked in.

I was in a high, high stairwell of metal and cement. Zig-zagging flight after flight of escalators rolled up alongside the green walls. There were people standing on each slanting length of moving stairs, riding up from the parking structure beneath the mall or descending back down into it.

I got on the first escalator up and started climbing the metal steps, weaving between the shoppers who were standing still. I glanced back behind me as I rose—and yes, there was Sera, standing below at the street-level doorway, watching me ascend.

His smile was gone. His pouting lips were taut. His cat's eyes were flashing. I knew from the look of him that he had, in fact, been about to kill me on the street. He was frustrated I'd managed to dodge him. He wouldn't kill me here with all these witnesses—or would he? Would anything stop him now? How crazy was he anyway?

I wasn't sure. I climbed the moving stairs. Up to the top of the first escalator, then whipping around onto the second, then climbing to the top of that to the third, pushing past the customers the whole way. I nearly tripped and fell as the next escalator ended. I stumbled off and saw an open doorway. I dashed through it.

I emerged from the darkness of the well into bright daylight: a scene both dazzling and bizarre. The mall seemed to have been cut in half. To my right was a vast expanse of bright white floors and storefront windows. Above me were rings of gallery walks under cascading skylight panels that were full of the bright blue sky. To my left, through a towering wall of protective glass, an open construction site was on display: a pit of dirt littered with abandoned bulldozers, a half-completed structure of iron girders and wooden planks, empty platforms on dangling pulleys between unidentifiable structures of cement. Either they were tearing this place down while shoppers rushed to consume the last of the merchandise, or building the place up while shoppers scrambled hungrily over what was already there.

The mall half was crowded with people, women mostly, walking purposefully past sleekly dressed mannequins, past window displays of glittering purses and jewels, past spanking new sports equipment and workout machines and electronics and toys and a featureless cafe of tall bland chairs and squat bland tables. Tinkling pop music filled the high spaces like a colorless mesmeric gas and settled over the shoppers like a pall.

I tried to vanish. I wove myself into the fabric of the crowd and threaded my way through it, trying to hide among the moving bodies and confound the searching gaze of my pursuer.

I looked around for him as I went. I couldn't see him anywhere. Maybe it was he who was confounding me.

I pushed on along the glassed-in edge of the open pit, hoping to find an exit, hoping to duck out of there before he caught me. But the place was built like a trap. They do that with malls. They make sure you have to walk the length of them before you can exit. The idea is, once you start shopping, you have to shop everywhere, shop the merchandise to its dregs before you can reach the open air again. I kept pushing through the crowd, but my wound had weakened me. I was already out of breath and losing energy quickly. I wasn't sure how long I could keep up my pace.

I almost made it all the way. I made it to where the shops curled around to meet the glassed-in construction site. There was a last string of well-stocked storefronts on one side, the wilderness of the open pit on the other, and between them a narrow hallway—a way out—maybe twenty yards ahead.

I pulled to a stop. I had to. I had to rest. I stood amidst the swiftly passing clots of people, my chest heaving as I gulped in air.

"Ausss-tiiiin. O-oh, Ausss-tiiiin."

He sang my name like plainsong, low and rhythmic, at such a key it was somehow audible above the footsteps and the voices and the pall of tuneless music. The sound sent a jagged bolt of terror through me. I raised my head.

He was right in front of me, coming out of the exit hall. How had he done it? How had he gotten around me so fast?

Never mind, there he was. Strutting toward me like a model on a catwalk, completely unimpeded by the wave of shoppers washing over him. They jostled each other, but not him, never him. He just passed right through them like a shark—like the ghost of a shark—coming at me.

He was seconds away. Moving fast. Drawing his hand out of his pocket so that already I could see the black grip of the gun between his fingers. I looked for a way out. To my left was the window on the pit. To my right: a shop. A storefront window. Two dozen TV screens within. Moving scenes of rushing silver rivers, waving meadows of yellow-green grass and purple Alpine mountains covered in white snow. Shelves and shelves of incomprehensible gewgaws and flashing gizmos, glittering contraptions and devices and their multi-colored cases and accessories. A confusion of electronic riches. No clue, in my panic, what any of it was.

Who cared? I just wanted to live. I charged toward it. Reached the store in two steps. Heard a woman scream. Thought: She must have spotted the gun.

I heaved the glass door open, expecting the blast any second, the searing jolt of the bullet, the long plummet into black and bloody death.

But I made it. I was through the door. Running . . .

In my mind, I kept on running, but no, I was getting nowhere. The world spun wildly. Disoriented, I thought the shop had tipped over and spilled me onto the floor. I was on the floor, anyway. On my back. In a pool of blood. So much blood. Sera must have shot me. No one could lose so much blood and live.

I heard another scream, a high scream ragged with anguish. Then Lady Betheray flung herself down on top of me, her tearstained face smeared with gore.

"No! You've killed him!"

I was back in Galiana, back in Netherdale, in the bedroom, on the floor where I had fallen after Sir Aravist kicked me off the length of his sword and through the door.

Hearing Lady Betheray scream, seeing the anguish on her face, I almost sat up, almost embraced her. I would have—I would have done it on instinct—if I hadn't been so disoriented and confused by the sudden change. But as I lay there dazed, as I only slowly began to realize what had happened to me, I caught myself. I kept still. I went on lying there.

Because I should have been dead. Right? I would have been dead if I hadn't just received ten days of twenty-first-century health care complete with expert surgery and enough antibiotics to kill every infection within a mile of me. Here in Galiana, though, Sir Aravist must have thought he'd killed me. Of course he did.

I let my eyes slip nearly closed. I stopped breathing. For another second—only a second—Lady Betheray bent over me, sobbing.

Then Sir Aravist loomed above us both. His eyes were hot. His cheeks were scarlet. He grabbed her arm. She cried out as he hauled her brutally away from me.

I turned my head just enough so I could watch it all through half-parted eyelids.

Sir Aravist was dragging her across the floor toward the four-poster bed. She struggled in his grip.

"Let go of me, you animal!"

But she was helpless. He was just too much stronger. He yanked her up and tossed her onto the four-poster as if she were a rag doll. She came up immediately into a sitting position.

"How dare you, you—"

"Shut up!" He slapped her.

The shock of the blow made her go still, wide-eyed.

"That's it! Not so fine a lady now, are you?" he growled.

"My husband . . . " she whispered fiercely.

Then she gasped as he grabbed a handful of her raven hair and pulled her toward him. "Don't you understand? Your husband's done with you, bitch," he said. "He gave you to me to do what I like with. To throw you out like the trash you are. But first . . . " He pulled her face to his and mashed his lips against her. She tried to turn away but he wouldn't let her, and the kiss hit her mouth like a blow. She tried to claw at his face. He pulled back and slapped her again, twice, a backhand then a forehand, harder. He leaned down over her, close.

"But first," he said again, very softly this time, "first I'm going to pay you for every superior sneer you ever gave me. I'm going to pull you down off your high horse and show you what my lowborn body can do to the likes of you."

With that, he hurled her back onto the mattress. She cried out pitiably and tried to roll away from him. He climbed on top of her and pinned her on her back. Then he seized the front of her gown and violently tore it open while she cried out again. He forced himself down on top of her as she struggled. Holding her by the hair, he buried his face against her breast.

She let out a ragged and awful cry: "God help me!"

By now, I had my sword. I had groped around and found it on the floor right by my hand. My hand, my arm, my body were all still clothed in the magic mercurial armor Queen Elinda had left for me in the Shadow Wood oak. It flowed with my body as I moved slowly—slowly so as not to draw attention to myself. My fingers closed around the sword's hilt.

I began to climb to my feet—still slowly. If Sir Aravist saw me, if he had time to turn, time to draw his own weapon, he would drive his blade into me just as surely as he had the first time.

But he didn't see me. He didn't turn. He reared up above Lady Betheray and tore her dress again and then again until it was in rags around her.

She let out a sob of anguish and despair. "No, don't."

The sound of her misery went through me like a kind of fire. I rose off the floor like a flame. I stood. Sword in hand, I started moving toward them where they struggled on the bed.

Sir Aravist looked down at Betheray's nakedness. He laughed. "You're no fine lady now, are you? This is the truth of you. This is how the world's supposed to be."

It was just then I reached him. I stretched out my hand. My fingers closed around his collar.

The captain of the guard let out a broken little noise of surprise and perplexity: "What . . . ?"

Before he could resist, I hauled him off the woman and off the bed and spun him toward me.

His face went as gray as the statue on the lid of a crypt. His eyes went as wide and white as supper plates. "But how . . . ?" he said.

I drove my blade straight through the center of him.

"The miracle of modern medicine," I said. "Now die, you piece of shit."

Skewered, Sir Aravist hung gaping on my blade. He tried to speak, but only his eyes could tell his horror: he'd been struck clean through by the risen specter of a dead man. His last sight on earth must have seemed to him like the very proof of hell and justice. For another second, our faces were inches apart, his agony and terror that close to me, and my hatred just as close to him.

Then he was gone wherever dead men go.

The dangling weight of his corpse drew my blade point toward the ground, and when the sword was slanted down like that, the body slid off it and fell to the floor with a liquid thud.

I stood over him, looked at him. I remembered in a flash the shock I had felt the first time I killed a man—moments ago in Galiana time, but a week and a half since to me. I remembered the moral immensity of it, the cosmic immensity of snuffing out a life, of ending a consciousness.

That was gone now. I was a different man. Maybe crueler, maybe just harder in this harder world, I couldn't say. All I knew was Aravist had struck Lady Betheray, he had tried to rape Lady Betheray, and I did not give a damn about him or his cosmic being or his consciousness or anything. He had earned this, and if I was the one to pay him off, then good for me. Let God forgive him. I didn't.

I turned to Betheray. Still lying on the bed, she was staring at me, as shocked to see me standing there as Aravist had been, so shocked she did not move to cover her nakedness.

Oh, it was beautiful, her nakedness. Milky and rose and shapely as distant hills, decked only with the golden chain and locket at her ivory throat. And I—I was full and flush with bloodlust and revenge and the sight of her filled me and aroused me and made me breathless.

I averted my eyes from her and sheathed my sword.

As I did, the blade seemed to melt into the armor, and the armor seemed to melt into me, and it was suddenly gone. I was dressed in my strange Galiana clothes again. Only there was a ragged gash in the center of my vest now, the place where Aravist's sword had gone in.

I stared into the candlelit shadows for a long moment until I had control of myself.

"Come on," I said then, my voice hoarse. "Dress yourself. Let's get out of here."

WE LEFT SIR Aravist dead in the room. We went down the hall past the other two corpses. Lady Betheray wore a belted robe now. She held a candelabra to light the way.

I followed her to a sweeping, majestic staircase, and down we went by flickering candlelight. At the bottom, we traveled along another night-dark hall. Went into another room finally, another bedroom, larger than the last, the master bedroom, I thought. It was vast, with large windows on the moonlit sky and cushions on the window seats and chairs against the walls and a canopied four-poster bed even bigger than the one upstairs.

Betheray set the candelabra on a table and turned to face me and I faced her. We stood like that a long time, silent, gaze on gaze. Her face was bruised from Aravist's blows. Her cheeks were still streaked with the tears she'd cried. But she was calm. I would have thought she'd be—I don't know—hysterical, sobbing, trembling, in shock. But she wasn't. She was calm and steady and regal and very fine.

"Are you . . . ?" she said after a while. Her voice was calm too.

And I said, "What? Am I what?"

"Are you . . . a phantom? Are you real? Are you alive?"

"I'm real. I'm alive," I said. "Look at me."

"But he killed you. I saw him kill you, Austin."

"No." I glanced down at the gash in my clothing. I gave a little laugh. "Well . . . almost, I guess."

"The blood though. There was so much blood."

I searched the air above me for an answer. I hadn't really thought about what to say. "My armor," I told her. "The king of the forest gave it to me. It has some magic in it. It healed me." It was the only thing I could think of on short notice.

It seemed to satisfy her though. She nodded. "Yes. Tauratanio has always been a friend of the queen and freedom. He's with us."

I smiled. I nodded back. It was kind of crazy when you thought about it. Magic and the forest king—that made sense to her. But if I'd told her about the hospital and antibiotics, she wouldn't have understood what I was talking about.

She went on standing there, studying me, thoughtful, silent. Then she closed the gap between us with a gliding step. She lifted her hand to my cheek, her cool hand. I leaned against it, comforted and stirred.

"He was going to kill me," she said. "Aravist. He was going to . . . use me and then kill me." She was still calm. Still regal.

I nodded. "Yes, he was."

"Winton—Lord Iron. My husband . . . gave me to him. Said he could do it."

"I know. I'm sorry, Beth."

We stood another long time, her hand on my cheek, my eyes on her eyes, and me breathing, trying not to pull her to me, thinking it would be wrong so soon after her trauma.

"But you . . . " she said. "You have never been anything but my hero." And then, as if it were an official decree, she proclaimed, "I am free of my vows."

And she came to me and kissed me.

There was no resisting this, not for me. I pulled her into my arms. Now we were together with my hands inside her open robe, and the feel of her flesh radiating through my fingers into my core. Kissing her, I backed her to the bed and she folded down on it and I folded down on top of her. My fingers twined with her raven hair, and my lips were at her breast so that it occurred to me I was in the exact same position Sir Aravist had been in a few minutes ago.

The only differences were my devotion and the free consent of her willing spirit.

20

FOR A LOVELY STRETCH OF NUMBERLESS MINUTES, WE lay together side by side beneath the canopy. Betheray had her head on my chest and her hair spilling over me and her softness pressed against me, and it was bliss. I didn't think at all, not for a long while. And then I did. And what I thought—what I wondered—was: *Who am I?* You know? That thing she said to me, that wonderful thing, that thing every man must want to hear, I think, from a woman like her: "You have never been anything but my hero." It wasn't true. Was it? That I had never been anything but. Hadn't I been other things? Hadn't I also been the Los Angeles man, the whining, lost failure of a Hollywood nothing who had come to this place through . . . God only knew through what? A brain tumor? A drug overdose? Magic? Madness? Really, God only knew. Another second, another hour, another day—who could say?—and I'd be back in LA running through that mall with Sera after me and I'd be that guy again. And I would know him as myself as I had always known him, while this guy—this guy right here who had braved monsters and pulled the sword from the oak tree and battled Sir Aravist and his men, this guy with this amazing woman in his arms—well, to be honest, I barely recognized him.

Still, here I was and I was him and we were each other. For now, at least. I did not know what to make of it. I did not know anymore which one of us was really me.

While I was thinking these things, Lady Betheray trailed her fingers down over my chest to my center, to the sickly white patch about the size of a saucer. She touched the ugly scar where they had stitched me up.

"It's . . . strange," she said. "It looks like you were sewn together. It doesn't look at all like magic."

I kissed her hair. "There are different kinds of magic, I guess."

My face still in her raven tresses, I breathed in deep. And all at once, with the musky perfume of her, there came another flood of Galianan memories, just as when she had walked past me in the tribunal hall. In the dark of my brain, there was a series of flashes. Images of events I had never lived through but that nonetheless were preserved in my mind, as if somehow I had come into my own story here midway.

I saw a tavern in the dark, a pewter tankard of frothing ale. There was the smell of drunkenness, the voices of drunken men, and then—a woman in the doorway, her face covered by a low-slung hood . . .

"You were right," I said softly.

"What do you mean?" said Betheray.

I saw the woman standing by me where I sat. Her head was down, her face hidden. Slowly, she looked up at me . . . I saw her frightened eyes . . . her hand coming out from beneath her cloak, an envelope in her fingers . . .

"Curtin did put a spell on Lady Kata," I said. "Lord Iron seduced her. She was lonely."

"Yes, of course. Her husband had been ill for so long. He was never a real husband to her. Winton took advantage."

"And once Kata had given in to him, he had Curtin go to work on her mind just like he did on yours. He used sex and magic to control her. Because he wanted to get the talisman."

Lady Betheray gave a little gasp of understanding. She tried to turn to me, but I pressed my face deeper into her hair. I drew in the scent of her, and with the scent, I set off a fresh set of flashing memories: *the envelope with Lady Kata's seal in yellow wax, the scrawled message on the page* . . .

"The talisman," Betheray said. "Kata was the one who had it all along!"

"The two of you were the only people the queen could trust to keep it for her. Her two ladies-in-waiting. She trusted you would bring the talisman to the emperor so he would know to come at the head of his armies to liberate you. She gave it to Kata because—"

"Because she knew my husband would get hold of it if she gave it to me."

"Yes. So when Lord Iron realized you didn't have it . . . "

"Of course. He guessed that Kata did."

"Kata gave in to him at first. But once she realized what he was really after, she fought him. She fought the spell, I mean. She resisted. She wouldn't tell him where the talisman was or even admit she had it. She gave herself to him, but she wouldn't give him that."

"She loved the queen more than anything," said Betheray proudly. "Even more than herself."

"She knew the talisman was the kingdom's only hope. No matter what Iron did, no matter how Curtin twisted her mind, she wouldn't tell them where it was."

"Austin." Now Betheray succeeded in pulling away from me. She leaned back, her face still close to my face. She lay her cool hand on my cheek again. "Austin, how do you know these things?"

As the scent of her receded, so the memories began to fade. A few last flashing images—*the tower stairs, Kata's frightened face at the crack in the door*—and they were gone. I leaned close to Betheray and drew in another breath of her, but the effect was over.

I was about to tell her the truth, about to tell her I could not remember anything else, when something else came to me.

I thought of Jane. Jane Janeway in Hitchcock's. I felt an interior punch of guilt as the image of her came into my mind, her sweet face flushed with pleasure at having helped me. I could imagine how that same sweet face would fall if she saw me here like this. Was it cheating to be with Betheray when I had never declared my feelings to Jane? Was it cheating even if I was in a fairyland brain-tumor hallucination that probably didn't really exist in the first place?

I couldn't work it all out now. I just remembered what Jane had said to me about Ellen Evermore: *If the woman actually wants your hero to find this thing, but she's in hiding because she's afraid of her enemies, would it be plausible for her to find a way to slip the hero a clue?*

That was it. That was what had happened. Jane had not only solved the mystery in Los Angeles, she had solved the mystery here at the same time. I remembered. She did leave a clue. Not Ellen Evermore, I mean, but Lady Kata, Lady Kata too.

"When Curtin forced her to lie to you," I said, "when he forced her to tell you that I was her lover, the idea was to drive us apart and hide what he was really up to. And it worked, but at the same time, it made Kata realize I was the one the queen had sent for the talisman. That was why Iron was trying to turn you against me. Once Kata figured that out, she sent a servant to me with a coded message—a message about the talisman only the queen's man would understand. She told me to meet her in the tower room."

"And Kata gave you the talisman there? What happened then? How did she die?"

I opened my mouth to answer, but I didn't answer. Because I didn't know. How did Kata die? How did she die when she was alone with me in a tower room behind a locked door?

"Austin?" said Betheray when I kept silent. "Did she give you the talisman? Darling, if she did, why are you still here? Why haven't you set off for the Eleven Lands?"

My lips moved, but still, I said nothing. I had nothing to say. What had happened after Kata opened the door to me? I did not remember.

Then something strange happened. I did. I did remember. Not the meeting in the room. Not the death of Lady Kata. Those things had happened before I—I, the real Austin Lively—came into this lunatic fairyland. What I remembered was something else—something that had happened after I arrived. Right after.

I had just walked through that door in the mazy Edison Building at the Global Pictures lot. Suddenly I was here, in Galiana, in the tower room, with the dead woman at my feet and the soldiers pounding at the locked door. Maybe the servant had betrayed Kata and informed Aravist. I didn't know. It didn't matter. What mattered was what happened just then, just at that moment before the door was forced open.

Yes. I had it now. When I first came to myself in Galiana, I was standing on the edge of a tremendous drop. I was right at the ledge of the window, leaning out the window, with blue sky and castle towers above me and water sparkling far below.

And something else. Something bright was spinning through the air beneath me, spinning down and down toward the water. It was the very first thing I saw after I stepped through that door.

"I dropped it. I dropped it out the window," I said—as much to myself as to Betheray.

"What? The talisman?"

"Yes! Aravist and his men were at the door. They were about to break in. There was no time to hide it. There was water below me so . . . "

I saw the thoughts unspool in Betheray's eyes. "So you dropped it into the moat."

I nodded, staring into space. That must have been right.

"And then Sir Aravist broke in and killed Lady Kata, is that it?"

My stare shifted to her, her valentine face, anxious to exonerate me. But Kata was already dead when Aravist arrived. "It . . . it was all really confusing," I said. "There were soldiers everywhere . . . "

"That must be what happened! I knew you couldn't have killed her. I knew it!"

I didn't respond. I only wished I knew as much.

Lady Betheray sat up, running her fingers through her thick hair. The sight of her nakedness in motion stirred me. She looked back at me, down at me.

"And that's why you came here," she said. "Of course! With everyone hunting for you, you needed me to get you back into the castle, back to the moat. You knew—because of our meetings—I was the only one who could get you past the guard."

"No," I said. "No, I came here for you." Because that was true, and because there was no way to explain to her that half of my own story had unfolded without me being here, that the details were locked away in my mind and that only her presence and my feelings for her brought them to the surface.

She shook her head. "No. No. I don't matter."

"You matter to me," I said.

"Austin, I love you, you know I do, but . . . I'm nothing. We're nothing. The kingdom is at stake. The people. Their freedom. The queen."

A high, noble enthusiasm flushed her cheeks, and she was beautiful. With the fresh hope and passion stirring her, she took hold of the locket that even now hung between her breasts. She lifted it to her lips and kissed it fervently.

Curious, I reached out and took the locket from her. She looked at me, her eyes shining.

"Is this the queen?" I asked her.

She nodded. She looked fierce and proud. "I've never taken it off. Not once. Even when my husband suspected what it was. I've worn it always. I've always known she would come back to us. And now she will. You'll bring the talisman to the Eleven Lands. The emperor will come. Oh Austin, he has to come. He loves her. And he'll restore her to the throne. The kingdom will be free again."

While she spoke—her voice trembling with love and patriotism—I took the locket in my hand and pressed the button on its side. The locket sprang open to reveal the miniature portrait within.

"Oh my God!" I said. I sat up quickly, propped on one hand, holding the locket before me with the other.

"What? Austin, what?" Betheray said.

But I didn't speak. I couldn't. I just went on staring—gaping—at the portrait in the locket's frame. It was the queen, all right. No one could think that she was anyone but the queen. She was young—in her thirties—but everything about her—the golden crown around her golden hair, the expression on her face, the look in her eyes—everything spoke of majesty and serenity and greatness. In the facing half of the locket, a coat of arms was engraved into the gold: a sword across an open hand. A motto: *Let Wisdom Reign and Each Man Go His Way.*

My gaze moved from the portrait to the words and back to the portrait.

"What is it?" Betheray asked me again.

But I shook my head. How could I explain? How could I tell her that the face in the locket and the face in the photo in Sean Gunther's phone were one and the same?

Queen Elinda was Ellen Evermore, the author of *Another Kingdom.*

21

HOW COULD IT HAPPEN? WHAT DID IT MEAN? WAS IT—
was she—the link between these two worlds, LA and Galiana? Had
she somehow created this bizarre disturbance in the fundamental
truth of things that had me ping-ponging back and forth between
one reality and the other?

Staring at the portrait in the locket, the same face I had seen
in Gunther's phone, I had the sense that I had stumbled onto the
explanation for this whole insane experience. I couldn't figure it out,
not just then, but the logic of it seemed to be all around me, an
amorphous cloud of unconnected fact waiting to resolve itself into
an answer.

But there was no time to work through it now.

Betheray took the locket back from me. She snapped it shut and
held it against her chest. "It's late. If Sir Aravist doesn't send word to
Eastrim by morning, my husband will come for us here. We have to
be gone. We have to hurry," she said.

And we did.

NOW I WAS dressed in the plain brown clothes of a stable hand, and she was draped in a great cape lined with ermine. Her hood shadowed her face so that she could've been any fine lady with any attendant traveling beside her. Lord Iron had taken care to leave us with no horses. We were going to have to travel on foot to reach Eastrim, a journey of days. This was our disguise.

We left the house and hurried away together through the moonlit night, the pile of Netherdale looming behind us. We came into that haunted garden where the shrubs and flowers seemed to have died of some poison in the air. We were halfway across it when I heard an ominous sound. I took Beth's arm to stop her. We both stood still amidst the scraggly, barren stems and branches. Staring into the moonlight, we listened.

Betheray whispered, "Horses!"

I listened a little longer. I shook my head. A small hope rose in me. "No. Just one horse."

Then I saw it. The black stallion thundering down from the ridge of the hill and crossing the valley to us. It seemed a thing out of legend or dreams—a literal night mare charging out of the invisible imaginary into the real world.

"It's mine!" I said, surprised—and relieved beyond telling.

The moon was rising up the arc of the sky, and all the dark was gray. As the stallion drew near, I could make out the shape of my rodent friend, Maud, sitting on the saddle pommel.

The horse drew close and stood above us. The rodent-woman looked down at us, her eerily human face disdainful as ever. But I was crazy glad to see her.

"I assumed you'd deserted me," I said.

"I assumed you'd be dead by now," she told me.

"It was your faith in me that kept me going."

She snorted. I grabbed hold of the pommel beneath her and tried to swing myself up into the saddle. Eventually I made it.

"For crying out loud," the rat-girl muttered.

"Oh, shut up," I said.

I stretched my hand down to Betheray. Maud averted her eyes as if she were embarrassed to see such a grand lady take the hand of the likes of me. But the lady did. I swung her up into the saddle behind me. She slipped her arms around my waist.

"Don't bother to introduce us," said the rodent.

"Lady Betheray, this is Maud," I said. "She's . . . what are you anyway?"

"I told you, long story."

"Hello, Maud," said Betheray gently.

The mutant rat nodded, mollified. I snapped the reins and shouted, "Ho!"

Off we rode toward Eastrim.

THE MOON ROSE high and the blighted land grew bright. The tortuous shadows of ruined towers appeared in the distance and then passed by. We cantered I don't know how long, and after a while, I saw the dark mass of the forest on the ridge to the right of us.

At that point, my friend the rodent-woman began to glow again. That rainbow confetti of light came off her and then quickly faded away.

Over the noise of the horse's rapid fire hoofbeats, the squirrel-girl called to me: "Pull up."

I drew back on the reins, and the stallion slowed.

"I have to leave you here," she said in her high buzzy voice. I looked at her, surprised and uncertain. But she added only, "Tauratanio . . ."

Then, before I could ask more, she leapt off the horse, flying, four legs akimbo, till she hit the earth and scampered away through the grass.

I sat astride the stallion and watched her go. I could see her glowing from time to time as she headed for the forest. Then she was lost in the dark and the grass and the shadow of the trees. I was sorry to see it. It felt as if more than just some odd creature had left me. The whole power of the forest and its magic seemed to have been withdrawn from our endeavor. I told myself I was just imagining it.

"It's all right," Lady Betheray said—as if she could hear me worry. "The forest king is always with us."

I sighed. "Let's hope."

I spurred the stallion and we were off again.

THE MOON HAD reached the top of its arc and begun descending through the white-washed sky when the city of Eastrim appeared ahead of us on a not-too-distant hill. The place seemed very quiet in the night, but I remembered the guards patrolling the walls, and I knew they would have orders to watch for me.

I slowed the horse.

"Won't the gates be shut?" I asked.

"Approach from the south," said Lady Betheray. "I have allies there."

I did as she said, but it was nerve-wracking, let me tell you. As the city's stone walls rose darkly above us, as the shapes of the guards became visible moving along the castellated battlements, I felt my mouth go dry and my stomach go sour.

I dismounted and led the horse by the reins, hoping to appear more like her servant. We came closer to the wall and then . . .

"Who goes there? Name yourself or die!"

The shout made me pull up under the walls. I could see the large, bearded guard looking down on us from directly above. I could see the shape of his spear and the shapes of the two men coming to flank him on either side with bows drawn and arrows pointed at my chest.

My immediate instinct was to turn and hoof it out of there. That's what Los Angeles Austin would have done for sure. But me— hey, I had never been anything but Betheray's hero. So I held my ground more or less heroically.

Lady Betheray called back to the guard over my head. "We only want to go our way."

I remembered the words in her locket—the words Maud had told me to whisper to the blacksmith who had given us the stallion. I understood now that this was the queen's password.

And it seemed to work. The atmosphere on the battlements seemed to change. The guard with the spear murmured to the archers. The archers lowered their bows.

"Are they your friends?" I whispered nervously.

"We're about to find out," she whispered back. "Go to the door beside the gate."

I tugged the horse forward. With every step, my fear grew stronger. I imagined a dozen scenarios of sudden disaster. Each scenario ended with me and Betheray dead in the dust. But at the same time, I was intensely aware of Beth's vulnerability up there in the saddle, of her ladylike frailty in the face of all these thuggish men. I couldn't have run away if I wanted to. I know this because I wanted to and I couldn't.

As we neared the large gate, I spotted the smaller door she'd told me about. I brought the stallion right up close to it and stopped. The horse nosed the earth as we waited in the black shadow of the wall.

My breath caught as a bolt was thrown back with a loud clunk. The door came open. I swallowed hard. A guard emerged, the one who had held the spear. He towered over me, almost a giant, with a giant black beard beneath grim eyes. Instead of a spear, he gripped a torch in his hand now. He held the flame out toward us. He studied my face, his expression grim.

With no urging from me, the stallion shifted. He turned sideways to the guard, showing him Betheray. Beth drew back the hood of her cape—not much, just a little, just enough. I saw the guard's eyes narrow as he examined her, his face flickering under orange torchlight. It was impossible to read his expression, impossible to guess whether he would let us pass or sound the alarm.

An endless moment passed and then another moment just as endless. Finally the guard stood aside.

"Let wisdom reign," he murmured.

I led the horse through the doorway into the city.

ONCE WE WERE out of sight of the wall, I hoisted myself back into the saddle. In tense whispers, Lady Betheray guided me around the edges of the sleeping streets and up the hill toward the castle. A cold mist, eerie with moonlight, gathered around us as we climbed an old cobbled path. The stallion began to make nervous, snorting noises. I could feel the beast's reluctance in the movement of his flanks against my thighs.

"What is this place?" I whispered.

"Don't you recognize it?" Betheray whispered back.

Weirdly, I did recognize it then. It was that strange sensation again of remembering what I did not remember. There were events that were not in my mind one moment, and the next moment, they were there, and I knew: this was the old castle cemetery where she and I had met in secret, where we had conspired to restore the queen, where we had fallen in love.

It was a field of monuments and steles and crypts from Galiana's ancient days. The place now stood abandoned and untended, the grass high where there was grass, the earth dank where there was only earth. The gravestones were moldy and slanted and so antique that whatever words had once been on them were now nearly worn away. Elsewhere in the mist, faceless saints and mourning angels stared at us empty eyed as we rode past in the silver darkness. Now and then—most terribly—as the horse snorted and tossed its head and stalled and then went on—the luminescent mist seemed to swirl into a drifting shape like a woman or a man. A clammy breeze would rise and the mist would thin and spread and the shape would soon be gone.

"What was that?" I asked the first time it happened. And when Betheray didn't answer, I asked, "Was it a ghost?"

"An emanation," she told me. "Don't you remember?"

And just like that, I did remember, though I didn't know how I knew. These shapes were shadows of the dead—those dead who lingered beneath the earth and yearned to live again. Their yearning manifested itself in these brief misty exhalations of being. They searched the air for life. They fed on souls.

The emanations kept appearing as we moved slowly across the field of graves. The sight of them sent a deep chill through me. I could feel the ache of the dead's desire as it shaped the mist, then sank away, unsatisfied. I remembered—remembered suddenly in chaotic flashes—how I would wait here for Betheray, hunkered in the chill mist with the yearning of the dead all around me. An unpleasant experience—very. All in all, I sided with the black stallion: I wanted to get away from here as much as the horse did.

"Here," Lady Betheray said.

The stallion stopped, still fretting and huffing steam. Lady Betheray took my hand and slipped off the saddle, dropping soundlessly to the ground.

"Follow me," she said softly.

I dismounted. By the time my feet touched the muddy earth, Beth was already gliding away from me in the twisting mist. I saw misty tendrils take the shape of hands and reach for her, but they could not seize her. She passed through them fearlessly, and they broke apart and were gone.

I hesitated where I was a moment, holding the horse's reins, uncertain where to tie him. Finally, I simply patted his flanks.

"Wait here," I commanded softly.

I released the reins. The stallion stood very still. Then his whole body stiffened, alert. He tilted his head in an unmistakable posture of listening. A second later and he snorted, lifted his head as if in a gesture of goodbye—and then trotted off through the mist the way we'd come.

"Wait! Stop!" I hissed after him desperately. How would we ever escape from here without the stallion?

But the damned horse never looked back. He couldn't get out of there fast enough. I couldn't blame him.

"Hurry!" came Lady Betheray's whisper.

She was now a mere shadow in the heart of the fog, getting fainter by the second. I could see the mist making figures all around her. I could see the figures waiting to grab me when I came.

I drew an unsteady breath and went after this brave lady.

I CAUGHT UP with her. We moved through the mist, hand in hand, shoulder to shoulder. A little ways and we came upon a tomb.

To me, it looked like nothing so much as a piece of scenery from a gothic horror film. It was a small house-like structure of streaked gray stone, gloomy and forbidding. It was fronted by a columned portico. Two cowled figures of bronze flanked the bronze doorway, which was itself cowled in fog. The morbid statues stood taller than me. Their heads were slightly lowered to reveal only ghostly emptiness underneath their hoods. The door between them had been carved with burial scenes which were green with verdigris and faded almost beyond recognition—they were just a suggestion of ceremony and grief. The inscription on the pediment was barely visible: *Here End All Things That Live.*

Lady Betheray, still moving fearlessly, approached this grim place. She lifted her hand and let her slim, white fingers play over the surface of the door. She found the spot she wanted and pressed it. The door clicked and swung in with the cheesiest creak of its hinges. As corny as the sound effect was, I have to admit it filled me with dread.

Lady Betheray slipped through the opening. I swallowed hard and followed her.

It was dark inside—black dark away from the moonlit mist. It was a moment or two before I could make out Beth's figure.

"Come on," she said.

"I can barely see my—"

Before I finished, there was a scraping noise, stone on stone. A spark. A blinding flame. She had a torch. I remembered: it was stored here for use during our trysts.

The flame illuminated a dreadful house of bones. Skeletons grinned at me out of low niches. Carved faces stared from the tops of tombs. Even Beth, in the firelight, in her cape, beneath her hood, seemed another monument, white faced, staring. It was almost startling when she moved again, as if she were a statue come to life.

She went to stand by a marble sarcophagus. Raising her torch with one hand, she touched a mechanism beneath its lid with the other. The lid sprang ajar. She raised it.

"Hold this." She handed me the torch.

As I watched with a feeling of mingled awe and disgust—awe at her courage and disgust at what I knew I was going to have to do—Lady Betheray climbed into the coffin. As her hooded head lowered out of sight, I moved to the edge of the box. My gorge rising, I looked down.

There was an open trap door in the bottom. Through the hole, I saw the gleam of Beth's living eyes looking back up at me. A superstitious aversion filled me. All the same, wincing with discomfort, I put my hand on the stone edge of the sarcophagus, took a deep breath, and climbed in.

Gripping the stone, I lowered myself through the trap until my feet found purchase. I was on a narrow, winding flight of stone stairs. Betheray was already descending below me. I carried the torch down after her.

Despite what Beth had said to me in the graveyard above, I was not prepared for what I saw down there. Nothing could have prepared me for such ghoulish malevolence.

WE STOOD IN an underground passage walled with dirt and stone. Lady Betheray led the way, and I followed close behind her with the torch. My eyes were so wide they must have looked like lanterns. I was flabbergasted by what I was seeing.

There were dead men down here. Dead men, and women too. Not skeletons as in the crypt above or "emanations" as in the mist, but figures of solid darkness—lost souls. As we hurried through the dank corridor, through a suffocating stench that came off the moldy stones, I caught sight of these creatures every few steps or so. I'd see one in the corner of my eye. I'd gasp and swing around, the torch held out in front of me. The thing would just stand there, staring back at me, holding me with its gaze. I would smell the rank smell of the grave on it. I would start to make out its features. And I would feel its hunger. That was the worst of it—the hunger. It came off the male dead as a kind of tremulous aggression and off the female dead as a hateful mockery of seduction. They wanted me—the men and women both. They wanted my life, my spirit, like a thief wants money. I could feel the men trying to seize it from me by force. I could feel the women trying to lure it out of me. It didn't matter how they did it. They would do whatever worked. They just wanted it, wanted the life-stuff of me, wanted to make my life their own and return with it to the world while I was left behind here to hunger forever as they did now.

"God," I heard myself say. The word was thick in my throat. "Are these the dead?"

"Don't stop!" said Lady Betheray urgently. "Don't look at them, Austin. Don't give them anything."

I knew she was right. That was exactly why the hunger of the dead was so horrifying. It went both ways. It was not just that these creatures wanted me, but that I wanted them somehow as well. I would see the shape of a woman—just a dark shape at first. But I was fascinated and I let my eyes linger on her. Soon, the shape began to flush with being and specificity. Features rose into her face, form rose into her figure. And she was beautiful. No, she really was. More than that. She was my dream girl. She looked like a woman I'd imagined. I could see in her eyes that she wanted to do with me exactly what I wanted to be done. I had to force myself to turn away from her, force myself to push on through the firelit shadows. But then . . . a man this time, just a silhouette, but I looked at him too long, and the black shape began to clothe itself from within with the aspect of a fatherly friend, the kind of mentor I'd never had. I began to wish I could remain in his company . . .

"Austin!"

Lady Betheray seized my arm and shook me from my trance. The fantasy friend in front of me subsided into a silhouette and slipped away into the darkness.

I blinked. I turned. I met Lady Betheray's living eyes. How had she had the courage to pass this way so many times? Every time we met to conspire to restore the queen to her throne, she had braved this danger.

"It's all right," she said.

She stood on tiptoe and kissed my cheek with her vital lips, the ermine of her hood brushing my face. The warm touch of her restored my mind to the moment.

I nodded. "Okay."

She went ahead. I followed.

AFTER A WHILE, the corridor slanted down. The walls ran with clammy water. Soon there were no more dead, but all the same, a new sense of depth and claustrophobia came over me.

"We're crossing under the moat," Beth whispered.

I had already guessed as much.

It seemed a long time before the passage began to rise again. Finally though, we came to the end: a faceless slab of stone. Once again, Betheray found the right spot with her fingertips. She pressed it, and the stone shifted. A doorway opened.

Beth took the torch from me and extinguished it in a murky puddle. She set the dead stick against the wall beside two others that were already there.

Then she gestured to me with her head and stepped through the open door. I was right behind her.

We emerged into a small niche hidden by a tapestry. Lady Betheray drew the edge of the arras aside and peeked out. She looked back at me over her shoulder and nodded: the coast was clear. We both stepped through into an empty hallway lit by flaming torches on the walls. It was a bright relief after so long underground. I could still feel the clinging desires of the dead. They were slipping off me reluctantly, like grasping fingers.

We held still, arm pressed to arm. Crouched, poised, listening. I could hear murmuring voices somewhere above us. Footsteps too.

"There are guards everywhere," she told me.

"Do you think the guy at the city gates might have alerted them?"

"Him? Not him, no. I know him. He's loyal to the queen. But the archers with him . . . I couldn't make out their faces at that distance. I didn't recognize them, and Winton does have his spies."

I gazed up and down the empty hallways, listening to those distant murmurs, those footsteps, the sounds of those guards. They could be anywhere, even just around the next corner.

I turned back to Betheray. I slipped my hand beneath her hood, beneath her hair, and touched her face.

"Maybe you should go back," I said softly.

I looked down at her looking up at me. What a noble creature she was. How full of courage and devotion. Here without a weapon. Without a man's strength. Oh, I know: in the movies women fight with swords and throw punches that knock grown men across the room. But not in life, not real life, besides the rarest exception. My lady's arms were slender and smooth. Her punch would have done little damage to a man's hard jaw. And she could not have wielded a sword in battle for more than a few minutes. I remembered how Aravist had overpowered her without breaking a sweat—how he tossed her light figure around like a doll. I'm sure she remembered it too.

Yet here she was. With nothing to protect her but me. And fearless just the same—in service to her kingdom and her queen—her people and their freedom.

Let Wisdom Reign and Each Man Go His Way.

I was certain of it now: I would die for her if I had to. It was not just a feeling, not just a principle. It was the truth.

"Go back," I said again. "Go back and wait for me. I'll do this."

I saw her consider it. Then she shook her head. "You would never find your way without me, Austin. You need me to get you there."

"Beth . . . "

"Ssh. We have to hurry."

I wanted to kiss her, hold her, even here, even now. I wanted to command her to leave. I wanted to make her go.

But she had already turned and hurried away, her cape flowing out behind her.

She went down the hall to an archway. Two wooden doors were flung wide here, fastened to rings in the wall that held them in place. Beth pressed close against the jambstone, and peeked around it—then pulled back quickly. She held a finger to her lips as I came up beside her.

I set my back against the open door, my shoulder against hers. I heard voices and footsteps around the corner: guards approaching. I held my breath as they drew closer. I saw Lady Betheray shut her eyes, her cheeks pale with suspense.

Then, the guards must have veered off, because the sound of their voices suddenly altered and began to fade. After a few moments, it was quiet again. Lady Betheray took a look then curled around the corner and was gone.

I went after her, through the open doors—and in an instant, I was dazzled by the white brightness of the light—so dazzled by light and mountains and trees and running rivers that for a second I could not comprehend where I was.

Then I did.

I was in the mall. I was in the electronics store with the TVs showing videos of woods and heights and waters. Confused, I turned—and there was Sera, right behind me, right outside the storefront, coming through the shoppers toward the shop's glass doors.

He was yards away. Closing fast. Lifting his hand from his side. Lifting his pistol.

Pointing his pistol directly at my chest.

A woman screamed out in the mall. In the store itself, a man shouted out a curse. I hurled myself sideways to the floor. There was a gunshot—suppressed—a whispered bang. On the nearest television set, the image of an eagle flying in a clear blue sky suddenly exploded in a shower of glass and fizzling sparks.

I rolled. I saw an aisle of toys—cars and drones and dolls and teddy bears and electric games. I leapt to my feet and sprinted for it. Sprinted down it. Sera charged after me. He planted himself at the head of the aisle to get his shot at my back. I sensed him there more than saw him. As I ran frantically for the end of the aisle, I reached up toward the shelf to my left and grabbed the first thing my fingers touched: an electronic teddy bear in a box. I swept the box into the air behind me, hoping to distract the killer, throw off his aim. I heard the bear say, "Hello, my name is . . . " But I never found out his name. Sera fired again, and the bear's voice died in a snowy cloud of stuffing and a hiss of static.

There were more screams. More shouted curses. A bell began to ring, loud as a siren: some kind of alarm. I reached the end of the aisle, came around it—and then, on instinct, pulled to a stop so abruptly I felt the shock in my kneecap, a jarring pain. But I knew Sera was still down at the head of the aisle. If I went to the next aisle over, all he had to do was take a sideways step and open fire. So instead, I stopped, then leapt back the other way, taking the chance he would not have waited for me.

I guessed right. Sera wasn't there. He must have gone on to the next aisle to set his trap. But now, I was dashing the other way across the store, aisle after aisle of TV sets, computers, video game consoles, whatever. But where was I going? How could I get out?

Sera commanded the front of the store. If I tried to reach the door, he would pick me off as I went past him.

The alarm bell went on ringing, deafening, scattering thought. Maybe the police were on their way. Maybe they'd rescue me. Maybe not. Serge Orosgo wanted both me and Sera gone. Who could tell what his friends in high places would do?

I was out of breath. The scar in my gut was starting to ache and throb. I had that feeling of hollow weakness at the center of me.

I had to get out of here, and fast.

Now I saw the checkout counter to my right. The cash registers, the hanging display of accessories on the wall behind, a little alcove just out of sight. Was there a door in that alcove maybe? Would it be open? Could I go through? If I went in, would there be a way out?

I had no idea. But it was the only chance I had.

I raced to the counter. The alarm bell rang and rang, filling my head with noise. Without breaking stride, I braced both hands on the countertop and with the strength of fear vaulted over it as if I were flying. The scar in my belly sang a high, bright note of pain. I felt the skin stretch. I felt like I might tear open and spill my guts.

Then—midair—I saw the store clerks hiding behind the counter, beneath me. There were two of them back there, a roly-poly young man and a diminutive girl. They were both crouching, cowering, their hands over their heads. I didn't see them till I was above them and then I couldn't stop myself.

I managed to land on the floor, on my feet, but the force of motion carried me forward. I went into the tubby guy. The girl screamed. I spun and stumbled, reaching out wildly for something to grab. I grabbed a game controller hanging on the back wall. It held just long enough for me to steady myself, then tore away in my hand so that I kept hurtling forward. Under the hammering sound of the alarm, I heard the girl clerk whimper and sob.

Somehow I managed to whirl between the two crouched bodies. There was the alcove up ahead of me. There was a door in the alcove—yes! I slammed into the wall beside it, the game controller jolted from my hand. I grabbed the knob. Turned it. Pulled the door open. Dashed through.

The clarion bell became muffled as the door slammed behind me. I was in a storeroom, a small space lined with shelves, all the shelves holding more electronics: boxed TVs and computers and toys and wiring accessories. Was there another door? A way out?

There was. I glimpsed it between the shelving.

Behind me, rising into the sound of the bell, blending with the sound of the bell, then rising over it, the girl store clerk shrieked in terror.

A voice rose above every other sound: "Out of my way!"

Sera. He must have seen where I went. He must have leapt the counter too. He must be only steps away from me.

I threaded quickly through the shelves to the exit. The entry door burst open behind me. I turned and there the kitten-faced killer was. His gun barrel scanned the little room, searching for me. He saw me. I grabbed the edge of a shelf and tilted it over. The boxes and gizmos slid off it with a crash. The crash was joined by a gunshot—that muffled blast. I don't know where the bullet went. The shelf must have blocked it.

I took hold of the knob of the exit door. I had time to fear it might be locked. It wasn't. I yanked the door toward me. Spun around the edge of it. Charged out.

And I was on a ledge above nothingness: a straight drop down into dirt and death.

I had come out of the mall into the construction site—or the demolition site, I still didn't know which it was. All I did know was that I was teetering on the edge of a skeleton structure of girders and wood, cement and rebar. Below me—four stories below me—was the dirt pit, the construction machines, rock, earth, a deadly fall, the end of everything. I hung over plummeting destruction for another second with, all around me, the weirdly quiet sound of air in motion and traffic far away.

Then I drew back onto the ledge. There was a narrow platform of wooden planks in front of me: a worker's walkway. It led to a broader platform of heavy metal plates on which stood a long, low wall of cement bristling with rebar. Putting out my arms for balance, I looked back over my shoulder. Through the door, I could hear Sera cursing—I could hear boxes crashing—as he fought and kicked his way across the little storeroom to the exit.

There was nowhere to go, nowhere I would be out of the range of his fire. But I had to keep moving. If I stood there, he'd be inches away when he came through the door.

And I had an idea. A desperate idea, but it was something.

Like a man on a high wire then, I began to edge out onto the walkway, barely balanced between the fatal fall to my left and the fatal fall to my right, the pit yawning under me. Swaying, unsteady, I took a step forward—then another step—then another—then three more quick steps that took me to the platform of metal plates, the cement with the rebar sticking out of it.

I found my footing. I grabbed a piece of rebar. Something to use as a weapon. I tried to pull it out. It was anchored fast. I could hear the crashing in the storeroom. Sera getting closer and closer to the exit. He'd be through that door with his gun any second.

I tried another piece of rebar, and another. The third one rattled in its hole. It was loose. I pulled on it, hard. Harder. It began to give, to slide up out of the cement. I twisted it and pulled it, grunting with the effort, fighting to keep my grip with sweating hands. I sobbed with frustration as the steel rod resisted, as it slid out only slowly, only bit by bit.

I'm not the one, I was thinking crazily. *I'm not the one to pull it free.*

And Sera was coming, coming. I looked back and saw the door knob start to turn.

I looked down at the rebar. Focus. Clear the mind. I pulled.

The rebar suddenly came out of the cement. I flew backward almost to the edge of the platform, almost plunging off into eternity. But I kept my feet. Now I had a yard and a half of steel rod in my hands. A weapon, such as it was.

The door to the storeroom swung open. I stepped back onto the wooden walkway, gripping the rebar in one hand like a sword. I started moving toward the door just as Sera stepped out of it.

Sera pulled up, shocked by the drop in front of him. Then he raised his eyes to me. Saw me coming. Grinned voluptuously. With confidence bordering on showmanship, he stepped out grandly onto the walkway. I didn't slow down. I kept on moving toward him.

"Darling," Sera said.

He raised his gun. His finger tightened on the trigger.

I whipped the rebar at him. A forehand slash down at his hand, just like I'd learned from the swordfight videos. The bar hit his wrist. The gun fired. The shot went wild. And just like in the videos, I swung the rebar up again, slashing it backhand across his face, opening a wide, raw diagonal gash from his chin to his eyebrow.

That second swing nearly sent me twirling off the walkway. I threw my arms out to my side, teetering there. I tilted back onto the planks and regained my balance.

Not Sera. The brutal blow to his head had sent his eyes rolling, his head rolling. I saw the dazed expression on his face as he swam at the very edge of consciousness. He staggered, gaping.

And he toppled off the walkway.

Standing on the boards, I watched him fall. Fall and fall and fall, it seemed, forever. He went down silently. Not a sound until the very end, and then only the pitiful start of a scream cut short by the brutal thud of his landing. Those sounds—the scream of terrified awareness way too late, the final impact—those sounds rose above the distant whisper of the traffic and reached me even where I stood.

Breathless, I lowered the rebar to my side. I gazed down at the broken body in the dirt below.

22

THE POLICE WERE WAITING FOR ME WHEN I CAME BACK inside. They had answered the alarm and swarmed the mall. They were just entering the electronics shop, guns drawn, as I stepped out of the storeroom, the rebar still in my hand.

"Drop it!"

"Put your hands up!"

"Freeze! Freeze! Freeze!"

Their shouts were almost drowned out by the deafening bell as it kept on ringing and ringing. It took a second before I could hear them, before I could understand what they were saying. If it had taken even a second more, I do believe they would have opened fire on me. I saw one cop's gun stiffen in his hand—until a husky, swarthy plainclothesman stepped forward and touched his wrist, gently pushing the pistol downward.

Finally, stunned and exhausted and half-crazy as I was, I got the idea. I dropped the rebar. It fell to the floor with a clang. I raised my hands above my head.

A pale, frightened uniformed patrolman and his dark, frightened uniformed partner trained their weapons on me as the big plainclothesman approached, opened the counter gate, and stepped through. He was tall and broad in the shoulders and round in the gut. He was dressed in a Spartans sweatshirt and torn jeans with his ID card on a chain around his neck and his gun in a holster on his hip. He had a hard-guy face with short sandy hair and a bushy mustache.

He grabbed me and spun me around roughly. He wrenched my arms painfully behind my back and handcuffed me.

Someone shut off the alarm. The quiet was almost as deafening as the bell.

"I'm not the bad guy," I told the plainclothesman over my shoulder. "The bad guy's dead."

He spun me back and looked me in the eye—a significant look, I thought, but I couldn't guess at the significance of it. Not then.

"You have the right to remain silent," he told me in a loud, clear voice.

I took the hint.

THE COPS DROVE me to a brick box of a police station somewhere in Hollywood. Two patrolmen hurried me through cramped hallways hung with fliers and bustling with detectives and uniforms. They hustled me into an interrogation room, a cramped cube of a place crowded with a long linoleum-topped table and a few plastic chairs. It looked like a broom closet they'd refitted for the purpose. One patrolman pushed me down into one of the chairs. He took off my cuffs. I rubbed my sore wrists.

The patrolmen left. Then my old pals Detectives Graciano and Lord came in.

I wasn't happy to see them. I remembered the way Lord had stonewalled me when I called her for help. I felt pretty sure now they were Orosgo's toadies, just like my brother and my parents were.

They stood over me, the short, blocky man and the large, oval-faced woman side by side. They looked down at me with sleepy, cynical, accusatory eyes.

A video camera hung in a corner of the ceiling. I couldn't help but notice it was unplugged. So it was just Graciano and Lord and me. No one else was watching.

"So why'd you kill him?" Graciano said casually, as if by way of making conversation.

I raised an eyebrow at him. "You've got to be kidding me, right?" He didn't answer. He wasn't kidding. "Half the mall saw him chasing me with a gun. There must be security cameras all over the place. There must be videos from every angle."

"You'd think so, wouldn't you?" he answered stolidly. "A place like that. You'd think there would be witnesses and videos and all that shit."

"Are you telling me there's not?"

"Just humor us, Lively, would you?" said Lord in her trademark impassive voice. "Just tell us what happened in your own words."

What was I supposed to say? I had lied to them before, back in the hospital. To protect Riley, I had left Serge Orosgo out of the story, just as my brother, Rich, had told me to. I could stick to that lie, if I wanted. It would be the easiest course. I could just repeat that Sera had come after me because I'd seen him murder Gunther. It would hang together with what I'd told them already.

But why should I lie? They'd already proved they were prepared to let me die no matter what I said. What worse could they do to me if I told the truth? Maybe if I showed them I was willing to name Orosgo, they'd be a little slower to mess with me. Maybe they'd realize I was dangerous to them alive, and that it would look bad if I turned up dead. Maybe.

Or maybe I just wanted to show them I wasn't afraid of them. Maybe I was just tired of being afraid.

So this time, I gave it to them straight, the whole story. How I was looking for the book, *Another Kingdom*. How Sera and the bald thug had broken in and shot Sean Gunther dead. I told them all about Orosgo: the mad billionaire descending in his helicopter, and the way I punched Sera in the face, and the crazy dinner on the patio, all of it. Well, almost all of it. I didn't tell them about Galiana. At one point, I rubbed my mouth wearily and, with my hand right beneath my nose, I thought I could smell the scent of Lady Betheray still on me. I thought of her where I'd left her, back in the castle, bravely leading the way to the tower room despite the guards everywhere. I didn't mention any of that either. I didn't want to give them an excuse to toss me into a madhouse somewhere and throw away the key.

When I was done talking, the tiny interrogation room was silent. The silence went on for a long time, so long it was unnerving. All the while, Lord and Graciano stood right where they were, right over me, looking down at me with those sleepy, cynical, accusatory stares.

At long last, Graciano said, "Uh huh." And then he repeated, "So why'd you kill him?"

I stared at him. "What?"

"Sera. Serafim . . . " He craned his neck to glance at Lord's notebook as if he needed to read the name. "Moran . . . Morana. Sera Morana. Why'd you kill him?"

"Are you joking?" I asked him.

"You think a dead man is a joke?" said Graciano. He turned to Lord. "Do you think a dead man is a joke, Detective?"

"Not me," said Lord. "Not my kind of humor."

"Yeah, I'm missing the laugh factor here, too, Austin. I gotta be honest with you, bud," Graciano said. He had that whole fake-friendly cop thing going on.

"He was coming after me with a pistol," I answered. "Everyone saw it."

"Yeah, you said," said Graciano.

"Because of the magic billionaire," said Lord as she jotted something down in her notebook.

"What magic billionaire? I didn't say anything about magic."

"Well, I just figured he was magic because he appeared out of nowhere," she said. "He wasn't there when you told the story before, now suddenly—*poof*—there he is. That sounds pretty magical to me. Doesn't that sound magical to you?" she asked Graciano.

"I'm personally amazed," he answered.

"This is crap," I said. "He shot up the store. Everyone saw him."

"I didn't see him," said Lord.

"We want to believe you, Austin," said Graciano in the same fake-friendly tone. "No, really, we do. You say a billionaire philanthropist landed in a helicopter and you had dinner with him on his terrace and then he sent this assassin Sera after you."

"I don't know if Orosgo sent him. I think Sera came after me because I punched him," I said.

"Right, you punched him. A . . . what'd you call yourself? A story . . . "

"A story analyst."

"A story analyst, right. And you punched an assassin after he killed the author but before the billionaire landed in his helicopter." Graciano and Lord exchanged an expressionless glance. Then they both looked back at me. "Of course we want to believe that, Austin," Graciano said. "It's a good story. Hell, I wish real life were actually that entertaining."

I saw how this was going. I gave them a full-fledged sneer, my teeth showing.

"The problem is, we've been doing some research," Graciano went on. "And this guy? This Serafim guy? He's not an assassin, Austin."

"He's good people," said Lord.

I sighed. There wasn't much point in answering. I could see that now.

"Well, he was good people before you knocked him off that walkway," Graciano said. "After that, he was dead people."

"He didn't work for Serge Orosgo either," said Lord, looking up from her pad to regard me with half-lidded eyes. "You know what he did for a living, Austin? He ran a literacy program for disadvantaged kids."

I actually laughed out loud. "I'll bet he did."

"He did," said Graciano. "No connection with Orosgo at all."

"Serge Orosgo hasn't even been in this country for the past three months," said Lord. "He's been at his mansion in Curacao the whole time."

"He has his headquarters there," said Graciano. "He stays there a certain portion of the year so he doesn't have to pay taxes."

I nodded. I was still sneering.

"What do you say to that, Austin?" Graciano asked me.

"What *do* you say to that?" asked Lord.

They both waited for an answer.

I gave it to them, right through my sneer. "You called Orosgo magic because he appeared out of nowhere."

"That's right," said Lord.

"That's right," said Graciano.

"Because I didn't mention him to you before today and then today I did."

"That's right," said Lord.

"So if I didn't mention him before, how come you found out where he was staying? The whole thing about Curacao and his taxes and whether Sera worked for him. Why would you research that? How could you know to do that? That sounds kind of like magic to me."

The next few moments were . . . I guess *uncomfortable* would be the word. Graciano and Lord kept looking down at me, and it's not that their expressions changed exactly, but something changed, something turned those blank stares from sleepy and cynical to angry and threatening. When Graciano spoke again, there was none of that fake cop friendliness in his voice anymore. Not in his voice, and not in his face either. There was nothing in his face but pure viper-eyed Mean.

"We're just telling you how it is," he said. "We're just telling you how it's going to be."

I looked at him. He looked at me. And I wondered: Was it possible? Could Orosgo really wangle all this? Change the records? Eliminate the eyewitnesses? Erase the security footage? Make it look like I'd murdered Sera for no good reason? Could he really be that powerful? The idea made my stomach churn.

Graciano was about to speak again, but I never found out what he was going to say. Because just then the door opened—flew—shot—banged open not like someone was just coming in but like someone was coming in with purpose, purpose and anger, like someone had said to himself, *That's it. I've heard enough!* and stormed through the door so fast and hard it flew and shot and banged.

It was my brother, Rich. He charged into the little room—and my mother and father were right behind him.

AT THE EXACT same moment, Detectives Graciano and Lord turned, presenting their profiles to me. They turned in unison, one motion together, stiffly, briskly. Like robots who had just received a wireless signal: *Turn.* Or like figures on a clock whose time to turn had come. As my brother and parents crowded the tiny room, the detectives marched out—first Graciano, then Lord—and were gone.

Thoughts whisked and ricocheted through my overloaded brain. Rich and my parents had been listening to the whole interrogation.

The whole interrogation was a charade put on for them. Not a charade, a test. To see whether I was committed to protecting Serge Orosgo even when the heat was on. It was a test, and I had failed it big time.

I didn't know these things, I just thought them. The thoughts just came to me. Maybe they were wrong.

My family, meanwhile, arrayed themselves around the room. My mother sat in the plastic chair across the table from me. She looked so thin and angular, I thought if she turned sideways, she would disappear. My willowy father began to drift about the tiny space like a dandelion seed on the summer breezes. He paused to examine the unplugged video camera on the wall, standing beneath it with his hands behind his back, looking up at it from one angle then another as if it were some ancient tablet thick with runes. Rich, the one substantial figure among them with his broad shoulders and three-piece suit and his great blond Viking beard, was leaning in a corner, watching me wearily as if my mischief had worn him plumb out.

I looked at them, one and then the next and then the next. And yes, my mind once again returned to that childhood memory: myself on the floor telling stories with figures. Lost in that stillness of delight and creation that was, I suspected now, my natural refuge from them, from this, from the truth of who my people were. As my thoughts swirled in my brain, so my emotions seemed to swirl in the heart of me, swirl together into some fathomless concoction of anger and disgust and grief—and more grief going deep into the fabric of my flesh and viscera. Was there any part of my life that was not a lie? I wondered. All this time, I had been worried that my adventures in Galiana had been a sickness and delusion. But really, wasn't it this, this other life, my real life, my childhood, my family, my upbringing— wasn't it all this that had been the delusion? In some ways, it seemed to me just then, Galiana was more real than reality.

"Well, you're getting yourself an awful lot of attention these days, aren't you?" said my mom with a disdainful little sniff.

"I'm being set up," I told her quietly. But I didn't have to tell her, did I? She knew. They all knew.

"Oh!" said mom, rolling her eyes. "Please don't be so melodramatic, sweetheart. It can't be good for you."

"Or for anyone," my father murmured, still studying the camera on the wall.

"They want to charge me with murder."

"No one wants anything of the kind," Mom said. "Do they, Richard?"

I looked at my brother—really looked at him for the first time since he'd come in—and he met my eyes. There was honesty in that exchange of glances at least, not like with my parents. He knew I knew, and I knew he knew I knew.

"Yeah, Rich, let's have it," I said to him. "What does he want? Your boy, your boss, your hero, Orosgo. What does he want from me?"

It was my mother who answered, though all the while Rich and I kept our gazes locked together, as if our mother's voice ran between us like a wall and we were looking over it at one another. "He wants to make the world a better place," she said. "Is that some sort of sin in your religion, dear? He wants to change the way people think. He wants to change the way people are, always fighting and oppressing each other, one better than the next, richer than the next, stronger than the next and keeping the other down."

As before when I heard of Orosgo's fantasies, what came into my mind was Eastrim, its heretics in cages, its guards with spears, its mobs crying for blood. I had already seen Orosgo's utopia, and it didn't work.

"He believes the world can be a better place than that, Austin," she went on. "If you believe in something so much finer, well, I for one would certainly like to know what it is."

There it was again, that question, the question I'd asked myself in Shadow Wood before the throne of Tauratanio, the question Rich had asked me in my hospital room. What did I believe?

Rich and I continued to look at each other across the wall of my mother's voice.

Without turning from him, I answered her. "I believe that people should be left the hell alone, Mother. That's what I believe. To hell with Orosgo. To hell with all of you."

"A very nice way to speak to your family," my mother said.

"Let wisdom reign, and each man go his way," I said.

Rich winced.

"Wisdom!" my mother said with a sophisticated little snort. "What's wisdom, I wonder?"

"Ay, there's the rub," murmured my father, studying the camera.

My brother only heaved a deep sigh so that his big shoulders lifted and fell.

"Here's the thing," he said. "A man is dead. You killed him, Aus."

I rolled my eyes.

"Well, it's a problem."

"Oh, fuck you, Rich," I said.

"A very nice way to speak to your own brother," said my mother.

"Adorable," my father muttered archly.

"I'm just saying," said Rich. "I'm just telling you. It's a problem—if you make it a problem."

"He was trying to kill me. I killed him first."

"Sure. But if you get charged with murder . . . Well, by the time you prove that, what's left of your reputation? Or your Hollywood career? Or your savings, for that matter?"

"If you have any savings," muttered my father. He was wandering away from the camera now.

"It's funny how this perfect Age of Orosgo involves so much extortion and murder," I said. "It's almost like it's the same as the age we live in now."

"He doesn't *want* to extort you," said Rich with some frustration. "He doesn't *want* to murder you."

"Well, that's nice, I guess. What does he want? That's what I was asking in the first place."

"He wants . . . " Rich searched the air for the answer. "He wants you on his team, man. Our team. He wants to be your friend, Austin."

"There. Is that so terrible?" my mother asked.

"Mm, very terrible, terribly terrible," said dear old Dad. Now he was studying the tiles on the wall. They were grimy tiles, once white. There was nothing to study on them, but he studied them anyway, his nose up close.

"He wants you to be part of the family," said Rich, with a gesture of his head at Mom and Dad. "Really. No matter what you think of him, that's the kind of guy he is."

I snorted. I couldn't meet his eyes anymore. I couldn't stand it. I looked away.

Rich wouldn't have it. He pushed off the wall and came to me. He leaned on the table. Hung down over me so that when I turned back to him, his big features and his big beard filled my vision, his hot breath washed over my face.

"I'm serious, Austin," he said. "*This* is serious. This is your life. You know? Your only life. What do you want it to be like? That's the question. You want your life to be about making movies? Orosgo owns a movie studio. The people who choose the projects and give them the what-do-you-call-it, the green light—they work for him. The journalists who'll interview you and give you publicity and write the movie reviews—they work for him. He can even make audiences turn up and love you, if it comes to that. All the best people know Orosgo, Austin. All the movie stars. All the important ones. All the important writers and directors and the big faces that talk on TV. All the people who can make your life happen and not happen, who can make it a success or one long slog of frustration and humiliation and failure and pain. Watch them. Listen to them. They all think what he thinks; they all say what he says. Are you gonna be the only one who disagrees? What do you think that's gonna be like? There it is. All right? Good life, bad life, brother. That's the choice you've got. You don't want to think about making the world a better place? Fine. But at least think about making your own world better. Okay? It's grown-up time, Austin, that's all. Good life, bad life. Time to choose."

You know what surprised me most about this? I'll tell you. What surprised me most was how hard the choice was. I mean, it's not like I didn't understand what was going on here. Of course I did. How many times had I seen this scene in the movies, or read it in books? The bad guy tries to bribe the hero. Tries to buy off his integrity, his honesty, his courage, the whole deal. And what happens? The hero won't surrender, right? He says go to hell, bad guy. Sure he does. That's what makes him the hero. And that's what I wanted to be too: a hero. Like in the movies, in the books. Like in my own daydreams. Isn't everyone a hero in his own daydreams?

But this wasn't daydreams, see. That's exactly what made it so hard. This wasn't movies or books. It was my life. Just like Rich said, it was my only life. And the truth was, I didn't want to spend my only life in failure and frustration. I mean, that's fine in books and movies, where the audience cheers, and in daydreams where you're your own audience and can applaud the courage of your own crucifixion. No one sells his soul in his daydreams.

But to live my real life that way? With no one watching? With all my ambitions thwarted? With every avenue closed to me, every door shut in my face? And that's if I was even allowed to live, if I didn't die one day in a car accident or a fall from a building or in a botched robbery that left me riddled with bullets with no suspects to take the blame. A funeral in obscurity and then forgotten.

Hey, what would it cost me to keep my mouth shut? Nothing. What would I gain from it? Success. Money. Everything. I knew what was right—of course I did—but I'm telling you, the choice was hard. That was the big surprise, how very hard it was.

Rich leaned over me, loomed over me, breathed over me. I looked down at the table. What would it cost me to do what he wanted? Nothing.

I rubbed my mouth with my hand, wrestling with the temptation.

And again, on my hand, I caught the scent of Lady Betheray. I breathed it in, a deep breath. I saw her face in my mind. I saw her face turned up to me in the torchlit corridors of Castle Eastrim. Depending on me. Expecting me to be—what?—her hero.

I closed my eyes. I leaned back in my chair. I laughed.

Startled, Rich straightened up off the table. "What?" he said. "What's so funny?"

I shook my head. I laughed again. I laughed because the choice wasn't hard, was it? Not really. Really it was easy.

I pushed out of my chair. I stood. I shook my head. I laughed.

"God damn it, Austin!" Rich said. His cheeks flamed red with anger.

"Tell Orosgo," I said. "Tell Orosgo I laughed."

And I walked out of the room.

BACK I WENT through the mazelike hallways hung with fliers and bustling with police. As I went, some of the cops—some of the uniforms and some of the detectives—stopped whatever they were doing to watch me pass. Every moment, I expected one of them to shout out or grab me. No one did. They just stopped whatever they were doing. They just watched.

Now up ahead, I saw the door to the outer lobby. Beside the door, there sat a uniformed woman in a high perch in a glass booth. She was the woman who had to buzz the door open in order for me to get through, to get out.

I reached the door. I stopped. I looked at the woman in the glass booth.

The woman hesitated, uncertain. I saw her lift her head and look over me from her high perch. I looked back over my shoulder to see what she saw.

There, behind me, were Detectives Graciano and Lord. They were standing shoulder to shoulder, gazing at me with those hard, cynical stares of theirs. Rich came up behind them as I watched, standing between them. He stared at me too, balefully. So did my mother and father, who joined them on their left and right. They all stood there in a cluster, a knot of hostility, staring at me. I didn't know what they were going to do: arrest me or let me go.

I turned back to the woman in the booth.

As I did, a large man came up beside me as if from nowhere. He took me firmly by the elbow. Startled, I looked up. It was the big, swarthy plainclothesman who had cuffed me back in the mall, the one with the Spartans sweatshirt and the mustached, hard-guy face. Holding me by the elbow like that, like I was in his custody, he raised his eyes to the woman in the booth. He nodded almost imperceptibly.

The woman buzzed the door. The plainclothesman pulled it open and led me through.

We walked together across the outer lobby. We headed over the grimy tiled floor straight for the glass doors that opened onto the street outside. It wasn't far, just a few steps, but the whole way the plainclothesman was talking to me in a low, rapid-fire murmur that seemed at first like little more than a hum of sound.

But then I listened more carefully.

"Get out of the city," he was saying. "Now, today, before nightfall. Ditch your phone. Don't use credit cards or ATMs. Go where you need to go, but go and go fast and keep moving, don't stop. You're a dead man in LA. You're a dead man anywhere they find you. Don't say anything. Don't look at me. Don't ask any questions . . . "

At that point, we reached the door. And despite his instructions, I couldn't help it, I did look at him. I looked up into his hard-guy face, into his glittering hazel eyes. He didn't even glance down at me. He gazed out the door at the street beyond.

"Just go your way," he said.

I blinked, startled. Had he meant to say that? Had he meant to say it in just those words? I couldn't tell. His expression was blank, unreadable.

I hesitated another second. Then I said softly, "Let wisdom reign."

He didn't react. He didn't even lower his eyes to me. He went on looking straight out the door, straight at the street.

I licked my lips. I faced the door. I pushed it open. I drew in a harsh, rasping breath of surprise.

Beyond the door—there was Galiana! I could see it! A soft, dim, faded image just beneath reality like pentimento. I could make out the torchlit corridors of Castle Eastrim. I could discern the blurred figure of Lady Betheray moving away from me down the hall.

My mouth wide, I glanced back at the plainclothesman again. Still—still—he was looking out the door of the police station at the street. Did he see Galiana there too? Impossible to know.

I faced the scene in front of me.

Go your way, I thought.

I stepped through the door.

"THIS WAY! QUICKLY!" Lady Betheray whispered. She took my arm as I stepped up to her, the same arm the plainclothesman had been holding. It was as if I had been passed from him to her.

We were in a grand hallway now hung with tapestries, their images alive with fluttering torchlight. Betheray was moving surely and swiftly, as if she knew her way well. I hurried along beside her. We reached a corner, an intersection with another corridor. I could hear the voices of the guards down there. As I reoriented myself, it came back to me: these were the guards who had just gone by us. Their voices faded as they retreated.

Lady Betheray pushed back the ermine-lined cowl of her cape, her black hair tumbling around her ivory cheeks. She peeked around the corner to watch the guards go. Then she held a finger to her lips and beckoned me to follow.

We went on beneath the torches in their sconces on the walls. We passed from one corridor to another. We came upon more guards, but Beth always seemed to know how to elude them. She seemed to have a sense of their schedules, habits, and routines. She seemed to be able to time our movements to sneak through the gaps in their patrols.

There was only one close call. It was awfully close though. We'd traveled a ways without incident and had gotten overconfident and careless, I guess. We'd begun moving very quickly and were heading full tilt down a hall toward an intersection when suddenly, a pair of swordsmen stepped out right in front of us.

If they had turned our way—if they had even glanced our way like people do sometimes when they come around a corner—if they had even caught a glimpse of us from the corners of their eyes, we'd have been done for.

But they didn't. They were moving as quickly and as recklessly as we were. They simply turned their backs to us and marched on without ever noticing we were there.

Lady Betheray and I stood frozen, holding our breaths, watching their backs as they walked off chatting together, their hands on the hilts of their swords. The second they passed the next intersection, Beth grabbed my elbow and we tiptoed down the hall at full speed, ducked around the corner, and hurried away.

At last, we came to a short hall that ended with a rounded protrusion of stone. There was a small wooden door set in the bend of it. Lady Betheray brought a heavy iron key from somewhere within her cape. She checked over her shoulder for patrols, then unlocked the door. We went through.

We came into a high circular room. I understood. This was the base of the tower.

There was a narrow stone stairway here. It wound up the curved surface of the wall to another door above. We climbed the stairs together to the higher door. Lady Betheray unlocked it with the same key.

I peered through and recognized the place. A broad, winding staircase, hung with faded tapestries and dimly lit by a torch or two. These were the steps to the tower room, the room where I had first come to myself in Galiana, the room where Lady Kata Palav had died alone with me behind the locked door.

"The only way to reach the moat without meeting the guard is through the window of the high room and down the wall. There's a path along the jutting stones. Like a ladder. You'll find it."

She pressed the heavy key into my hand. I looked down at it, surprised.

"You're not coming?" I said.

She shook her head. "The guards pass through here on patrol. I can't make the climb down the wall, so I'd be in plain sight the whole time. I'll wait for you here."

I nodded. I gave her one last glance—that is, I meant to give her one last glance. But when I saw her, her valentine face, her bright, clear eyes eagerly looking up at me, when I caught the scent of her and remembered the scent of her on my fingers and how it had cleared my mind in the police station with Rich, I took her by the shoulders, pulled her to me, and kissed her—kissed her and breathed her in, that same perfume, and the same courage that came with it.

When we broke apart, I tried to think of something to say to her, something worthy of the moment, you know, but I had nothing. I tried to put the meaning in my eyes. She smiled up at me. She touched my face.

"Go!" she said.

I went.

I CLIMBED THE tower stairs quickly.

"What have I done? What have I done?"

It began to happen again. I don't know what triggered it—Betheray's kiss, the scent of her, or just the fact that I was in the tower—but memories that were not memories, images of that last time I had climbed these stairs, though I had never climbed these stairs, of that time I met with Lady Kata before the time I came here at all—all these scenes began unspooling in my mind like a movie I had never watched before.

"What have I done?"

We were in the tower room together. Lady Kata was crying.

"What have I done?"

She was already brandishing the dagger at me. She was frantic, her eyes wild, her beautiful face flushed, her cheeks streaked with gray tears, her golden hair in disarray. The knife flashed in the torchlight. Was she going to kill me?

"It's all right," I kept saying to her. My hands were lifted to her, palms out. I was trying to steady her, comfort her. "It's not your fault, Kata. Lord Iron seduced you."

"How is that not my fault?"

"He bewitched you! He stole your will. That wizard of his. Curtin."

A febrile light came into her eyes. Her wild gaze seemed to fix on a spot in eternity.

"Yes! Yes! That's it! The wizard. He enchanted me! He stole me from myself!" But even as she said the words, her voice broke. She shook her

head. Her eyes glistened with guilty tears. "But I was the one who did it. I loved him. I needed him. I wanted him. I always had the power to resist, but I didn't."

"You did resist, Kata. You held on to the talisman."

"I betrayed my queen!"

"We can still make this right. We can bring the talisman to the emperor. Anastasius has armies. He'll restore Elinda to her throne."

Lady Kata looked around her, her eyes darting crazily here and there as if a thousand invisible demons were jeering at her from all directions.

I urged her back to herself. "The talisman, Kata!"

"The talisman . . . " She breathed the word to herself as if only now remembering. And then, as if fighting against some force that constrained her, she struggled to lift her hand and extend her finger. "There! I hid it there!" A wild, desperate expression of defiant joy came over her features. "No matter how he bewitched me, I would not give it to him!"

I followed her gesture. Low on the curving tower wall, just below the window, there was a tile mosaic. It showed a scene of a queen enthroned. Men and women in various forms of dress were moving toward her to bring her tributes: grain, wine, a lyre, and so on. I didn't know if it was a picture of Queen Elinda or an allegory of some sort or both at once, but there was no time to worry about it. Because now, the distraught Lady Kata cried out—words that sounded as if she had forced them from her throat.

"Behind the throne!"

I went to the mosaic. I knelt before the image. My fingers traced the tiles that made the throne. The slab of stone that held them wobbled, unsteady. I worked my fingernails between the tiles and pried the stone away.

And there it was! There, in a small niche: the talisman. A glittering pendant with an S-shaped bolt carved into its golden center.

My heart sped up as I put my fingers on it. I had risked my life half a dozen times to get this. I had worked my way into Lady Kata's confidence, praying all the while that she would not betray me to her lover, slowly talking my way through the spell that had taken over her will.

Now I had what I had come for. I could bring it to the Emperor. Anastasius would restore the queen and save the kingdom.

I stood up. I turned around.

I saw the dreadful thing.

While I had retrieved the talisman, Lady Kata had plunged the dagger into herself, plunged it in to the hilt. Her mouth was open. Her eyes were wide. But in her expression, I thought I saw something like relief. She had finally freed herself—from her desire for Lord Iron, from the spell his wizard had cast on her. She had taken her life but reclaimed her soul.

I rushed to her. I grabbed the hilt of the knife. Even as I did, she fell to the floor, dropping away from me with so much force that the blade came out of her. I stood there, staring at the dead woman, the bloody knife in my hand.

And I heard the thundering footsteps of the guards on the tower stairs.

I knew I only had a second. I knew there was only one thing I could do.

I leapt to the window and threw the pendant toward the moat. I watched it turn and fall, glittering in the air. Then, even before it hit the water, I swung back to the door with the bloody dagger still in my hand, swung back just in time to see Sir Aravist and his guards come bursting through . . .

NOW I REACHED the tower room. I used Lady Betheray's key to unlock the heavy door. I pushed in. As soon as I crossed the threshold, the memories crowded in on me like hungry beggars desperate for a scrap of bread. I only had a second to take in the place where it had all happened. The bloodstain on the stone floor. The tapestries on the wall. The mosaic with its empty hiding hole . . .

Lord Iron and his men had not found the talisman and so they had tried to use the law to torture its location out of me. If Tauratanio had not sent Maud to help me, I would've died in the executioner's chamber with no one to protest or care. Or maybe they would have locked up what was left of me in one of those cages so the guards could spear me to death there while the people cheered.

I crossed quickly to the window. I felt full of energy and daring. I had not realized until now how heavily Lady Kata's death had weighed on me. I could never quite believe I had murdered her, but I could not figure out how she had died. Now I knew, and the freedom from my own suspicions made me feel light and high, like a kite carried on the wind.

I reached the window and climbed over the edge. The moon was low. Its light lay in a broken silver line over the water of the moat. It whitened the outer stones of the tower. I could see where the stones jutted. As Lady Betheray had said, they made a ladder almost to the ground.

I lowered myself from the window to the first step then began to make my way down, crawling over the surface of the tower swiftly and surely. It was a long way, but it only took a few moments. I dropped the last few feet onto the soft, damp earth.

I moved toward the water's edge, panning my eyes over the surface of the moat as I approached. I was looking for any signs of the talisman, but what was the use? How would I ever be able to see it where it lay deep beneath the night-dark surface, far below the blurred gleam of the moonlight?

And yet, I did see it! How weird! The moment I stepped to the edge of the moat, I saw it through the murk. It lay at the bottom, half sunk in mud. But it was glowing. Its jewels, its gold, its S-shaped bolt—all were illuminated by a light from within.

When I knelt in the grass and bent over the water, that light grew brighter. It was responding to my presence. It was glowing for me. I was meant to find it.

I held my breath. I was afraid the light would go out, afraid the thing would vanish before I grabbed it. I couldn't tell how deep it was. Would I have to swim down for it?

I reached an unsteady hand toward the moat. Even before my fingers touched the surface, the talisman trembled. It broke from the mud. It rose up through the water.

It burst out into the air, shedding moonlit droplets as it flew.

It leapt on its own power right into my hand.

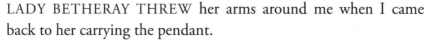

LADY BETHERAY THREW her arms around me when I came back to her carrying the pendant.

"God bless you!" she whispered in my ear.

She took the talisman from me and slipped it over my neck, tucking it inside my shirt. Then she drew back. I could see there were tears in her eyes, tears of gratitude and admiration. They caught the yellow glow of the torchlight coming through the open door. I felt my heart grow inside me until it seemed too big for my chest. I wished every moment in life could be like this one.

But even the next moment wasn't like it. Already, fresh worries flooded my mind. "The stallion—my horse—he ran off. He wouldn't stay in the graveyard. How are we going to get out of here?"

"I have friends in the city," she told me. "They'll hide us until we can get another mount. But we have to hurry, before the next patrols."

We hurried. And, in fact, we made it back through the corridors without encountering even a single guard. We slipped back behind the arras. Passed back through the secret door in the stone wall. Betheray relit her torch, and we traveled back through the underground hallways where the hungry dead—the yearning silhouettes of what had once been men and women—appeared by firelight, trying to seduce us into giving them our lives.

We reached the winding stair beneath the sarcophagus. Lady Betheray handed me the torch and went up first. I lit the way for her so when she reached the top, she could work the mechanism that undid the lid. The lid went up. She climbed out, her cape flowing after her over the edge of the death box. As I came up the stairs, she reached down and took the torch from my hand. I climbed out.

In the crypt now, we shut the sarcophagus lid. I looked around again at the skeletons grinning out of their niches in the flickering flames of Betheray's torch. I saw the stone coffins with carved figures on their lids that seemed to move and live with the life of the fire. God, I would be glad to get out of this place, away from all these dead.

"Quickly," Beth whispered.

We moved together to the crypt door. I pushed it open for her and she went out, then me.

The moon was almost gone. The mist was dim and gray. The ancient graveyard had almost vanished into its own shadows. But as my eyes adjusted, the strange and slanted shapes of the monuments and steles and broken sculptures half emerged out of the night fog. Once again, I saw the drifting tendrils of mist caressing the gravestones and slithering over the weather-worn statue faces. Again, I saw the mist take the shapes of the hungry dead below, momentarily drifting into the human form of their desire, striving against dissolution for a second, then vanishing with a whisper that might have been a moan or just the wind.

Then, as my eyes adjusted further, I saw the others. Lady Betheray saw them too. She gave a small, gasping cry of despair.

I should have known that we would never make it out of here alive.

"Well, well, well!" came a booming voice from the darkness.

A shadow moved forward out of the crowd of shadows that we could now see ringing us round.

"My spies on the wall were telling the truth," the figure went on.

From every side of us, there came scraping noises. Sparks. Flames. Torches. We were at the center of a ring of torches held by some of the dozens of soldiers standing everywhere among the monuments. The night took on the color of a hellish day as the mist-tendrils swirled and curled around the red and yellow flames.

By that sickly light, I could see it was Lord Iron approaching— Lord Iron and, in his wake, nearly hidden by his bulk, his little raisin-faced wizard with his indigo robes flowing like liquid night.

On instinct, my hand went across me to my belt line. For a moment, I felt the scabbard there take shape. I felt the hilt of my sword come into being within my grip. I felt my helmet and my armor begin to ooze out of my flesh and encase my body.

But what was the point? There were too many of them. My arm went slack and fell to my side. The sword faded. The armor withdrew into nothingness and was gone.

Lord Iron now stood before us. His tall, broad-shouldered figure went bright and dark as the flames of the torches played over it. He was not dressed for action. He wore black leggings and an embroidered shirt fringed with white lace and open at the throat. His only weapon was the dagger at his hip. He gazed down at his wife with high disdain. She lifted her chin and glared back at him with righteous defiance.

"And here you are," he said.

The wizard Curtin hung behind him like a shadow. His beady eyes were moving over me, examining me, searching me. I could feel him looking for a chink in my mind, a way into my will. I steeled myself against the creeping, probing fingers of his malevolent thoughts.

Lord Iron drew his eyes from Lady Betheray to afford me a quick, dismissive glance.

"Sir Aravist?" he asked.

"Dead." I spat the word at him. "And his goons too."

He smiled a little, but his eyes didn't smile. "I'm impressed. He was the best swordsman in the country."

"Was," I said.

He snorted. Turned back to Betheray. "And you. Look at you. You still claim to be faithful to me?"

She drew in a breath, her eyes on fire with torchlight and anger. "Faithful, yes. But no, not to you."

He nodded. "And you have the talisman, I suppose. That's the only reason you would have risked coming back here."

Neither of us answered.

"Never mind," he said. "It'll be more amusing to have it tortured out of you."

Now, after the first shock of the ambush—after the first paralyzing wave of helplessness and defeat—my brain was beginning to work again. It didn't have a lot to work with. We were surrounded by dozens of men with swords and bows. There was no chance we could escape, no possibility we could defeat them—and no way we could hide the talisman from them. Once they had us in chains and in prison, there'd be nothing left for us but agony and death and the final knowledge that we had failed the queen.

As I say, not a lot to work with. But there was one thing. One advantage I had, if you can call it that. Lord Iron didn't know—none of them knew—that I was armed. My sword was invisible and wouldn't come into being until I went for it. Which meant . . . what? Not much. I had a single chance to draw and strike at Lord Iron. If I could kill him . . . well, it would give me some satisfaction before the soldiers' arrows shredded me. And at least Beth and I would die fighting instead of howling on the executioner's rack.

So that was something. The only option, really. Still, it was hard to act on it. Like the choice back in the police station. I knew it was the best thing to do, but in the moment, it was hard to decide to die.

Lord Iron was not focused on me at all anymore, only on his wife. He was looking down at her from his greater height with an expression of cold hatred—that icy hatred a man feels toward a woman he admires when she has made him seem small to himself.

"I would have made you the first lady of this country," he said. You could tell he meant it to hurt her. He meant her to regret the opportunity she'd missed.

She laughed once, harshly. Then she spat in his face.

I knew right away that was my moment. I could see as Iron's features twisted, as his eyes blazed, as his skin reddened, that he was about to lose control. He wiped the spittle from his cheek and his eye, and then the fury exploded in him.

"Bitch!" he shouted.

He drew his dagger and brandished it above her.

I made my move. I reached across myself and, yes, there was Elinda's sword. It gave a steely whisper as I pulled it from its scabbard. I swung the silver blade toward Iron's neck, meaning to behead him in a single swift stroke before the archers could draw and cut me down.

But my arm froze. The sword froze—inches from him. My whole body was suddenly held there motionless by an overwhelming and invisible force.

It was the wizard. Curtin. He had lifted his hands, his fingers like talons. I could see blue sparks dancing round his long, pointy, filthy fingernails. My muscles locked. My mind disconnected from my body. He shrouded and bound my will with his own. I was held fast. Try as I might, I could not finish the blow and kill my man.

With my surprise attack foiled, the soldiers all around us in the torchlit cemetery had time to react. Some drew their swords. Some raised their bows and aimed their arrows at my heart.

But Lord Iron held up his hand and stopped them. No one attacked, no one let fly.

Iron looked at me as I stood there helpless, still mid-blow, my hand shivering with the effort to strike. He examined me like I was a specimen in a lab. He sneered.

"You love her," he said. He sounded startled. Then he gave a quick laugh. He lowered his dagger. Sheathed it. "Good. I'll make you watch her suffer before I kill you."

I struggled with all my might against the force of Curtin's magic. I felt his will tremble against the rebellious force of mine. But still he held me. He was strong, very strong.

Lord Iron, meanwhile, gestured. Four nearby soldiers lowered their swords and moved out from among the graves to come toward us.

"Take them to the dungeon," Lord Iron said.

Two of the soldiers grabbed Lady Betheray by the arms. She struggled uselessly as they lifted her off her feet and began to half carry and half drag her away. The other two soldiers moved toward me.

I was still struggling against Curtin's unbreakable chain of will.

But then, as the soldiers came toward me, I stopped struggling. I saw . . . something. Something over Lord Iron's shoulder. Out beyond the crowd of soldiers. Beyond their torches. At the edge of the graveyard. In the darkness, through the mist.

I saw a little confetti-like sparkle of colored light.

Maud!

A bolt of hope and energy lanced my spirit and enflamed my will. I broke from the power of Curtin's spell on the instant. I stepped away from the oncoming soldiers and swung my sword in a wild arc to hold them back.

At the same moment, a chorus of twanging bows sang out in the reaches of the night. Arrows arced up into the sky and fell like stars. All around me, Iron's soldiers began screaming, collapsing. I saw eyes go wide by torchlight, mouths open in shock and pain, men dropping to the earth with blood spurting from the shafts buried in their necks.

The two soldiers who were coming for me stopped in their tracks. They looked around in confusion—and as they did, one caught an arrow in the eye and keeled over, dead. Lord Iron crouched low, afraid. The wizard was searching the night for a target. Who was attacking them?

A shout came out of the distance: "At them!"

And fast after came the thundering hoofbeats of a stampede.

Tauratanio's centaur army charged through the mist, their dark faces jacked wide in the frenzy of attack. Their swords were uplifted. Their blades caught the last light of the moon and flashed. Their muscular flanks flowed as their horse-bodies carried them into the cemetery.

The Eastrim guards saw them coming, panicked, and lost control. They loosed their arrows wildly. They spun wildly this way and that. Some ran. Some lifted their swords clumsily, trying to get ready for close action.

Another second and the two armies crashed together among the graves. Blades rang on blades. Eyes blazed. Blood flew in arcs across the white mist. Dozens of war cries—dozens of high-pitched screams of agony—filled the boneyard darkness.

All this I saw in a second, but there was no time to take it in. Lady Betheray was being dragged off through the graveyard. The second soldier who had come to grab me now collected himself and charged. Our fight was over in an instant. I ducked beneath his swinging blade and drove my sword straight through the core of him. But as he gasped and died on the steel, Lord Iron seized the moment. With a beckoning gesture to his wizard, he rushed away into the night, following the soldiers who were carrying the struggling Betheray away.

I kicked the corpse from my sword and charged after them through the battle.

Arrows flew. Swords clashed together. Everywhere men and centaurs fought among the graves. I crouched low, my liquid armor flowing over me, my helmet taking shape around my head even as I hurried after Iron and his wizard and the men with Betheray.

And all around in the melee, I saw the flame-lit mist congealing here and there—and there and there—into human shapes, the emanations of the hungry dead. I saw those shadowy emanations reaching for the fleeing souls of falling soldiers, seizing those souls and dragging them down below the earth into their dank, toxic, miserable maze of corridors even as the now-inanimate soldier bodies hit the ground and were left behind facedown in the mud.

I rushed through it all, after Lord Iron's party. Under the wizard's protection, they were slipping unharmed through the chaos, heading for the verge of the graveyard, for the heavy wall of fog that hid the field beyond. I went after them full speed. I reached Lord Iron first. Roaring with rage, I whipped my sword around in a murderous sweep at his head. Near him, Curtin, the wizard, didn't even look back at me. He merely gestured behind himself carelessly. Some invisible force flew from his fingertips. It shielded Lord Iron and deflected my blade so that it flew past him by at least a foot. The wizard's will staggered me, and I fell back as Iron hurried his escape, putting distance between us—he and the wizard and the soldiers with Beth all moving away from me.

Over the battle cries and the sounds of hoofbeats, I heard her call out to me, "Austin!"

But I was losing them in the mist. Their shapes were growing dim in the fog and darkness. Looming centaurs and struggling soldiers were creating a mad confusion of shapes and action all around me.

I killed a man who stepped in my way and rushed under the rearing hooves of a centaur just before they dropped on top of me.

Where was Iron? Where was Betheray? I had lost them. No, there they were. I spotted them through the battle madness. Lord Iron seemed to have stopped. He seemed to be confronting Betheray where the soldiers held her between them. He had his hand on her face and his own face pressed close to hers, his features gnarled with rage as he spoke to her.

The mist closed over them, and the action swirled before me, and I lost them again, but I fought forward, blocking a sword that swung for my head, kicking a soldier out of my way.

In another moment, I burst from the fog into a little clearing, a calm eye in the torrent of battle where there was only the night and the last moonlight and a headstone and a statue of an angel weeping and tendrils of mist winding through it all.

And there was Beth. She was standing alone.

My heart leapt up as I saw her. The soldiers had let her go. Lord Iron and the wizard had deserted her. I could just see them retreating into the further darkness and the furthest mist. Never mind them. Beth was free.

I sheathed my sword. I rushed to her side. I took her arm. "Beth!"

She turned to me. Raised her face to mine. She smiled a little, her eyes glistening. I started to smile back. But then I realized something was wrong.

Her valentine face was stony white. Her breath was rattling in her throat. Her lips were moving as she tried to speak—but she couldn't speak. She didn't have the strength.

As the truth washed over me like a black wave, my eyes traveled down to where her two hands clutched at her center. Blood was pumping out between her fingers. I could see the ragged wound where Lord Iron had plunged his dagger in.

"No!" I said. "Beth! No!"

As I took hold of her arms, she made a move to bring her lips closer to me. She whispered: "My love . . . the emperor . . . the talisman . . . go . . . "

I caught her as she collapsed, and the weight of her carried me down to my knees. I knelt among the gravestones with her body in my arms. I saw the light of life in her eyes for one more second—a last look of sweet devotion—then the light went out and she was gone.

Roiling grief filled me. I cried out high and wild. Tears pouring from my eyes, I reached to touch her face—and as I did, through the mad sorrow clouding my vision, I saw the mist stir and swirl and gather around her and then rise up off her like a pillar of steam. The pillar took shape. Her shape: her rising emanation, the very image of her, revealed by the white drapery of the fog.

And even as that image rose from the corpse in my arms, other shadowy gray shapes began to move in around it. The dead. All the dead. Their misty figures came closer. They reached to seize her emanation, to drag her soul down with them into their yearning labyrinth.

Supporting her body in one hand, I drew my silver sword again with the other.

"Get back! Get away!" I shouted. I slashed at the gathering shapes, trying to keep them off her.

It was useless. They had no substance. The blade went through them like the mist they were. They didn't even slow. They just kept moving in on her, reaching for her. I stared up into the night in horror as the circle of lost souls closed in on the mist-made shape of Lady Betheray.

But they never reached her.

As I looked on helplessly, the body in one hand, my sword in the other, some faint whisper of whirling wind rose up above the bloody sounds of war. Where the wind went, the mist was dispelled until a black border of crystal clear night formed around Lady Betheray's ghostly emanation. The dark shadows of the hungry dead could not breach that border. I saw them reaching, striving to cross it, but the shapes of their grasping hands were swept away to nothing by the breezes.

In the next second, the image of Lady Betheray began to rise higher, and as it rose, it lightened. The dark fog that formed her caught first the red flames of the torches as it lifted up above the general mist. Then, rising even higher, her emanation turned pure white from some mystic source of illumination that was not the moon's.

With my head tilted back to follow her ascent, I saw her figure turning white against the open air. I saw the hands of the dead reaching up after her helplessly. And then I saw . . .

I wasn't sure what I saw. Lady Betheray's emanation never lost the shape of herself, never faded, never vanished, yet as I looked up at her, she became so much a part of the fabric of the night that I could no longer distinguish her from the starry sky.

She was gone.

I lowered my eyes to her body. I lowered her body to the ground. For a second, the lingering impression of her image rising into the stars stayed with me, mitigating the hollowness of my grief. But then I looked up.

Here—here on earth—there was only chaos amid the graves. The centaurs and the soldiers traded sword blows in the mist and mud, churning both together into a swampy vortex. The horsemen's front hooves kicked the air as the strange creatures reared and fought against the soldiers' slashing blades. The swarming shadows of the dead seized hold of the souls of the fallen and carried them below. Torchlight stained the mist with red, and puddles of crimson blood collected on the earth.

I felt alone and hopeless. The loss—and the injustice of the loss—and the rage at the injustice—rose up out of my heart and curled around my throat and closed around my throat like an iron ring, strangling me on my own hot passion for revenge.

I climbed to my feet, my sword gripped hard in my hand.

"Iron!" I shouted through the noise of melee. "Iron!"

My eyes searched the night for him, but he had escaped through the mist. I looked the way he had gone. He couldn't have gotten far. I would hunt him down. I would kill him. I would kill him if it cost me everything I had. I took a step, a single step, in his direction.

And suddenly my black stallion raced in front of me, rearing, blocking my path.

Maud balanced on the pommel of the saddle, sparkling, as the horse's hooves kicked at the air.

"Get out of my way!" I shouted at her.

"Mount! We have to go!" the mutant rodent shouted back.

"I'm going after Iron. I'm going to kill him!"

"You can't. You can't defeat Curtin. He's too strong."

"I don't care! Get out of my way!"

The horse's hooves came down. The beast snorted, its head twisting, its eyes rolling.

"There's no time for this!" the rodent said. "Our armies are at the walls. The gates are open. But we can't hold the position much longer!"

I stood there panting with anger and frustration. The raw force of my rage was spurring me to vengeance, but Maud's words held me where I was.

"The only way you can have your revenge," she said, "is to bring the talisman to the emperor."

I looked up at her, furious. I wanted blood. Not later. Now. Not through the emperor. By my own hand.

But even as I tried to convince myself to brush past the stallion and go after Lord Iron, a thought was forming in my mind.

The mutant rodent spoke the thought aloud, the very words. "It's what she wanted. You know it is."

I stared into the night. It was true. It was what she wanted. Not just revenge. The queen restored. The kingdom restored.

I let out a ragged, tremulous breath. Slowly, as if against my own will, I fitted my sword back in its sheath. At once, sword and sheath and armor all melted away. My helmet too. Maud had the good manners to avert her gaze from my tearstained face.

I grabbed hold of the saddle, stepped into the stirrup, and swung up into the seat. My heart was in ashes.

"Ride," I said.

We raced away through the darkness.

AFTERWARD, I COULD not remember the journey to the city gates. Even as I rode, I had only the vaguest sense of the wind on my face and the fields before me and the streets of the city rising up around me. Mostly, I was aware of the pain and rage inside me. That last look Lady Betheray had given me. The weight of her dead body in my arms. The living warmth of her naked flesh only hours before. All that—the pain, the memories—was far more real to me than the passing scenery.

Then I heard Maud say, "Whoa. Whoa."

The stallion slowed to a stop. I looked around as if coming out of a dream. Up ahead of me, I saw the gates and the battle for the gates, ten or fifteen centaurs holding off half an army of men, as more and more soldiers poured into the fight every minute. I saw the colored lights of fairies swarming around the winches to protect the peak-capped trolls who were keeping the gate open. I saw the soldiers slashing at the fairy lights with their swords.

"Look at me," said Maud.

I looked. The mutant rodent's bizarrely human, bizarrely female face was set and grim.

"I have to go," she said. "I have to organize the retreat."

I blinked, coming to myself. I shook my head. "But . . . "

"You'll be all right."

"I don't know the way."

"Keep the north star on your left shoulder, then follow the rising sun across the Eleven Lands. You'll find it."

I swallowed. "All right," I said uncertainly.

"You will. The emperor will call you to him. Just head in his direction, and he'll bring you home."

"All right," I repeated, a little more convincingly this time. Then I gazed into that strange face of hers. "Thank you for everything. You know?"

"Yes. I know." She turned to jump off the saddle. But she hesitated. She turned back to me. "You're not as big a pansy as I thought you were."

Even in my sorrow, I laughed a little. Maud gave me a last quirky smile then leapt off into the night.

I faced forward.

Already, the battle for the walls was lost. The centaurs were being driven back by the soldier reinforcements. The fairy lights were faltering. The fresh soldiers were hacking their way toward where the trolls worked the winches. The gate was beginning to descend.

"Hurry!" Maud called to me from the darkness below. "Go your way."

I nodded. I drew a breath. "Let wisdom reign," I whispered.

I spurred the stallion and charged through the falling gate.

AND IN A vastly disorienting snap of consciousness, I found myself walking on the sidewalk outside the Hollywood police station. The world of Galiana that had been so utterly real a split second before was utterly gone.

No. Not utterly. The grief—that was still there. The grief and the fever for revenge. A second before, I had been on fire with my mission. To find the emperor. To bring him the talisman. To call him back with his armies to overthrow Lord Iron's council and restore Elinda to her throne. And now . . .

Well, maybe Galiana was a dream of some kind—a hallucination, a symptom of insanity, it felt like it had to be something like that—but the grief, the rage, the fever for the mission—all that was real, still with me. The frustration at having been called back to Los Angeles before I could cross the Eleven Lands. The idea—the fact—that I would never see Lady Betheray again—never, neither here nor there . . . It was all like a cloud of darkness inside me that swallowed every lighter thought and feeling. In that moment, I felt like I would never be happy again. And how crazy would that be? To spend the rest of my life mourning for a woman—and for a kingdom—that may never have been real in the first place?

I was walking without looking, lost in thought. I nearly stepped off the curb without noticing. A truck went speeding by me, the trailer sidewall inches from my face. I staggered back onto the sidewalk, shaking my head, coming out of my daze.

I remembered. The last thing that had happened here. The assassin falling to his death at the construction site. The cops bearing down on me in the interrogation room. My family . . . Orosgo . . . The plainclothesman at the door . . .

Get out of the city. You're a dead man in LA. You're a dead man anywhere they find you.

Right. Right. I was in danger here. I scanned the dingy streets. The white walls of the buildings, the murky recesses of the storefront doorways. Gabbling knots of tourists went past me on my left and right. Cars zipped across my eyeline in front of me, their drivers hidden behind dark windshields. Was anyone watching me? Was anyone after me? Was one of these people Orosgo's agent, sent to find me? Kill me?

Confused, I stood where I was. My head was filled with thoughts that all seemed to crash into each other like a pileup on the freeway. What was I supposed to do now? Run? Hide? Find the emperor. No, find my sister, Riley. Destroy Lord Iron, or defeat Orosgo. And what about Jane . . . Jane Janeway? If I became a fugitive, how would I ever get back to her? And if I did get back to her, would I still be able to have feelings for her, or would there only be this deadening sadness in me and nothing else from now on to forever?

Was this going to be my life? This grief, this fear, this confusion? Was this the rest of my life? No dreams, no home, no friends, no family, no career. Just nights on the run and days on end tangled in the web of a conspiracy I didn't even understand. A mad billionaire after me. An evil wizard. A conniving lord. My parents. My brother . . .

As I stood there, overwhelmed, someone bumped into me from behind, a shoulder hitting my shoulder, jarring me. I looked up in time to see the figure of a woman heading away from me along the sidewalk. She was wearing jeans and a light khaki jacket against the autumn chill. Her golden-blond hair hung straight down past her shoulder blades. In my dazed state, it was a moment before I realized she had slipped something into my hand.

I lifted my hand and looked down at it. A noise came up out of my throat.

The locket! I was holding the locket! Betheray's locket. The one she wore around her neck. There was no mistaking it. It was the very one with the picture inside, the portrait of Queen Elinda, Queen Elinda who was also . . .

I looked up, looked for the woman. She was just turning the corner. As she did, she glanced back at me.

Ellen Evermore!

The words came back to me—the words of Magdala, the forest queen, speaking of Lord Iron and his fellow conspirators: "*They tried to kill the wisest queen in all the world . . . They would have succeeded too, if my husband had not used his magic to transport her to another kingdom.*"

Another kingdom: right here!

"Wait!" I shouted.

I ran after her. I reached the intersection, turned. A little wave of tourists washed over me, surrounded me. I looked over their heads along the sidewalk, searching the crowd. I did not see the gold-haired woman anywhere.

Where did she go? Baffled, I looked around me.

And suddenly, with a screech of tires, a long-snouted silver Camaro pulled up at the curb and stopped short, the passenger door right beside me.

"Get in!" the driver screamed frantically. He shoved the door open toward me.

I stooped and caught a glimpse of him behind the wheel: a wolfish Latino, his neck tattooed, his eyes full of panic and fear. I knew him from somewhere. Where?

Then it came to me. Marco. It was Marco, my sister's boyfriend.

I took one last look around the street for Ellen Evermore. She was gone. So I jumped into the car.

The Camaro fired away before I could get the door closed. It flew out of my hand, and I had to reach out of the speeding vehicle and dangle perilously above the racing pavement before I could grab the handle and yank it shut.

Marco was weaving the silver car through the traffic at a reckless speed, his frightened eyes locked on the scene through the windshield. I struggled to get my seat belt across me and get it locked in.

"What the hell are you doing? Where's my sister?" I said. "Slow down!"

"She needs you!" Marco shouted over the roaring engine. He was clearly terrified. The Camaro's tires screeched again as he drove around the corner and rocketed on.

"Where is she?" I said.

"I don't know."

"What's wrong?"

"I don't know! I don't know!" His voice was high, strained, hysterical. "It's all real! It's all real! They're trying to kill us!"

"Kill you? Who?"

"I don't know!" The whole car tilted as he took another corner at high speed. "It's about the book!" he said.

"Slow down!" I shouted.

But he didn't slow down.

"Has Riley got the book?"

"I don't know! I think so! She told me to find you!" He glanced up frantically in the rearview mirror. Then he said, "That's it! I've done it. I'm done!"

I was thrown hard against my seat belt as the car sliced into an open no-parking zone at the curb and stopped short. Then I was hurled back against my seat again.

"I have to go!" Marco said, grabbing the door handle.

"Go?"

"They'll kill me! They'll kill everyone!"

"Marco, wait!"

Too late. He had thrown the door open and leapt out of the car.

"Hurry!" he shouted to me over his shoulder as he ran away. "They'll kill her too! Hurry!" And with his knees pistoning high, he took off, running as fast as he could.

For a long moment, I sat where I was, dazed. Then I looked down. My hand was balled into a fist. My fist was pressed against my belly. I felt a strange, radiant heat pulsing against my palm. I opened my fingers. I saw the locket. Some power was coming out of it, seeping into my flesh—into my mind.

I touched the latch. The locket popped open.

There she was. Her portrait. Queen Elinda. Ellen Evermore.

I could hear Lady Betheray's voice in my mind. Her last words.

My love . . . the emperor . . . the talisman . . . go . . .

I could hear Marco.

Find Riley. They'll kill her. They'll kill everyone.

I looked up through the windshield at the traffic going past me. The heat of the locket radiated through me. My thoughts were clearing. My heart was clearing. I was beginning to understand.

Ellen Evermore. Queen Elinda. LA. Galiana. It was all one story. My story. My madness maybe, or maybe my mission. I didn't know; I wasn't sure. I only knew—I finally understood—that Galiana and this place, reality or LA or whatever you want to call it—these two worlds were connected, and the book—*Another Kingdom*—was the portal between them.

Queen Elinda—Ellen Evermore—had been sent here by Tauratanio's magic, exiled here to save her from being murdered in Galiana at Lord Iron's hands. Fearing for her kingdom, a kingdom stripped of its heroes, she had created the book as a kind of passage back. Reading it would shape a mind, the proper mind, the mind of a fighting man of brave heart and right belief—it would shape that mind so that that man could find his way between one kingdom and another, so he could bring the queen's talisman to the emperor, who would return with his armies to save her country.

The queen—Elinda, Ellen Evermore—had searched in our literature for signs of such a mind. She had found Sean Gunther and then realized that alcohol had destroyed him. He was no longer able to serve. She had found me in my script among his papers. She had sent me the book and then withdrawn it when she saw that I worked for Orosgo. I had not read enough of the book for it to change my mind fully, only enough to make a beginning, to give me this strange, uncontrollable power to pass from one realm to another.

But who was Orosgo, then? Why did he want the book? And what was the connection between Elinda's world and mine? If Galiana fell, would this world fall too? If I saved one, could I save them both? And if I lost one, what then?

I didn't know the answers. I didn't know what would happen next. I didn't know what Orosgo was planning here or how the book figured into his plans. I didn't know if I was the right man for this job or just a sad and comic mistake.

I only knew I had to stay alive. I only knew I had to find the whole truth. Somehow, someway, I had to do the work that had been given me to do. Whether it was Orosgo after me or Lord Iron or some phantom of my imagination or all of them together, I had to stand against them. I had to beat them, stop them, bring them down.

I snapped the locket shut. Its heat faded. I slipped the chain over my neck. I climbed over the center divide and dropped into the driver's seat. I took the wheel in one hand. I took the gear stick in the other. I put the car in drive.

Find Riley. Find the emperor. Find the book. Save the kingdom.

God, I sounded crazy even to myself!

I didn't care. I would do it. Somehow I would do all of it. Somehow I would be what I was called to be: a fighting man of brave heart and right belief. I would not be stopped. I would not turn back.

I would go my way.

I nodded once. I drew a breath.

"Let wisdom reign," I whispered.

I hit the gas and sped off through the city.

THE END

Acknowledgements

This novel reached its first audience in the form of a podcast, which would not have happened without the help of some true and talented friends. Michael Knowles delivered a wonderful performance as Austin Lively not to mention all the other characters; he brought the story to vivid life. Scott Immergut latched onto the podcast idea immediately and he and Rob Long gave it a platform at their website *Ricochet*, with the able assistance of Max Ledoux. Then, for no other reason than friendship, love of the arts and a very paltry number of bucks, the podcast was assembled, edited and refined by Mathis Glover, Jonathan Hay and Mike Coromina while Cynthia Angulo provided the logo.

In novel form, Robert and Mark Gottlieb at Trident Media found a wonderful publisher at Turner, and everyone there — from Todd Bottorff to Heather Howell to Stephanie Beard and Madeline Cothren — provided the kind of support most writers only dream about.

Finally and always, I have to thank my wife Ellen, my first and best reader, my steadfast supporter, and still, after all these years, my muse, my song, my only-ever love.